WIND AND SHADOW

WIND AND SHADOW

PHILIP J. CARRAHER

To order additional copies of this book, contact:
Xlibris Corporation
1-888-795-4274
www.Xlibris.com
Orders@Xlibris.com
24246

Dedication:

To Ellen Rawdon Carraher, my mother;

To Tommy Carraher, my brother,
who lived a too brief, too brave life;

To Rose Rawdon Mahaney and to
James Mahaney;

To Philip Mahaney and Patrick Mahaney, cousins and
brothers; and to Kathy Mahaney; cousin and sister;

To Thomas and Gail Carraher and to their son, Peter
Carraher, who also lived a life that was much too short;
and to Michael, Peter's brother;

To Robert and Ann Carraher, and Fred Carraher;

To William and Sarah Stuart, and Mary Stuart;

To Josephine Mahaney;

To Marybeth Mahaney,

And to my wife Ann; the best person I know.

Introduction

1946. The horrors of World War II ceased officially the previous year with the signing of a formal document of surrender by the Japanese. The tender promise of world tranquility born with the signatures placed upon that document now seems to be present everywhere, having mysteriously seeped into the world's atmosphere, into the very sunshine, as though the world itself had been placed in a warm, golden room of peace.

Much of Europe lies in the rubble left behind by the terrible conflict and poverty, another consequence of the war, is rampant throughout the continent. Many nations in Europe look to the United States for aid, and many receive it, benefiting from that nation's generosity in victory.

The newly created United Nations has just accepted a gift of millions of dollars from John D. Rockefeller, Jr., so as to be able to purchase land in New York City for the building of a permanent headquarters. Tests of atomic bombs are being made by the United States at Bikini Atoll in the Pacific Ocean. ENIAC, the first electronic digital computer, containing approximately 18,000 vacuum tubes and weighing almost thirty tons, has been built, the first small step taken toward the future computer age.

The "promise of peace" not withstanding, the seeds for a newly developing Cold War have already been sown, as have the seeds for violence elsewhere in the world; as, for example, in Northern Ireland, between the Protestants and Catholics living there.

And Ellen Rawdon, a thirteen-year old girl living on the family farm in Donegal, Ireland, has just finished milking the two family cows, one of her daily chores. She will take the milk into the house, hand it off to her mother and will, in turn, receive a kiss on the cheek for a job well done. Then she will be off to school.

Ellen's world is physically restricted by the boundaries of where she lives. The county of Donegal is in the extreme northwest of free Ireland, resting in the province of Ulster. Land bounded in the north and west by the Atlantic Ocean and on the east by *Lough* Foyle and the counties Londonderry and Tyrone. To the south are Donegal Bay and the counties Fermanagh and Leitrim. The nearest town to the Rawdon farm is a village named Moville, a small town with two primary streets running through its middle. The only place Ellen has ever visited bigger than the rather miniscule Moville is Letterkenny, the largest city in Donegal having a population, at the time of her visit, of approximately nine thousand people, a teeming megalopolis by Donegal standards.

While what will be deemed "history" roils on about her, while nations many times bigger than her own stir themselves to war and threats of war, nibbling away at the sense of golden peace so prevalent after World War II, while future legends and so-called movements stretch and groan to come into existence, pushing other legends and movements aside, little Ellen is contemplating her own small dreams, her own individual hopes for her life. Like young children everywhere, she dreams of her own particular ready-to-blossom future, of what she will be when she is grown.

Ellen's future will be one that will run parallel to what will be deemed the historic and noteworthy events of the times and, being parallel to them, will have little or nothing to do with them. Like most of us, she will live outside the occurrences of what will selectively be declared "our history". Ellen's existence will therefore be ignored by historians. Her life will be, by the standards of the commentators of "great events", a rather ordinary one, a life unworthy of analysis or consideration.

If the sun were to rise only once and never do so again, how much would we marvel then at the glory of its light? It however rises every morning and the very repetition of that wonder breeds our nonchalance of it. A one-time miracle is a cause for awe, while a multitude of those same miracles produces a shrug of the shoulders and a desire for something else. Similarly, how many "common miracles" reside in what the chroniclers of history deem *ordinary?* How much excellence of the human spirit sits outside the "great events" of our times, outside the cloth-bound covers of the archives that sit gathering dust on our bookshelves?

Isn't there much unheralded grandeur in the world? Don't we see it resting in the eyes of parents as they gaze with love at their children? Isn't it present in the determined faces of firefighters as they rush into blazing buildings to pluck a trapped stranger from a furious death? Don't we see it in the concern offered by a good-hearted caregiver treating the sick in a hospital room? Or in the strength of character exhibited by some of those very same patients as they battle the illnesses and misfortunes that have attacked them, as they face their adversity with a bravery that at least matches, and at times surpasses, that exhibited by any general or soldier standing on a field of historic combat?

The true history of humankind is told only in part in the tales of the "great events" that make it into our archives. Much of the true merit of humanity, perhaps even at times the best part of it, rests in what is accepted as common and ordinary. Like the daily sunrise, we take much of what is wonderful around us for granted, while writing down notes furiously to record what is often the worst about us.

Ellen's dreams are modest by the standards of some, for she dreams not of achieving great glories and amassing vast riches, she hopes not for fame and adulation by strangers, not of conquering or destroying nations or philosophies, but of simply growing up and being loved, of marrying and achieving the joy of raising her own small family, of loving her own children, of living in peace, of being happy . . .

. . . a common, ordinary dream . . . as common as radiant sunshine . . . .

Chapter One

The sun, weary of its daylong contention with the clouds, crawled toward the horizon like a fatigued plowman stumbling toward bed. Pale streaks of washed-out yellow streamed across the pewter sky, edging the dark-bellied clouds with little more than a vague hint of its true golden glory.

Ellen ran toward that gray-golden sky, racing through the wild grass and heather, running and enjoying the simple delight of running, hurrying up to the crest of the hill that leaned into the cloudy gray sky.

The sea breeze rushed against her freckled face as she ran, pushing its windy fingers through her long wheat-colored hair, causing it to wave like a ship's flag behind her, a flag that pointed the way back to her home, the family farm, a mile or so from the hill's bottom. Blades of wild grass brushed against the lower calves of her thin athletic legs, as if attempting to grab hold of her and stop her in her dash, wanting her not to simply run past but to stay and play in their midst. Ellen ignored their silent plea and continued racing up the hill.

She ran without fear of tripping and falling, being as familiar with the countryside surrounding her home as the gulls overhead were familiar with the wind's currents. She came to this hill and ran up its side often, too often to fear falling.

Cliona's Hill. Not the hill's true name, not the name the locals knew it by, but rather Ellen's own made-up designation for it. She had christened the rising slab of land with that name the same day her father related to her the tale of the legendary Cliona, the beloved goddess who'd drowned in the ocean eons ago, the goddess for whom the waters of the world continued to lament to this very day.

Nearing the hill's crest, she perceived, as always, an alteration in the sounds that came to her. Now she could better hear the soft lapping of waves landing against the rocks that formed the base of the hill's other side. A mournful sound, that of the water, like the dropping of many tears, lamentations offered for the lost goddess, Cliona.

Reaching the hilltop, breathing deeply but effortlessly, she gazed down at the harbor dotted with its small fishing boats. Braids of green, woven between the rocks and crags of the sloping seaside wall, trailed down to the rocky shore below. The gray slabs of rock, black where stained by the water, formed a long broken band that reached into the sea, bits and pieces of a great stone necklace that might have been discarded by the legendary giant Finn M' Coul himself. A faraway mist sat on the horizon where the water met the sky, a fog of gray-green distant smoke that sat sprawled across the world like the haze of many dreams.

The reason for Ellen's run up the hill was already gliding past in the harbor: a tourist ship. A few of the passengers, some waving to the strangers gazing at them from the shore, could be seen standing along its railings. Members of the crew were at the forecastle. Ellen stretched her arm high and waved back, although at this distance and in the dimming twilight she doubted she could even be seen.

She'd raced up the hill for no other reason than to watch the ship go by.

Below her and to her left, past the giant's discarded stone necklace, a small plank pier jutted out toward the horizon, held above the water's surface by two lines of wooden columns. When the tide was low as it was now, the columns would gain in height and that part of the wood formerly under the water could be seen. Ellen saw that wood now, its endurance rewarded by an encrustation of snails and a green coat of slime. A lone boat was moored to one of the columns, a small fishing boat looking rather forlorn and old with its green and white paint peeling off its wood. As Ellen's eyes went to it, it began to bob gently in the water, prodded into motion by the swells of the passing ship. That motion seemed to be a greeting of sorts, the boat saying hello to Ellen with its movement, like people you pass on the street nodding their heads to you as they go by.

Ellen loved this hilltop. Being here gave her a sense of open freedom. Sometimes, when running up this hill as she'd just done, she felt as though she could continue up and up, past the very crest of the hill itself, racing straight into the midst of the open sky, there to dash and play among the clouds, like a colt frolicking in an open field amidst mounds of white hay.

The crest upon which she stood offered a sense of direction as well as a sense of freedom, pointing as it did toward the horizon in the distance, toward America where, Ellen had come to believe, her future was packed up in a bundle and stored away waiting for her. Her life, her future life, was there in New York City, waiting to be picked up like a checked bag of luggage sitting in a bus depot locker.

Leaving was a necessity for her, as it was for many, for the town and countryside here in Donegal held too poor soil in which to plant and grow futures, not futures with any expectations of success anyway, financial or otherwise. Consequently, many people here, indeed many in all of Ireland, left the land they were born on, the land they loved, as soon as they were grown and able, going to other places to find their fortunes, or, if not a fortune, at least a livelihood, a job that let you pay the bills and raise a family. Dreams of a good life, even a grand life, could come true on the other side of the horizon, on the other side of the smoke-like mist that today hovered in the distance. Here in Donegal, in the small town of Moville, dreams only went to the pub to have a couple of pints and make empty talk of What Could Be.

If Ellen turned her gaze away from the water, which she did not, and her eyes wandered to the right a bit, she would have viewed the old warehouses and the aged railroad depot now standing silhouetted against the darkening sky. At one time the wharf was a beehive busy with the freight carried by the many ships that docked there. But that hustle and bustle was years ago, history as ancient as the Druids, or so it seemed to Ellen. Ships coming to Ireland had virtually ceased to be an event with the terrible sinking of the British passenger ship, the Athenia, by a submarine in 1939. After that tragedy, most ships that were not military did not dare to ride the waves as long as the war went on. At least they didn't dare if the destination was Donegal, Ireland.

Truth be known, Moville had stopped being a major port even before the Athenia's sinking and, even with the war's end, there was no real hope that anything would change for the better anytime soon. Many of the Moville train tracks were overgrown with smirking weeds that mocked the rails disuse while the cargo and tourists ships went elsewhere now with their burdens – mostly to Killybegs on the other side of Donegal. As a result of their betrayal, the prosperity of Moville had shrunk and shriveled to the size of a wrinkled pea. Wealth in Moville was now little more than a stray and hungry dog with its ribs showing, roaming the streets of a town that had few bones to be found.

The surviving local pubs continued to do their business. It seemed no matter how poor people got they could still find the pence needed to pay for a pint of the Black Stuff or for a shot of good Irish whiskey. Perhaps they needed it more then; the effects of the drink a compensation of sorts for the lack of hope for a better tomorrow.

But despair was an unknown entity to thirteen-year-old Ellen, as foreign to her as the opposite side of the moon. She had her dreams, the young always do, and she held tight to the hope, no, to the *certainty*, that those dreams would come true one day to become her personal reality. One of the mysteries of the top of Cliona's Hill was its ability to grant Ellen's dreams the freedom to soar. The view here, the open expanse of water and sky, was as a race jockey's whip provoking her imagination to full gallop. Here, her hopes for the future were somehow made more solid and the romances of her youthful heart could take wing and ascend into the clouds to fly alongside the gleeful gulls.

Her future happiness was on the other side of the horizon, just a boat ride away.

Her dreams varied in their cosmetics while remaining solidly the same at their core. She would marry a man she truly loved and who truly loved her back. They would not be rich except in that love, but they would have enough to live on and be happy. And she would stand by his side when he needed her and, in those few bad times, she would be strong of heart and brave, like the heroines in the books she read and those she saw in films. Just like the princesses and maidens in the tales her father told her.

Would a royal prince on a white horse come to the farm and fall in love with her? Maybe, but probably not. Pragmatic by nature, she understood that such a possibility was very unlikely. No one she knew had ever seen a prince in any part of Donegal. Could you imagine it? Becoming the Serene High Princess Ellen Such and Such? How impossible was that?

She didn't really care about being a princess. She didn't care to marry a prince in title, but she definitely would marry a prince in spirit, a good and kind man, a wonderful man, a man like her father.

Their home would be their own. Nothing too grand but it would be just fine even if it was a little drafty. Sure it'd need work just like the home she lived in now always needed work. But there'd be a big garden bounded by a white picket fence – all the homes in America had big gardens and white fences – and in that garden, beneath a warm sun, she would cut colorful flowers that she would put in a vase and then place upon the dining room table. There she would sit and enjoy dinner with her husband and her own fine rosy-cheeked children.

Or maybe they wouldn't own a house, perhaps it would be too dear in cost and they'd always be too poor to buy one. That would not be as fine as owning a house but it would be all right too, for they would have Love.

The man she married would love her so much, with all his heart and soul, that he wouldn't be able to think of life without her. She would be loved absolutely, remarkably, and she would love with all her heart in return. Her love would last forever, like the loves in her father's tales, like the love of her own parents. Her love would be a Forever Love. That was the solid core of all her dreams, that her love would be everlasting, that her love would be forever.

The hooting sound of the passing ship's whistle came clambering up the hill to tap her on the shoulder, to take her attention away from daydreams and thoughts of love. She saw an emission of steam from one of the ship's smokestacks swirl up into the sky where, caught by the breeze, it dispersed and was gone, its wisps becoming lost in the clouds.

Ellen's eyes remained fixed upon the tourist ship as it moved casually by, heading toward Magilligan Point, dissolving into the gathering darkness of twilight and the smoky haze resting on the faraway water, becoming little more than smoke itself as it disappeared into the mist and was gone.

She turned and went back down the hill, walking now, a happy skip to her step, returning to her home, trailing dreams behind her.

Chapter Two

Ellen was drawn out of her light sleep by a sound that startled her, a dull scraping noise like a knife cutting wood that produced in her a slight tremor of fear. *Something's in my room! A Cluricaune?! No, can't be. There's no drink in the room for it to steal. A Far Darrig? That'd be worse! The evil thing might want to hurt me!*

Ellen's father, a born *shanachie*, was constantly relating tales of the legends of Ireland to his children and had this night sent her, her brother and sisters too, off to bed with a tale of revenge taken upon a luckless Moville resident by a particularly nasty *Far Darrig*. They were mean and nasty goblins, too wicked to be taken lightly.

Another sound. Softer this time. Disoriented from sleep and fright, a moment or two passed before she realized the noise was coming from outside her room rather than from the foot of her own bed as she first feared. It came from the small landing on the other side of her door. She tossed off her blanket, padded to the door in her bare feet and opened it as silently as a thief. Peering out into the darkness, she just caught sight of her brother Jim's shoulders and head disappearing from view as he slowly descended the stairs.

James Rawdon, Ellen's only brother, seventeen years and some months old, almost four years older than Ellen, was a stocky, scrappy looking boy of medium height with a face splashed, like Ellen's, with a line of freckles. His hair was rough, unlike the shiny and smooth locks of each of his four sisters, a red-brown unruly bit of haystack that stuck out wildly in all directions. It looked like a demented sheaf-tosser had gone completely wild on his noggin.

Despite the horror of his hair, Jimmy was a good-natured boy, but he was also endowed with a mischievous streak that constantly prodded him into trouble. When years younger, his rear end had often suffered for his pranks and disobedience, his father believing that the sins of the soul of his "sonny boy" could be burned away by making his son's "arse glow like a red coal". Still, the fear of punishment seldom deterred Jimmy from doing what he wanted, not if he wanted to do it bad enough. Although it's equally true that he never consulted his rear end to determine what it might have thought of his shenanigans.

Where is he off to now? Oh, Da'll be so mad . . .

Jim was too old for spanking now. Punishment inflicted now was in the form of imprisonment, in his being confined to his home and forbidden to leave to meet his "carousing hoodlum" friends. He was (or was supposed to be) suffering under such a restriction now, a punishment for a previous offense, and by his daring to leave the house this night, a figure of shadow on the stairs, he was compounding that offense. *Da would howl like the devil if he caught Jimmy now*, thought Ellen. Her brother's disobedience, in his creeping out of the house at this late hour, almost eleven P.M., was shocking to Ellen who would never dream of going against her father in such a manner. A whispered call to Jimmy almost popped out of her mouth, a call to summon her brother back to his senses and back to his room, but she checked herself and the words rolled to the back of her tongue instead where they were then swallowed and gone. Instead she silently closed the door, knowing that Jimmy wouldn't listen to her if she did call to him. And if, by calling out, she woke her parents, Jim would blame her for his being caught.

Returning to her bed, she wondered again where it could be that her brother was going, so late at night. Putting the palms of her hands together, she murmured a prayer to God above to please keep Jim safe, wherever it was he ended up, whatever it was he was going off into the night to do.

*   *   *

A shimmering sliver of crescent moon, a pale glowing grin of a lantern in the inky star-dotted sky, offered Jim some dim light to walk by as he went down the dirt road that led away from the Rawdon farm to the paved Derry Road. The empty wheelbarrow he pushed before him bumped along the rutted *boreen* until he reached the paved route that would transport him and the barrow smoothly the rest of the way to Moville. He'd taken the barrow from the barn for good reason; he and Sean would need it – if all went well. It was part of the plan.

He made his way across the small bridge that passed over the Moville River, hurried by "the haunted spot" at Piper's Hill – Da had told him of the horrors that could befall a person foolish enough to dally there at night – and continued on for two miles until he reached the main street of Moville. His destination, the narrow alley directly opposite the Red Rooster Public House, was now in sight.

"Sean?" he whispered to the darkness as he approached the entrance to the alley. The obscurity shifted and a silhouette appeared, moving closer until Jim could make out the face in the wan moonlight.

"Lo, Jimmy."

A grin broadened Jimmy's face. "I've brought the barrow as you wanted. Took it from the barn." With this pronouncement he pushed the wheelbarrow into a shadow in the alley and released its handles. Sean responded with a grin of his own and, placing both hands inside the large pockets of his jacket, produced and displayed for Jim's eyes two bottles of (apparently) good Irish whiskey. "Here they be, James," he declared, his eyes glowing with delight. "We're all set."

Sean O'Reilly, a few months younger than Jim, already exhibited a confident maturity and self-assurance that commanded respect even from boys and men older than himself. Sean, at the age of sixteen, carried a natural sophistication of character and intelligence that installed in most who met him a sense of admiration. He did nothing outwardly to be so highly regarded and indeed, in his own odd way, was a modest young man. He presented a handsome face to the world, one endowed with fine, well-shaped Celtic features, and looked at events and people with penetrating green eyes that seemed to take in everything around him. His hair was black and shiny as a raven's wing. He was book-smart too, and did well in school, pleasing even the most violent of the nuns teaching there.

Broad at the shoulders and tall, his height already approaching six feet, Sean was reputed to be the best fighter among the boys his age and, for this reason, seldom had to fight. A circumstance that was good for him for he held an innate distaste for what he considered the nonsense of brawling for the sake of it. Although he had no compunction in putting fist to chin when necessity absolutely required it.

Sean held one bottle higher than the other and shook it about to slosh its contents. "This one's got the tea in it," he told Jim. "This other I've filled with part good whiskey for the taste, and with three-quarters pure alcohol with some paint remover thrown in. It's worse than any *poteen* he's ever drunk. When he downs this it'll kick the *omadhaun* clear up to the Big Dipper."

"*If* he drinks it. If it works as you think it will," returned Jim.

"'Twill. 'Twill," replied Sean. "Have a little faith, heathen. Everything is possible if you believe." He offered Jim a smile of confidence and then, turning to gaze at the entrance to The Red Rooster, punctuated his words by making the sign of the cross.

Jim's eyes located a small crate in the gloom of the alley and went to it to sit. Across the street the wooden sign of the Red Rooster, pushed by the strong breeze of the night, swung beneath the iron bar that held it aloft above the entrance to the pub. The boys could hear the creaking of the swaying sign in the alley clear across the street.

"He *is* inside, isn't he?" piped up Jim suddenly.

"Sure. Before you came I went up to the window and looked. He's in there, belly to the bar."

"The Rooster's been known to stay open well past the singing of the anthem," came back Jim. "So we might have us a bit of a wait."

"Not so," returned Sean, his whispering voice suddenly tense with excitement. "Look over. There's the big bag of manure now."

Jim jumped off the crate and stood beside Sean, gazing across the street. The object of the young boys' less than affectionate thoughts had indeed just exited the pub. The emerged bag of manure's name was William O'Mooney; a large man of twenty-six years of age who appeared older than his years. A man whose muscle was already being transformed into barstool fat. A protruding belly evidenced his love for food and pints, and his ruddy face displayed the telltale signs of the inveterate drinker he was. Although he had no way of knowing it at that moment, standing in front of The Red Rooster, Bill O'Mooney had already achieved the apogee of his life. From here it was downhill, a spiraling descent down Whiskey Slope to a life befogged by drink, a continuous decline into the life of an alcoholic blowhard.

But for now, to do him justice, he was just about the meanest and toughest son-of-a-whore in the town of Moville, a poisonous snake with plenty of venom in his fangs, to be approached only with great caution and a long stick.

O'Mooney liked to be called "Billyclub", an appellation bestowed upon him by his most ardent admirer: William O'Mooney himself. He thought it conveyed the appropriate sense of tough manliness for which he wanted to be known. As expected, he was basking now in his preferred condition, deep drunkenness, as he exited the pub. A condition that gave Sean and Jim great pleasure as they watched the man from the alley. It was part of the plan, to get to the man when he was less than sober.

O'Mooney stood, his small eyes gleaming out over his round cheeks into the street, looking like a hog that had just eaten a truffle, his face beaming in its alcohol-inspired sense of well-being, unaware he was being watched and conspired against.

"Oh damn," muttered Jimmy as the door of The Red Rooster opened once more and another pub denizen joined "Billyclub" on the sidewalk. "That tears it. If they walk home together, it's all off." Both boys breathed a sign of relief when the second man bellowed a loud drunken laugh, slapped O'Mooney on his wide back and returned alone into the pub.

O'Mooney's habit, after a night at The Red Rooster, which is to say each and every night, was to utilize the alley in which the boys now stood as a shortcut to his home. As expected, he started across the street now, heading for the narrow alley.

"Get ready, Seano," muttered Jim. "Oh, piss, I sure hope this works."

O'Mooney was humming to himself as he stagger-walked across the street. Nearing the shadows of the alley he pulled up at the edge of its entrance, hearing sounds from within. Standing still, he straightened his back and squinted into the darkness. He listened, and then smiled as he realized that the sounds he'd heard was that of voices in conversation.

Two boys, both laughing over how they'd stolen some good whiskey. Careful not to be seen, O'Mooney went to a wall and craned his neck so that one eye was able to view the length of the alley while his body remained hidden. No small accomplishment. In the dim moonlight he saw Sean and Jim, each holding a bottle of good Irish whiskey. *Boys out on a toot*, he concluded. *What a waste of fine whiskey.*

O'Mooney, if then placed on a boat and ridden on a rough sea would have made sloshing sounds like a three-quarters-filled cask of aged scotch. Still, full of whisky as he was, he suddenly had an overwhelming desire to drink some more. In what he imagined was a dazzling display of athletic speed he was suddenly upon Jim, pouncing upon the boy nearest to him. Grabbing hold of Jim's arm with one hand he yanked the bottle away with the other. Jim surrendered the prize without resistance, then twisted out of O'Mooney's grip and took a few steps deeper into the alley to get away from the threat of the man.

Step one of the plan was complete.

Jim yelled at O'Mooney, called him a thief for show, and then ordered him to give the bottle back, precluding his demand with a curse.

O'Mooney offered the boys a good imitation of Kelly's pig as he snorted derisively in response to Jim's demand. He lifted the prize, the whiskey bottle, high overhead so that it caught some moonlight, and stared with admiration at the label. "I b'lieve this stuff's too good for little snot-nosed children such as yourselves. It's a man's drink. I think I'll keep it for meself."

"I thought you said it was a man's drink?" stated Jimmy.

O'Mooney slid his worshipping eyes off the bottle's label and looked at Jim, trying to comprehend whether or not he'd really just received the audacity of an insult.

"Give it back," demanded Jim. "That's stealing."

O'Mooney grunted. "So what? Didn't you just steal it yourself? And what'll you do? Run home and tell your mum? Or maybe you'd like to try to take it back?" He glared threateningly at both boys and then grinned as both simply stood their ground without moving. "No? Didn't think so."

There was a moment of silence before Sean's voice came low out of the dark. "You mucker. That stuff's too good for the likes of *you*. Give it back."

O'Mooney stared at the silhouette that was Sean, surprised by the direct insult and the threatening tone of the voice. "Huh? What'd you say?"

"You heard me. That whiskey's too good for a plonker like you. Give it back."

O'Mooney's eyes narrowed and a hand, the one not holding the prized bottle, curled into a large fist. If his hand had still held Jim's arm, the bone would have been crushed. An incensed light came into his wolfish eyes. "Oh, I'm going to beat you for your smart mouth, little boy," he snarled. "Beat you black and blue."

Sean took a step back. "*Pougue Mahone*. You're not so tough. All talk. The word is that your father and mother are dumber than retarded hens and that you're even dumber than they are. It's said that you can't even hold your whiskey. *Why, even I could out-drink you.*" He held up the bottle in his hand, displaying it as a challenge. There it was, the trap, placed with these last words before O'Mooney's feet. Would he walk into it? A thrill of fear went through Jim and he gathered his legs so as to be ready for flight, to flee, in the event the man decided to fight rather than drink.

O'Mooney might have been offering proof of Sean's slur of his parents as his eyes then grew wide as hen's eggs and he gazed at him like a one-year-old trying to comprehend the rules of chess. "Can't hold my whiskey?" he growled at last. "Oh, a real smartmouth. All right, boy, let's have us a contest. First we'll drink and *then* I'll beat your damned head in." He spat against the alley wall as Sean smiled in beatification. O'Mooney had just stepped full into the snare.

With a pleased glance of the eyes toward Jim and a smile curling the corners of his mouth, Sean twisted the cap off the bottle of tea in his hand. Raising it to his lips he turned it bottom up and swallowed half of its contents in a few great gulps. Even in the dim light, O'Mooney could see the bubbles rising in the bottle as Sean drank. "Now you, you great blowhard," he challenged, looking victoriously at O'Mooney and lifting the bottle overhead to better exhibit the fact that it was now half-empty. "Let's see what you can do."

O'Mooney stared incredulously and with admiration in spite of himself. "Well, boy," he muttered at last. "You *can* drink."

"Better than you," came back Sean with a sneer on his face. "Let's see what you can do. Or I'm going to spread it all over Moville that you ran away. I'm telling the whole town I beat you."

O'Mooney responded by twisting the cap off the bottle he held, tossing it away and raising the bottle up to his lips. Wrapping his lips on the bottle top and swallowing in huge gulps, he consumed in seconds the entire fiery contents it held. Sean's smile broadened, his expression the happy face of a cat with canary feathers falling from its mouth.

"How's that you little piss," barked O'Mooney through a loud belch and a crazed madman's grin. He threw the empty bottle to the side where it shattered loudly against the wall and, hitching up his pants, he growled, "Now, children, I'm going to break your wonderful young faces."

Sean and Jim would never forget the joyful moment that followed on the heels of O'Mooney's threat. Their scheme had gone as smoothly and as effortlessly as possible. In the next tick of the clock, O'Mooney's regal threatening smile dropped from his face as though the corners of his mouth had been pulled by lead weights. His eyes opened wide and the pupils rolled up and disappeared into his head, his eyes now spelunkers deciding to explore the empty caverns of his skull. The boys could see the whites of the man's rolling eyes, a gift of the moonlight. Then, like a tree axed at its foundation, O'Mooney fell forward, already senseless, to the ground. He landed with a soft thud, his protruding belly serving as protector of his face as it helped to partially break his fall. Face down in the dirt, he lay with his arms spread-eagled out, his fingertips nearly touching the walls of the alley on either side of him.

That soft thud of O'Mooney's landing was the sound of glorious victory, the sweet grunt and thump of success. Surely, there were unseen rainbows glowing in the night sky and somewhere nearby the Cloughaneely Band was playing joyously. The boys gathered closer to the fallen man and, gazing at the huge lump in the darkness, let out a whoop of victory. "We did it, Sean!" cried Jim. "We beat him! We beat him!"

"Shh, quiet," cautioned Sean. "We're making too much noise. Come on, we've still got a lot to do."

The boys bent over their prize and together turned it face up. There was a line of blood on O'Mooney's upper lip, resulting from a bloody nose and a scrape on his chin when his face hit the ground. The man appeared twice as fat now that he was prone on his back, looking like a beached whale.

"Go on, Jim. Get the barrow. We'll put him in it." Jim rolled the wheelbarrow over to the stupendous mass of fallen O'Mooney and the two boys, with no small effort, lifted the heavy man off the ground and transferred his bulk into it. Once there, O'Mooney looked as peaceful as if sleeping in his favorite armchair.

"Do you think we'll make it to the church without being seen?" asked Jim.

"We'll make it. The angels are with us," replied Sean with confidence. "We'll keep off the main street." He gripped the handles of the barrow. "Check the back of the alley. Make sure all's clear. Watch for the *Garda*."

"Clear," called back Jim in a whisper and with that Sean lifted the rear of the barrow, his young muscles springing taut as, with a soft groan of effort, he began rolling the massive unconscious O'Mooney out of the dark passageway, heading out of town, toward Saint Mary's Church.

*   *   *

One half-hour later, Jim and Sean were walking together, walking away from Saint Mary's and returning to their homes, Jim rolling the now O'Mooneyless barrow casually before him. The animation generated by their night's work had dissipated and they were content for the moment to walk in silence, savoring the sweet success of their plot. Half-success, at least. There was another chapter to be written in order to complete their small book of reprisal. If all went well, that chapter would be penned tomorrow, Sunday, within the holy space of the church.

"Maybe we should have taken him to the Presbyterian Church, Sean. It seems almost – evil – to drop him in Saint Mary's, doesn't it?"

"Not to me. Besides your father won't be going to the Presbyterian Church tomorrow, will he?"

Jim hissed a chuckle as he recalled once again the sweet moment when O'Mooney's eyes rolled up into his head and the man toppled to the ground. "Oh, it was priceless, Sean," he pronounced gleefully. "O'Mooney almost couldn't believe his eyes when he saw you downing that tea. I tell you, Sean, when he fell I thought his belly put a dent in the ground." Both boys laughed.

"I've got to hand it to you," continued Jim with clear admiration in his voice. "The way you planned it all like you did. No one but you could have thought it all out."

Sean shrugged off the compliment. "Ah, it wasn't much. I actually got the idea from a story I heard your father tell. He's great – spinning tales. Better than listening to the radio."

It was an outrageous remark made by O'Mooney against Jimmy's father that had prompted the boys to plot their act of revenge.

"I just had a bad thought, Sean. What if O'Mooney wakes up in the middle of the night?"

Again Sean shrugged. "He could. We have no control over that." Then, flashing a moonlit grin, he added, "But if there's a God above, he won't. He'll stay sleeping in that confessional until we're ready for him."

"Were you scared at all? Did you think for a time it wouldn't work?"

"You mean when he started coming at me?"

"Oh Sweet Mary. I thought he was going to grab you and pound you purple as a plum. Were you scared at all?"

"Not a bit. I just thought I'd pee a river in my pants."

The two friends mixed their laughter and then grew silent once again. The barrow hit a bump on the paved road and Jim had to steady it. In the night the shadows of the trees were black on either side of them for a time. Then the road began to turn down between wide-open fields. He and Sean reached the fork in the road where they had to separate and each bid goodnight to the other. "See you tomorrow in church then," said Jim as he pointed the nose of the wheelbarrow away from Sean. The crescent of moon, which had been smiling at them as though a comrade sharing their happiness, here too bid a goodnight to both boys as it chose that moment to disappear behind a bank of heavy clouds.

"Tomorrow I'm going to be more religious than a nun," replied Sean, now nothing more than a dark shadow. "See you at church early."

Jim pushed the barrow a few steps ahead before stopping and turning around again, himself a black shadow in the deep night. "We did it Sean!" he cried enthusiastically. "We did it!"

Sean had to imagine the grin on Jim's face as darkness obscured any view of it. "We sure did, Jimmy," he called back. "And if all goes well, tomorrow'll be more fun than tonight. See you at church."

Tomorrow O'Mooney would receive his much-merited comeuppance. Tomorrow the undeserved insult to Jim's father would be avenged . . . tomorrow . . .

. . . if only the blessed angels in heaven above continued to smile upon them. And they must. After all, justice was on their side and justice is loved by God. An uncalled for slander against a good man, or woman if it comes to that, could not be tolerated. Sean looked up into the dark sky overhead as he walked away from Jim, going toward his own home. The dark clouds scudded by and the curve of moon abruptly reappeared overhead, tucked in the midst of a group of sparkling stars. Surely, thought Sean, it was not just the moon that was smiling at him now. At least a few of those sparkling stars had to be glints of light reflecting off the toothy grins of satisfied heavenly spirits. "We did God's work today," he murmured to himself.

Tomorrow. Tomorrow O'Mooney would truly pay for his sin.

Chapter Three

The sun rose as weary as it had gone to bed, screening its rise behind a veil of mist and white clouds, a shy maiden peering over the hills of Donegal. The sunlight, accompanied by an abundance of chirps from twittering birds, crept softly into Ellen's room and fell, barely warm and scarcely bright, upon her face. Despite the tentative touch of the sun's fingertips, her eyes blinked open and she was immediately wide awake. Once bathed and dressed, she bounded down the stairs toward the delicious aromas of Sunday breakfast, of rashers and eggs, of fresh bread and jelly.

The Rawdon house, a two-story home of white-painted stone, was shielded overhead with a blue-green roof that held two chimneys, one at each end. From a distance, Ellen thought the chimneys made the house resemble the head of a mythical flat-headed horned beast, an image provoked by one of her father's tales. According to her father the house they lived in actually was, in the time of the Druids, a living creature, a former mythical creature transformed into an immobile pile of house by Christian magicians chasing evil from Ireland. But the family was safe inside it, despite its past, as the house could not come to life again – unless inhabited by wicked children.

That particular tale was told to Ellen when she was just six, and she for years made certain that the terrible possibility of the house coming alive would not occur due to anything she did, although she fretted constantly about Jimmy making it happen. Now, more grownup, she knew the story wasn't true. The house coming alive couldn't really happen, at least most likely. Just another of her father's tales. But, last night when watching Jimmy creep out of the house, she was not entirely certain that the floor boards beneath her feet were not beginning to tremble with the movement of their coming back to life, despite her grownup attitude toward the tale.

An evil beast at one time? Probably not. But a good home now for certain. The house, occupied with Ellen, her sisters Maggie, Rose and Teresa, her brother Jimmy, her parents and the dog Tinker, was more often then not filled with the sounds of activities, of expressed personalities and opinions, of wants and needs and squabbles and conflicts; with the tension of sibling rivalries and with parents' scoldings and parents' teachings, but above all this there was, in abundance, the warmth of affection and love.

Maggie, Rose and Teresa, five, three and two years older respectively than Ellen's thirteen years, were already seated at the table eating. All Rawdons present, including Ellen, were dressed in their Sunday best, ready to journey to church. Jim's chair was empty, he an absentee.

Didn't he come home last night? Ellen held onto her question, not wanting to get her brother into trouble by revealing she'd witnessed him slithering out of the house in the dark of the night.

She gave a good-morning peck on the cheek to each of her parents, her mother by the stove breaking an egg into the frying pan and her father sitting at the table, and settled into her seat, already salivating over the smells of good food. As a plate was placed onto the table before her, her father, with a sigh of exasperation, spoke up: "Mary, someone better have Jimmy shake his tail and get down here. I'll not be late for Mass." The words were ostensibly for his wife, but were in fact meant for his children, a request for a volunteer to rise from the midst of his pack of daughters, run up the stairs and rouse his sleeping son.

Ellen inhaled deeply. *Time to tell. Da'll be mad.* Her mouth opened, prepared to spill the secret it held. The first words of betrayal were about to emerge and show their faces between her parted lips but before she could utter them her sister Maggie spoke up first, and, hearing Maggie's voice, the words of betrayal stayed put, to bide their time until Maggie had her say.

"Oh, sorry," Maggie said, "I forgot to tell you. Jim's up and gone already. He told me he was meeting Sean O'Reilly and going to the early Mass with him."

Ellen's mouth clamped shut, and, as with her almost-call to Jim last night, her words were gulped down, this time with a forkful of scrambled egg.

Philip Rawdon stared at Maggie as if she'd suddenly stood up and declared herself a lost daughter of the English monarchy. "W-What?"

"Jimmy's gone to – "

"I heard you, Mags," interrupted her father, leaning back in his chair. "Now give me a moment to fully comprehend this wonder. My boy, my beloved son who normally has to be dragged from the warmth of his bed on a Sunday as though he was a tick hiding in Tinker's anus, has suddenly this day decided to rise with the dawn and go off to early Mass with the O'Reilly boy. Is that what I'm hearing you tell me, Maggie?" He shifted his eyes then to Ellen who was suddenly taken with a giggling fit. "What are you laughing about, El?"

"You said Tinker's anus," replied Ellen, still giggling. She reached out and grabbed a scone off the plate in the middle of the table.

"He was wearing his suit," came back Maggie with a shrug of her shoulders "He said he was leaving for church."

"Well, my son must think me ignorant entirely. But then maybe, just maybe, the boy was indeed blessed by a holy saint while he slept and has actually gone off to church as he said. You can bet I'll be finding the truth of it. Well, all right then, we'll finish our breakfast and be off." His eyes held a twinkle in them. He didn't entirely disapprove of Jimmy's high spirits, believing the nature of the boy to be an inheritance received from him. "Ah, well," he mumbled to himself. "I was a devil meself at his age."

With the finish of breakfast, the family squeezed themselves into the big, old banged-up convertible that was the family car. The top was down due to the mild day. Like the old man it was, the auto moved slowly and carefully down the rutted dirt path leading to the Derry Road, advancing as though fearful of tripping and breaking a hip, its bones and joints popping and creaking all the way to the paved road. Only there did Philip Rawdon allow it more speed.

Ellen's parents sat in the front, this day enjoying the roominess offered by Jimmy's absence, while the four girls sat pressed together as usual in the back seat, looking like cigars pushed into the breast pocket of a tight-fitting shirt. Four Irish cherubs sitting side by side.

Ellen liked Sundays. And absolutely loved Saint Mary's Church. A sense of admiration filled her as she passed through the regal entrance of the holy place and stepped onto the gleaming blackened wood of the aged floor. She was impressed by the height of the ceiling overhead, by its grand wooden beams. So big and so high, so unlike the cramped quarters of her own home. She liked too the impression of quiet worship the church held. The interior contained a strong sense of comfort, as though it truly held in its heart something holy and celestial. Ellen believed it did.

And Sunday was the one day her father dressed up, put on his best (and only) suit to look like what Ellen knew he truly was, a man of quality.

Philip Rawdon was a man in his late fifties now, with deep black hair just beginning to surrender to silver, but he was so strong and vigorous, and so youthful in appearance, that most thought him to be years younger. All who knew him thought he'd live past one hundred, maybe past a thousand. A man tough and strong, and real and true and tender as well. Ellen loved him with all her heart.

Her mother too always dressed in her best on church days and, on those days, looked to Ellen to be all courtly elegance. A queen could certainly look no better. Ellen thought them both to be the handsomest couple in the parish, in all of Donegal and, most likely, in all of Ireland.

Inside the church she always sat next to her father on his right, while her mother was on his immediate left. Ellen felt a sense of privilege in sitting there, thinking she was usurping the rights of her brother Jim and her older sisters to gain the seat by her father's side. She didn't care if she was a thief, it felt good to sit close to him, this large, handsome man with the smiling gentle eyes who was her father. Her sisters and brother would have a no-holds barred, teeth-gnashing fight on their hands if they dared tried to move her.

This particular Sunday the family car held another rider, Doubt, the unseen but palpable family doubt as to the truth of Jimmy's story. It filled the space in the front seat as completely as would Jim's physical body if he was present. So it came as much a surprise to them as not, parents and daughters alike, when, in approaching the church with its high steeple, they actually saw Jimmy standing on the stone steps with the O'Reilly boy.

"Look, there's Jimmy!" shouted Rose. "By the steps!" Her arm shot out from behind her father to extend past his right ear and waggle a finger in the general direction of her brother.

"Aye, I see him, Rosie," said her father.

"Oh, he *is* with Sean O'Reilly," remarked Rose in a hushed tone soaked with worship. If her voice had legs, its knees would have buckled.

"Isn't he a dream?" whispered Maggie. "Too bad he's so young." Teresa giggled and Ellen looked at them all, her three sisters, with bewilderment. Then she turned to scrutinize Sean, wondering what the fuss was about.

The church named Saint Mary's was a church within a church, or rather a church within the ruins of a church. The original structure had been destroyed during the great famine suffered by the Irish in the Nineteenth Century, during a time when much of what food was able to be provoked out of Irish soil was exported away from the starving bellies of those doing the growing. Cruel times. Terrible times, and the priests of the old Saint Mary's church had offered fiery sermons against the sins of those in power who literally were taking the food out of the mouths of the hungry, not only allowing but actually compelling the Irish to starve. In response to the priests' condemnations, the powers-that-be not only continued to procure much of the available food but took the church as well. The original Saint Mary's was set ablaze to teach the starving to keep quiet about their hunger pangs, a concept of threat conceivable only by those with full belching bellies.

Portions of the stone walls of the original burnt structure remained, a piece of nave and most of the great tower. These remains, offering a dim glimpse into the past glory of the destroyed church, could be seen standing behind the newer smaller building erected on the same consecrated soil. Thus, the new church stood in the dual shadows of the other's ruin and its grim history.

The land surrounding the church-within-a-church was a graveyard, and was sprinkled with monuments designating the graves of the departed. Many of the stone markers were so eroded by the elements, so gnawed upon by the teeth of time, that their inscriptions were all but totally erased. Some were indeed totally illegible. A few older graves were marked with thick wooden crosses carved crudely with a farmer's axe, the only monuments the poverty at the time of their deaths could provide for the loved ones buried there.

Many of the local residents talked of seeing in the darkness of the night's shadows the specters of ancestors skulking through the graveyard or strolling through the ruins of the old church, crying and moaning like *banshees*. Lost souls seeking absolution for sins still unforgiven or attempting to find for themselves the pathway to heaven that, for whatever reason, remained hidden from their preternatural eyes. Ellen, years ago, had asked her father if the stories of spooks roaming the church graveyard were real, if such things as ghosts were even possible, and he replied that of course they were.

The family climbed out of the car and went as one to the church steps. "Well this is a grand day," called out the father to his son as they approached Sean and Jim. The family went up the steps, Mary and the girls continuing by and entering the church as Philip stayed behind with Sean and Jim.

"Is it not a grand day? My Jimmy – " here he placed his big hand on his son's shoulder, " – is abandoning his heathen inclinations – inherited from his mother's side of the family I might add – and is making his way to God." He gazed with suspicious eyes at both boys. "And you too Sean. When's the last time you saw the inside of Saint Mary's? When Noah was putting his nails to wood? Now a more cynical man than meself might be asking why his son, having already gone to early Mass, is still hovering about the church even after that Mass is ended. One would think he would naturally already be on his merry way." He paused, letting the silence form the question mark to his request for information.

"Well, sir," replied Sean, seeing Jim fumbling for words, "actually we're waiting for you. We decided to stay for the next Mass 'cause Jim wanted to wait for his family, and I decided to stay with him. He said going to Mass without his family just didn't feel right." He beamed a sunny grin at the elder Rawdon.

"Well, you have been licking at the teat of the Blarney Stone, haven't you?" responded Jim's father, staring into Sean's face.

"I'm glad you're here," offered Jim, picking up on Sean's lead. "I missed having the family with me. Now we can go inside." He imitated Sean's grin.

Philip Rawdon's eyes widened. "Well now, what *is* this all about? What is really going on, I'm asking."

"Really," said Jim. "We're just going to church."

His father eyed him skeptically. "All right, son," he said finally. "Have it your way. But the name of Rawdon better not be blackened today, nor any day – " He turned to look at Sean. " – nor the name of O'Reilly for that matter, or there'll be the devil to pay." He punctuated this declaration with a sharp nod of his head and then stepped by and into the church.

"Sean," said Jim after his father had passed through the church doors, "He knows something's up."

"He likes O'Mooney even less than we do. He'll love what's going to happen."

"O'Mooney slept right through the first Mass, He might just as well sleep through this one too."

"I thought of that too. Where do you think I went when I left before? I got a bottle and filled it with water." He opened his jacket to reveal the container to Jim. "I'll pour this on the pig's head. It should wake him up."

The two conspirators went up the steps and into the church together, Jim going to the pew in which his family was seated while Sean stayed alone in the back near a confessional.

The sermon that day was an inspired one, filled with threatening gestures and allusions to the terrors of hell and torment. Father Cullum grew red-faced as he narrated and gesticulated with unusual heated spirit. His literal torrent of impassioned speech held the congregation in awe and wonder (and some in fear that the clergyman would suffer a stroke right on the altar) as he orated with wild energy, carried away by the fervor contained in his own rising voice.

No one noticed Sean as he went casually to the confessional stall furthest from the altar and surreptitiously extended an arm past the curtain shielding the interior from the church. Unseen, he poured the entire contents of the bottle of water in his hand over the head of the slumbering O'Mooney. It was here, to this confessional stall, that the boys had hauled the man in the barrow the previous night.

In moments, Sean was rewarded for his effort by the sputtering and coughing that emerged from behind the curtain. Hearing the sounds of the man rousing himself from sleep, seeing the curtain quiver with movement, he quickly withdrew, stepping far away from the confessional and its awakening contents.

Father Cullum's arm was extended high overhead, pointing a finger to the glory of the heavens, speaking at the very height of his oratory splendor when he abruptly halted in mid-sentence and stood absolutely frozen, appearing as though he'd been transformed on the instant to solid stone by the gaze of an unseen Medusa. He was a petrified priest, the only movement that gave the lie to his having been turned to stone was that of his mouth dropping open. Some parishioners swore afterwards that they saw his jaw actually hit the bible in front of him before bouncing up again. Some wondered for a few seconds if the man was experiencing a heavenly vision while others were certain that their priest had indeed, as feared, burst a conglomerate of blood vessels in his skull. Surely he would in a moment drop dead to the altar floor.

By a miracle of God he remained standing. "O Heavenly Father – " he muttered at last, words whispered rather than spoken aloud and so words heard only by those in the pews nearest him. His raised arm came down to his chest to make a hurried sign of the cross.

Now the more perceptive members of the congregation realized that their priest's eyes were fixed not upon a miraculous vision occurring only for the holy man's holy sight but rather upon *something else* immediately behind them. Heads began to turn, the eyes of the parishioners following the priest's gaze to the rear of the church.

William O'Mooney, goaded out of his drunken slumber by the water Sean had spilled over him, had stepped from the darkness of the small confessional and now stood in the light and holiness of the Mass, standing in front of a stained-glass window as naked as a newborn baby, looking like a drunkard's mockery of a holy baptism. A sight O'Mooney was, but a sight sorely lacking an infant's charm. The remnants of the water Sean had poured over him dripped from his head and shoulders, and left his hair plastered flat to his skull. He might have been some unholy creature just risen up from the depths of a corrupt sea. The red flush of his face contrasted with the extreme pallor of his body so that it looked like a huge fresh-picked tomato had been placed upon a snowman's body to serve as its head. The pale white of the swollen globe of his belly hovered like a large pallid jellyfish preparing to attack his genitals as he took a step forward, moving on legs so unsteady it was questionable for the moment whether or not he would remain standing. His bleary eyes stared about him, attempting to send perception and comprehension to his swirling, befogged brain. The man, it was clear, had no idea where he was.

His legs did manage to continue to hold his weight and he stepped slowly down the side aisle, bumping now and then against the wall, walking with a baby's steps toward the altar, muttering to himself in an unknown alien language, a naked madman speaking in strange tongues.

The stunned hush of the church gave way to shrieks of horror and shouts of anger. Some men and many children laughed. Women screamed. Candles flickered and the entire altar, some said later, took an appalled step back. The loud uproar caused O'Mooney to instinctively halt in his steps. He comprehended there were people about him, the realization coming to him even through the fog of his blurry sight and more blurry brain. Further awareness somehow pushed itself into him and a glance down at himself brought to him at last the comprehension of his own blatant, screaming nakedness. With a shocked gasp, he fell stupefied against the church wall, pressing his body against it as though wanting to pass through its stone to the other side. His jaw flopped down just as Father Cullum's had done seconds earlier, and his mouth transformed itself into a verbal sluice out of which gushed a river of confused gibberish. More speaking in tongues.

Delight danced up the spines of Sean and Jim. This was better than they could have imagined. Both were laughing wildly, wiping tears from their eyes.

A woman's voice, an elderly woman by the sound of it, was heard shouting in a voice clear and strong over the uproar: "Shame on you, William O'Mooney! And in the house of God for Heaven's sake! You damned shit-for-brains pervert!" Shock and admonition rode upon her voice.

Suddenly fully aware of his humiliation, O'Mooney started running for the nearest exit. An old woman, perhaps the same one who'd shouted shame at him, hit his rump hard with her blackthorn cane, the sound a sharp slap that resounded through the church like a rifle shot. Now even many of the women who'd first shrieked their horror were roaring with laughter. Philip Rawdon placed his hands over Ellen's eyes, regretting he didn't have hands enough for his other daughters' popping eyes. "Maggie! Rose! Teresa! Look away!" he shouted. The giggling girls ignored him.

O'Mooney ran and burst through the nearest exit, the dusty blackness of the soles of his feet and the pale flesh of his rump, now bearing a red stripe from the slap of the woman's cane, were the last images the people saw of him as he disappeared from their sight. O'Mooney was certain that even the stone statues of the saints were laughing at him as he fled, his breasts, belly and ballocks bouncing, from the holy shadows of Saint Mary's.

*　　*　　*

O'Mooney's humiliation was a momentous event that provided the pubs in Moville, and in surrounding towns as well, with much reason for laughter for many nights after. He achieved fame of sorts as it became a standard local expression in many a pub to scold a foolish person with the declaration: "You have the holy sense of O'Mooney's white arse". Many assumed that Billyclub's drunkenness had made him appear in church that day (O'Mooney himself believed it as well as he had no recollection of meeting Sean and Jim the previous night) and the two boys responsible for his everlasting mortification didn't tell anyone otherwise. Not for years afterward at least.

O'Mooney disappeared from the streets of Moville. Some believed he changed his name when he left for he was never heard from again.

Some say he went down to Kerry to live in a cave, others that he went to live with monks in Tibet while still others were certain he gained passage on a ship and traveled straight to the Outback in Australia. Whether or not the tale of "O'Mooney's white and holy arse" had made it to the aborigines living there was not known, although those in town who spoke of Australia were fairly certain it had.

Jim's father of course suspected that his son and Sean were somehow responsible for the man's disgrace but he never pressed either for the truth. When he did speak of "O'Mooney's naked jaunt through Saint Mary's Church" afterwards, and he did so often, it was always with much glee. He usually concluded the short history with the words: "Ah, and it was a wonderful moment. A rare moment, the kind of moment that warms one's heart to love the whole of the world. The kind of moment that confirms one's belief in a loving and kind God."

Chapter Four

A full year passed by, and another few months as well. Maggie suddenly announced to the family that she would be leaving for America, there to earn a real living. And, within weeks, the eldest sister made good her words and was gone from home. The hope she expressed in leaving was fulfilled quickly as she obtained work immediately upon arriving in New York City. Soon the family was receiving monthly checks from overseas to help pay the bills. Money very much needed.

Ellen remained in school, education being a priority (as much as economics permitted it to be a priority) in the Rawdon house, while many of her friends had "finished" their "learning" and had gone off to seek work (beyond the boundaries of Moville). Continuing on in school gave Ellen a jabbing sense of guilt for she would have liked to have been earning money instead of just going on to the next level of education. Only her parents' insistence kept her in school.

Winter came, the Mummers made their appearance and then were gone again. Spring followed, this time dragging after it a summer of unprecedented heat (for Donegal). For a full four weeks in that blistering summer it was "hot enough to char the tops of trees", as some declared. The Donegal cows shunned the open fields, collecting in small groups in whatever patches of shadow they could find, seeking shelter from the blazing sun. Unless absolutely necessary the men of Donegal followed the lead of the cattle, abandoning their tasks during midday to also seek relief from the heat. Each day the sun rose hot and bright to bake the houses in Donegal as if they were loaves of bread put into a brick oven.

During those sweltering days, a breeze was considered nothing less than a heavenly gift offered by holy angels to the truly suffering.

Back in January, on Saint Brigid's Eve, the Rawdons had made a few Saint Brigid's crosses and hung them in the byre. The crosses were believed (by some) to have the power of keeping animals from harm and perhaps that power was being shown now in the summer's heat, as the two Rawdon cows were doing well.

After a month, the swelter at last packed its unmentionables into a traveling bag and abandoned the north of Ireland, much to the relief of all. The cool was welcomed as thoroughly as a train carriage filled with a multitude of rich relatives arriving from the States, all bearing gifts.

Ellen, just completing the last of her chores that first wonderfully cool day after the hot spell, went to her room and placed herself down on her bed (just for a few minutes) so as to enjoy the frosty feel of the breeze as it curled in over the windowsill of her room.

With the passing of the last year and few months, the once skinny Ellen had quietly transformed. No longer a gangly young girl, her lanky tomboy quality had slowly modified itself into a youthful elegance. Nearing the age of fifteen, Ellen was showing signs of becoming a young women of wholesome beauty, albeit, for now, it was a beauty still only partially complete, still in the midst of being formed.

In bed, enjoying the cool breeze, she heard her parents' voices coming up the stairs, soft and indistinct at first, then louder, the tone vaguely disquieting, sounding troubled. *Are they worried about money again?* She sat up, then jumped off the bed and went out of her room to greet them, and was startled to see a thin line of tears sitting on the lower lid of her mother's eyes.

"Mum, what's wrong?" she asked.

Mother and father exchanged glances. They had not expected Ellen to be in the house. "I'm going to lie down," said Philip as he released his wife's eyes. "You might as well tell the child."

Ellen stared with concern at her father's back until he disappeared into his bedroom. *Da's not feeling well,* she thought. She and her mother stepped into Ellen's room, her mother sitting on the bed and Ellen doing the same, following her mother's lead. The two sat in silence until Ellen prompted her mother to talk: "Mum, what is it you're worried over? Tell me. You and Da have been acting odd for days now."

"All right, Chickie," responded her mother, and, with a deep breath, she began: "Your father and I were trying not to worry you and the others, so we didn't say anything but I suppose now it's time. It's your father, El. We didn't go into Letterkenny to shop three days ago, nor the week before. Your father saw a doctor there, the same who'd operated on him years ago. You were just a babe then. Years ago they discovered a tumor in his stomach and they operated and took it out. For years he's been fine – but now – "

Ellen's heart lurched inside her. She was suddenly more afraid than she'd ever been before in her young life.

"The doctor," continued her mother, clutching herself now, "made – some tests – "

"Da, sick?" Ellen stared at her mother. "But what, what is it?"

Her mother, pausing, stretched out her hand and placed it tenderly over Ellen's, a soothing gesture, which served only to increase Ellen's fear. "Oh baby!" blurted her mother, her composure abruptly gone and tears springing out of her eyes, "The doctor says it's the cancer again! Worse this time . . . ."

Cancer. The word pounded fright straight into Ellen's soul. Her heart was suddenly twisting inside her chest like a madman looking to escape from a straitjacket. She stared wildly, disbelievingly, into her mother's weeping, moaning eyes. "Cancer? No. No that can't be!" The words jerked themselves out of her. "It *can't* be!"

Ellen knew of the horrors of cancer. She'd watched her Uncle Terry being eaten up by it just a year ago, growing weaker and weaker until he required a cane simply to cross the room, until he had trouble climbing in and out of bed. Ellen, looking into her mother's devastated eyes, saw now the image her uncle's wasted face, gaunt and gray, the hollow cheeks barely supporting two grim eyes that seemed more like two stones resting at the bottom of two dry wells.

"Even if it is cancer, it can be fixed. They can operate, Mum. Then he'll be fine again. Isn't that so?"

Her mother released Ellen's hand and turned away. "Oh, Chickie, they can't fix him. H-He's going to die!" With that she buried her face in her hands, sobbing, releasing her sorrow onto the palms. Ellen stared at the back of her mother's dress, the cloth pulled taut across the shoulders. She wanted to comfort her but couldn't.

"Die . . . ? Mum, they're wrong!" she declared to her mother's back. "You'll see. They're wrong!" *It has to be a mistake. Da's so very strong.* Her father was unassailable and invincible. A rock.

Her mother continued to sob. "They're wrong!" Ellen insisted again, shouting the words this time, even as a profound bubble of sorrow welled up inside her to mock her declaration. In the next moment she leaped up and ran from the room, fleeing the house as though believing it was possible to run fast enough to leave a terrible truth behind her forever.

*　　*　　*

Ellen stood on top of her hill, staring down at the harbor. The morning clouds were gone and the gold of the sun floated in broken shards upon the expanse of water before her, a sight now dulled by her tears. She used the sleeve of her shirt to wipe her face and then wiped it again. The sour taste of bile sat in the back of her throat and her ribs felt as though a monster was caged behind them, a creature with powerful teeth that wanted nothing less than to tear her up. Years ago, Da had told her the story of the legendary Daire who was swallowed by a monster and, to save himself, had cut himself free, but here the monster was inside her instead of the other way around, and it was the monster doing the ripping and cutting. How do you save yourself from that? A gentle breeze came off the water but seemed now to carry only misery with it, a mocking charlatan imitating the tenderness of the friend of her past.

Hugging herself, she dropped to the grass and sobbed, pleading for the world to change back to the way it was, praying to God to *please change it back*, praying harder than she'd ever imagined she was capable of praying.

Da can't die. He can't! He can't . . .

And, inside her, the hateful creature that was her dread raked her ribs with its claws and mocked her prayers, all the time screaming an opposing truth at her terrified and distressed young heart.

Chapter Five

The days were now traitorous carriages carrying hours that were thieves with neither mercy nor compassion, hours that held the sinful souls of purse-cutters and pickpockets, thieves coming to steal pieces of Philip Rawdon's robust health and snatch away bits of his wellbeing. Time can heal all wounds, it is said, but in Philip Rawdon's case Time was nothing less than a heartless destroyer.

These filchers had their hands in the pockets of Ellen's heart as well, stealing away fragments of her hidden hope for a magical cure for her father, robbing her little by little of the faith that God would somehow answer her many prayers.

In a few months, her father transformed from a man of health into an emaciated mockery of himself, the horrible alteration taking place right before Ellen's disbelieving eyes. The once cheery character of the Rawdon home slowly transformed as well, becoming a looming, heavy thing, an atmosphere of misery seeping into every corner and crevice of the house. The very Angel of Death might have taken up residence there, sitting in the easy chair with feet up and enjoying a few pints, waiting patiently until the time came to step forward and lay official claim to Philip Rawdon's life.

Ellen, despite the waning of her hope, beseeched God each day. *God. Please make Da well. Hear me. Listen to me. Please God. Please! Da, fool them all and get well. We all love you. Get well. Please. Please Da . . . .*

What good is a deaf God?

*   *   *

On one fine day, months into her father's illness, Ellen, with her mother and father, made a trip to Doon Well, a natural spring in Donegal reputed to have special healing powers. Da, although much wasted away, was still well enough to drive and this he did, traveling to the well at the insistence of his wife. Once there, Mary tore a strip of cloth away from a sleeve of one of his old shirts (they'd taken an extra shirt with them) and hung it on the bush beside the well. Another kind of prayer.

On the bushes at Doon Well there hung, like clusters of buds on fertile rosebushes, a profusion of pieces of fabric from the clothes of other pilgrims who had also come to the well, all seeking cures. Stuck in the ground were many walking sticks and crutches, their great number creating the impression of an odd kind of dead hedge. Whether those leaving these fragments of their sicknesses had walked away cured, or had taken an extra crutch and stick with them before setting out, wasn't clear, although Ellen hoped that at least some represented a true cure.

Philip Rawdon went to the Doon Well to please his wife, not believing God would be found there. More superstition here than religion, in his opinion. Being a teller of tales, he thought he knew a tall one when it was presented to him. So he expected no true cure to come from his visit although, for his wife's benefit, he pretended he did. Sometimes the pretense of hope is better than its absence.

Philip Rawdon was a man with an innate sense of dignity, with a sense of wanting to hold his head up high no matter what, and even now, in the throes of this terrible disease, that innate dignity was one of his true strengths. His body had failed him, even betrayed him, but there was little fragility to that inner desire to maintain as much as possible his own sense of self-respect. He would face his destiny, cruel as it was, with as much pride as possible. This was his own internal well to which he wandered often, now a thirsty and weakened man, there to withdraw sustenance and strength from its depths. It would serve him better than would the waters of Doon Well.

To alleviate the gloom in the car on the return trip, Ellen's father reached into that internal well to withdraw some humor. "Hear 'bout

Paddy Muldoon and his mother?" he asked Mary as he drove the road back to Moville. Paddy Muldoon was an inveterate drunkard well known in Moville.

"W-What? No, what?" asked Mary, drawn out of her sad silence by the inquiry.

"His mother asked him why he didn't give up the drinking 'fore it's too late," said Philip.

"Nothing new in her saying that," responded Mary. "Poor woman."

"He told her it's already too late."

"He would."

"She then says to him, it's never too late. Know what he said back to her?"

"No, what?"

"Well there's no rush then."

Mary chuckled. "He would. Man is incorrigible. Always full of drink. Is that story true or did you make it up?"

"True as anything I've ever said," replied Philip. He heard Ellen chuckling behind him in the rear seat. "Did you hear of the miracle that occurred at the Monaghan funeral?" he asked his audience.

"Miracle?"

"This fellow, Pete Monaghan was his name, lived in Greencastle; poor fellow was found dead in his barn. As it was during that hot spell we had a while ago the wake was held down to one day, so that his mortal remains wouldn't take a bad turn you see. In the morning the box was nailed shut and the pallbearers carried him down to the churchyard. One of the bearers was none other than our Paddy Muldoon from Moville and he was, as usual, drunk as a lord. As they all enter the graveyard through the gates what does Paddy do but drop the box – "

"Da, you're making it up!" interrupted Ellen from the back seat.

Her father ignored her. " – and what then but suddenly there's a loud knocking from inside the box! Pete Monaghan was alive! They pry out the nails, open the box and sure enough he sits up, smiling and happy like he just lifted his head from the bar. Where's me drink? he asks. A miracle, says the priest. A true miracle. Praise God. Pete Monaghan is taken home and the rest all went to the pub to rejoice, but no sooner are they on their second pint then they learn that Pete has died once again. This time for real. They rush from the bar and put him back in the box and start once more for the graveyard. But as they're ready to go through the gates, the priest puts up his hand to stop them. Know what he said?"

"I'm sure I have no idea," responded Mary, already smiling.

"'Get somebody up here to take Paddy Muldoon's place,'" he says. "'We'll not be dropping the box and having any more shenanigans from Pete Monaghan today.'"

Ellen and Mary laughed. "I swear, Phil," said Mary, shaking her head, "After all these years I'm married to you I still don't know when you're telling the truth or fibbing through your teeth."

"Truth can be a tiresome thing," replied Philip. "Best to dress it up at times. Makes things more interesting."

Truth can be a terrible thing too, thought Ellen, the judgment coming to her unbidden after hearing her father's last words. Sitting in the back seat, with that conviction prodding her, she began to cry, shedding her tears silently and privately so as not to have her sorrow come between the smiles of her mother and father. Smiles were too rare between them now.

Ellen's tears were a silent secret she kept to herself the rest of the ride home. They dripped down her cheeks and were periodically wiped away by the backs of her hands as she kept her eyes focused on the passing scenery offered by the road taking her and her parents away from the hope of Doon Well, returning them to their sorrow-filled home.

*   *   *

After that trip, her father deteriorated at a faster pace, the ticking thieves stealing more and more of his wellbeing, filling their pockets greedily now with his health. Ellen's bedroom was transformed to essentially a hospital room and given over to his care, so she moved in to sleep with Rose, filling the empty bed left behind by Maggie's long-ago departure.

Ellen had been permitted the luxury of having her own room ever since she was a child as Maggie had years ago decided she didn't want it, preferring the company of her sister to privacy. Maggie and Rose were extremely close and both were in the habit of chatting away in their room with each other for hours at a time. "Talking 'til late night like magpies living on coffee beans" as their father said to them more than once. The beneficiaries of the close affinity of the two eldest girls were the two youngest, Teresa and Ellen, who obtained separate rooms that otherwise would have gone to Rose and Maggie.

With Philip now confined essentially to bed, Ellen's mum devoted herself almost entirely to his care, nursing him without complaint. Many neighbors admired Mary for her devotion while others considered her foolish for her sacrifice. Oblivious to opinion, Mary considered her devotion to her husband as something natural, loving him too much to conceive of doing otherwise.

Other than palliative treatments to minimize pain and elevate the patient's mood, there was nothing more to be done medically. Philip Rawdon had endured months of experimental x-ray therapy and radium treatments of ever increasing dose rates. The cancer mocked all attempts to either cure it or stem its spread.

The treatments begun with hope months ago, albeit slender hope, had become a suffering ordeal offering no hope at all. They were battles fought in a war by a lone soldier standing on losing ground, suffering wound after wound from enemy fire, and so finally the man said enough. One day, after receiving his latest radiation treatment he went home knowing he'd never have another, prepared at last to grant himself the peace of accepting the inevitability of his own death.

Although exhausted from the many months of caring for her husband, although weary to her soul from breathing in the exhalations of sickness and decay and from existing every day in the depths of the deepest sorrow, Mary could still look at her Philip's now wasted, shrunken body, gaze into his less than clear eyes, and manage a tender smile, a smile of unconditional love. An amazing phenomenon, that smile, under those conditions. More miraculous in its own way than a burst of energy from the sun and a truer statement of her affection than artificial words. Each night the woman still kissed her husband's sunken cheek before she retired to her own room, there to place her own fatigued body into bed.

Ellen's love for her father, as great as it was, wasn't strong enough to stop the spread of the cancer within him. His once poetic tongue, a talent she wished now she had more fully inherited, the storyteller's magic way with words, also faded away, stolen by the disease that was killing him. Ellen wished she had her da's gift for words so that she could pray better. Maybe God would listen to her if she could find the right words to say her prayers better.

Her father's ability to speak, largely gone, was another theft accomplished by the ticking thieves. Now when he did talk, when he gathered the energy to even attempt to speak, the words came out as barely more than slurred noises, punctuated by thin lines of drool falling from a drooping corner of his mouth. A mouth only sometimes capable of presenting a soft smile to those he loved.

One day the inevitable occurred, the cancer spread to the brain and Philip Rawdon, now on the very threshold of deliverance, motor skills largely gone, the man incontinent, had to be transported from Moville to Mercy Hospital in Buncrana, the trip along the lower road necessary as there was no hospital in the small town of Moville capable of caring for the dying man. He would have preferred passing on in his own home, but God said no to that small wish.

He entered this hospital this time knowing he would not be cured, knowing he entered simply to finish his death. This was a truth, although an unspoken one. A silent reality that no one cared to give breath to.

*   *   *

Jim, Rose and Teresa visited their father whenever they were able but daily visits by them were not possible as their time was very much needed at home, to do what was necessary to keep the farm functioning.

While not all family members could take the time to visit Philip every day, Mary granted herself the freedom and time to do so and Ellen was designated by all to be the child to be with her, the others all agreeing that their mother should not travel alone. Ellen received a special dispensation from her own school to do "God's work" and so it was that each day, without fail, the two, daughter and mother, went together to visit the ailing storyteller, the failing father and husband, as he lay in his death bed in Mercy Hospital.

Two weeks passed by, and than three; Philip Rawdon's strong heart refusing to let go of life even while the rest of him continued to surrender to death. Each and every day while he lay in his bed in Mercy Hospital Mary and Ellen together rode the morning bus to appear before his bed.

Ellen got in the habit of going to the window by the side of the hospital bed so as to describe to her father the sights occurring outside that he could no longer rise to see. She would speak to him of the way the wind was bending the trees, or of the passing of a young couple walking the street holding hands, or of the color of the sky on that day, the shape of the clouds at that particular moment.

Today, Da fell asleep as Ellen stood looking through the window, telling him of the flight of a few birds in the distance, puffins she thought, a few birds she saw fluttering up into the sky. They reminded her of the gulls she watched from Cliona's Hill.

Turning to the bed and seeing that her father had dozed off, she abandoned the window and, after a moment, walked to the room's door. Her mother, sitting on a chair by the bed, reading prayers from her prayer book, looked over to her. "Where're you off to, El?"

"Just outside."

In all the days of coming here, Ellen had never explored the hospital and now, prodded by curiosity, she wandered through its corridors. All mostly alike to her eyes. Most of the doors to the patients' rooms were open and, looking inside each room as she went by, she saw either the sick resting prone in their beds or empty beds awaiting the arrival of new patients to hold. There was, here and there, the sounds of disease, a coughing fit, a moan. Ellen heard someone laughing somewhere, faraway it seemed, and was troubled by the sound. Laughter here seemed odd and out of place to her, distasteful, like a comedian doing a comedy routine at a funeral in a church cemetery.

How could anyone be laughing here? In this place? The laughter struck her as a kind of personal insult, to her father, to her and her family.

She stopped and peered into a room to watch a nurse offer a pill and a cup of water to a very frail and aged woman with white wispy hair. As Ellen watched, the nurse, seeing her, reached up and, with a sweeping motion of her arm, pulled a curtain around the bed, a demand for privacy.

Why keep the door open if you didn't want people to see? wondered Ellen.

By the time she returned to her father's room her mother was standing in the hall outside the hospital room, her coat already on. "He's asleep," she told Ellen. "We'll catch the early bus back home today." She smiled, a smile floating in a pool of sorrow, and handed Ellen her coat.

*   *   *

Her mother would return home from the hospital each evening to sit in her chair, silently reading from her small prayer book, whispering novenas and mumbling appeals to Saint Jude. Ellen sometimes just sat and watched her, feeling prayed out herself. Why keep talking to a God who doesn't answer?

Perhaps Mum is utilizing the wrong prayers, saying the wrong words? Like me. Is it possible we're both praying wrong? Her mother seemed to her to be a sad, trapped creature, hunkered in her chair like a sparrow with a broken wing sitting in a corner before the glittering eyes of a bristling cat, wishing for flight from a place from which there was no escape.

It would be wrong to say there was only sorrow for Ellen during all this time, during the many months of Da's illness. Ellen did not always exist in absolute sadness. There were happy moments as well, the normal moments of which a childhood should be composed. At times these periods of happiness served to both alleviate the sadness and, perversely, to accentuate it as well. For on the heels of the happy moments, afterwards, sometimes, Ellen would suffer a pang of guilt over her small and fleeting joy, feeling that somehow it was wrong, perhaps even evil, to experience any happiness at all while her father was so gravely ill.

Ellen had difficulty in reconciling the neglect of God with His reputation for goodness, for compassion. God's silent disregard toward her prayers, even if she was praying wrong, didn't fit with the powerful, loving image of the Almighty she held. *Why doesn't God help Da? Why doesn't He?*

Why doesn't God like us?

Death. As a farming family they were all familiar with it. They all knew the cost paid by some creature to allow them to eat a meal at the dinner table. But human death, the death of a loved one, was something that formerly always happened to others. Up to the time of her father's illness, Ellen had thought of her family as something indestructible, something permanent, a thing that had always existed and would always exist. This new and terrible knowledge that her father was to die was a frightening, unfamiliar creature, an evil monster emerging from dark shadows, standing before her and confronting her with rage and too-sharp teeth. No one she loved had ever died before.

Unbeknownst to Ellen, other prayers were being whispered in contradiction to her own, prayers that begged for the sick man's release from pain, for the peace and mercy of his death.

*   *   *

Then one day, a Thursday, the prayers of Mary Rawdon, prayers whispered in direct contradiction to those of Ellen, were answered. On that Thursday Philip Rawdon passed on.

Mother and daughter were there in the hospital room when he went, Ellen standing again at the hospital room window, describing once again what she saw through the glass to her father, not certain if he was capable of listening anymore but telling him anyway. Her mother sat in a chair at the foot of the bed, exhausted as always with sadness, reading from her prayer book, listening to her husband's rough breathing, a steady yet uncertain rhythm.

Suddenly the man's eyes moved beneath the thin blue-veined parchment of his eyelids and opened. "El," he called softly.

Was that a smile on his lips?

Ellen went to the side of the bed. "Da, here I am," she whispered. Seeing his daughter, Philip's mouth sought to say something but failed. Ellen wanted to throw herself upon him and hug him.

In the next instant her heart leaped into her very throat in fright. Her father's expression twisted horribly, his nostrils flared and his eyes snapped wide open to stare wildly, protruding as though wanting to spring from their sockets. "Da, what's wrong?! What's wrong?!" shouted Ellen, horrified by the change in her father's face.

Philip abruptly bolted up to a sitting position on the bed. "The *Dubhlachan!* Mary!" he yelled, finding his ability to speak clearly again with his last seconds of life, the words literally exploding out of him. "The *Dubhlachan!*" In the next instant he dropped back into the rut of the mattress as though hit in the forehead with the blunt end of an unseen Viking axe.

"Philip! Philip!" Mary leaped up from her chair, her prayer book dropping to the floor forgotten as she rushed to him, pushing past Ellen to reach his side. Ellen, paralyzed, stood without movement, staring at her father, too frightened to move, understanding that her father's soul had just then left her, forever.

Da's gone.

She stared at her mother, now crying softly over her husband's body. Ellen hugged herself, her body suddenly trembling to its bones.

Philip Rawdon was a storyteller to the last. The *Dubhlachan*, the phantom driver of the death coach, the *Coach a bower*, had, by his own final words, come to him to carry him away, away from Ellen, away from his family, out of their lives, forever.

Da is gone . . . .

At last pushing herself to movement, Ellen rushed to the door and called for the nurse to come. Then, waiting, still trembling, she turned to look back into the room, staring at her mother who continued to cry over the sheet-covered skin and bones of her husband's chest, oblivious to anything but the totality of her own sorrow.

Ellen, who in her shock had not yet begun to cry, hugged herself once more and suddenly felt her own hot tears flooding down her cheeks, the water rushing out of her eyes as though the tears were living creatures with minds of their own. She barely knew she was crying. There was, at that moment, only the pounding intensity of one overwhelming and terrible truth . . .

Da's gone . . . forever . . . Da's gone . . .

Chapter Six

The open grave stretched out half in sunlight and half in the long shadow being thrown upon it by a nearby tree, the shadow resting like a black coat tossed over the back of a bench. The daylight and the shadow split the grave into equal parts of light and dark. Avoiding the shade, the casket sat by the side of the open grave in full sunlight. Ellen stood nearby quietly staring at that box, her mind oddly unable to focus upon its purpose, to fully comprehend it. It seemed somehow less than reality that the coffin could truly be holding the body of her father.

There were moments when she half expected to feel her father's arm fall reassuringly around her shoulders, strong as it was before the cancer, offering her some affectionate comfort.

Behind the graves, a short distance away, an ancient stone wall curled around them. That wall made Ellen think of her father as he was in his prime: powerfully built, strong as stone, with hands as large as dinner plates and a ruddy face glowing with good humor and kindness. Before he got sick. Sick with the cancer. Her mind tried to step quickly pass the image of him in his final days, when he was eaten by the terrible disease, for it was not the way she wanted to remember him, but the image insisted on being seen.

Those last days and weeks of his life, Philip Rawdon was little more than a living skeleton with skin stretched over the curves and crevices of his skull, a shadow of the robust man he'd been before. His eyes were without luster, his hands gnarled, the veins on the back of them standing out, raised like worms against the pale, almost translucent, skin. Not like stone at all. He was born just fifty-six years ago. Not like stone at all.

Ellen stood at her mother's right hand, between her mother and Jim, holding tight onto one of Jimmy's hands, so like her father's hands before the sickness. Rose and Teresa were on their mother's left. Sean O'Reilly was there too. Almost like a second son to the Rawdon family, he'd left his college studies to return to Moville for the funeral. Maggie could not return from America and had spent an hour on the telephone last evening with her mother, crying tears of regret and sorrow over being so far away from home.

Despite the sun, Ellen felt cold, and the shawl over her shoulders pressed down upon her as though it'd been woven with threads of granite.

The funeral was a town event; every citizen in Moville who could attend came to the Mass. Others came from Greencastle, from Malin and Bridgend and all places in between. Even through her sorrow, Ellen had felt a surge of pride at the sight of the crowd attempting to squeeze into the scented church interior. Many were forced to remain outside, standing on the steps and beyond, spilling into the graveyard and onto the road. Most of Moville's stores and shops were closed for the Mass and funeral.

A gust of wind swirled in a circle by the casket and a few dead leaves rose up and twisted in its eddy. *An angel dancing,* thought Ellen as she watched the floating leaves and swirling dust trembling on the wind. Da would have said as much. *Perhaps Da really is in heaven and maybe he is happy, just as the priest said in his sermon during the Mass: Happy in God. But not here with us.*

The wind died down and the fluttering leaves settled back to the earth, the angel departing. Ellen again felt a chill sweeping over her, and felt empty again, uninhabited except for cold and sorrow. She let go of Jimmy and brought her hand up to her face to wipe away some fresh tears while Father Cullum, standing in the shadow of the tall tree, began to intone the final prayers that would ever be spoken while Philip Rawdon's body remained above the ground.

Chapter Seven

Two nights following the day of the funeral, Ellen stood alone in the dark, the night so deep around her that she thought at first she must be underground. Then vision came closer to her, presenting her with the realization she was standing not in the black of a cave as she first thought but rather upon a dark road – a road without beginning or end – an incomplete path resting beneath the canopy of a thick and virgin forest. *How did I get here?* she wondered.

Abruptly the black-as-pitch night was pierced in the distance before her by a shaft of moonlight, the beam of light suddenly appearing in front of her through the treetops. A length of moonbeam that came offering her no comfort or calm but rather pulling further terror behind it.

For, to her horror, the trees blocking the path before her were suddenly being split as though the very light of the moon held the teeth of a carpenter's saw. Crack! Crack! Crack! Sounds such as might be made by a maddened street worker with a colossal jackhammer. Crack! Crack! Crack! The sounds came to her ears as the tall trees in the distance snapped and fell, popping at their roots, the large trees being crushed and flattened as easily as if the wheel of a great unseen wagon was rolling over little blades of grass, clearing a swath, a path, through the woods.

Something, something vaguely terrifying, emerged out of the distant charcoal sky in the midst of the cleared path, a black swirl of smoke rising up in the moonlight, rising as if from a great fire burning on the ground, or, perhaps, and more frightening, from flames raging in the fires of hell itself.

Although Ellen couldn't make out exactly what the smoke was, she understood instantly it was something *more* than mere smoke and the sight of it filled her with dread. Instinctively she understood something bad was filling the sky. As if to confirm her fears, the smoke gained the *intent* of movement and began to swirl *forward*, coming toward her, coming *at* her.

Moving forward, it congealed into a distinct shape, or rather distinct *shapes*. Out of the black smoke there evolved the forms of horses pulling a carriage, great coal-black steeds pulling a coach of glistening ebony. The horses, horrifyingly, were headless, with nothing but the bloodied stumps of their necks atop their bodies. They galloped not upon the snapped trunks of the crushed trees that now formed a roadway through the woods but rather *above* them. They were flying, steeds and carriage, flying toward her with breathless speed through the breech cut in the forest by the teeth of the moonlight.

It was the *Coach a bower*, the coach of death.

As it came nearer, Ellen heard the scream of a banshee from somewhere behind her, the spirit shouting doom to her from somewhere inside the dark of the inky night at her back. The spirit's screech crawled up her spine like a living thing under her skin.

The form of the headless coachman, the *Dubhlachan*, made itself known to her sight and Ellen felt to the marrow of her bones the terror of the emptiness above the phantom's broad shoulders. Like the steeds, the man was headless.

The curtains of black silk covering the coach windows flapped in the force of the wind, making a sound like that of a devil's laugh, mocking her fright.

Quickly the coach came nearer still. Now, Ellen could see the long whip in the gloved hand of the *Dubhlachan* being waved in the air and then being brought down upon the backs of the horses as the demon sought to drive the animals to even greater speed. The staccato cracks of the whip exploded in the night air, sounding as though the very bones and skulls of the unseen dead were bursting like chestnuts left too long in the flames of hellfire.

It's coming for me!

The breech cut through the woods, a river of night and liquid moonlight, had the coach riding its current, adding its own speed to that of the river, hurtling toward the gaping, terrified Ellen with ever increasing velocity. Run! But, attempting to race away, she discovered her feet were rooted to the ground and she was unable to move! All she could manage to do was turn her head to the side, her attention drawn there by the new sound of running water. In doing so she saw that where before there had been only forest there was now a rushing stream and, spanning its width, a small stone bridge, reaching from this side to the other.

The coach of death cannot pass over the barrier of a running river. Her father had told her that years ago. With effort, she shook off the shroud of paralysis enwrapping her, turned and ran, making for the bridge, seeking safety from the *Dubhlachan* and the coach that, she was now certain, wanted nothing less than to steal her life, just as it had stolen that of her father's. Frightened half to death, she ran, making for the safety of the other side of the bridge . . . and the coach came closer . . . she ran, hearing the crack of the driver's whip coming nearer behind her, nearer and nearer until almost atop her. She reached the bridge – but too late . . .

. . . and she woke up, sitting up in her bed with a shout.

A few seconds passed until the dream, so terrifyingly real, began to fade and Ellen, panting like her dog Tinker after a long run in the fields, began to accept the fact that a dream was all it was. Yes, she was in the familiar darkness of her room, and there was no frenzied *Dubhlachan* and headless stallions here seeking to take her life. With a sigh she fell back, putting head to pillow again.

Was the dream a story from her father? The storyteller still telling his tales even from heaven? *If so, then why such a scary one? Da, why scare me like that?*

Ellen slept poorly the remainder of the night and awoke in the morning more tired than rested. She lay in bed awake for a time before finally summoning the energy to get up, to wash and put on her clothes and at last go out of the room.

Downstairs, she was surprised to see her mother sitting alone, slumped asleep in her father's favorite chair. The morning sun eased bright illumination through the nearby window and fell on her mother's head and shoulders, producing a halo of white light that glowed in the edge of her tangled gray hair. *Did she sleep down here all night?*

Her mother looked so small now sitting in the big chair. Ellen could see the tracks on her cheeks where tears had rolled down her face. *Was she crying all night?* Her mother still held the handkerchief she'd used to dab her eyes, the cloth balled in a clenched hand resting in her lap. Beside the chair, on a small table, was a framed picture of her parents as they looked on their wedding day, smiling and happy, their lives still before them.

"Mum?" whispered Ellen, going over to her and speaking in a subdued voice so as not to startle her. The stricken woman's eyes fluttered open. "Mum, are you all right?"

Her mother gazed up at her with red and swollen eyes. It took her a moment to realize where she was. "El," she responded at last. Ellen bent down and kissed her on the cheek, wanting to comfort her, to make all the pain go away, but knowing that the miracle of such a tender mercy was a task for God, not in her ability to achieve.

"What time is it?" asked Mary, sweeping her eyes across the room, not taking anything in, seeing only more shadows and sorrow.

"Early, Mum. The sun's just up a little while. I could check the clock in the kitchen if you want."

"I never wore a watch. Your father always told me the time," stated Mary. "I-I suppose I should get one now." Then, suddenly, as if a switch had been flipped, her sorrow broke out and ran in a spasm over her features, contorting her face with grief. "He's gone!" she blurted out. "Gone forever! What'll I do without him?" She began to weep without restraint, uncontrollably, large tears bubbling out of her eyes and streaming down her cheeks, glistening in the golden sunlight. "Oh, I want to die!" she moaned. "I want to die too!" The distraught woman rocked in her husband's chair, her sobs raw in the extremity of her painful sorrow.

Ellen's eyes widened with astonishment and she flung her arms around her mother, hugging her around the neck. She'd never seen her mother carry on so and was as much frightened by it as made compassionate. "Oh Mum, please don't talk like that! Please, please don't!" She too began to cry. "Oh Mum, please . . ." Ellen had never before seen her mother so vulnerable, had never seen anyone at all in such total despair. "Please, oh please . . ."

Jim, who'd been out milking the cows, came into the room. Ellen was relieved when he came over and gathered their mother to him. "I'll put her to bed," he told Ellen and then, supporting his mother's weight as she leaned on him, led the sobbing, distraught woman slowly up the stairs to her bed.

*   *   *

Ten minutes later, Ellen and Rose were at the table in the kitchen when Jim came down the stairs and into the room. "How is she?" asked Ellen, forcing her voice past the constricting lump of concern in her throat. Her own eyes were red from crying. Rose had a consoling arm across Ellen's back.

"Falling asleep. At least I think so."

Ellen nodded her head, not convinced. "I'm going to sit outside with Tinker for a while," she murmured as she got up and started wearily for the door, walking as though the weight of her grief over the loss of her father, and now the pity and concern for her mother were actual physical burdens placed upon her young slim shoulders. Tinker, hearing his name, rose up and followed behind her, dragging his tail, sensing the sorrow in the room.

Jim poured himself a drink of whiskey and sat down at the table. "There's still work to be done," he announced to Ellen's back. "I did the milking but there's also clothes to be washed and hung on the line. I'm going out now and work on the lorry."

Ellen turned and stared at him.

"I'll do the clothes," said Rose. "El's tired."

Jim shrugged. "I'm tired too. There's other jobs to be done as well. The farm still needs to be looked after. Life's got to go on."

Ellen nodded her head. "Y-Yes, I know, Jimmy. I'll do the wash. In a few minutes. Just a few minutes . . . ."

She turned and went out the door, Tinker following her out. She went to the barn, walking like a sleepwalker, feeling like a North Pole explorer passing over tall, hypnotic drifts of ice and snow, as cold and numb, as disoriented and uncertain, as if the Rawdon farm had been transformed to a polar icecap and she, alone and lost, was walking toward a frozen death.

Entering into the shade of the barn her gaze happened to fall upon the milking stool sitting by a stall and she went and placed herself on it. The barn was cool with shadows filled with the pungent scents of the animals they sheltered.

Tinker came to her, sympathizing with her sadness. The dog's head snuggled into her lap and Ellen started to lightly stroke behind one of its ears. In response, Tinker's tail began to sweep the floor of the barn. *It's not fair,* thought Ellen. *Da shouldn't have died. He shouldn't have.* She put her hands to her face and began to weep softly. Tinker's tail ceased its back and forth swing.

A few minutes passed before her tears subsided and, wiping her eyes and cheeks with the backs of her hands, she glanced over at the cows. They had three now. One, the oldest called Biddy, stared back at Ellen with big naive eyes. The cow was old, but its milk was still good, which is why they kept it. Biddy gazed at her with her large eyes as though questioning Ellen's sitting presence here in the barn without milking to be done.

Ellen recalled the day the cow had last given birth. She remembered standing by and watching as her father helped the cow deliver; remembered seeing his arm disappear into the beast, reaching for the calf, then pulling it into the world of life and death in rhythm with the mother, until finally the newborn emerged before Ellen's awestruck eyes. Soon the calf was resting on a bed of hay in the barn, blinking the bewilderment of its new life,.

Old Biddy still offered the farm good milk. The day the cow ceased to do that, it would be butchered for the meat. *Life goes on.* That's what Jim said and he was right. Ellen offered Tinker a final pat on the head and stood up. "There are things to be done," she announced firmly, speaking to herself as much as to the dog, and, as though her words were a command from a superior officer and she a new recruit, she stepped out of the barn.

Outside, Jim was already working on the lorry. Old when her father had purchased it, it hadn't grown any younger since. It consisted of a large cab that seated two, running boards on both sides and the back for carrying the load. Once its paint was bright blue but the color had paled with age, washed out with years of the sun burning its shine and hue away. Inside the cab, the aged cracked leather seat was held together with strips of duct tape. A large round bonnet covered the engine. Jim had it raised up now and was working on the very tired and old insides. It was a talent just to keep the old banger running. The lorry and the family car, two old men weary of too much work.

Sweat glistened on Jim's forehead and seeped from beneath his uncombed hair. It darkened the front and back of his shirt. His body was spotted like a leopard's as he worked in the dappled sunlight pressing past the leaves of the tree by which the lorry was parked. A sunny and warm day was blooming.

Ellen watched as Jim climbed into the cab and started the engine. The motor retched and groaned, coughing as if suffering with consumption. Probably should be in a hospital ward. Jim turned the ignition key once more and this time the engine roared to life. Ellen watched her brother settle back into the cracked and taped leather seat, relaxing for the moment in pleasant satisfaction over his success.

Life goes on. *There is work to do*, thought Ellen and, prodded by that thought, she started back toward the house.

Chapter Eight

Sean studied the old photo, a snapshot of him at the age of fourteen standing with the Rawdon family. They were all grins and smiles then. Now the old man was gone. Sean had thought at the time that Jimmy's father would live forever. The man seemed as permanent as any of the hills of Donegal.

Poor Jimmy. If his old man had lived he'd be here in the university with me. But with his father's illness and his passing, and there being no man left to tend to the farm, Jim had to stay home. Everything has its ramifications, doesn't it? How much of our own lives, our destinies, do we actually control?

The door to the room opened and in walked a fellow student, a tall drink of water named Tyrrell Ross. A long streak of piss, to those who didn't like him. Sean put the old snapshot back into his wallet and returned the wallet to the pocket of his U.S. of A jeans. He was seated in a chair with his feet stretched out onto the edge of his bed and he lowered his feet now to grant the visitor a place to sit.

"It isn't fair," complained Tyrrell, pushing some books aside and throwing himself onto Sean's unmade bed. He stared at Sean, his face pale and oblong, his mouth sitting on an unfortunate jaw that was a bit too long, even for Tyrrell's horse-like face. If Sean sketched that face in an art class the teacher would give him a failing grade for his lack of a sense of proper proportion.

"Birds chirp and Tyrrell laments," said Sean, chuckling in response to the other's complaint. "What's wrong now?"

"It isn't fair," repeated Tyrrell. "I slaved over my paper for two weeks while you scribbled yours in a couple of days and you end by getting a better mark." He shook his head. "Something's wrong."

Sean chuckled again. "From what you said, it seems you believe a grade should be rewarded based on effort rather than quality," he declared. "If that were so than the least able would always get the highest marks since they must always work harder to keep up. If that was so, the mule would be more highly regarded then the thoroughbred horse, wouldn't it it?"

Tyrrell shook his head and smiled. "You bastard. So I'm a mule, am I? You should be in Parliament the way you can toss words around. Well, I may not the best student in this stinking college but I might be the best lover. Tonight the girl of my dreams will be mine. I feel it in my bones. She's succumbing to my charms."

"You mean your charm, don't you? You have only one."

"Oh, and what's that?"

"Your virginity, of course," responded Sean, laughing. He ducked as Tyrrell picked up and threw a pillow at him.

"Enough," said Tyrrell, seeing that Sean was rising to come at him. "Truce. You and Claire coming to the pub with us tonight?"

"No. I'm going to the other side of the Liffey, to the Abby Theatre, alone," came back Sean, a cloud descending over his features. "Claire and I won't be doing anything tonight. Together that is."

"You two split?" asked Tyrrell.

"We won't be seeing each other anymore. It's over."

"Too bad. God, what a beauty she is, Sean. She could make a poet out of even a mule like me. What happened?"

Sean shrugged. "She started to talk about marriage, commitment and that kind of garbage. Christ, I know her just three months. Even if it was three years, I'm not ready to settle down. I mean, that's it, isn't it? Being married means the end of possibilities, doesn't it? Being married means spending the rest of your life *being married*. We argued over it and she left."

"The end of possibilities? I don't know. I could imagine a lot of possibilities with Claire," declared Tyrrell, widening his eyes and lowering his voice to suggest lasciviousness. Then, in all seriousness, he added quickly. "Sean, she looks like an angel."

"Angels are for dead people," stated Sean with a shrug of his shoulders.

"You're smart and all that, but sometimes you talk like you're dumb as a baboon's rear end," declared Tyrrell, pushing himself up off the bed. "Well, I'll be off. See you tomorrow then."

"Yeah, be seeing you. Good luck with your lone charm and all."

Marriage, thought Sean, thinking of the argument he'd had with his girlfriend. *That's a place you finally end up in. I'm too young and life's too short for me to be landing already in the last place I'll be.*

Sean felt he had a great gift being presented to him. The future. He was not about to surrender it. Not yet at least. Not even to an angel.

Chapter Nine

Seven weeks passed by. Ellen began to wonder if her mother would ever be the same again. With the death of her husband something had been withdrawn from her mother, something precious. She was now a different person, a woman who never laughed, a woman peering out at the world through eyes that were nothing less than pure pools of perpetual sorrow, a woman transformed, maybe forever.

That was the frightening thought, her real mother might never come back to her. Lost, just like Da. Lost in a kind of living death.

Mary Rawdon, in her sorrow, slackened in her desire to keep herself groomed and presentable and her daughters had to now fuss with her to force her to keep herself clean. The distraught woman often sat in her husband's chair late into the night and remained there well into morning. Mary's hair was left uncombed unless someone else took the time to brush it. Even then, while her hair was being brushed, Mary's green-gray eyes stared vacantly in front of her while her hands kept fingering her rosary beads, her mouth almost silently mumbling prayers. At times Mary Rawdon appeared to be little more than a dazed hollow-eyed specter, sitting and disregarding anything said to her.

Ellen, horrified by this change in her formerly so meticulous and vivacious mother, tried many times to talk to her, as did Rose, Jim and Teresa, to convince her to pull herself together and revert to her old self. These attempts failed, the talks either degenerating into argument or simply fading away, absorbed into her mother's weary depression like smoke from a chimney dissipating into a bleak, starless night sky.

Ellen tried diversion as well, thinking, plotting really, of ways to inspire and avert her mother's mind away from grief. In the first few weeks following her father's death, she many times made suggestions of ways to spend a day, to get her mother out of the house, to get her thoughts away from her agonizing loss, but Ellen's attempts were almost always met with rejection. "No, Chickie," her mother would reply in a blurred voice, looking at her daughter with blurred eyes. "I'm not up to it today. We'll do that some other time."

Even on those few instances when the family succeeded in getting Mary out of the house on some little journey the end result would be a joyless trip from which the woman returned the same as before.

The daughters took turns bearing the responsibility of cleaning the house and preparing the family meals. As they ate their dinners, they found themselves often sitting in a smothering shroud of silence. Gone were the days of her father's tales and his funny jokes. There was little conversation, talk being difficult to achieve beneath the sadness that spread away from them on all sides. It was as though they were nothing more than a printed design on a large white tablecloth and their sorrow a massive stain of ink that had spread over them to the four corners of the linen. Their meals were now joyless affairs, accompanied only by the clatter of utensils and dishes and the sounds of their eating.

Jim too changed. Formerly a good-humored, joking young man with a mischievous streak he became sullen, carrying anger and surliness around with him like two of Paidir's bags of skin.

Ellen thought her father's death to be everywhere and all pervasive, dominating the house and all their lives.

She was affected also. There was a new awareness within her that all things loved and cared for will in time pass on. All things are perishable and so all joy, all happiness, carries within itself the potential sadness of its loss. *What then, is the value of joyful things?* Now, when Ellen walked to the top of her hill and stared out to where the sky and water met, she was aware of a dark threatening shadow at the edge of her thoughts, a growling at the borders of her dreams and hopes. Her dreams of a happy future now also held a vague anticipation of future sadness as well, of pain that would be born out of a storm not yet imaginable.

Her mother had been happy, her mother had dreamed of a happy future when she was young just as Ellen did now, and her mother's dreams had come true. But her mother's happiness was gone now, wasn't it? Dreams realized, like all things, past on. They're here and then gone, as temporary as newly formed buds appearing on a rosebush, that open and fall to the ground to ultimately become dust and less than a memory.

*   *   *

A miracle. One cloudy day, four months and six days following the death of her father, Ellen woke, washed and dressed and, going downstairs, was astounded to see her mother busy at work in the kitchen, sweeping dust out the back door. The black garb her mother had taken to wearing was abruptly gone, Mary abandoning the color of grief to instead, this morning, don a brightly colored print dress that she wore beneath her old apron. Breakfast was already cooking on the stove. Preparing the morning meal for the family had been Ellen's job for weeks now.

A miracle. Nothing less. Ellen's heart leapt with joy at the unexpected sight; she could actually feel it doing handsprings behind her ribs like a gymnast on a floor mat. Halting in her tracks, she stared at her mother as though expecting the image to vanish like an illusion, a nasty leprechaun's mean trick.

But the sight of her mother remained to smile at her. A smile more like her Mum's old true smile than the wan imitation the woman had managed now and then to force upon her mouth since her husband's death.

"How did this kitchen ever get this dirty?" said her mother, ceasing for the moment to sweep the floor and looking over at her daughter, a look of complaint in her eyes.

Oh and how wonderful was that look of complaint! Ellen emitted a peep of joy, ran to her mother and flung her arms around her neck. "Oh Mum, thank God." She had tears in her eyes when they separated.

"What's this?" said her mother, still smiling. "Don't be making a great *cooramuch* now. Let me get on with my work. I've a family to care for. And you get on with yourself too. Since this kitchen looks like the barn, I can only imagine what the barn looks like."

The recovery, seemingly so startling and magical, had in fact been taking place unseen over the past weeks, a healing being performed slowly within her mother's heart and soul but unseen to others until now. So it appeared this morning, to Ellen's eyes, as though nothing less than an astounding transformation had occurred, a change as magical as if the shards of a broken vase had suddenly drawn together on their own, reassembled themselves and stood whole again before her.

Ellen found herself humming a little song as she left the house and went to the barn to milk the cows, her step suddenly light enough so that she thought she might rise from the ground and glide on the breeze, as though the pull of gravity itself had for the moment relinquished any claim of power over her.

Now she understood the full truth of the knowledge that *all* things perish. *All* things, even the most severe pain of the greatest sorrow.

And in that full truth resides not only a possibility of potential suffering but also a promise of the rebirth of hope and happiness.

Chapter Ten

With his father gone, the responsibility for the day-to-day running of the farm was deposited like a bag of bricks upon Jimmy's back. Times continued to be nothing but hard in Moville and it was Jim, working the farm, who increasingly felt the strain of trying to choke enough money out of the land to pay the family's bills. Too many days he felt like a mule pulling a heavy wagon of dirt up a steep hill, the only reward for making it to the top being another wagon of dirt to pull up the same hill on another day.

His father at times used to say: "Money's scarcer than knobs of shit from a starving goat's arse." Da usually spoke the words with a smile but now, months after his father's death, Jim began to appreciate that the words contained more worry than humor.

Sean was gone, off to the start of better things in his life, and Jim brooded over the loss of his chance for a similar new beginning. Maybe not in a university like Sean, but going off to a place where hard work at least paid better. Boston or New York City in America. Staying behind was a true sacrifice, one he'd have preferred not to have had to make but he was needed here, on the Rawdon land, and so on the land he had to stay. Any ambitions he once held to his heart were forced to bend a knee and yield to that conquering need. *I have to stay. That's the start and end of it. I have to stay.*

No other option existed for him. Not now.

Stay a year or two or three and then leave? No, there was no hope of future change coming toward him. None he could see. Not unless the plow hit a leprechaun's pot buried on Rawdon land. It was clear to

Jim that no matter how hard he worked the farm, things wouldn't be getting any better for him. Next year, and the year after that as well, would bring him nothing but more work, more wagons to pull up the hill and another year nearer his grave.

When not brooding over lost opportunities, he worried about money. The constancy of bills to pay was like being surrounded by little men prodding him with the points of knife blades each day. He sought out additional work on the Moville piers and now and then was able to get it, rare occasions as work at the largely unused docks seldom arrived there seeking company. The extra money he earned went directly to the family, excepting what he kept to pay for pints at the pub. Ellen, Rose and Teresa also helped out whenever possible, managing to earn a few shillings here and there by taking odd jobs in the few shops in Moville that offered them. Such work was scarce and the pay meager even when it did appear.

Maggie still sent money home, whatever extra shillings, or rather American dollars, she found herself in possession of at month's end. But all in all, money came in paltry amounts to the farm.

His sisters and mother never knew of Jimmy's conflict, of the disharmony caused by what his life actually was and what he thought it should be. Of course Jimmy worked the farm. What else would he do?

* * *

Although it wasn't as clearly evident in his demeanor, Jimmy being a Stoic by nature, he missed his father as much as did his sisters, perhaps even more so. Unknown to the others, once or twice a week, it became his habit to walk the road to Saint Mary's and, alone, visit his father's grave. This he did usually at night when the day's hard work was done, going there after his supper to express what was in his heart and/or to offer a silent prayer to his father's soul. These conversations and prayers were usually not spoken aloud but expressed in thought, in silent contemplation, Jim being certain that souls in heaven did not need sounds to hear what was whispered in the human heart. On his first few visits he questioned the "why" of his father's death. Why did God bring such a terrible disease to such a good man? Why bring down such suffering to his father, and to his mum who was still suffering in her own way? Both such faithful followers of the Church? Was there a hidden reason for causing the good to suffer so, a concealed purpose known only to God Almighty?

If he truly expected to receive answers to his questions he was disappointed, discovering very soon that graveyards didn't offer any additional passage to the solution of mysteries than did any other location, not to the living in any case. Of late, when he came to the grave, he put such mysteries aside and would simply sit on the ground and let himself feel the nearness of his father, imagining conversations, how his father would respond to his words.

The logician would say that such conversations, prayers really, to the dead could be spoken anywhere and have as much chance of being heard in heaven as words uttered on a grave's edge, but it wasn't logic that brought Jimmy here to the gravesite, rather his own need and faith. Talk to his da seemed more intimate here, more real here.

One balmy night, remaining late in the graveyard, the grounds dimly lit by a glowing, grinning moon, Jimmy heard the sounds of people whispering in the dark. The noise surprised him as he imagined he was alone this night as he normally was on others. Was it someone else visiting a grave, holding a conversation, as he was, with a loved one no longer living? Curious, he leaned toward the whispers, listening more intently. No, not a conversation between a departed soul and one who pined for a loved one's loss, rather talk between a man and a woman. And neither God nor holy souls had anything to do with their conversation judging by the sounds of lascivious hisses and passionate groans that accompanied their whispered words. Whoever they were, more than simply talking was taking place in the shadows. A man and a woman come to the graveyard to kiss, and perhaps do more than kiss.

Jimmy listened, the sounds growing more passionate as the minutes ticked by. Both man and woman were in their cups, he realized. Drunk as the forsaken Billyclub on a bender. He crept closer so as to see better and in the moonlight discerned the woman's face. He realized he knew her: Lucy Moran, Loosey Lucy. An old schoolmate from years ago.

She was seated on one side of the horizontal of a large stone cross, with the man standing and bending over her, smothering her face and upper body with kisses. Immediately Jimmy thought it strange that Lucy would come to the graveyard at night, even for doing what she so liked to do, as she was superstitious as all get-out and always feared the possibility of running into one of the dead souls she believed walked the graveyard grounds. She'd always been scared of the graveyard, especially at night.

Her drunkenness no doubt offered her the courage to spit in the eye of her superstitions, at least temporarily, but it was still not quite courage enough for it was clear to Jimmy that she remained skittish. Periodically she would halt in her ardor to question a sound in the dark. "Hush, hear that? What was that? Something's out there!" Her fears would be summarily dismissed by the man as, "just a noise" or "bloody birds and animals, is all", then he would pull her back to passion.

Who was Lucy with? Jimmy thought it had to be Peter Shea, another friend he knew from his days in school. Weren't Lucy and Pete going together for the last few years now? A known "item", the two of them. Who else would it be but Peter?

Surprisingly, presented by chance with this opportunity, there arose in Jimmy the sense of the mischievousness that had so dominated him for most of his growing up years but which of late had been absent.

Acting on impulse, he scooped up a couple of handfuls of soil and smeared his face with dirt. The ground was damp, as it usually is in Ireland, and clung in streaks to his skin. He ruffled up his hair and then bent down and pulled up a large clump of grass, a divot, which he placed on his head like a Chinese cap. Removing his jacket and draping it over a headstone, he rubbed more dirt on the front of his shirt before pulling it loose from his pants, letting it hang like a shroud to mid-thigh. This wouldn't be his joke alone, the local myth of ghosts roaming the graveyard would be his collaborator tonight.

He emerged from out of the dark shadows like a body just risen from a grave, his arms extended straight out from him like an accident victim wearing elbow splints, emitting moans as though auditioning for entry as a soprano into a banshee's choral group, walking slowly, haltingly, toward Lucy and Peter.

Lucy broke free of the man's embrace, pushing him away, and leaped up from her seat on the stone cross, popping up as though she'd accidentally sat down on a red-hot iron skillet. Here, striding toward her, was the sum of all her fears of the graveyard. She stared in absolute horror at the sight, her eyes as wide as eggs dropped by hens training for the Chicken Egg Laying Olympics. The apparition, with flesh peeling from its bones (or so she imagined, thanks to the dirt smeared on Jimmy's face), was nothing less than a demon escaped from hell. Stunned and paralyzed she could, briefly, do nothing but ogle fixedly at the creature advancing slowly toward her, temporarily frozen as though encased in ice, certain that the demon she saw had risen from the dead to claim her own soul. A few additional ticks and the ice broke, Lucy screamed, a procession of short shrieks that erupted one by one from her mouth like bullets from a rifle barrel, yelps of fright that startled even Jimmy. Her eyes, incredibly, widened even further, dramatically, until they appeared they might now actually explode from their sockets like corks from mishandled and over-shaken bottles of champagne. She took a step back, moving out of shadow and gaining more light on her upper body. Jimmy saw now that her blouse was open, her brassiere under her chin being worn like a necklace, exposing her ample chest to the night. He gaped at the sight. Gaper gaping at gaper. That exposed chest was abruptly heaving with deep fright, making her look like an asthmatic struggling for air, and then she fainted dead away.

Jimmy dropped his arms and stood, mouth open, gazing at the fallen woman. Never did he dream she would react so dramatically to his prank.

"Who the hell are you and what the hell do you think you're doing?"

Jimmy had forgotten all about the man, and, prodded by the growl of the voice, moved his eyes from the fallen Lucy to the figure standing beside her. The first thing Jimmy realized, with a shock, was that it was not his friend Peter, but rather a stranger unknown to him. The second thing he realized, with increasing shock, was that the man, no longer bent over Lucy but standing up and displaying his full height and breadth, was as big as a pillar of rock at Stonehenge, larger than even Bill O'Mooney, who was the biggest man Jimmy had ever seen until now.

The third item of interest that Jimmy comprehended was that, unlike Lucy, this behemoth was not taken in by his feeble attempt to mimic the best of Shakespearian acting. His performance did not seem to impress Mr. Stonehenge at all as the man did not applaud and was offering no accolades, instead he was angry, livid in fact. Suddenly this little joke seemed like a truly stupid idea.

"Ah, lovely night?" said Jimmy, backing away. "Sorry about this. Thought you were somebody else."

"I'm going to teach you, Sonny," snarled the Stonehenge pillar. Then, realizing that, like Lucy's chest, a certain part of his anatomy was exposed to the night, he dropped his hands down to zip up his pants prior to beating Jimmy to a pulp. His rush in doing so was Jimmy's savior and the man's undoing, for that part of him he sought to tuck away was abruptly snagged in the zipper's teeth. Suddenly Mr. Stonehenge Pillar was howling in excruciating agony, hopping and twirling about like a panic-stricken bear that had played with matches and accidentally set the fur of its lower half on fire. Then, the pain evidently increasing, the man's knees buckled and he fell onto the ground where he rolled onto his back, still screaming his anguish to the dark sky, his cries rising up to the smiling moon and the indifferent stars. His hands remained where they were most needed, his fingers struggling to pull down the tormenting zipper, which, despite his best frantic efforts, remained resolutely in place, smiling a sideways toothy grin in imitation of the moon above. Neither sympathy nor pity seemed about to be offered by either the zipper or the moon.

Jimmy stepped back a few yards, reclaimed his jacket, and hid behind a tombstone.

Lucy woke from her faint, and, seeing her would-be lover prone on the ground and howling his lungs out, was immediately certain that the malevolent spirit she'd seen had entered her man and was struggling with him for control of his holy soul, attempting to possess his body. A wild look of fury came into her eyes. "Let my Danny go, you devil!" she screamed at the top of her voice. "You'll not possess his body and turn him to your evil!!" She looked about for a weapon to fight the demon with and, spying a wooden cross about three feet tall, immediately decided there would be nothing better than that for beating back the fiend. Rushing to it she, with some effort, managed to tug it out of the ground. Running back to Danny Stonehenge, she immediately began beating him black and blue with it, believing she was in fact thrashing the now unseen demon attempting to possess him. "Back to Hades with you, you stinkin' devil! Back to Hades! Back to Hades, you evil spirit!"

"Stop hitting me, you stupid cow!" shouted Danny in between screams, wishing he had two more hands, a pair to tug at the zipper and another pair to protect him from the wooden cross being hammered down on him.

"Unclean! Unclean! Back to hell with you!" screamed Lucy. She continued to beat Danny Stonehenge without mercy or letup, undeterred by his pleas.

Jimmy, bending low, careful to avoid being seen, crept out of the graveyard, leaving Lucy beating her man over the head and body, the man fighting to stop the pain of both cross and zipper, and Father Cullum storming out of the rectory to see what unholy and unnatural terrors were occurring in the church graveyard, the priest adding his own screams to the night.

Jimmy was halfway home when he promised himself that tomorrow he would return to Saint Mary's, the church and not the graveyard, and there offer prayers of thanks to the majestic wisdom of God for granting humankind the ingenuity and creativity that enabled the invention of the zippered fly.

*   *   *

That little burst of the "old" Jimmy, the youthful, mischievous Jimmy, was also a farewell of sorts to his former self. A closing of a door on the past, a shutting out of his previous self from himself. Jimmy had changed due to the death of his father, becoming more somber, more bitter, less fun-loving, and that change was increasingly dominating him. His old sense of play had surged forward that night, perhaps even seeking release from its captivity, but in doing so it had not achieved freedom but rather used itself up, depleted itself, leaving more room in Jimmy's heart for his ever growing anger and resentment. Rather than a sign of recovery from the sufferings of his father's illness and loss, as one might have supposed if present in the graveyard that night to witness the final boyhood prank of his life, it was in fact its opposite, a final emptying of sorts, a shedding away of the playful boy he once was.

*   *   *

One year following the day of the funeral of Philip Rawdon, the family went as one to visit the man's grave in Saint Mary's churchyard, respecting the anniversary. Some words were spoken to the stone marking the grave, a few tears shed and a few prayers murmured. Then they walked away. All told, the family spent less than a quarter-hour at the site.

Ellen found it difficult, painful, to reflect upon the fact that the bones of her father were now actually residing in a box beneath the grass she stood on. The image of him in his Sunday suit, sitting beside her in the church pew, the way he was for so many Sundays in her life, came into her mind and rested there, a friend to her now, chasing away less pleasant thoughts.

The night of the anniversary visit to the Rawdon grave found Jim, as was now increasingly his nightly habit, leaning against the bar inside The Red Rooster. He stood beside a seated Michael Duffy, a young man who had, of late, become his nighttime drinking companion. A short, stocky, red-haired man with a round baby face, Duffy looked like a medieval choirboy searching for a church to sing in even while he was half drunk.

Jim called to the bartender for a whiskey, forgoing his usual ale. "It's better for keeping the chill outta your pants," he told Duffy when his friend asked him why he was changing drinks. "If it's any of your business." He was falling into a dark mood.

Duffy decided to lighten his friend's frame of mind with a joke. "Did you hear the one about Sean and the priest?"

"I had a friend named Sean . . . once," responded Jim, shaking his head. "He's gone off to be educated . . . and here I am, still picking potatoes and cleaning muck."

"We'll make the name Luke then," responded Duffy. "Anyways, Luke, filled with drink to the eyes, as was usual for him, is staggering home one day when he meets his priest. He – "

"What's the priest's name?"

"What's the difference?"

"Every priest has a name, doesn't he?"

"Father Murphy. Luke meets Father Murphy while staggering home and the priest stops him and tells him, you can't keep drinking like you do. Know what happens to people who drink as much as you? They keep getting smaller and smaller, shrinking and shriveling away to nothing. Keep drinking like you do and you'll soon be as small as a mouse. Luke's eyes get big. Noooo, he says to the priest. Father Murphy says it's so. As God as his witness. Small as a mouse, Luke. You've got to take the proper steps now, 'fore it's too late for you. Luke nods his head, now has tears in his eyes, and thanks the priest for his kindness. You've saved me life, he tells Father Murphy. You've saved me life."

"He gave up drinking?" asked Jim.

"No, he went home and killed the cat! Ha ha ha . . ." Duffy was guffawing at his own joke as though it was the first time he'd ever heard it and the ending was a surprise to him. Jimmy laughed as well in spite of himself. The bartender, who had listened in on the story, spoke up, telling Duffy, "That joke was old when Saint Patrick was tending sheep in his knickers, but you told it well enough. Have a round on the house."

Duffy and Jim thanked him and in moments the promised two drinks were placed on the bar.

The smile on Jimmy's face slid away as his gaze then fell upon the sight of two well-dressed young men sitting at a table by the hearth. He hadn't seen them there when he entered and concluded with undeniably perfect logic that they must have entered the pub afterward. The fire they were seated near burned bright, sending a rhythmic ebb and flow of light gliding over their faces and bodies. Strangers to Moville. Or at least to Jim who had never seen them before.

Immediately the sight of their clothes, fine and tailored, became a visual irritant to him and he began to resent the sense of economic wellbeing the two men exuded. One of them wore a thick chain of gold around his neck. *No doubt rich boys come to a poor man's pub for the adventure, slumming for the night in Moville.*

"Damned pigs," muttered Jim into his drink. "With wallets as big as cows' utters, no doubt." The presence of the two men was quickly taken as a personal affront. He turned to Duffy. "Those two look ripe for the picking," he growled with a tone of contempt. "What say we shake their tree when they leave?"

"What!" exclaimed Michael. Then, in a barroom half-whisper, "You mean you want to rob them?"

"Sure and why not? They look like they've got enough to be able to spare a little. They're half-drunk and skinny twits to boot. No doubt thinking we're a bunch of bog-trotters here in Moville. Probably against a united Ireland too. It'd be like taking candy from babies."

"You're not serious, Jimmy? Robbery! What the devil are you thinking?!" Duffy stared at Jim as though he'd suddenly sprouted a pair of horns on his forehead.

"Can't use the money, Michael?"

"That's not it. Can always use money. Jimmy, you're not truly serious, are you?"

"Why not?"

"Why not!?" sputtered Duffy. "Why you'd end up behind bars! That's why not! Besides neither of us are brigands. And it isn't right! Lord, what would your mother be saying if she heard you talking about beaning people on the streets so as to steal their money?"

Jim stared at Duffy, thoughtfully. "Of course I'm saying a joke, Michael," he responded at last. "I was just trying to see if your flaming red hair stood up on the back of your neck when you get riled up."

Duffy startling chuckling. "You had me going there, Jimmy. But I knew you weren't serious. Robbery. Why, you'd have to be totally daft."

Jim ordered yet another drink for himself and another ale for Duffy. And for the remainder of the night he allowed their conversation to concentrate upon other things besides the contemplation of thievery, even while his gaze, now and then, drifted back to the two strangers sitting across the room.

Chapter Eleven

Ellen sat on the step outside the entrance of her home, Tinker at her feet, watching the hazy curls of gold and red clouds in the distance as the sun moved slowly behind the trees, setting for the day. A blur of a quarter moon and a few pale stars, misty ghosts of stars actually, could be seen in the still sunlit evening sky.

Ellen thought again of what her friend Lauren had told her earlier and considered once more her own reaction to her friend's revelation. At the time, she'd stared open-mouthed at Lauren, disbelief stamped on her face. *How naïve I must've looked.* Now she shook her head at the memory and scolded herself. She'd behaved very unsophisticated. Like a real *culchie*.

The inside of the house smelled of the mutton in the kitchen, her mother cooking chops for supper, and Ellen could catch the smell of the meal being carried to the doorstep. Tinker was inhaling the odor of food too and, already drooling, was preparing his dinnertime strategy. Needing a friend at the table, he gazed up at Ellen with imploring eyes that pleaded: You'll remember to slip me scraps from your plate at dinnertime, won't you? You and me, El, friends to the end.

Ellen's thoughts were not in line with Tinker's mealtime desires but, shifting away from her memory of Lauren's words, went toward consideration of her mother now preparing supper. *How much better Mum is now.* Once more Mary was the mother Ellen had known before her father got sick. A little sadder perhaps, still heartbroken over Da's passing, but heartbroken in a different, softer way. Ellen missed her father too. She would always miss him. How much more then did her mother yearn for him?

A memory of Da came into her mind, gently, as though floating on the same air that carried the scents of dinner to her. In that image, Ellen was just eight years old, lazing on her father's favorite chair, pretending to be fully asleep but secretly watching her father through the slits of her almost-shut, half-dreaming eyes. Seeing her in his chair, he at first frowned down at her and, bending down, was prepared to pick her up to move her but then changed his mind. Believing her to be asleep, as she pretended she was, he instead chose to let her be. Peeking through her eyelashes she watched him as he turned on the radio, leaving the sound low so as not to disturb her, and then placed himself into another chair other than his favorite, where he unlaced his ankle-high boots.

There was love in that. Her father forgoing his favorite chair for her and tiptoeing to another, not wanting to wake her. *He loved me. He did. Da loved me.*

The memory rolled out again for her, repeating itself. And two moments in her life coexisted for a time on the doorstep. One a picture of the past and the other the reality taking place now. Da sat once more before her mind's eye, removing his boots even as she listened to the sounds of her mother preparing dinner inside the house. Similar kitchen sounds as she'd heard then while still snuggled in her father's chair. She'd felt so warm and protected then, half-asleep in her father's chair, so long ago. The world was perfect then.

Tinker whined up at her and rolled over. Ellen, with a laugh, began to rub the proffered belly. A minute later her mother called her to supper and Tinker's head lifted, the dog staring at Ellen as she ceased rubbing and stood up. Tinker continued to remain on his back as she started to go inside. A few seconds had to pass before the dog at last accepted the fact that there'd be no more rubbing of his belly right now and he flipped over and trotted into the house after her.

Jim and Rose were already seated at the table when Ellen entered the kitchen. Teresa was helping set the table. Tinker walked to a spot by the wall and plopped down as Teresa deposited the last dish to be served, a large bowl of potatoes, on the table and Ellen placed herself in her seat. The family, together as one, said grace.

While the others chatted over their meal, Ellen found her thoughts drifting back to her friend. Lauren's revelation had somehow shocked her although it probably shouldn't have. In fact, after absorbing the initial shock, she had to admit that part of her wasn't surprised at all.

Ellen and Lauren were friends who'd once spent a lot of time together, but then Lauren discovered boys and Ellen's father had gotten sick. Over the months of her father's cancer, the two friends had seen less and less of each other.

Lauren was a pretty girl a year younger than Ellen. Plump with brown hair and striking green eyes. The tips of the corners of her mouth were curled up slightly so she looked as though she was always thinking of something that was about to make her burst out laughing. She had a wart on the side of her jaw, a birth defect that, years earlier, had caused many of her schoolmates, both girls and boys, to dub her "Laurie the Wartie". Then, with the filling out of her body, that name ceased to be used, at least not by the boys when talking directly to her. The eyes of the boys went to gaze upon Lauren's newly developed, and ample, "diddies". The wart was no longer even noticed or, if noticed, was deemed of no earthly importance whatsoever.

Dinner ended and Rose and Ellen helped to clear the table. Their job tonight included the cleaning and drying of the dishes. Jim, despite his mother's request that he remain at home, grabbed his coat and left the house for the pub. Teresa went inside to listen to the radio.

"How do you know when you meet the right person?" piped up Ellen as she dried a dish handed to her by her sister. Her question was directed toward her mother sitting at the table, sipping a glass of tea.

"Now don't be telling me you've met a young boy you like," replied Mary with a smile.

"N-No, I was just wondering . . . ." Ellen could feel her cheeks redden over her mother's words.

"Talking about boys. It seems only yesterday you were a bundle wailing in my arms, your father looking at you with a big grin on his face that stretched from ear to ear. You children, you all grow up faster than you know."

"When you met Da, did you know that he was the man you'd marry? Did you know right away?"

Mary smiled at the memory evoked by Ellen's question. "Yes. With your father, I knew the moment I saw him he was the man for me. It took me a little while to convince him I was the girl for him though. He was a slippery one, your father."

"Why Mum? If you knew you loved him right away, why didn't he feel the same about you?"

"Only because he didn't. Life isn't simple as that. Not always. Nice and neat. Sometimes one falls in love with another and that person never returns your love. There was a girl I knew had that misfortune when we were young. She loved this boy so much she went nearly mad when he couldn't love her back. Tried to drown herself in the *lough*. Sometimes it takes time. Love can be fast and sudden for some, and slow, but in the end just as strong, for others." Mary Rawdon had been looking at her teacup as she spoke but now she turned her gaze directly onto Ellen. "Why all this talk, El? Is there someone you're liking?" Rose stopped washing the dishes and stared at her sister. Ellen's cheeks flushed red once more under the scrutiny.

"She does!" declared Rose, laughing. "She does like someone!"

"No I don't," protested Ellen. "No, it's Lauren. She thinks she's in love. We were talking today and she told me."

Rose grunted. "That tramp. What are you doing with her? Stay away from her. You don't want people thinking you're like her."

Ellen, frowning, went to the task of drying another dish Rose handed to her. She wanted to retaliate to her sister's words, to defend her friend, but didn't know how to do it.

Mary eyed her daughter. "I know Lauren. She's got a head full of foolishness tied together with strings of nonsense. A lot of times, when you're young, you think you're in love but it's not real. Just a passing fancy."

"Lauren passes her fancy to just about anyone," grumbled Rose. "Little tramp is all she is."

"That'll be enough of that talk, Rose," stated Mary firmly. "Be Christian if you have to talk about people."

"How do you know when it's real, Mum?" persisted Ellen. "Does it feel different? How can you know?"

"Ellen, you're growing up. You're a young woman now and if you're anything like I was, you've got a head packed with romantic dreams. If you haven't met a boy yet, you will. I just want you to remember to be responsible. You can listen to this too, Rosie. Be responsible. Your father told me once years ago that young men are after one thing. I suppose that's as true now as then." She shook her head and smiled. "Lord knows, your father should know about that. Before we were married, he broke a heart or two."

"Da?" Both daughters stared at their mother with eyes opened wide.

"Of course Da. What do you think? He was born old Da?" Mary stood up and brought her empty teacup and saucer to Rose. She turned and, putting a gentle hand on Ellen's cheek, kissed her on the forehead. Then she kissed Rose also. "My little chicks. I'll repeat to you what my own mother once told me. Your love. Your physical love is a gift. It's the greatest gift a woman can give a man. But that gift will be valued by a man according to the value you yourself place upon it. So don't give yourself away cheaply. Love can be glorious, but it can be, and sometimes is, dangerous as well. I've seen more than one young woman broken by it. I've seen lives ruined by it. Be careful, darlings. I only hope that when you do meet someone that he loves you as much as your father loved me . . ." Tears began to spread across the lower lids of her eyes. ". . . and as much as I loved him."

"Oh, Mum," murmured Ellen, her brows knitting in concern. "Mum . . . ."

"Hush, I'm fine," said Mary, pushing away the hug offered her by Ellen. "My little girl, grown up." She gazed into Ellen's face. "Your freckles are gone now you're grown. Do you remember how much they upset you when you were small?"

"Upset me?" replied Ellen. "Did they?"

"You came home one day after some of the other children made fun of them, crying and wishing them off your face. I told you I loved your freckles. I didn't lie to you. I did love them. And you told me you hated them anyway."

"Did I?"

"I told you that when I was a little girl I always wanted freckles and felt bad that I couldn't have them. I told you that freckles are beautiful. Then I asked you to name me one thing that could possibly be more beautiful . . . and what you told me in return I always carry in my heart. It was a gift to me. I'll always treasure it."

Ellen stared at her mother. "What I told you? Why? What did I say?"

"You looked up at me and said: "Mothers. Mothers are more beautiful than anything.""

They stood gazing at each other. Ellen contemplating how her words, lost to her own memory, had remained bright and golden in her mother's heart.

"Now," spoke up Mary, "I'm going to have another cup of tea and listen to the radio for a bit."

"I'll make you another cup," offered Ellen. "Rose, I'll finish up the dishes. You go with Mum."

Left alone, Ellen saw Lauren's face again and recalled once more how shocked she was when she first heard her friend's confession. Lauren had pulled Ellen to the side with a request to talk. "Well, El, I did it," she told her.

"Did what?" asked Ellen, not understanding at all what her friend meant.

"Slept with Timmy," responded Lauren, smiling.

Ellen's mouth popped open, forming a perfect O of surprise and she stared at her friend, for the moment unable to speak.

"Shut your mouth," said Lauren. "You don't have to act so surprised. I told you I was thinking of it."

Lauren went on to tell Ellen about her walk down Ballynelly Lane the previous night, she and Timmy going to a small private glade near the old fortification. Timmy had brought along cigarettes to smoke and wine to drink. "It seemed so romantic, under the stars," explained Lauren. "So I let him." There was a superiority in Lauren's words that both surprised and confused Ellen.

Now, reviewing Lauren's act against the words her mother had just spoken to her, Ellen decided that Lauren had done something very foolish. She shook her head and began to giggle when she thought of

Timmy, Timmy Kane, thin as a rod, with drooping shoulders, a long face with skin spotted with acne. *Certainly nothing to look at. Lord, I can't even imagine . . . .*

Ellen decided she couldn't do what Lauren had done. All of her dreams of romance, of finding and marrying the perfect man, couldn't be surrendered for a jaunt to Ballynelly with a clod like Timmy. Love for the first time wasn't just something to run past, was it? Just something to get done and be over with? Ellen wanted something more out of Love than that, and she was willing to wait to get it.

Chapter Twelve

Jim came rattling home late at night, after staying late again at the pub. Forsaking bed he went instead to the kitchen and poured himself one more drink. His mother, hearing her son in the kitchen, an unusual enough occurrence to provoke her curiosity (and apprehension), came down the stairs to see if anything was wrong. And, if truth be known, to scold him (once again) for keeping late hours at the pub.

Jim sat at the table, a tumbler of whiskey in front of him, his face awash with something akin to self-pity and self-concern. *Something's wrong.*

Seeing her, he, without a word, turned away and raised the glass to his lips. She noticed his hand was trembling, a sight that made her stomach sink. For a moment she was standing on windy precipice, looking at the sheer drop at her feet.

"What's wrong, Jimmy?" she asked, placing herself into the chair beside him.

He simply looked at her.

"What's wrong, Jimmy?" repeated Mary. "Nothing bad happened, did it?"

Jim, whose eyes had hooked onto the glass that held his whisky, now moved his gaze to his mother's face. "No, nothing's wrong," he said quietly. "Why'd you come down?" he complained. "Can't I have a drink by myself?" He turned away, running a hand through his rough hair, at the look of hurt that came onto his mother's face. "Sorry, Mum. I didn't mean anything."

She felt another twinge of sorrow for her son, what loving mother could not when sadness sits upon a child's face? "Tell me what's wrong, Jimmy?" she asked once again, more a plea than a question now.

"Ever notice," said Jim after a few moments of thought, "how some people have so much? And others so little? Why is that, Mum? It's not their hard work. No one worked harder than Da and you. It's because they hold the cards, Mum. Some are inside and others are out. And those that are in don't let you in. We could struggle for years and not make what some others make in a month. It's not fair." His eyes, filled with gloom, returned to the glass.

"Not fair? And don't I know it? Life's not a magistrate sitting on a bench, making decisions based on what's right, is it? We're getting by, Jimmy, and that's better than some are doing."

"Getting by. And that's all. And just barely. Ever think about having more, Mum? Maybe some extra money to hire help, to make life a little easier? How about a new lorry, or tractor?"

"Aw, Jimmy, I know how hard you're working. I – "

"Not just for me, Mum. I'm not thinking just of me. For you and the girls."

"Sure sometimes I wish things were easier. But if wishes were horses then beggars would ride, isn't it so? We have to make do. That's the way it is."

Jimmy took another swallow of his drink.

"What else? Jimmy. What else is wrong?"

Jimmy stared at her and then made up his mind to tell her what he had intended never to give voice to: "There . . . was a man tonight, Mum. A man drinking in the Rooster. Reeking of money, he was. I-I followed him out the door when he left. An easy mark. A bop on the head and I'd have his money – "

Mary stared at him aghast, momentarily too shocked to speak. "You tried to rob a man?" she said at last, her voice containing true horror. He might have told her he was burying bodies on the farmland for the IRA. In the next moment her shock turned to anger "Now you tell me why my son, raised to be a Christian, suddenly takes to robbing people in the streets! You tell me that, young man!" She beat the words down upon him as though hitting him with strokes from a *shillelagh*.

"I-I didn't rob him, Mum. I followed him, but I couldn't go through with it." He snorted a hollow laugh. "Want to hear the funny part? He actually fell down, he was so buckled. What did I do but help him up. Brushed off his fancy jacket and sent him on his way."

"Well, thank the Lord for that." Mary exhaled a great sigh of relief. "You did the right thing, James. Thank God."

"Did I, Mum? Do the right thing? Why the man was so drunk he would probably think he'd lost his money if I had taken it."

"No good comes from no good. And did you give any thought to your family while you were planning your evil horrors? You wanted easy money! That's the heart of it! And what would happen to your family? Did you think of that? Your family that depends on you to keep the farm going? What would happen to the farm if you were sent to the jailhouse? Did you give any thought to that? Did you?!"

Although rough in his exterior and, to a degree, in his behavior, Jim was in fact a sensitive young man. Suddenly oppressed with shame, he slumped back on the chair, and stared with sad gloom at his mother. "I-I suppose not . . . I'm sorry, Mum," he added in a voice that contained little power. "I'm sorry." Despite his efforts to contain them, two tears, one from each eye, escaped and rolled down his cheeks.

Mary put her arm around him and pulled him to her so that his face was nestled against her shoulder. "You're sorry," she said softly. "And I believe it. But sorry doesn't fill the barn, does it James? God bless you for doing the right thing. And you promise me now you'll not be thinking of such a thing ever again. You promise me that, Jimmy."

James looked up as though he was six years old again and seeking comfort against the pain of a bruised knee. He nodded his head.

"You're a good boy, Jimmy. A good boy. That's what God reminded you of tonight. That's why you helped that man. You're a good boy, Jimmy."

Jim let himself be held as though he was a child instead of the young man he was.

*   *   *

Some miracles come and go so softly they often pass unnoticed. After that night, Jim was a different man, or rather was again much the person he'd been before his father's death, the angry edge to his behavior, increasingly evident in the last few months, suddenly gone. He'd been at a crossroads of sorts for a time now, standing at the nexus of two paths, deciding which life he would choose for himself, one of honest work or one of crime. Sometimes lives are determined by small fleeting events, and what appears to be an insignificant occurrence to an outsider is one that has tremendous effect upon the person inside the moment. Was it the small scolding Jim had received from his mother that night in the kitchen that served to nudge him to the right road? Or had he already chosen it himself, in that moment he'd bent down to help the man he'd followed with the intent to rob? Or was it a combination of the two? Whatever the answer, on that night the weight of Jim's anger, the weight of the profound resentment he'd carried with him for so long following his father's death, was lifted off his confused heart. Suddenly it was all gone, vanished as though it had never been.

He settled back into the routine of his former life, holding tightly onto a newfound appreciation for it, and Michael Duffy had to find a new drinking partner for his nights at The Red Rooster, Jim's trips to the pub ceasing almost entirely.

Talk of Jimmy's failed attempt at robbery, or rather his failed attempt at the attempt, never made it past his mother's lips, remaining a secret between mother and son.

Chapter Thirteen

The days went by, turning into weeks, which transformed then to months. Routine made up the bulk of many of the days of Ellen's life, her time growing up. It was so before her father's illness and as true after. To a large degree repetition controlled her existence. Many days were, by necessity, a kind of reiteration of the previous ones, the same chores and tasks having to be completed with each dawn. There was a certain monotony to it but there was comfort in it too, that routine. It held safety in it.

Sure there were days in which the routine of daily living was broken as well. Days few and far between, thank God. Days in which difficulties of weather afflicted the farm or a new need for money pushed the normalcy of habit aside to demand full and immediate attention. Days in which fresh problems had to be dealt with and solved. And, most rare, days that presented changes that would be permanent and everlasting.

Today was like that, a day of permanent change.

*　　*　　*

"Not a cloud in the sky," murmured Ellen to herself as she gazed out to the horizon from the ridge of her hilltop. Sitting down on the grass, she briefly closed her eyes and let the warmth of the sun float over her face.

The years had been kind to Ellen in physical terms; she'd grown up well. She was the prettiest young thing in Moville, and, to the minds of many, pretty enough to win the gold cup if a contest were held to find the fairest lass in all of Ireland.

The ship that had brought her here to her hilltop was still a distance from the horizon, still visible as it floated away from Donegal. One of a very few that still docked in Moville, even if only briefly.

Ellen opened her eyes again to see it. The ship's nose was now nudging the blue edge of the sky, moving into another existence, becoming part of a different world.

Rose and Teresa were aboard that faraway ship, going to America, to New York City. Rose and Teresa were going to be gone, for always. Just like Mags.

Sure it was expected, but like many things expected it came still as a shock of sorts when it occurred.

The family had been saving every extra penny that could be salvaged over the time since their father's death. Now they finally had enough to pay for a single fare to America. Lo and behold, when going to make the purchase, the ship company offered them a second passage for an additional nominal fee. So cheap a deal it had to be taken. A call to Mags netted them the extra money needed. Now instead of just Rose leaving, it was Rose and Teresa.

Sad to say goodbye to them, but exciting too.

Excitement lost on her mother. Less than an hour ago, her mother was all tears as she bid her middle daughters farewell, hugging each in turn as though fearful, if once she let go, they'd be grabbed up in the tentacles of some hidden sea monster and dragged to the bottom of the waters, never to be seen again except for the bleached bones that would float to the surface and wash ashore.

But Rose and Teresa wouldn't let their mother's sadness dampen their sense of excitement, their sense of new adventure. They shed tears only at the last moment, when Jimmy, Ellen and their mother, abruptly the last remnants of the Rawdon family remaining in Ireland, had to at last depart the ship and leave them. This sadness on the part of Rose and Teresa, sincere as it was, was momentary and brief, leaving as quickly as it came, lasting only until their family was walking down the gangplank. Before Mary, Jim and Ellen reached the shore all sadness Rose and Teresa felt over leaving home was pushed away again, crowded to the back of their hearts by the internal commotion of excitement they felt.

The Rawdon remnants stood on the pier, looking up and waving their hands as Rose and Teresa waved back from the ship's railing. The strong breeze off the water whipped their hair about their faces as though their long tresses too were filled with the excitement of the moment and doing a jig of joy on their skulls. Their faces were all bright eyes and smiles.

Off to a new life.

Odd, all the times Ellen had dreamed of going to America she'd never considered the possibility that she would be the *last* sister to go. Being the last, it now occurred to her that she would have the hardest time leaving. With all the girls gone, who would help her mother with the chores? Who would help do all the things that had to be done on the farm? Wasn't it true that Rose and Teresa could leave now, almost carefree, without a thought, only because she was left behind?

Jim and Mum had gone straight back to the farm after leaving the piers but Ellen couldn't go with them, not right away, not while she could run to her hilltop to view the ship as it moved toward the horizon, not while she could still rest her sight on the vessel that was carrying the last of her sisters away from home.

She kept her eyes on the ocean liner as, enwrapped in its own silence, it moved slowly over the horizon, dropping off the world it seemed. In minutes there was nothing left of it except its smokestacks. Then those columns too disappeared from sight and were gone as well. For a few minutes Ellen could still see the smoke they threw off, then she was staring at vacant sky and water.

Rose and Teresa gone . . . .

"Not a cloud in the sky," murmured Ellen again. She said it as though reciting a prayer that her sisters would enjoy nothing but bright, sunny days when they arrived at their destination, at their new home.

Fragments of sunlight floated upon the surface of the water and presented a carpet of dancing diamonds for her eyes. The warmth of the golden sunlight on her face was luxuriant and part of her would have liked to stay longer to enjoy it, to close her eyes again and rest under the golden glow, but she couldn't. Time to go home.

There was much to do.

She pushed herself up off the ground, presented her back to the carpet of diamonds and started back down the hill, returning to a house more empty now than when she'd risen from her bed in the morning.

Chapter Fourteen

Ellen, with school a thing of the past, had to try to find work locally, and, after only a short time of searching, amazed herself by being successful, obtaining a clerk's position in the sole existing Moville law office, a skeletal survivor of better times. Obtaining the position was a stroke of good fortune equivalent to winning the Sweepstakes as decent jobs continued to be as rare in Donegal as wedding rings in a *bairin breac*. Sure it was just part-time work, but it offered enough money to help pay some of the bills.

What was it Da said once? If a Help Wanted sign was hung in a store window in Moville, the neighbors would be certain the proprietor had a pistol clapped to his head and was being robbed. No one would believe there was a job being offered.

The work enabled her to make monetary contributions to the family welfare but not all her salary was given away. Each week Ellen tucked away what little bit of her money could be spared into a small purse she kept (sort of hidden) in a dresser drawer. This hoarding of funds was done with some guilt, with her feeling a bit like a thief, but could she always be financially dependent on others? Wasn't "saving for a rainy day" a good thing? She sure wasn't going to marry into a fortune, was she? What was wrong with putting away a little personal dowry?

A dowry, as if she'd ever need one. Marriage looked to be a skittish cat hiding under a bush. For a time now, Ellen's good looks attracted the attention of the local young men, many of whom looked her up and down, head to toe, and decided she was a sweet thing indeed. More than one earnest attempt was made to try to bed Ellen, but all such attempts met with failure, there being no young man she could truly give her heart to. It was slim pickings in Moville as far as Ellen was concerned.

Jimmy had better luck. He'd met a young girl, a Kerry girl, and it looked like marriage was in the future for him. A happy thought, and a scary one as well. The house that was Ellen's home had been transformed by her father's death, and then again by her sisters' leaving. Soon Jimmy would be married and the house would be changed into something else once more. For, after Jimmy brought a wife home, wouldn't she, Ellen, be more in the way then anything else? That was no one's fault, it was just the way things would be.

There'd be a new lady of the house. And then she, Ellen, would be a third wheel. But there was another thought that came with this one. With Jim's marriage she, Ellen, would no longer be required to stay. She could join her sisters in New York City.

She might need her savings then to leave home, maybe by then she'd have enough to go to America. Or maybe by then Rose and Teresa and Mags would be sitting pretty and be able to send her the cost of a fare. If they did that then, when the day of her leaving came, and if she saved more than she needed, she'd give what was left over to her mother, a goodbye gift. It was a plan of sorts, as vague as it was.

Then her mother was stricken ill and everything changed once again.

* * *

A grimace of pain passed over Mary's face as she sat at the kitchen table enjoying a cup of tea. "'Tis nothing," she declared stoically when asked by Ellen if something was wrong. "A neck ache." The next moment following this declaration, Mary fell to the kitchen floor, tumbling off her chair.

A stroke. Caused by a "subarachnoid hemorrhage" said the doctor. A leak of blood that spilled onto the area surrounding the brain. This leaking was followed by a condition called "vasospasm" or a narrowing of some of the blood vessels irritated by the hemorrhage. Mary Rawdon had a slight (the doctor said it might have been a lot worse) "hemiplegia" or paralysis to her left arm. There were also some "spacial and perceptual problems manifesting themselves" in her behavior.

Suddenly her mother, her independent, strong mother, was no longer the same person she was before. She had difficulty reading and writing, trouble guiding her hands to perform simple tasks such as picking up a kitchen spoon or fork. She suffered from "left-side" neglect as well, a condition in which objects and people on her left side were forgotten. Ellen and Jim had to remember, if they wanted to hold their Mum's attention at all for any length of time, to stand and talk on her right side.

Her mother, made less independent and more frail by the stroke, needed care and looking after and so it fell to Ellen to offer her mother the necessary aid she now required. As with Jimmy years earlier, now with Ellen. A sense of duty and responsibility kept her bound to her home as sure as leather straps and locked doors, and kept any personal wishes she may have had at bay. Brother and sister had more in common with each other than they fully realized, more than either ever gave voice to.

It would be wrong to assume that there was resentment in Ellen over the task she was offered by circumstance. Such was her love for her mother that she considered it nothing more than right that she should care for her. To do otherwise was a thought that never even crept into her mind. As her mother had cared for her father, so Ellen now cared for her mother.

Jim, for whatever reason, perhaps to concentrate on caring for his mother, perhaps for other unspoken reasons, continued to postpone any plans for marriage.

*　　*　　*

A couple of months passed by. The days again settled into a routine, albeit a new one; there was Ellen's work at the law office, her work on the farm and her caring for her mother, and little time for anything else.

*   *   *

The arrival of the year of 1951 had not brought better times to Moville with it. Economic conditions in Donegal were growing sterner day by day and more and more businesses found it necessary to close up shop, being unable to make ends meet. Beyond Ireland's borders there came pronouncements of the possibility of a Third World War, news that was terrifying to listen to. Chinese Communist troops had entered the Korean conflict and American casualties were said to number more than 100,000 men. A phenomenal number! Why that many men might be more than lived in all of Donegal for the past few centuries, thought Ellen when she heard the figure given. *Why can't people get along? How much killing can the world endure?*

One evening, after working her normal day in the law office, a job she'd held for just a little more than four months now, Ellen was surprised when Mr. O'Hannon called her into his office to announce that, "due to falling income", the firm could no longer afford to employ her. "I regret losing you," he told her with true sincerity, "as you're a fine employee".

A fine employee now dismissed, her departure an "unfortunate necessity".

She walked home, stunned by the loss, feeling like a hospital patient who, against doctor's orders, leaves the hospital room while still in the midst of illness. Her distress over the loss of her job was even greater because it had been totally unanticipated. She felt like it was her fault she'd lost the work and thought herself to be a total failure. Sadness made her cry walking home, wiping tears from her cheeks all the way. *How can I tell Jim and Mum that I'm no longer working?*

Unanticipated. *Didn't Da always say it's the thing you don't worry about that comes up behind you and sneak attacks you?* His own cancer was proof of that, Mum's illness too. Now her own firing, completely unexpected.

Of course the first time Da had spoken of "the thing you don't worry about", he wasn't tossing out the aphorism for the sake of imparting wisdom, rather as a prelude to his telling one of his tales, the story of the "Nightmare Steed", the demon horse, the *pooka*.

Da, I miss you and your stories. Why did you ever have to leave us?

The *pooka*, a large terrible black steed, composed more of wind and shadow than skin and bones, a beast that always made its appearance at night, seeking to approach unsuspecting innocents and trick them into climbing upon its wide back. A terrible ride would follow, a horrifying rush through bogs and woods, over boulder-covered hills and rushing rivers. A wind-whistling journey deep into thick forests where people seldom wandered due to good sense. The demon horse would whinny a continuing mocking laugh as the branches of the trees raked at the rider's eyes and face, tearing the skin away as the rider screamed his fear and pain from behind the flowing black mane. Try as the rider might, he couldn't climb or jump off the steed's back, stuck there as if nailed on. He would remain so for the duration, until either the *pooka* or death released him.

Life is like that, isn't it? Sometimes it just grabs you up and no matter how much you don't like where it's going, no matter how much it hurts, you can't get off the ride.

The *pooka* could be cruel and didn't concern itself at all with how much pain and brutality was inflicted upon the rider on its back. It just ran and ran, and in the act of running, mocked the terror and tears of the rider it held.

Just like life.

A gust of wind blew over the dirt road. *Cold.* It raised dust for a moment and Ellen could see the sun reflecting golden off the cloud as the wind held it. Then the brisk breeze was gone and the dust settled back to the road. The trees lining the path down to the farmhouse on either side of her were filled with hopping and chirping birds singing joyously to the world from behind the glossy leaves of the trees. The world was happy. Her sadness was for her alone.

Ellen saw her brother once again working on their old and battered truck behind the barn and wiped away all tears. He didn't look up and so didn't see her approaching the house. Ellen didn't interrupt his work to greet him but went straight to the door and into the house. *Jimmy would just ask how come I'm home so early. How do you tell people bad news?*

You just tell them. That's what Da would say. Tell Mum first. Ellen decided she'd better get it over with and let her mother know right off she'd lost her job.

Inside, Ellen saw her mother asleep in the same chair her father used to doze in. Eyes closed, resting her head half upon her shoulder and half against the wing of the chair. She appeared so relaxed, so peaceful, that Ellen decided not to disturb her but instead tiptoed into the kitchen. She'd make some tea for her and her mother.

When she returned to the parlor, carrying a serving tray with two cups of tea, she observed what she'd failed to see previously. Her mother had been knitting and the ball of yarn had fallen and rolled away from the chair. Ellen noticed too, with a sudden twinge of fright, that her mother's hand, lying on her lap, appeared to be *wrong*. It was resting palm upward.

And she was still, so very still. A chill trickled down Ellen's spine, cold points of ice stinging each vertebra. *Something is wrong!*

Placing the serving tray with the tea on the table near the chair, she stepped over to her mother slowly, almost cautiously. Her hand fluttered down to her mother's arm.

"Mum?" she whispered. A shadow of agony passed briefly before her eyes as she saw no reaction to her touch, not the slightest bit of movement. She noticed there were small bubbles of saliva sitting in one corner of her mother's mouth.

"Mum!?" repeated Ellen. A cry of shock this time, a sound half-pleading. "Mum!" A call louder this time. Then another plea, another cry. She shook the old woman, but still there was no response. Ellen, discerning the truth at last, threw herself upon her mother's body, flinging her arms around the woman's shoulders as tears burst from her eyes, comprehending her mother's death on the moment even as a part of her continued to beg God to let her mother please be alive, even as she released her mother and ran to the door to scream to Jimmy to get into the house to do something to save her. Even as she did all this, she understood that her mother was gone from her forever. Just like Da.

Ellen had the sensation that she had been placed outside the world, or rather was still in it, but was now no more substantial than a dust particle floating in a beam of sunlight, like the dust on the road she'd seen when coming home. She watched as her brother stepped into the parlor, as he stopped and stared and knelt down before his mother's body. Her own heart thumping in her chest was the most real thing about the scene before her.

Jim put his ear to his mother's chest and then placed his fingers on her neck, feeling for a pulse. Ellen felt as though she received a slap from a devil's unseen hand when her brother turned his head and made a motion of finality toward her, a silent indication, confirmation really, that their mum was gone. A new explosion of grief burst from her and Jim stepped quickly over to her to put his arms around her, hugging her close to him, attempting to comfort her, attempting to comfort himself as well.

He directed Ellen to a chair and she found herself sitting, still sobbing, as he returned to their mother, their wonderful, wonderful mother. *Oh God!* Ellen watched as he picked Mary up, the woman's head rolling and falling backwards as her son hoisted her into his arms.

"I'm going to put her in her bed," he told Ellen, talking over his shoulder, his own voice groaning with controlled sorrow, he now shedding tears as well. His leg bumped the little serving table near the chair and one of the two teacups that Ellen had just brought into the parlor fell from its saucer and tumbled over onto the floor, spilling its contents onto the rug.

Chapter Fifteen

Mary Rawdon's coffin was brought out of the church shadows and into the sunlight to the sound of the church choir singing "Our Lady of Knock". Six men, one of whom was a teary-eyed Jim, carried the casket the necessary few yards to the church graveyard. There it was placed beside the open grave that would be Mary's place of final rest, beside her husband, beside him in death as she was in life. The day glowed bright with golden sunshine flowing out of a crystal blue sky.

Behind the graves, a short distance away, sat the stone wall that appeared to be as ancient as time, already old before the era of Saint Patrick, at least to Ellen's mind. She'd seen the wall many times in making her visits to her father's grave. There was, strangely, something comforting about that wall now, about the existence of that wall.

Slim comfort; she had to be held up by Jimmy as she walked from the grave.

* * *

Ellen lay in bed in the darkness of her room. How vacant, how cold the house was without a mother's love to warm it! And how much she'd taken that warmth for granted over the years, not appreciating its true importance until it was snatched away. An orphan now, she experienced a sense of disconnection with her world, a sense of being bereft, cut off from the past and her own heritage, feeling like a small fishing boat that had lost its moorings and, pilotless and unconnected to the shore, was floating, drifting out into dangerous waters.

In her bed beneath the covers, feeling empty except for the ache of sadness inside her, she stared at the dark shadows floating on the walls of her room, incapable of thought, her mind little more substantial than the shadows surrounding her.

She stayed in bed until the first hints of daylight began to peek through her window and the sound of birds fluttered into the room with the dawn. Sounds incongruous to her mood but she found herself not only listening to the joyful chirping but actually enjoying hearing it.

Throwing the covers off, she got up and, feeling the hit of the pristine chill of the morning air on her body, put on a robe before going to her parents' room, a room now empty but for memories and the ache of loss.

The thin lace curtains glowed in the sunlight. A sense of fragility floated about the room now, or perhaps the fragility was in Ellen's eyes only, residing, like beauty, in the eyes of the beholder.

She gazed at the bed, and saw in her mind an image of her mother resting upon it, appearing as she did on the last day of her life, when Jim had placed her on the bed. Mum's face, with its finely etched lines of age, appearing peaceful, as though Da's arms were around her when she died.

They must have been. Da's arms around Mum. They must have been.

Although familiar, the room seemed now a strange landscape, barren and subtly changed.

A framed photograph of her parents, taken when they were first married, sat on the bureau. Ellen reached out, picked it up and, after staring at it for a time, returned the smile she saw on the faces of her parents. *How happy they seemed then. So much younger. How much they changed over the years . . . .*

Replacing the photograph to its place on the bureau her hand brushed against the old and tattered bible her mother had kept for years, for as far back as Ellen could remember. Opening it, she found tucked within its pages, at various intervals, small funeral cards giving the dates of the deaths of relatives and friends who had passed away over time. Some were protected with plastic, a few contained photos of the deceased, a bodiless face floating above the words of a prayer. Some of the cards were very old. Ellen had the sense of holding in her hands not a bible but rather a miniature paper graveyard, with little paper tombstones appearing every few pages.

She saw a photograph of her grandmother staring solemnly at her from behind small, old-fashioned black-rimmed spectacles. *Sacred Heart of Jesus. Have mercy on the soul of Catherine Rawdon, Ballybrack, Greencastle, Co. Donegal.* This small prayer was followed by the date of death and her grandmother's age when she passed away: eighty-seven.

Another card brought back a childhood memory of an old neighbor, a warm-hearted elderly lady who had once in a while sat with Ellen when she was a child and read tales out of a book to her. *Aged one hundred years when she died. Had she really been that old?* Ellen's childhood fondness for the woman curled the corners of her mouth with a forlorn smile.

A protruding edge of white paper caught her eye and Ellen withdrew it from its place among the pages of the bible. A letter, folded in half to fit within the book's pages. Unfolding it, Ellen recognized her mother's neat and elegant handwriting. A letter addressed to her father, dated shortly after his death, a letter written to a beloved memory, to a soul in heaven.

Feeling a touch of an eavesdropper's guilt, Ellen took it over to the bed where she sat down and began to read:

> *Dearest,*
>
> *I am writing to you knowing that somehow my words, my thoughts, will find you. I miss you. There is no place, no spot I can go to, no house I can enter, no friends I can visit, no place I can be, and not think of you. I see you everywhere. Everything recalls a memory of you. Even the sight of our children makes my heart ache for in them I see you. I am trying very hard not to be sad and perhaps one day I will succeed, but now I weep. I cannot stop. I don't know where to find the strength to combat my sorrow but I pray to our kind Lord to offer it to me and perhaps one day I will be granted that strength. For now I can't stop crying, I miss you so.*

The letter ended there. Unsigned. Ellen wiped away some teardrops from her eyes and cheeks, then folded it in half again and replaced it in the exact spot from which she'd taken it. With trembling legs, she took the photo of her parents and the bible with her back to her room and there placed them on the top of her bureau, wanting them close to her.

Everything recalls a memory of you. Even the sight of our children makes my heart ache for in them I see you . . .

Sorry, Mum . . . sorry.

Ellen felt hot tears streaming from her eyes and wiped them away, not certain at all why she was crying, whether for loss of her mother, or for her mum's sorrow over the loss of her beloved husband.

Chapter Sixteen

Ellen stepped outside the house, leaned against the white wall of her home and gazed at her brother's back as he walked to the barn. The warmth of the stone wall, gathered from the sun's heat, seeped into her shoulder blades as she watched Jimmy step into the barn. It felt good on her back.

Once again, watching Jimmy, she experienced a pang of guilt over the resurgence of her desire to leave the farm, to follow her sisters to America, as though the wanting of it was itself something shameful.

The ambition to leave – to escape, really – had steadily gained strength within Ellen over the weeks since her mother's passing. She had not wished for her mother's death but it came nonetheless, and now, weeks later, Jimmy had proposed to his Kerry girl. They'd be wed in six months. Now Ellen accepted the increasing authority of her own desires, no longer bound by any sense of obligation to remain. She was no longer *needed* here.

I'll be little more than excess baggage once Jimmy is married.

I'm around now doing little more than cleaning and cooking and mucking out the barn. And that's little enough reason to remain even if he doesn't get married.

Since the loss of her job, on the same day her mother had passed on, she'd not been able to get another. That would change in America. There was money to be earned there.

What she had here now at home was not enough for true happiness, was it? If she stayed and even if she eventually married she would, she thought, always regret never having experienced anything different.

And who in this place would she marry anyway? No local boy she could think of appealed to her. That much had stayed the same.

There were few ways to meet boys in Donegal, in school at one time, or maybe at play, but the days of school and play were gone. Now the best chance was at the few church dances that occurred each year, the events always well supervised by nuns or priests. There the boys would line up on one side of the room and the girls on the other, the great expanse of floor in between daring them to cross it like a scowling bully, until a boy or two got up the nerve to actually do that and ask a girl to dance. More often than not it was girls dancing with other girls. The best thing about the dances was that you got to see who, what, was available. A poor crop, in Ellen's opinion. Oh, she danced when asked, never said no so as not to hurt anyone's feelings, but there was no boy there who took her breath away, that was certain.

She adhered to the idea that her future was somewhere else, in America, waiting for her to cross the sea. She had believed that for as long as she envisioned a future for herself, for her entire life.

Anyway, I'd be of more use to you, Jimmy, if I was earning money and sending some home, like our sisters do.

Two weeks ago, Ellen had been on the telephone with Rose, discussing her hope to join her sisters in New York. Rose encouraged her to come and told her that she, and Maggie and Teresa, would scrape up the money needed for her fare. "Don't let the money stop you, Ellen," Rose had told her and Ellen listened. Rose was married now and living with a husband! How quickly things can change.

It was Rose who told her how to apply for an immigrant visa, a step Ellen had days ago taken. Rose would act as her "sponsor", assuring the American authorities that she wouldn't become a burden to the country.

Could she travel alone? she had asked.

"Sure and why not?" said Rose. "No one bothered us a'tall. Anyway, we'll get together the cost of a plane ticket instead of a boat. You'll be safe on a plane and you'll be here before you realize you left."

A plane? The very thought of flying made Ellen's heart beat faster.

Jimmy would miss her. That she knew. He would also miss the work she did around the farm, at least until he was married and his bride moved in. But that wouldn't be long. She was already thinking of herself as a third wheel in her own house.

Could she simply wait around until the wedding? She'd considered it, and rejected the idea. Jim's waiting a half-year in tying the knot didn't mean she had to put her own plans on hold, did it? She'd had enough of that, letting her own desires play second fiddle to her sense of responsibility, strong as that sense of responsibility was.

No, no more waiting. Time to go.

Still, although she'd reasoned it all out in her head, a part of her continued to scold her for wanting to leave. Her heart, almost nonsensically, considered it as a kind of abandonment of her brother. They'd grown closer than ever to each other over the time they'd shared caring for their sick mother. They'd borne so much pain together, for so long.

I'm sorry, Jimmy. I'm sorry. But I'll soon be leaving.

*   *   *

Ellen waited until the next day to tell her brother of her plans to leave, apologizing to him at the same time for wanting to go. Jim, his eyes brimming with tears to match her own, simply put his arms around her and held her to his chest for a few moments. "If it's leaving that will make you happy," he told her, "then that's what you must do. And it's not unexpected, El. I'll miss you, more than anything, but you've got to follow your heart to be happy."

You've got to follow your heart to be happy . . . .

*   *   *

Ellen was giving up the only life she'd ever known, and, although that abandonment was her choice, somewhere in her heart she regretted it. She loved the farm, the house. Almost every memory she had up to now was part of this place, or at least connected to it in some way. She would always love her home, but she understood that she was at a place in her life where she could no longer be satisfied remaining in it. She stayed this long only because her mother needed her. If she continued to stay now she would be throwing away all hope for something different, something possibly better, than what she had now. She'd be taking the spade to any dreams and hopes she ever had. No Prince Charming was going to ride into Donegal to sweep her away to his castle. She'd understood that fact years ago and saw no reason to change her mind about it now.

Leaving home may ultimately not produce a better future for her – there were no guarantees in life – but it would at least give her what she didn't have now, the *hope* of a better life, the chance of grabbing onto a better future. If she didn't take even the chance now, how much would she regret it when she was old and, in her dotage, sitting in a rocking chair, thinking of what might have been?

All of the years she'd been alive she'd been unable to control the events shaping her existence. The circumstances propelling her days along cared little for her sentiments of them, simply carrying her along as if she was little more than a raindrop in a racing river. But now, in finalizing her decision to leave, she felt she was at last taking her future into her own hands, into her control, or at least as much control as it was possible for her to have. Leaving might be ultimately prove to be a mistake, but it felt correct and proper now.

The same day she told Jimmy she'd be leaving, Ellen again called her sister Rose in New York. Rose repeated her offer to make room in her apartment to give Ellen a place to stay until she was "situated". They had an extra room that could be given over to her.

And with her saying goodbye to Rosie over the phone, it was done and made final. Set in stone. Ellen would leave her home and go to America. It was there, in a new land, that she would attempt to build herself a new life, it was there she would attempt to become the Ellen she should be.

You've got to follow your heart to be happy . . .

. . . and any regrets that might come from doing that . . . well, let them come.

Chapter Seventeen

The day for her departure arrived and Ellen sat on the old sofa, nervously fidgeting while Jimmy pulled the lorry up to the front of the house, the lorry being used as the old auto was out of service for the time being, until Jimmy could get it running again. Her things, everything in the world that could be called a thing of *hers,* were packed into a lone suitcase sitting by the door. It held only two items that were once the property of her parents, the wedding photo and her mother's bible. The Holy Book still shielded in its pages the unfinished letter her grieving Mum had written after Da's death, a love letter to a soul in heaven, and the book would hold it until she, Ellen, died herself, if she had her way.

She felt like a little child, feeling the same kind of anxiousness she experienced as a toddler whenever she lost sight of her mother and father. *Is it happening? Am I really going? Am I really leaving?*

Her sense of excitement, of disbelief, had kept her from sleep most of the night. If she'd gotten more than an hour's total rest it was a lot.

Jim entered and bent down for the suitcase. "Well, come on, El. We have to be off. The train'll be leaving soon." With that pronouncement, Ellen's bag in hand, he turned and went out of the house again.

Time to go. Ellen took a deep breath and pulled her purse to her as she prepared to stand. Inside was a small sandwich for eating later. There was very little cash tucked away in it as she had very little money to her name. The cash she'd tried to save over the few months of her employment was long gone, having been spent to pay some of the medical bills incurred while taking care of her mother. Her sisters, as promised, all chipped in to pay her for her passage, sending enough money to allow her to purchase an airline ticket. She was the first in her family who would travel to America in a plane.

I'll leave Ireland this morning, and be in the U.S. by evening . . . . Her heart raced at the thought of such swift change.

All those years on her Cliona's Hill, she'd always expected she'd leave in one of the great ocean liners, never for a moment had she imagined a flight to America. Never once. She'd always gazed at the water in front of her when she thought of the future, never did she stare up at the clouds

Still sitting, she sent her eyes around her house for what she thought would be the final time, for a very long time at least. *Will I ever be back?* Almost desperately, her eyes sought to etch the room into her mind, her heart wanting to remember it vividly. The rug, the curtains, the table, the forlorn radio, the sofa she sat on, the pictures on the wall in their old frames, she took them all in, fixing them in her mind. Then, still clutching her purse close to her, shutting her eyes to the room for a moment and opening them again, she stood slowly and stepped toward the door.

Will I ever be back?

She didn't look back at the house when she reached the door but simply opened it and walked through to the outside. A different *outside* greeted her today, a new outside. She thought she could feel the very existence of her home sealing itself up behind her as she walked away.

Tinker, resting on the ground, his snout going gray now, a slight limp in a front leg, rose up and walked to her, whimpering as though comprehending she was leaving and would not be coming back. Ellen crouched down and hugged the dog goodbye. With tears in her eyes, she let his tongue lick at her face.

Climbing into the passenger seat of the lorry, she turned her head and stared through the dust-streaked rear window to view the exterior of her home, keeping her eyes fixed on it as Jim started the engine and they began to roll away. Tinker, after a moment's hesitation, ran after them, racing in the center of the dirt road, ears flapping with each stride, the pink tongue that had just licked her face (and had licked her face so many times over the years) dangling from the open mouth. Ellen watched as the old dog fell further and further away, diminishing in size as they picked up speed and gained more distance. Now and then, with the rocking movement of the lorry, the glass would catch the early morning sun and her view of the road behind her would be obscured, the glass opaque with the bright glow of sunlight. Then another rocking motion and Tinker and the road would abruptly reappear. She kept her eyes tight on the sight of the old dog, panting after her, running as fast as possible, running and limping not fast enough, until the lorry reached the paved road, rounded a curve and both Tinker and the Rawdon house, her home no longer, were gone from sight.

Gone.

Facing front again, Ellen gazed out of the dusty windshield and locked her eyes onto the road before her.

*   *   *

Ellen sat on her suitcase, her skirt spread and covering her legs, her eyes gazing at the curve in the train track in the distance. Soon the train would come roaring in and she would board it to be taken away. She was leaving behind the *lough* as seen from the top of her hill, leaving behind her home, her past, her parents' graves, abandoning her life as lived up to now, exchanging it all for an unknown, hoped-for future. A future that existed only vaguely in the dreams of her heart but, if it came to her as fair and friendly as she imagined, would be a fine future indeed. She had no fear of it, feeling the same kind of thrill she had as a child when she'd first run up to the crest of Cliona's Hill and there gazed out across the water toward what could be.

Jim stood beside her, alternately watching for the appearance of the train and gazing at his sister. He was going to miss her. Ellen was his favorite of all his sisters. Always had been, and his affection, his love, for her had only deepened as they, together, cared for their mother. They were a *team* of sorts, weren't they?

A tumbling breeze gusted on the open platform and Ellen had to push a disobedient lock of her wheat-colored hair away from her eyes now and then. Her hair was almost golden with the sun shining strong upon it. Her hand then went down to her skirt to push it back into place. More than once she had to force it to behave, the cloth attempting to hold hands with the wind and dance and play with it, refusing like an energetic child to remain where it was told.

A few other passengers dotted the station here and there at various intervals, all strangers to her.

"Guess who I saw yesterday," said Jim, breaking the silence between them. "Old Miss O'Connor. Remember her? You and me both had her for a teacher years ago, in different years. Remember I warned you about her? She's come back here for a couple of weeks. Visiting her sister."

Ellen smiled. "I remember her. She taught me in the third year of school. She was always nice."

"Nice! She was always reporting me to Da. I remember her always punishing me for forgetting my lessons or for some other reason or another. Half the time I swear I didn't know why she was rapping my knuckles with that ruler of hers. Whap! Whap! Whap! Back then I thought she was the meanest person in the world. With her bony face and her hair pulled back she looked the part. Paint her face green and put a wart on her beak and she'd make a right good witch in a flick."

"Ellen laughed. "Well you weren't exactly the perfect student, were you? You know what I remember about her? She teaching all the girls about sex. What stuff. I remember her telling us never to wear patent leather shoes as boys would use them to see the reflection of our underwear in them. Is that true?"

"Don't know. No girl in Moville ever wore patent leather shoes. Now I know why. Because of her."

"Did you say hello?"

"Sure, but I made sure to keep my hands in my pockets when I was talking to her. She still frightens me. I was afraid she'd yank out a ruler and start pounding my knuckles bloody." Then he dismissed his words with a chuckle. "No, actually she was nice. She remembered me and you as well. She told me to say hello to you, which I forgot to do until now. I told her you were off to America and she wishes you the best of luck. She said if she was young again she'd be going there too. Dublin's as far as she ever got."

In the distance, the arrival of the train was announced by a whistle blast. They both turned to look once more at the track just as the dark serpentine form of the rail cars and locomotive came into view around the curve. Ellen stood up, excited at the sound. As the train came closer, she could see it more clearly, an older engine but to Ellen it appeared marvelous with its sleek shining black paint, gold trim and gleaming metal.

Coming for her.

The train slowed and crawled into the station and, coming to a stop, sat hissing and growling like a fierce beast wanting its freedom to run again. Its whistle blew once more, the sound piercing now that it was so close, a scalpel blade of a sound slicing the air.

"Well El," said Jim, placing his hand on her arm. "It's time to say goodbye." There were tears in his eyes and Ellen's throat constricted at the sight of them. Her own eyes filled with tears as well.

"Oh, Jimmy, I'll miss you so much," she told him. He pulled her to him and gave her a mighty hug of farewell, kissing her on the cheek as he released her.

"I feel so bad," said Ellen, "that it's you who has to stay, to keep up the farm and all." She was at last giving voice to her sense of guilt, the fact that she was able to grant herself permission to leave while Jim was forced to stay.

He waved away her words. "No, El. Sure I once thought of going too but now that's changed. I left that idea behind somewhere and can't find it to pick it up again. It's fallen under a rock somewhere and let it stay there. I know now I won't ever leave. I'll stay here and be glad of it. I'll just be a *culchie* the rest of my time. A hick, they'd call me in America. But I just want to live the life I was born into. It's a good life as hard as it is sometimes. But that's me, El, and you are you. Don't be feeling guilty over leaving. You've got to go and God go with you with the going. There'll always be a place for you here if you should ever want to come back. That's true of all the Rawdons." He smiled down at her, a trace of sadness in the smile. "Although," he added, "given the behavior of our sisters that doesn't seem too likely. Once gone for a short while, gone for all time it seems."

"Seems . . . ." responded Ellen. *Will I ever see you again?*

"May the good Lord be kind to you, El. Best of luck. And call. Now we've got a phone, we should use it." He bent down, picked up her small suitcase and gave it over to her.

Halfway into the train Ellen turned to look back at her brother. He was wiping a tear away from his cheek. She smiled one last time, threw him a little wave of her hand and then disappeared inside. In a few seconds she reappeared behind one of the windows and waved again to be certain he saw her. He smiled and wiped away more tears as he walked the few steps necessary to be directly beneath her window.

The train's schedule did not allow for a long stop in Moville, they were lucky it still stopped there at all, and in another half-minute the stationmaster's voice was shouting a notice of departure above the noise of the train. It started up with a jerk that made Ellen gasp and then it started rolling out of the station. *I'm leaving! God!* Ellen waved a last time at Jim who was now waving energetically at her and walking to keep pace with the moving train. As it gathered speed he slid away, falling behind her and out of view, just as Tinker had done an hour or so earlier.

Bye, Jimmy . . . .

Ellen moved away from the window and settled back into her seat. She thought she could feel the excitement of the many miles traveled by the wonderful old train that now carried her. The carriage seemed to hold the aroma of motion as much as the scent of old wood and leather.

An old man sat in a seat across the aisle, his face pinched and gaunt and with such deep indentations below the cheeks that he made Ellen think of a skull's head. He gave Ellen a quick look and turned away. She wasn't displeased with his reticence for he didn't appear to be a pleasant man and besides she didn't feel like entering into conversation right now, wanting instead to be alone with her thoughts for the time.

Bye, Jimmy, goodbye Moville, goodbye Tinker, goodbye home, goodbye hilltop . . . .

The last small houses of Moville went by and she was in the countryside. *What will it be like?* wondered Ellen once again. She shivered slightly, her excitement now told to sit down and behave by a nebulous forlorn sadness demanding her attention. *I'll not see Donegal for a time . . . for a long, long time . . . if ever again . . . .*

What will it be like . . . in America . . . ?

*   *   *

Ellen, lost in thought, was suddenly surprised to see the train pulling into Derrylin in Fermanagh. *Have I been riding that long?* It seemed she'd only just gotten on the train. The stop in Derrylin was as brief as in Moville, just long enough to allow its passengers to hop aboard or depart, then the train was off again.

The old man with the skull-like face was replaced by an elderly, very plump, gray-haired woman. On her nose sat gold wire-framed spectacles that made her eyes appear large and owl-like. Sitting, she smiled at Ellen. "Where you off to, child?" she inquired, her voice pleasant and soft.

"To America. First to Dublin now, on this train. From there I'll be catching a plane to New York City. I have sisters there."

"Oh, America. I've never been that far," replied the old lady, smiling at the enthusiasm so noticeable in Ellen's voice. "And to fly there! It is exciting isn't it? The furthest I've ever been is to London. I still remember it, the museum, the Tate, the marvelous stores. Oh I had such a good time. I'm just on this train to the next stop. I was visiting my sister in Derrylin."

From that point on the endurance of Ellen's ears was put to the test as the pleasant gray-haired lady continued to talk without letup. Words fluttered out of her mouth like pigeons flying from a coop kept by the Almighty, a coop of infinite size and infinite capacity. She talked without letup, telling Ellen all there was to know about the private lives of her sister and her sister's husband, who was of no good account at all, a rogue. She talked continuously, stopping only now and then, to catch her breath or to giggle like a small girl at something she said. She talked until the air around Ellen's head seemed filled with the confusion of the flapping wings of the blather-birds fluttering about her. She talked until Ellen was silently begging for relief even as she continued to smile politely at the never-ceasing-to-talk woman.

Thank the Lord. Relief finally arrived when the train pulled into the next station. There the woman stood up, shut down the infinite pigeon coop, offered a quick farewell and departed, the fluttering blather-birds exiting the train car with her.

To Ellen's relief, no one filled the vacated seat. Sitting alone as the train pulled out of the station, Ellen never thought an empty seat could look so good.

As the train rolled along its way, the steady rhythm of the movement began to lull her to sleep, her lack of rest during the night now catching up to her. Her eyes shutting, she twisted herself around a bit to allow her cheek to press against the cushion of the seat. At first she was merely half-asleep and, in that somnolent state, remained aware of the movement of the train, of the sound of its wheels pressing on the tracks, taking her to Dublin, but then she drifted off, descending into deeper slumber.

When she awoke she sat straight up, afraid for a moment as she'd forgotten where she was and was startled by the strange surroundings. Then, looking about her, she relaxed and settled back into her seat. A fat, jolly appearing man now sat across the aisle and Ellen, seeing him, suffered a twinge of embarrassment over her having fallen asleep on the train. The man, seeing Ellen awake, smiled, nodded a silent greeting, and then turned his head to gaze out the window. *Not a conversationalist, thank goodness.* Ellen had still not recovered from the continuously talking woman who'd gotten on in Derrylin.

Ellen shifted her eyes to the window beside her and, to her surprise, saw that the train was now entering the city of Dublin. *We're there. Goodness, how long was I asleep?* A fresh wave of excitement passed through her, the first leg of her journey to America completed.

Dublin. The sight of the city brought a fragment of another of Da's stories bubbling up out of her memory, the story of the druidess Dubh. Slain with a stone from a sling, her body fell into a large pool and sank to the bottom. The water into which she'd fallen was named *Dubhlinn* or Dubh-pool, and it was that very pool of water that gave this city its name. Dublin was named for a pagan druidess who was killed with a rock and had sunk to the bottom of a pool.

Da, miss you. Always will.

*　　*　　*

Hours later and Ellen was asleep again, the excitement of being aboard a plane dissipating into absolute boredom after the first two hours of flight. A slight tap on her shoulder roused her from her nap and she lifted her head to glance up at the stewardess leaning toward her. "Please fasten your seat belt," said the attendant with a smile. "We'll be landing in New York City in just a few minutes."

Ellen nodded her acquiescence even as a new rush of excitement coursed through her, sending her heart to beating faster. *I'm there!* Fastening the belt around her waist, she turned her head to stare out the window. It was night, and below her she saw Manhattan Island, or rather saw the strings of the sparkling bright lights of the city laid out below her, looking like long strands of diamonds exhibited against a background of black velvet.

The sight of so many lights, stretching out in all directions as far as her eyes could see, momentarily snatched her breath away. "Sweet Jesus, it's so big," she whispered to herself. "It's so very big."

In a few minutes the plane touched down. Ellen felt the bump of the landing wheels through her shoes as the plane reestablished contact with the ground and decided on the instant to give that bump a special meaning, a special significance, deciding it would be the very moment of the start of her new life. That small bump as the plane first touched the ground of the United States was officially her new *beginning*.

*   *   *

Such hustle and bustle! So many people! Ellen had never seen anything matching the activity she now watched as she stood in Idlewild Airport. *I didn't know so many people could be together in one place!* So many, all rushing in different directions. She had presented her papers to the officer after departing the plane, nervous that, for some reason, she'd be told she couldn't enter the country, that she'd be told to turn around and go back to where she'd come from. To her relief, she was passed through in moments. Now she stood in the large terminal, off to the side so as to be out of everyone's way, scanning the crowds for her sister's face. Pressed against a wall, she felt as if she was standing on the banks of a river, searching for one tadpole in a rush of many frog-babies passing by in the current. An impossible task. Without her thinking about it, her hands attempted to smooth her jacket, her traveling clothes a bit crumpled from the long journey. *Rose, where are you?*

No, not an impossible task after all. Finally she saw her, her sister Rose, wrapped in a little pocket of people, also scanning the crowds, looking for her. "Rose, Rose, over here!" she called out, waving her arm. "Over here!"

Rose at last heard her name over the noise of the crowd; in moments Ellen was encircled by her larger sister's arms and was standing in the center of a warm smiling hug.

"El, it's good to see you," gushed Rose. "It really is." Rose's eyes, gleaming with sisterly love, wove a comforting reassurance around Ellen that immediately shooed away the nervousness and fright that had begun to nibble at her heart while she was standing alone in the large terminal.

"Oh, Rosie, it's so good to see you too. I'm so happy to be here."

A broad, well put together man, a little shorter than Rose, suddenly appeared beside her sister. Brown hair, thick and trimmed short on the sides, topped a face composed of pleasant features and supported by a firm, strong chin. A nice face. He looked at Ellen with fine, gentle Irish eyes. Smiling eyes. Ellen liked him at once.

"This is my husband, James," introduced Rose. "James Mahaney. I'm a Mahaney now. But you know that. I sent home pictures of the wedding. I only married him as he has the same first name as our brother, and it would be an easy name for me to remember."

James, smiling warmly, extended his hand to Ellen and she immediately accepted it in her own. "My name can't be that easy to remember for Rosie calls me by many others much of the time," he told her. "Some of them would make the devil put his fingers in his ears. Pleased to meet you. All Rose has done for the past few days is talk about you."

"It's nice to meet you too," responded Ellen, feeling a bit awkward now.

"And now," said James, "Pleasantries made, I think it's a good idea for us to go and claim your bags and get you home. You must be worn out after your long trip."

Ellen nodded her agreement although at the moment she was experiencing too much happy excitement to feel the slightest touch of weariness. "I have only one bag, she told him. "That's all I have."

*   *   *

The hour was late, half past eleven at night, and it was turning cold when they arrived at Rose's apartment. The chill however was left standing on the building's steps as inside there was comfort and warmth. Rose showed Ellen to the small room surrendered for her use and helped her unpack her bag. She told Ellen that Maggie and Teresa, sharing their own apartment on Seventy-eighth Street, would be coming over tomorrow evening to visit, after they finished working. "They wanted to be here tonight," she said, "but I couldn't guarantee we'd be here even by this time. Who knew the traffic would be so good."

James, declaring his weariness and stating his need to get up early in the morning, went off to bed. Rose, having taken the next three days off from work, without pay, had no problem staying awake and she and Ellen moved into the small kitchen where they chatted over tea, cake and cookies, reminiscing about the past and discussing the events of their younger days. Events that, over the passage of time, had acquired a dreamlike quality. They sat, talked, sipped tea and laughed until three in the morning when, exhaustion at last conquering Ellen's excitement and beginning to close Rose's eyes also, they were forced to their respective beds to sleep.

I'm in America, thought Ellen as she pulled the blanket up to her chin. *I'm in America*. This last thought on her mind bid her goodnight, and she closed her eyes and drifted off to sleep.

But when she dreamed, it was of what she left behind, visions of the Rawdon farm and the view from her Irish hilltop filling her head the first night of her life in America.

Chapter Eighteen

The relative silence of the night was broken by the early morning sounds of the great city stretching its limbs and waking. Ellen opened her eyes and briefly carried the illusion that she was home in Donegal before recalling that Ireland was now as far away from her as America once was.

The sounds! The growling of motors, the grumbling of trucks and cars, the squealing of their brakes. The activity of the wakening city came through the window together with the illumination of the morning sun. "It sounds like a great contraption festival outside," murmured Ellen as she went to the bedroom window and, parting the curtains, looked outside and down into the precipitous valley below that was Lafayette Street. The apartment was located there, on the edges of "Little Italy", "the Bowery" and "Soho", just north of "Chinatown". It was, at that time, not yet a fashionable place to live.

Many people were already hustling off to work, making their way to the subway entrance or the nearest bus stop. Some marched like soldiers going off to battle, others walked wearily, as though already thinking of the rest they would enjoy at the end of the coming day.

Ellen went back to her bed, covered her head with a pillow and almost immediately fell back into her sleep and dreams. It was after ten when, wrapped in a robe, she emerged from the bedroom to be greeted by a "Hello, sleepyhead," from her sister Rose.

On the radio in the kitchen played a Bing Crosby song, the crooner's voice, soft and silky, pleasant to listen to. "Nice song," said Ellen.

Rose nodded. "One Irishman doing well."

"I guess I was more tired than I thought," said Ellen as, in obeisance to her sister's motion telling her to sit, she placed herself into a chair at the small oval red Formica-top table that took up most of the space in the small kitchen. "It's not too late for an egg and bacon," said Rose. "And some toast too. If you're hungry that is."

"I'm famished."

"After breakfast, or I should say brunch, I'll show you the lay of the land. We'll walk around the neighborhood. Then tonight, when Jim comes home from work, and our sisters come visiting as well, we're taking you out to dinner. To celebrate your arrival."

Ellen emphatically shook her head. "No, Rose, I can't let you do that. It'll cost too much. And I have to think about going out and landing a job."

"There's time enough for the job hunting," returned Rose just as emphatically. "And we're taking you out. That's all there is to it."

*   *   *

Two hours past noon, Ellen and Rose left the apartment to walk the neighborhood. The streets seemed crowded and tumultuous by Ellen's standards of experience, the city an overpowering vast maze of complexity and activity. *It's a place big enough to swallow you up whole!*

Ellen was silently thankful she had her sister beside her. A significant part of her felt as small and helpless as a toddler. All around her the volume of the noise of the city played in her ears, a consistent, indistinguishable mixture of sounds. This grumbling background noise of urban life in New York being as much a part of this city as were the sounds of the countryside part of farm life in Donegal

A beautiful clear day, the sky above a cobalt blue marred only by a few smears of white cloud. Ellen found it chilly in the shadows cast by the tall buildings but pleasantly warm when they passed through the dark into the light of the sun. Her eyes went from store window to store window, enthralled by the multitude of objects they held. Furniture shops, hardware stores, fabric shops, book stores, hat stores, electrical stores, smoke and news stores; there seemed to be an endless array of places to purchase anything a person could possibly conceive of buying. Quantity was the word that came to her mind. *There is so much here!*

One shop they passed held a vast selection of gifts, statues and ceramics and more. *Unnecessary extras,* Ellen considered most of the items, no matter how pretty they were. The store's display window sparkled with variety and color. All things that people didn't need, but might spend money on "just for the wanting".

Sitting in the lower right-hand corner of the window, she saw a series of music boxes. They were so unusual that they immediately captivated her eye. So many, in all shapes, sizes and colors. She'd never seen a music box that wasn't in the shape of a box before. *They're called music boxes after all.* One had a quartet of ducklings sitting in a circle in a barrel of water. Although the box was not wound up, Ellen could imagine them swimming about. *Wonder what the song is that they swim by?* Another had a nightingale sitting on a perch in a wonderfully ornate golden cage. Next to that was a medieval knight on horseback riding on a track that circled a castle. Above the knight was a figure of a woman standing atop a rampart, waving down to him. *A knight and his love.* At least that's what Ellen decided. "It's sad," she said to Rose with a wan smile. "He'll go around that castle forever. They'll never get together."

"I suppose," replied Rose with a shrug.

Ellen's mouth dropped in astonishment when she saw the price tag on one of the displayed objects. "Why, that'd be enough to run the farm for a good part of the year," she told Rose.

"That's why I never get past the looking in the windows of some of these stores," responded her sister. "New York has everything, but as long as you don't have the money, a lot of it will always belong to someone else. Come on, there's cheaper stores along here too."

During that initial walk on the streets of lower Manhattan, Ellen saw evidence of another side of life in New York as well, an indication that the city could be cruel to those unable to give it proper effort and labor. A derelict, shabbily dressed, grimy with grease and dirt, was rummaging through a garbage can, scanning its contents with sunken, desperate eyes. He looked up at the passing women, and suddenly those eyes tightened on Ellen. As he stared straight at her, the hollowness withdrew from his gaze to be replaced with an angry, hard expression that radiated animosity. Ellen, frightened by the glare of the man's eyes, was glad and relieved when she and Rose had achieved the security of walking some distance beyond him.

Why is he mad at me? she wondered.

"There's more than a few like that here," said Rose, seeing Ellen's reaction to the derelict. "The Bowery is just over a couple of streets and there are a lot of what they call flophouses there. You'll get used to seeing them."

"Goodness, no one ever went through garbage in Moville," said Ellen. "That man looked at me like I did something to him."

"Some of those poor people look at everyone that way, Ellen. Some aren't quite right in the head. Don't be taking it personal. Come on, let's head for Delancy Street. There's lots to look at there. More bargains too."

Going through garbage....

Ellen held no illusions about what it would take to survive here in New York City. The same effort it took to survive anywhere. Hard work. The same sweat and toil required to force a living out of the farmland in Ireland. She had left the farm behind but not the need to toil, that obligation traveled with her, stuffed in her little suitcase beneath her changes of underwear, carried on the plane to America in lieu of the silver spoon she wasn't born with. *The sooner I get out and start earning a living, the better off I'll be.*

For a brief moment, once again, she was frightened by her audacity in coming here, filled again with a child's fright at simply being so far from *home.* An instant of apprehension rolled through her, as though her bones were narrow streets assailed by sudden gusts of a frigid wind, that sense of fear momentarily so strong it made her heart pound inside her. But the instant of self-doubt was fleeting and fled as quickly as it had come, to be replaced by another thought: *This city, so vast, holds so much. So very much. Surely it can spare a little of its abundance for me ...*

... and not force her to go rummaging through its garbage cans to get it.

Chapter Nineteen

Ellen looked over her breakfast at Rose. "I have to find work," she stated flatly. "I've been reading the Classified Ads in the paper and I'm going out today to your Wall Street. I surely will find something there."

"*My* Wall Street," replied Rose. "I wish it was mine. Now you know there's no hurry with your finding work. This is just your third day here. It's a big change from Donegal. Take time to get used to it."

"Three days is long enough," declared Ellen. "I only hope I'm good enough to get work."

Rose put her coffee cup down onto the saucer and snorted a laugh. "You? Good enough? Why half the people in this city, and many of them working, communicate with scratches, grunts and belches. You're well above them. You'll do fine."

"Thanks Rose. But it is a bit scary. I-I feel so . . . so *small* here."

"All right, El. But put it off one more day. This is my last day off. We'll go out shopping today and get you a good outfit. Interview clothes. A good outfit will make you feel better about yourself. Tomorrow will be soon enough."

Ellen nodded her head and smiled her appreciation to her older sister. Taking a sip of coffee she wondered what ever would she have done here in this immense city without help. She thought once more how much harder it must have been for her sisters to have come here first.

"Thanks, Rose," she responded gratefully. "Tomorrow then."

*   *   *

Tomorrow dawned grayer than the day before, thanks to the thick clouds that rolled in overnight. Ellen, clad in her brand-new outfit, walked to the Prince Street Station of the Double-R train and went down the stairs, her token already in her hand. *Hope I get something. What will I do if no one wants to hire me? What if I never get a job? What will I do?*

She exited, as Rose had told her to do, at the Rector Street Station and ascended the stairs. Only the walls surrounding Trinity Church stood between her and Wall Street when she emerged again into the gray morning.

The financial district, of which Wall Street was a primary artery, seemed to Ellen to have the energy of the city condensed to electrical force. The street might have been a wire upon which were running currents composed of living human beings. And the buildings here made dwarves out of the others she had thought so tall. *Higher than the hills of Donegal!* The city here was a mountain range, so very, very big, and she, standing at the roots of the buildings that stretched up to the clouds, felt as small and insignificant as an ant sitting between an elephant's toes.

Everyone moves so fast here! She found herself having to pick up speed just to keep up with the swiftness of the others. And it was impossible to walk a straight line, constantly she was forced to step first to one side and then to the other to avoid having people bump into her.

The great number of people rushing about frightened her more than a little bit and she decided to stand in the safety of a doorway just to get out of traffic and calm herself.

Reaching into her purse, her trembling hand pulled out the page she'd ripped from *The New York Times* that morning and she pretended to confirm to herself the address of her destination. *So many people!*

She wandered about, walking in a circle for more than fifteen minutes, before daring to stop a total stranger to ask him would he be so kind as to tell her exactly where was Water Street? He blurted a direction to her and then quickly walked away, as if stopping to speak to her even for that brief moment was an expensive extravagance, one she was incapable of appreciating and one neither of them could truly afford.

*   *   *

Entering through very large and heavy doors, Ellen was directed by a security guard in the lobby of the building to a line of elevators that would take her to the personnel department located on the fortieth floor. This was the first time in her life that she rode in a "lift" and the first time she'd ever been so high above the earth (while not seated on an airplane).

"Goodness," she exclaimed when, having exited the elevator, she passed a window and peered through its glass to the streets below. A great angel might have piled four additional Cliona's Hills on top of each other, and then picked her up and placed her on top of number five. She was astonished at how far up she was, how far below her the ground was. She might have been a cloud in the sky looking down at the earth! The people and traffic below looked as small as bugs crawling on thin slats of wood.

Her heart was thumping strongly as she walked through the door with the brass plate holding black lettering declaring the place to be the "Personnel Department". An application was handed to her by a rather curt woman seated behind a wood desk and wearing an equally wooden expression. Ellen completed the form as requested and handed it back to the wooden lady, then she was asked to wait until she could be interviewed.

Placing herself into a chair she sat nervously, trying not to chew her lip and feeling very out of place.

But by the time she was called into her interview she'd harnessed the strength to push her nervousness and insecurity aside. Almost to her surprise the interview proved to be pleasant and, better still, grandly successful. She was then and there offered an entry-level position with the firm which she happily and immediately accepted.

Glorious! A job on the first try.

How wonderful the return walk to the subway was! Ellen virtually floated down the streets, less crowded now that the rush hour had passed, feeling like an Olympian champion preparing to accept a gold medal, as though she'd just won a major victory with surprising ease of effort. *A job! And on my very first try!* In Moville it would have taken her weeks of effort to *not* find work.

Even the day seemed now to want to celebrate her good fortune as the clouds departed and sunlight filled the sidewalks upon which she so happily walked. The streets, for the moment, were ablaze with the flood of golden light and Ellen, walking through that sunshine, felt as fortunate and as blessed as a princess protected by the Little People in one of her father's old tales.

She could hardly wait to tell Rosie and her sisters of her good fortune, and then spend money to call her brother Jimmy up and give him the good news as well. A pang of guilt went through her again as she thought of her abandonment of him just a few days ago, when she left him alone on the farm.

It'd be good to talk to him again. She hadn't done so since calling home the night she'd arrived in New York, to tell him she'd made the trip safely; and then she'd spoken to him less than a minute so as not to run up Rose's telephone bill.

Riding the Double-R back to the Prince Street station, she had one dominant thought frolicking in her head: *A job! On my very first try!* It was all she could do to keep herself in her seat and not jump up and dance a jig in front of the other riders.

A salaried job. And on my very first try!

Chapter Twenty

Ellen's sense of being flattered over gaining employment very quickly faded, washed away by the daily routine of nine-to-five work. And she was very shortly disappointed to discover that what seemed to her to be a substantial amount of money (by Donegal standards) was not a whole lot in New York City. Wanting a place of her own, she began checking the newspapers for the price of apartments and was drop-jawed astounded by the amount of dollars each cost. Rents here were astronomical. *Why, to afford these places a person has to go to a landlord carrying bags stuffed with gold and diamonds!*

As more time passed and the weeks became months, she felt more and more to be an imposition to her sister. Rose was now pregnant and expected to give birth in a few months. Ellen would truly be in the way then. *Maybe I should move in with Teresa and Maggie? No, with just the two of them they're already cramped for space. Me there too and the walls would be bulging.* Ellen recalled the small third-floor walk-up apartment she'd visited on 78th Street, with its screen down the middle of the one bedroom to create separate spaces. There was no space for another sister there. Rose, living here so close to the Bowery, had a much larger apartment for less rent.

In any case, Rose would not hear of her leaving and insistently told her she was not an interference at all; she was welcome to stay as long as needed. In fact, Rose told her, the share of money she put toward the rent was helping her, Rose, in paying her own bills. "And there'll be more bills to pay when the baby comes. Besides, a woman living on her own could have problems in this city."

Ellen appreciated her sister's kindness but remained uncomfortable with remaining with her, with her own lack of independence.

Coming from a background in which money was scarce, Ellen held a healthy regard for its use. Frugal by nature and not materialistic, she didn't "need" (want) expensive things just for the sake of having them. Her father used to say: "People need flashy things in direct proportion to how little they think of themselves." Ellen didn't need fancy jewelry or fur coats. With very few exceptions, her money was spent on necessities and, consequently, she saved much of her income. Soon, even with New York prices, she hoped to have enough to allow her to grant herself true independence, to find her own place to live.

*   *   *

Five more months went by and Rose gave birth to twins, fraternal twins, two boys she and her husband named Patrick and Philip. The second child to be born appeared as a complete surprise after the arrival of the first. An unannounced guest to the house. No one, not doctor nor parents, had any idea that twins were on the way.

Ellen was an aunt. *Aunt El.* Here was a term she could hardly believe applied to her. It sounded too grown-up, more grown-up than she felt herself to be.

*   *   *

Rose's own birthday was suddenly approaching with the coming month of October, and Ellen, as a gift, purchased tickets to an off-off-Broadway play to give to Rose and her husband as a present. The play was a slight but critically approved comedy entitled *The Bum's Rush,* being performed in a small theater located in Greenwich Village very near the Playwrights' Playhouse in which the plays of Eugene O'Neill had been performed years earlier. Ellen was convinced to obtain the tickets on a recommendation by a coworker, and by the added knowledge that the playwright of *The Bum's Rush* was as Irish as was O'Neill. She therefore could offer Rose and Jim the unique experience of a day at the theater while also supporting the Irish Arts.

Presenting her gift, she told Rose and Jim she'd be taking them both to dinner as well once the play was over. "Don't worry about the babies," she told them. "I'll watch them while you're at the theater and Teresa has already agreed to come over and sit with them while we eat supper. So everything's arranged."

Two extravagances in one day, a play and a dinner, but Ellen thought her sister and her husband to be owed them. Rose objected, being as frugal as Ellen, but Ellen insisted, refusing to take the tickets back.

"How do you know the play is any good?" asked Rose.

"It's written by an Irish playwright," said Ellen emphatically, putting an end to the discussion.

The tickets were for a Saturday matinee and, as the day approached, Rose actually began to look forward to the day out. "Just to get away from the bawling babies will be a blessing," she declared. "Why the two of them always go to the bathroom at the same time is beyond me. It must have something to do with being twins."

The Friday prior to the matinee Jim came home with the news that he would be forced to work that Saturday, compelled to submit to the whim of an unsympathetic foreman. So there'd be no trip to the theater for him. Rose was certain he'd bribed his foreman into telling him he had to work, Jim preferring toil to the theater. If that was indeed the truth of it, Jim wasn't saying.

Rose would not go to the theater alone and so, in order not to waste the tickets, it came to pass that Ellen and Rose went to the play together, Teresa coming over to watch the babies a few hours earlier than originally planned.

How arbitrary Life can prove to be at times. In going to the play that day Ellen couldn't know that she was taking the first step onto a path of linked circumstances that would profoundly alter her life. Had Jim not had to work that particular Saturday, Ellen's life, her future, would not have unrolled in the same way it did. Indeed it might have been entirely different.

On such small occurrences destinies at times are set into motion and nations may sporadically rise or fall.

And Love, for better or worse, may enter our lives.

*   *   *

Despite it being mid-October, the Saturday was pleasantly warm, a benefit of an Indian Summer that arrived the week before. Ellen and Rose walked the distance from their apartment to the small theater on MacDougal Street only wearing jackets for the walk, the winter coats put away again for the time. It was as nice as a day in June

Unlike the top-of-the-line showplaces uptown on Broadway, seating was on a first-come basis and holders of tickets simply selected the best vacant seat they could find after entering. Rose and Ellen arrived early enough to have their selection of the best seats in the house and picked two in the middle of the fifth row from the stage.

The building, in a previous life, had housed a saloon. Ellen, curious, gazed about the interior and saw some evidence of its past as a drinking place – a sign on the wall advertising beer at $0.25 per glass particularly caught her eye for she wondered why it wasn't taken down – but for the most part the place was bare walls and bare floor. The original tin ceiling remained overhead, holding a few yellow lights, the same ceiling that no doubt looked down on a bar brawl or two in its time. The chairs were the metal folding kind, no plush theater seats here, but were padded and comfortable enough. *I'm glad I'm taking Rosie out to dinner as well,* thought Ellen. *If the condition of the play lives up to the condition of this theater, it'll be a pretty poor birthday present otherwise.* Her faith in Irish creativity was being tested.

As Ellen looked around the theater's interior, she saw, to her surprise, a face familiar to her, a young woman she knew casually from work. Bonnie was her name. Seated in the last row of seats she was just fifteen rows back as the whole place held only a total of twenty rows of metal chairs.

Seeing the familiar face, Ellen smiled and waved. Bonnie, after realizing who it was who was waving to her, returned the greeting and flashed a big grin. Since Bonnie was alone, Ellen motioned for her to come closer to the front and sit with her and Rose. To this Bonnie shook her head, indicating she preferred to remain where she was.

"You know her?" asked Rose.

"From work," replied Ellen. "Odd, why would she want to sit in the back when there are better seats down here?" She felt a little hurt, thinking that perhaps Bonnie stayed in the rear of the theater for no other reason than to avoid her. That would be unlike her though as the girl was friendly and gregarious in the office. A kind of effervescent flake actually. At least to Ellen's mind. Bonnie's personality was exhibited in her personal style of make-up, which was loud. Her lips were usually covered with a bright colorful glaze, her eyelids coated with a deep iridescent blue or green. They were intelligent eyes however, sparkling with friendliness and good humor. Ellen got along well with Bonnie in the office. Or at least she had thought so. But why didn't Bonnie come down and sit with her?

Ellen watched as a small string quartet (composed of music students instead of professional musicians) entered to fill a small corner just off the immediate right of the stage. The violin player began to test and tune his instrument and, with the sound, an air of happy anticipation began to circulate through the gathering audience. The theater was now almost completely filled with patrons.

Introductory music from the quartet and a dimming of the theater lights signaled the start of the play. A hush fell over the audience as the curtains parted, and all eyes went to the stage prepared to be entertained . . . and gazed . . . and gazed . . . and gazed . . . .

The stage remained resolutely vacant and silent. It began to be believed by some in the audience that the stage before them was not a stage at all, but rather an oil painting of a theater stage, one rendered by an artist incapable of drawing people.

After a fairly bewildering minute of silence, two young men entered the theater from the back and marched down the aisle on the far right, arguing loudly. At first it was thought that they were new (and obnoxious) members of the audience, but when they continued to the front of the theater and then up the steps and onto the stage, the truth was realized and a smattering of applause arose from the audience.

"What the hell kind of play is this?" wondered Rose, whispering the question into Ellen's ear.

Ellen didn't have a chance to reply. A scream, a shriek, came from the back of the darkened theater, the sound so startling it made Ellen gasp.

She and Rose (and the rest of the audience) turned their heads around toward the sound and Ellen's heart flipped over in surprise as she saw that the person doing the yelling was none other than her office acquaintance Bonnie. Having leapt out of her seat, she was screeching and pointing an accusatory finger toward the stage. "That's the father of my baby! That's the father of my baby! You stinking bastard! You stinking bastard! I love you! I love you!" She screamed so forcefully the veins in her neck protruded.

The entire audience sat frozen, stunned by the sudden infusion of hysterical histrionics into their midst but began to chuckle and laugh as they realized that this display was also part of the entertainment. The young woman was neither an escaped lunatic (as some feared) nor a frantic abandoned mother (as feared others) but rather another cast member of the comedy.

"Lulu?" inquired one of the actors on the stage, squinting into the darkness.

Bonnie was already walking swiftly to the stage, screaming insults at the top of her lungs with every step. "You no-good toilet rat! You heartless piece of goat manure – "

"It sounds like your mother," declared the second male actor as Bonnie went storming up the steps to the stage, her feet slamming hard as though upon each step sat a cockroach that had to be stomped into flat extinction.

"What the hell kind of play is this?" asked Rose again. Ellen remained silent, not certain of the answer.

At the play's finale, Ellen sat, wondering if she enjoyed it or not. She wasn't certain. Parts of it were quite funny, some of it she didn't understand at all.

"What the hell kind of play was that?" asked Rose as they stood up to leave, the sneer in her voice leaving no doubt as to how she felt about the play. "Are you certain the writer was Irish?"

Ellen shrugged. "I'm sorry you didn't like it, Rose." Then, deciding on the moment to go backstage to see Bonnie, she spent the next minute convincing her sister to go with her. "I want to congratulate her on her performance," she said.

"Congratulate . . . for that . . . ?" said Rose. Ellen persisted and at last Rose relented. Together the two sisters went to the stage and then to the rear of the theater.

After a bit of confusion, they found Bonnie standing in the midst of a cluster of actors and stagehands. Ellen, with a reluctant Rose in tow, joined the cluster and complimented Bonnie, who was thrilled to receive the good review. "If only you were a movie director," she told Ellen, grinning at her, her eyes sparkling from within the iridescent green portholes in which they resided. "You don't know any movie directors, do you?"

"N-No," responded Ellen. "I'm sorry."

Her full name was Bonnie Stevens. Her pretty face was framed by dark brown hair twisted into very tight curls, so tight that if hair had nerves the tresses might have been screaming in pain. Her dedication to dancing lessons and exercise classes was testified to by her firm muscular legs and her flat stomach, now largely revealed and on display as the robe she wore was not closed. A small rose tattoo sat on her upper right thigh.

"Tansy, can you come over?" The request was issued by a man fifteen feet from where Ellen stood, and, to Ellen's surprise, Bonnie turned and responded to the summons. "Be right there." Then, turning back to Ellen and Rose: "My stage name, dahlings. Bonnie's a little plain, don't you think? Must go. Thanks for the compliments."

"Bye, Bonnie, ah, Tansy," said Ellen as Bonnie walked away.

"What an odd duck," whispered Rose into Ellen's ear. "What kind of name is Tansy? And did you see her standing around half undressed? She must be as loose as that robe she has on."

"Oh, don't be such a *culchie*," responded Ellen. "That's just the way theater folks dress around the stage."

Rose smiled at the rebuke. "Well, aren't you the sophisticated city mouse all of a sudden," she said. "Come on, let's go and eat. You still owe me a dinner."

* * *

At the office the following Monday, Ellen, on a trip to the ladies' room, ran into Bonnie and, recalling the reprimand she'd received in the theater, greeted her with a "Hi Tansy". She was swiftly corrected once again.

"No, here I'm Bonnie," she told Ellen. "Tansy's for outside." Her face held a glorious smile. Bonnie seemed to always wear the expression of a little child playing a secret and private game. "Out there, in the theater I mean, I'm the other."

"It's like you're two different people," responded Ellen, returning Bonnie's smile.

"In a way I suppose I am," said Bonnie. "But only two. I think anyway. At least that's what all the voices tell me." She giggled and then went on, "I think most people are at least two people. Wouldn't you say? Hey, you eating lunch with anyone?"

"W-Why, no."

"How about going with me? I know a nice place close by. And it's cheap."

Ellen shrugged her shoulders. "Sure, why not?"

*　　*　　*

They became friends. It's said that opposites attract and the truth of that old adage was amply displayed in the friendship of Bonnie and Ellen. Bonnie had no use for churches or religious institutions of any sort (substituting Tarot Cards for belief in God) while Ellen was fiercely religious. Indeed, Ellen, at the ripe old age of twenty, still said her prayers every night before closing her eyes in bed. Bonnie had little use for the conventions of Society as well, often mocking its rules, enjoying nothing more than metaphorically sticking her tongue out at its accepted proprieties, an attitude foreign to Ellen, who would never think of offering such disrespect to the values of others.

Bonnie's attitude toward love, physical love, was another contrast between them. Bonnie lived a life of rather casual morality, falling in and out of love (and correspondingly in and out of bed) with some regularity. This fact Ellen didn't discover until later, and it was shocking to her when she learned of it, believing it to be a sinful way of living. Still, discovering it, she didn't condemn her friend for what she believed was immoral behavior. She remained Bonnie's friend. "Hate the sin but love the sinner" is a Christian aphorism and Ellen believed it to be a good one.

There were other differences between the two as well: frugality on Ellen's part versus Bonnie's extravagance and Ellen's modesty of appearance versus Bonnie's abundance of makeup and often revealing dresses serving as two more examples, yet, despite the differences between them, the two became good and fast friends.

Different, yet the same. For, in important ways, beneath the contrasts of their lives, the two were not that unlike at all, a fact not readily apparent when viewing the surface dissimilarity of the two. Each was innately good-hearted, honest to a fault, and kind and charitable to those who needed compassion and generosity. Beneath the surface characteristics of the two there was thus concealed much that was the same, the apparent contrasts resting upon foundations that were more identical than not.

"More than anything" Bonnie hoped to become a movie star, to become a famous icon of the silver screen. "That's one reason I had to leave my home," she told Ellen. "My old man was driving me nutso. Telling me to get married, to forget my *craziness* of being an actress. Blah, blah, blah. I was the steady topic of conversation in my house and always I was *wrong* about something. I dressed wrong, looked wrong or said things wrong. I must be retarded because I was wrong so much. He'd tell me to forget about being an actress and settle down. Forget, forget, forget. Blah, blah, blah. Do this, do this, do this. I don't know why my dad, who was so miserable in his own marriage, thought he knew so much about what would make *me* happy. Or maybe he wanted me to be miserable too. God, they hated each other. My mom and dad. Always arguing. Even hitting at times."

"That must have been terrible for you," stated Ellen sympathetically. Bonnie was speaking of a marriage, a relationship, so different from that of her parents' life together that it seemed she might be describing the habits of a different species of life.

"No, it was actually *good*," came back Bonnie, refusing to relinquish her smile. "I'd stay in my room to get away from the fighting and I'd pretend. I taught myself how to act that way. Acting is just pretending. God, I'd like to make it in the movies. Like I said, to be a great actress, a new Bette Davis or a new Harlow. Nothing could be better. I like the old-time actors and actresses. They had style. That's what I want. Style.

Sometimes I do get depressed though, thinking I'll never make it. That's when I start bingeing on food, like now. I usually end up gaining ten or fifteen pounds before I catch myself and start dieting again."

Ellen told her of her own dream, much less ambitious, to meet someone, get married and raise a family. Bonnie stared at her for a few seconds before offering a perfunctory: "That's nice." Immediately she resumed rambling on about her own dreams for the future.

The red faux-leather of the booth was comfortable and soft and, as Bonnie had promised, the food wasn't bad, being more than a single notch above edible. Bonnie was eating now as if she was very depressed indeed, shoveling food into her mouth with a startling insistence, stopping her mouth from eating only on those moments when she used it to talk.

Suddenly, in the middle of listening to Ellen talk of her hilltop overlooking the water, Bonnie dropped her fork onto her plate, so hard (dramatically) that it rang like a chime.

"What's the matter?" asked Ellen, thinking she'd said something wrong, that somehow she'd insulted Bonnie.

Ellen needn't have worried. Bonnie, her cheeks puffed out with food, simply declared the obvious: "I'm eating like a pig." Then, swallowing what was in her mouth and pushing the remnants of her meal away, she added, "Got to stop eating. At least for now. Would you believe I used to have anorexia? But thank God, I've got it in remission. *Total* remission. What you said before about getting married, that's not a real goal, is it? I mean, *everybody* gets married. It's no big deal. Don't you want to *do* something? Something special, I mean."

"Oh, I don't know," replied Ellen. "I think finding the right person is a goal worth going after. It might even be true that if you don't have that, nothing else really counts for much. At times I'm not certain it's going to happen. It's hard to find the right person, I think. Sometimes I think that."

Bonnie chuckled. "Sure, but only if you have standards. One blind date I had was so bad he was super-baaaaad. Guy was so fat he couldn't get into the door in my apartment. Ugly too, he had a face that looked like a rat. That's literally what he looked like, a rat head peeking out of the top of this giant round roll of cheese that was the rest of him. God, it was terrible. He did do one good thing though."

"Oh, what was that?"

"He cured me of blind dates forever," responded Bonnie again punctuating her words with her infectious laugh. "God, it was horrible. Say, speaking of blind dates did you hear about the girl who actually liked her blind date?"

Ellen shook her head.

"She liked him so much she went to bed with him," said Bonnie. "Then, after they finish doing *it*, she says to him, I'm afraid you now have the wrong idea about me. I'm really not the kind of girl who sleeps on a first date. The man then says he believes her and she starts to cry. Really sobbing. What's wrong? asks the man. You're the very first one, she tells him. The very first. Now he's amazed. He's the first one? The girl was a virgin? I'm the first man you've ever slept with? he asks. No, she tells him, still crying, you're the first man to ever believe me when I tell him I don't sleep on the first date!" Bonnie, thrilled with her own joke, laughed wildly. Ellen joined her, laughing not so much at the small joke as at Bonnie's joy in having told it.

* * *

Over the next few weeks they met now and then, to shop, see a movie or simply to talk. Here too there was a contrast between the two but one that contained its own compatibility, for Bonnie liked to talk very much, and Ellen didn't mind being a good listener.

By December they had become close enough friends that it was Ellen whom Bonnie called on a Sunday afternoon to tell of the loss of her latest boyfriend. "He just dumped me! Just like that!" Her words were dropped into the phone between tremendous sobs, Bonnie crying as though her heart would be broken forever. "I saw him for two weeks! I thought he loved me!" Ellen was surprised to hear that a fortnight was sufficient time for Bonnie to have committed herself body and soul to someone.

That evening, in an act of Christian compassion, Ellen walked the distance to Bonnie's Village apartment (the first time she'd ever gone to it) and, together with Bonnie's roommate, another wannabe actress named Trolla Travis (real name Patricia Moran), spent the evening sipping wine and eating cheese smeared on crackers while listening to Bonnie's ranting complaints. Bonnie cried and talked, her tear-filled conversation that night kept from being totally rambling only by its sole underlying connective theme that the Male of the Species was something to be condemned unconditionally for having the audacity to exist.

*   *   *

One month and nine days following that night, Bonnie's roommate, Trolla, abruptly abandoned New York to travel to Canada to join up (once again) with a mechanic named Zeke, who "looks so much like Farley Granger, it's scary". Discarding her previous agreement with Bonnie that "all men are dirt" Trolla hastily went off to reside with the clump of sod named Zeke, Montreal being Trolla's paradise, as long as her rebel Zeke was there.

So Trolla was gone, just like that, without even the courtesy of a wave and a fare-thee-well. Worse, she left without regard for paying her share of the rent on the apartment she and Bonnie shared. Trolla, in answering Zeke's call, left behind an old cat named Soft Thing (that she formerly absolutely could not live without) and an IOU for her share of the last two months' rent. An IOU she had no intention of honoring.

In sticking Bonnie with the responsibility of paying her rent, Trolla had accepted as true one of the primary guiding principles that Bonnie lived life by. In this case Trolla's disregard for the "conventions of society" included the social convention of treating your friends with at least a modicum of consideration. Bonnie, although she couldn't see it, had in effect been hoisted by her own petard, or at least a petard she voiced a general belief in. The rebellious attitude of disregarding "rules", having been accepted by her roommate, had come back to slap Bonnie in the face when manifested in Trolla's total disregard for the task of paying her bills.

Understandably, Bonnie exhibited a cache of bad feelings and anger when she mentioned to Ellen that "the bitch left" and now she, Bonnie, would need to scrape up more money to pay the coming month's rent and "find ASAP another roommate" to help with the rent in future months.

Ellen impulsively (and as much to her own surprise as Bonnie's) immediately offered to be that new roommate.

*　　*　　*

So it was, in mid-February, as the city was looking forlornly to the coming of spring, that Ellen was preparing to live in the city's Greenwich Village. Or, as Rose called it: A "modern-day Sodom and Gomorrah", where "freaks walk about like ants let loose in a bag of sugar".

Why did Rose feel that way? To Ellen, on her few visits there, the Village seemed nice enough, offering her a bit of the feel of a small town in the midst of a rather overwhelming large city. To her it appeared to be as good a place to live as any in New York and better than many. She was pleased by the physical size of many of its buildings, a lot of which, at least off the main avenues, were three and four-story townhouses. While there, in Greenwich Village, she didn't feel so small. There, she was more the right size. Rose's talk about its being populated with "freaks" seemed to be nothing more than a bad tale told against it.

Just two days after offering to be Bonnie's new roommate, Ellen, carrying all her possessions in two small suitcases (the extra suitcase evidence of her prosperous life in America) said goodbye to Rose, Jimmy and the boys, hailed a taxi, and rode up to Christopher Street in the heart of the Village. The entire cab ride took less than five minutes.

Exiting the taxi, she was forced to step past two men holding hands and kissing! – *Sweet Lord, Rose's right! Sodom and Gomorrah!* – to go up the steps of her new building to reach its entrance. She was glad when the two men, still holding hands, moved off the steps and walked on down the street.

This is my new home, thought Ellen as Bonnie buzzed her past the security of the front entrance. With one suitcase in each hand, she ascended a flight of narrow stairs, went down the short, dimly lit hall and, resting one suitcase on the floor, rapped lightly on the door of apartment 2B. The door was pulled open and she was standing in front of her friend's beaming smile of welcome.

Stepping through, Ellen officially assumed the status of cotenant with Bonnie, wondering (silently to herself) if she really knew exactly what in the world she was doing and already questioning her impulsive decision to do it.

Chapter Twenty-one

The night of the "big move" Bonnie took Ellen for a walk to show her around the neighborhood. While it was February the weather was comfortably warm for walking, with the temperature holding in the low forties even with the setting of the sun. They wore light coats and no gloves as they took their stroll, Ellen wearing the same coat she'd worn in October when taking Rose to the theater.

Thanks to the warm weather, all snow that had fallen from two January storms was melted away, the only evidence of a total of fourteen inches of snow a few scabs of icy slush and surrounding blotches of moisture on the sidewalks.

Bonnie pointed out four stores near the apartment building, the deli, the supermarket, the dry cleaner's and the liquor store. "Those are the most important stores to know," she declared. "They supply the necessities of life. Now let me give you a tour."

The always busy streets of the Village were made even more so this evening by the pleasant weather. Some of the pedestrians were students (of New York University), strolling the streets in their jeans or, in a few cases, rushing to night classes with books in hand or leather briefcases banging their legs. Others were neighborhood residents who were, like Bonnie and Ellen, taking a walk in their neighborhood. Many others were visitors from other New York neighborhoods come to the Village for the nightlife. One young man stood out from the pack and, in passing, immediately snagged Ellen's attention for, seeing him, she instantly thought there was something wrong with him. He was young, lean and tall and dressed entirely in black. His skin was so pale he might have had chalk in his veins instead of blood and his brittle eyes seemed to be searching for the energy to fully focus upon the world. He walked as though his thin arms contained bones of lead and were too heavy a burden for his sloping shoulders to carry.

"I wonder if he ever goes out in daylight," said Ellen, after the man was well past them. "And did you see that look in his eyes? He might be ill."

"Drugs," responded Bonnie with distaste. "An addict. Stay away from people like him – no good."

Drugs? "Do you know him?" asked Ellen.

"Well enough to want *not* to know him," replied Bonnie. She offered no further explanation of her obvious aversion for the man except to add, "I know his type."

A group of young men wearing expensive suits strolled past, Wall-Streeters who'd come up to have a good time in the Village clubs, their collars open now that they were away from their desks. Two of the group looked over Ellen and Bonnie as they went by, obviously liking what they saw, but there was no lewd advance and the men simply continued on without a word. Bonnie feigned disappointment over their failure to make an advance toward them.

"I could see you going wild with one of them," she declared to Ellen in a low whisper.

"I beg your pardon?" responded Ellen, half in shock, her voice a pitch higher. Bonnie chuckled over Ellen's words and the expression on her face, enjoying the impact of her statement. Ellen was thankful for the increasing darkness of the night as Bonnie could not see clearly, in the gathering shadows, that she was now blushing pink.

Maybe Rose's right, thought Ellen. *Maybe this is a mistake. Maybe I don't belong here.*

The streets were lined by a variety of restaurants and nightspots, by stores and shops. As with the area around Rose's apartment, there was so much here, but it was a different "so much". This area held many more restaurants, small and eccentric shops and places of entertainment.

They passed a small art gallery and Ellen, attracted by the colorful paintings she viewed from the street (and by the polished wood of the glistening floor of the gallery) insisted on going inside. The painter being exhibited was inspired by the Impressionist and Expressionist schools of art and combined the two styles expertly into his work. Some of the paintings were quite beautiful and Ellen was actually tempted to consider purchasing one, a portrait of a young girl with blond hair and a sad Mona Lisa smile, but her temptation to buy was swiftly and rudely shown the exit door by the price indicated on the portrait. The cost took Ellen's breath away. Feeling suddenly very out of place, like a pauper who'd invaded a king's castle believing he could purchase the king's carriage for a couple of pence, she (with Bonnie following) scurried out of the gallery just as someone, a tall beanpole of a woman clad in a sleek ebony dress, was emerging from the shadows in the back of the gallery, walking over to them no doubt to inquire as to whether they saw anything they wanted to buy. They were laughing when they reached the sidewalk again.

"Goodness," said Ellen. "Did you see how much those pictures cost? They must be painted on gold."

"I'm used to it," replied Bonnie. "Almost everything I want costs more than I have."

Ellen recalled her sister Rose's very similar complaint when they were looking at the window display in the shop on Lafayette Street.

A short distance and they were passing by the Victorian-Gothic style building that was the Jefferson Market Library. It looked out of place in the midst of the modern boxy apartment buildings and half-century-old walkups that lined the avenue, a structure from a different land, a different culture. "That's a library now," said Bonnie. "It used to be a courthouse. Mae West once was brought here because they brought obscenity charges against her."

"Really? How do you know that?"

"I used to go out with a guy who knew everything. Or thought he did. He didn't know as much as he thought but at least he knew a lot about the city."

They passed a small restaurant, a sidewalk cafe with tables and chairs on the pavement separated from pedestrians by a small wrought iron fence. When the winter got more serious again about its bringing cold temperatures, those tables and chairs would disappear but tonight was a good night for dining outside. They continued on past to the next building, a townhouse housing a small theater in its basement. It sat in silence now but as they passed it by, the soft sound of music, drifting out of a nearby Blues club just two more doors along the street, came to their ears. "That's pretty music," remarked Ellen.

"Let's go inside," suggested Bonnie. "My feet are tired. These shoes are murder on my hammerhead toes. I could never be a ballerina. We'll sit at a table, have a drink and listen to the music."

They made their way past a small knot of people lingering outside the door and entered into the dimly lit interior of the club, the sound of the music growing louder as they went inside. A good sound, a soothing jazz dominated by piano and bass. Luxurious music. The dark interior was lit (barely so) by a soft bluish light that floated in the air like fog. With a little effort, they found a small table (the table-top just a little bigger than a serving platter) pushed against a wall and placed themselves into the two chairs that stood on either side of it, Bonnie emitting a sigh of relief as she settled in.

A waitress almost immediately descended upon them and Bonnie ordered a carafe of house wine with two glasses. "Let's get a little stinko," she said to Ellen with a smile.

Around them were people staring at the musicians, seemingly transfixed by the music; others were less absorbed and were engaged in whispering conversations. At a nearby table, a man and woman were doing more than talking, enwrapped in slow and sensual explorations of each other. Their activities caught Ellen's eye. "Goodness, look at them," she exclaimed, appalled by the sight. "They're like barnyard animals in heat."

"Yeah," came back Bonnie. "I wouldn't mind trading places with her." She threw a Groucho Marx leer across the table to Ellen.

"Oh, you don't mean that," said Ellen.

"Sure I do. Why not? He's good looking."

"Well, you can't just sleep with anyone who comes along just because he's good looking, can you?" responded Ellen.

"No. Unfortunately some of them don't like me." Bonnie burst out laughing at Ellen's expression of moral shock just as the waitress returned bearing their carafe. "C'mon, have some *vino*," she said, grabbing up the carafe and pouring the wine. "Boy, you should see your face. You really did grow up on a farm, didn't you? I didn't think people like you still actually existed." She punctuated her words with such a pleasant and warm smile it was impossible for Ellen to be offended.

"Father Cullum would be upset," murmured Ellen, more to herself than to Bonnie. Somewhere deep inside her, on a level as much subconscious as not, Ellen had the sense that there was an opposing army lining up along the borders of *what she was*, that some kind of internal lines of separation were needed as long as she lived here. She took a healthy swallow of wine, following Bonnie's lead.

"I was a waitress once," said Bonnie over the rim of her glass. "Lousiest job I ever had. Money was good. You can make a lot. But I couldn't do it. I'm a control freak. Don't like to take orders too much. Don't like to take guff either. I was fired when this guy aggravated me and I told him to kiss my ass. The guy wasn't too upset but the owner was and fired me on the spot. That guy, the customer I told off, well, he comes over to me and talks nice. He asked me out and I said OK." Bonnie took another swallow of wine and started giggling. "After a few dates I ended up one night over at his place on Third Avenue. Funny how things happen some times. He ended up doing exactly what I'd told him to do when I got myself fired." Bonnie snorted another laugh and raised her glass once more to her lips.

Ellen shook her head and took another sip of wine.

The two women stayed in the club until well after midnight, going through another carafe of wine (mostly drunk by Bonnie) before finally deciding to leave and go home. Bonnie, for all the wine she'd drunk, barely looked tipsy. As they left, going through the door, they were fairly pushed to the side by a young man and woman going in, the two arm-in-arm. The woman was tremendously heavy with brassy blonde hair.

"Goodness," commented Ellen, after the couple had gone by. "That's a true *Ballybos* girl, isn't it?"

"A Bally-what girl?" asked Bonnie.

"*Ballybos*. Oh, that's an Irish term for a measurement of land. It's the amount of land necessary to feed one cow."

Bonnie burst out laughing so loudly that people turned to stare. "That's great," she told Ellen. "*Ballybos*. I have to remember that one."

The edges of the world on the return trip were comfortably soft, the city streets made less harsh now as a result of the wine and the deepening of the night, the darkness hiding from sight the city's scars and grime.

Even the building in which they lived seemed more charming now, its defects concealed beneath the pancake makeup of the night. A red brick building at least a century old if a day, but sturdy and well maintained. They entered and ascended the stairs to the second floor. Ellen thinking that the old corridors and stairs, unlike the halls and stairs of many apartment buildings, offered a mystical sense of comfort. Ellen had liked the old building the very first instant she saw it, on her first visit to Bonnie's apartment. It was one of the reasons she so quickly offered to be Bonnie's roommate.

The two chatted until the hour grew late and then bid each other good night, going off into their separate bedrooms. Ellen pulled out a fresh pair of pajamas from her still half-unpacked suitcase, changed into them and padded to the bathroom to brush her teeth. Bonnie was already asleep in her own room, Ellen could hear her snoring.

She returned to her own bedroom and climbed into bed. *This is my home now.* She laid her head on the pillow of her bed and gazed at the darkness of the room. *My home.* The thought didn't frighten her.

"It's not Donegal," she told herself. "That's certain."

And with that whispered opinion of the obvious, she mentally offered up her bedtime prayers, requesting God to please keep her safe. Closing her eyes, despite her misgivings, she drifted off into peaceful sleep.

*   *   *

The romantic social idol of the day was that of the brooding, sullen artist (or actor or poet) contemptuous of the social mores held by others. That mythos was nowhere more prevalent than in the Village, a primary thread of commonality running through the collective consciousness of the area. A good reason why Bonnie fit in so well. Many young "rebels" migrated here to "be true to themselves" or, at least, be true to the image of the rebel they imagined themselves to be. In the coffeehouses they talked of their distaste for McCarthyism and materialism, and expounded upon their fear that the world would very soon be blown to bits by A-bombs built by capitalists. For many, or so Ellen eventually came to believe, what was rebelled against was of less importance than the attitude of rebelling. Many here wore their sense of contention toward the *bourgeoisie* and the ruling government bureaucracy like a favorite red scarf, as something placed around the neck to add a splash of color to their otherwise drab outfit.

While the rebels were expressing their distaste for conformity, most dressed the same, wearing black turtleneck sweaters and jackets, black pants and shoes, in imitation of the fashion that was then the rage in Paris's Left Bank. The nonconformists conforming, and blind to their own hypocrisy.

Ellen, after a time, privately considered most of them to be little more than heathens and atheists, an opinion not too much unlike the one her sister Rose had voiced to her when Ellen first told her she was moving to Christopher Street.

Ellen didn't know it, but the current sense of contentiousness existing in the Village around her was nothing new. In growling at society, the place was being true to its history. This small section of New York City had a past dominated by "counter-culture" rebellion going back decades, back to the "Socialists" at the turn of the century, to the "Bohemians" of the 1930's and 40's and now to the "Beat poets" and coffee house existentialists who voiced their discontent to almost anyone who would listen. The Village had, over the course of many decades, gotten into the habit of wearing a supercilious and contemptuous snarl that it directed toward those they decided were the villains of society. Sometimes it snarled with good reason, and other times, as Ellen perceived so quickly, it snarled just for the sake of snarling.

Chapter Twenty-two

Bonnie was enamored of everything electric and simply "had to have" any electrical gadget or appliance that met the simple criteria that she both liked it and could afford to buy it. Many items she purchased at a small secondhand shop on Sixth Avenue, a repair shop that took in broken appliances (paying a few pennies on the dollar for them), mended them and then placed the reincarnated results on a store shelf to be sold again.

Ellen was astounded at the number of electrical devices her new roommate had accumulated for herself. She never knew so many electrical tools and appliances even existed. There was the imported Morphy-Richards Atlantic Model iron, sold as "the iron with the butterfly touch", the large and noisy Duco hair dryer, the electric cooker (What's wrong with using the stove? wondered Ellen), the Toastmaster toaster, the Swan Mayfair coffee-maker with the "Pyrex" glass insert, the Pifco chrome plated curling tongs with the red plastic handle, a necessity for Bonnie's hair, and, usually resting on the Formica topped table in the kitchen, the electric Vactric hand duster.

A Crosley 10 inch television sat on a small table in the living room but all other electrical items, including the hair dryer, were kept in the kitchen. The hair dryer was not used in the bathroom so as not to hog the toilet and keep someone else (a roommate) from being able to use it.

Bonnie warned Ellen not to use too many electric appliances at the same time as they were all hooked up to one electrical socket. The old building, erected just after the end of the Civil War, was not originally designed for electricity, that convenience added years later. There were two outlets in the kitchen but only one of them still worked and there were so many wires now plugged into the working socket that it looked like a small squid had taken up residence in the corner.

"Don't ever use the radio and the toaster and the iron, or the coffee-maker and the iron and radio, at the same time, for instance," said Bonnie. "And when you use the hair dryer, don't use the cooker and keep the radio on. Otherwise you'll blow out everything."

One month or so into her new residency, with Saint Patrick's Day past and Easter approaching, on a Tuesday, Ellen came home from work a little earlier than usual and went into the old black and white tiled bathroom to take a quick shower. Then, feeling happily clean, putting on her robe, she went to toast some bread. Forgetting the rules, she made the mistake of also putting on the radio and attempting to dry her hair with the dryer, all at the same time. Immediately, the apartment was plunged into darkness.

"Drat," she murmured, "Bonnie told me not to do that. Where did she say the fuse box was?" Getting up, she immediately banged her knee against a chair that was cloaked now by a shadow, a hidden obstacle in the dark. "Oweee!" she yelled with the pain. "Drat, drat, drat . . . ."

She heard shouts now from the hall outside the apartment. Cries of "Where're the lights?" and "What the hell happened?" came muffled through the apartment door from the other side. She opened the door a bit to peek outside, staring into the hall like a little child supposed to be asleep in bed, peeping into a room occupied by adults. The landing was dark as pitch. A couple of Bonnie's neighbors (her neighbors too now) had their doors opened and were talking across the hall to each other. "My lights just went out!" said one, a middle-aged transvestite named Warren (and known by no other name, at least to Ellen). He was speaking to Mr. Burnside who was standing in the doorway in his own apartment directly across the hall from Warren. "Mine too," came Burnside's voice. "What the hell is going on? I think the whole building is out!"

Ellen silently closed her door, hoping no one would discover the loss of power in the building was her fault. "Oh, goodness, where are the fuses? I've got to put a new one in and get the lights on again." She scurried anxiously back to the kitchen and began rummaging through the kitchen drawers almost frantically, searching for the box of fuses that Bonnie kept for just such an emergency. "Where are they?" she grumbled in frustration. "Where are they?"

Bonnie chose that moment to come home. "Ellen, are you all right?" she called out into the darkness of the apartment.

Ellen came out to her. "Oh, Bonnie, I messed up," she declared in a contrite and frightened tone. "I was drying my hair, and I put the radio on and was toasting a slice of bread and blew out all the lights all over the building. I'm so sorry."

Bonnie giggled, understanding at once. "It's not you. There's something wrong with the electric line into the building. I was just talking to the Con Ed' people outside. It'll be fixed in a few hours they said."

"It . . . *wasn't* me . . . ?"

"No, you silly. Come on, I have some candles somewhere. Let's get some light in the apartment. And my little transistor radio is around somewhere. If the battery is still good, we can get some music."

Ellen and Bonnie lit a few candles and, by their flickering light, tried to get Bonnie's small Japanese-made radio to work. They couldn't do it. Either the battery was dead or the radio had long ago lost its ability to make sounds. "Oh, the heck with it!" declared Bonnie, throwing it onto the sofa. "Let's go out," she suggested. "We can sit in a restaurant as easily as we can sit here. What do you say?"

Ellen said it was a great idea and went to throw on some clothes while Bonnie dug out an old flashlight. Together they went down the dark stairs, following the flashlight's beam.

*　　*　　*

They were nearing the small lobby when they saw an elderly woman, obviously fearful of tripping in the dark, trying to make her way up to her apartment on the unlit stairs, a bag of groceries in one hand. "Mrs. Staffutti," said Bonnie to the white-haired woman, "Hi, it's me, Bonnie. Are you going up to your apartment?"

Mrs. Staffutti nodded her head and Bonnie grabbed her arm. "Come on. We'll walk up with you. We have this light. This here is Ellen, my friend. She'll carry your bag for you. Your apartment's on the third floor, isn't it?"

"Oh, this is so good of you," said Mrs. Staffutti, offering Bonnie a smile. She turned her head to face Ellen and handed her the shopping bag. As Ellen accepted it, the elderly lady smiled once more. She had a sweet face and smiled with her eyes as well as her mouth. "I can't quite see the steps. I'm afraid I'll fall."

They walked to the entrance of the woman's apartment where Ellen returned the shopping bag to her. After accepting a genuine thank you, they turned and went back down the stairs. "Have a good Easter," the elderly lady called down the steps after them. Her apartment door slammed shut before they could turn and wish her the same. Once again, they were following the flashlight beam down the stairs, descending the steps carefully. This time, not meeting another Mrs. Staffutti, they made it to the lobby and out of the building. Outside, they extinguished the flashlight and stood on the steps, now faced with the decision of where to go.

"How about that little club we went to last time? suggested Bonnie. Ellen shrugged. "OK," she said.

"No," returned Bonnie, rejecting her own suggestion. "We'll go to the Village Vanguard on Seventh Avenue. You'll like that place. We can listen to bebop."

"OK," said Ellen, wondering what "bebop" meant.

They were at the Vanguard in minutes and inside and seated at a candle-lit table in just a minute more. "It's nice in here," said Ellen, letting her eyes wander around the dark, roomy club. There was, at the moment, no entertainment on the stage. A flickering candle was placed in the middle of every table.

"Let's order some wine," said Bonnie. "I'm thirsty. And food. I'm hungry too. I skipped lunch."

A waitress came over and asked them if they were ready to order. Bonnie ordered the wine, a carafe for two, and a steak, medium. Ellen ordered fish, the salmon.

In a minute, the waitress reappeared with the wine and two glasses.

"The food will be along in a little bit," she told them and then walked away.

"Hmmm, I want some of this," said Bonnie as she poured the wine into her glass. Then she filled Ellen's glass. "Here's to having candles when it's dark," she said, raising her wine in the gesture of a toast.

"To candles," responded Ellen, returning Bonnie's smile.

They enjoyed their small meal, ordered a second carafe of wine, which quantity was once again primarily consumed by Bonnie, and then paid their bill and started back to their apartment.

"Goodness," said Ellen, "I hope the lights are fixed by now."

"Me too, I want to watch the television. It's Tuesday, right? That Texaco Star show with Milton Berle is on, isn't it? I love him. He once dressed up like Carmen Miranda, made him look like Warren across the hall . . . ." Bonnie punctuated her opinion with a soft giggle.

"Hello, Bonnie."

Both Ellen and Bonnie turned around to see the speaker. Walking behind them, just two steps behind, was a young man, tall, thin and wiry, clad in the faddish black uniform of the Beat generation, turtleneck and pants covered by a long wool overcoat, also black, that went down to the ankles. His black hair was greased back, his eyes were brown and friendly.

"Hey, Paul," returned Bonnie, stopping in her tracks and turning fully around. "How're you?"

"Good. Long time, no see."

Bonnie tilted her head to the side a bit. "Now, who's fault is that, Paul?" she said, an "It Girl" pout appearing on her mouth.

"Mine, I suppose."

"Right. Oh, this is my friend, Ellen. Ellen, this is Paul."

Ellen and Paul quickly shook hands and then Paul dismissed her to turn his full attention back to Bonnie. "Hey, I was just heading down to Louie's Café," he told her. "How about coming along? We can catch up on old times."

Bonnie giggled. "Is that *all* you're after, old times?" she purred.

Paul put his head back and laughed. "There's no game-playing with you, Bonnie. That's for certain. You're looking fine, that's certain too."

"Thanks, Paulie. You're not looking so bad yourself."

"So how about it? The café, I mean."

Bonnie turned to Ellen. "Do you want – ?"

Ellen put her hands up, palms forward. "No thanks, Bonnie, but you and Paul go on. I'm feeling a bit tired and I just want to go home."

"You don't mind?"

"No, not at all. Go ahead. I'll see you later."

Bonnie handed the flashlight off to Ellen and then stepped forward and linked arms with Paul. "OK, Louie's Café, here we come."

"Nice to meet you, Ellen," said Paul and with that serving as their dual farewell, he and Bonnie presented their backs to Ellen and were off down the street. Ellen watched their silhouettes, close together, moving away into the distance for a few seconds and then turned and continued on her way home.

As she hoped, the power was back on in the building when she returned and so, once inside and settled on the small sofa, she turned on the little 10 inch television to keep her company. By eleven o'clock there was no Bonnie and by twelve there was still no Bonnie. Ellen went off to bed. In the morning she discovered that Bonnie didn't return to the apartment the entire night and she could only assume that Paul had indeed "caught up" with more than simply old times.

At work, in the office, Bonnie made her appearance, still wearing the same outfit she'd worn the night before. She shrugged her shoulders and smiled when she saw Ellen, offering her a "What can I say?" expression that held more contentment than regret in it. "Hey you only live once," she said, and, offering no further explanation, went off down the hall to return to her desk.

Chapter Twenty-three

Ellen did not condemn Bonnie for what she saw as a lack of morality, not absolutely, but neither did she condone Bonnie's behavior. What Bonnie did was wrong, pure and simple. Ellen was reminded of her childhood friend Lauren back in Ireland and her not infrequent excursions to the countryside or to a haystack inside a barn. She was reminded too of her mother's words: *Your love. Your physical love is a gift. It's the greatest gift a woman can give a man. But that gift will be valued by a man according to the value you yourself place upon it.*

What value did the men Bonnie slept with place on her? Both friends, first Lauren and now Bonnie, ultimately produced more puzzlement in Ellen than rebuke. *How could they do that?* she wondered, thinking about the various partners that came and went. *You give the milk away and no one will buy the cow.*

She didn't often spend her free time going out with her roommate after that evening. She liked Bonnie still, very much, but it was clear to Ellen by now that Bonnie was looking for different things from "going out" than she was, and some of those different things were too opposed to what Ellen believed was right and good to be easily accepted by her, or for her to even casually be a part of. Besides, people judge you by your friends, isn't that so? And if Bonnie was giving the cow's milk away wouldn't it mean (to others) that she was also? Especially if she and Bonnie were out together at night in a club.

The two women remained good friends and would talk the night away when home together but when the weekends came, or when Bonnie decided to go out during midweek, she would do so with other friends while Ellen, invited to come along, would opt to remain at home alone. Ellen was soon considered by most of Bonnie's friends as the "square one".

Sometimes, alone, Ellen would stand in front of the full-length mirror she discovered attached to the inside of her bedroom closet door and study herself. *I'm not bad looking*, she thought. *Not too bad anyway.* It was an underestimation. She was beautiful.

Sometimes she would put some music on and would waltz around the room, pretending that a man had asked her to dance and was embracing her, whirling her around the floor, putting her own arms, for lack of those of a man, around her waist.

There were times over the next few months, not too often (thank the Lord!) when Bonnie would come home late with a "friend" and Ellen would lie in her bed in her room, listening to them through the wall. (No other choice – they were so loud!) At such times, Ellen could not help but feel that the sins being committed on the other side of the bedroom wall might sizzle the wallpaper right off the plaster and blister the paint on the ceiling. Sometimes she covered her head with a pillow to muffle the sounds.

On such nights Ellen felt her own loneliness more than ever, the ache of being alone lashing out at her, mocking her languishing heart.

*   *   *

"Look at me!" cried Bonnie. "Look at me! I'm breaking out!" Having made this declaration of mortification to Ellen and displaying her face for Ellen's view, Bonnie ran back into her room. "Oh why today? Why God?! Why!" Bonnie's voice was muffled now, coming from within her bedroom. "I wish I had some reefer. Got to calm down."

Ellen, dressed and ready to go, sitting on the sofa and reading a magazine, smiled at her friend's nervousness. By now she'd learned what a "reefer" was and was not at all pleased to hear Bonnie talk of using it. Looking over to her friend, she told her so. "I thought you didn't like drug users," she shouted to Bonnie.

"Oh, reefer isn't real drugs," came Bonnie's voice from the bedroom. Ellen frowned and returned her attention to her magazine.

A soft May morning light came in through the nearby window accompanied by a breeze that made the curtain flutter almost continuously. The morning sun entering through the window offered Ellen sufficient light for reading.

Suddenly Bonnie reappeared. "Oh God El. The audition is in one hour and my face is blotchy as hell. Look at me. I look like the volcano-birds of volcano-land laid volcano-eggs on my face!"

Ellen chuckled. "You look fine."

"Do I?" beseeched Bonnie.

"Yes, now get away before your face explodes all over me."

"Oooh you – " Bonnie grimaced, stuck out her tongue, turned and ran back into the bedroom. "Thanks for coming with me," she called out to Ellen. "I need you for moral support. Thank you. Thank you."

"No big deal," returned Ellen. "I had a day off from work coming to me anyway. It'll be fun. I've never been to an audition before. And you look fine."

"Today is my day! I can feel it. And my horoscope said so. It's in the stars. It's in the stars. It's my day! My day!" Bonnie was so excited that each word, each syllable she spoke, popped out of her mouth as though her tongue was a trampoline. "I'm beautiful. B-E-utiful! I'm going to be simply great at that audition today. The best! Oh God, is that another blotch! Please no more blotches! Please!"

*   *   *

They rode in a taxi to Eighth Avenue and Eleventh Street and together entered a small theater, almost run-down, the place wearing a disheveled appearance that spoke more of poverty, a lack of funds, than creativity. Here was a theater dedicated to experimentation, to an ideal of the dramatic arts rather than the tried-and-true of Broadway proper, and it paid the price for its intentions. Like any artist dedicated more to a vision than the business of making money, it wore shabby clothes.

Inside, a young man, so thin his skeletal structure might have composed of paper-clip-wire instead of bones, came over and handed Bonnie a fact sheet. He pushed one toward Ellen too but she shook the offer away. The interior of the theater looked like someone's cellar, a disorganized unkempt cellar.

"Oh God," moaned Bonnie as she held the sheet up to Ellen's eyes. "Look how many others are here."

"Do you want to leave?" asked Ellen, disappointed for her.

"Leave? Are you insane? I want this part! It's a good role. A really good role. Oh, I want this part! I want it!"

They sat and waited, Bonnie so nervous she *didn't* speak, tapping her right foot on the ground, looking around now and then like a puppy sniffing the air for the scent of food in the bowl. A half-hour passed by; and when Bonnie's name was suddenly called she leapt out of her chair as though someone had pushed a needle through the bottom of the seat, surprised by the sound of her own name. "Yes, yes, I'm here!"

"We're reading from page twenty. Go inside to center stage."

Bonnie turned to Ellen. "Wish me luck again." Then, without waiting to have her request fulfilled, she scurried away to her destiny, leaving Ellen alone, with only a magazine on her lap keep her company and fill the time.

A few minutes after Bonnie's departure a man walked over to Ellen, a man with a light step for Ellen didn't hear his approach, or perhaps he was unheard because her thoughts were focused more on Bonnie and the pictures in the magazine than upon her surroundings. The man cleared his throat to announce his presence and Ellen, hearing the sound, lifted her head, surprised by his closeness to her. Looking up, she found herself staring into a pair of dazzling, very blue eyes. At the sight of those eyes and the handsome face in which they resided, something inside of her was suddenly, powerfully, overwhelmed.

"I startled you, didn't I?" he said to her. "Sorry. I just noticed the empty chair. Would you mind if I sit?"

"N-No, of course not," replied Ellen. She avoided looking at him after speaking to him, nervously alternating between staring into space and placing her eyes onto the magazine on her lap. She felt suddenly awkward, and, out of the corner of her eye, thought she could perceive his appraisal of her. He was looking at her, she could sense the sight of his blue eyes upon her, and, sensing those eyes, could feel her cheeks flooding with embarrassment over the awareness of his gaze.

"Are you here to audition?" he asked, after what seemed to Ellen an uneasy millennium.

She turned her face to him. *My, he's very attractive.* "Me? Oh no. I don't act. I'm here with a friend. She's trying for a role. I'm with her for company and for moral support."

He smiled and Ellen felt the smile go rolling straight to her heart. "I didn't think you were an actress," he told her. "Oh, don't misunderstand me. You're pretty enough. But you don't . . . you don't exactly *behave* like actors do."

"How do actors behave?"

"Well, let's see, how can I say it? You're . . . more *subdued* than a lot of these others."

Ellen considered his words, smiled and nodded her head. There was a lot of fire and excitement crackling around the room, generated by an anticipation and anxiousness of which she wasn't a part. She knew what he meant.

"May I introduce myself?" he asked, extending his hand toward her. "My name is John, John Madden."

She accepted his hand. "Ellen Rawdon," she said and felt her face flush with new energy, her cheeks suddenly feeling as if the bones had just been surgically removed and replaced with two steaming radiators. *Let's roast some marshmallows.* Inwardly, she was embarrassed by the tug of attraction she felt for him. His blue eyes held intelligence and good humor, Ellen thought, and kindness too. There was a sense of prosperity about him, the suggestion offered by his well-tailored charcoal gray pinstripe suit and silk tie. He looked like some of the more successful men on Wall Street Ellen saw each day at work except there was a red carnation in the lapel of his suit. She seldom saw anyone on Wall Street add such a touch to their all-business appearance. On his wrist she noticed a bracelet of thick gold.

"Very pleased to meet you, Ellen." His voice was gentle. "May I ask, if you're not an actress, what do you do for a living?"

"I'm working right now for a company on Wall Street."

"Ah, a business woman."

Ellen had never thought of herself as a businesswoman, but upon consideration, thought it might describe her now as well as any other classification. Should she correct him and say she was a transplanted farm girl? "I suppose," she responded. "In a small sense, that is. At least I do work *for* a business. What about you? Are you an actor?"

He threw a smile at her. "Well, we're all actors, to some degree. But a professional? No, I'm not."

"Johnny!" a man's voice came between their conversation. "Johnny, come on!"

Frowning at the interruption, John Madden turned toward the sound of his name. Ellen's eyes followed his gaze and saw a short, stocky man, swarthy with broad features, waving an arm, beckoning the man with the dazzling blue eyes to leave her and join him. "Business summons me," John said to her. "Business can be a pain. Ellen, how about having dinner with me tonight? I'd like to continue our talk."

He noticed Ellen's knitted brow of doubt in response to his invitation. "I understand," he said, obviously disappointed. "You don't know me and – "

"No!" blurted out Ellen, much too loud and too fast. "It's just I'm not used to – but yes, yes I would like to have dinner with you tonight." Someone in the furnace room of Ellen's heart turned up the gauges and her radiator-cheeks glowed with new heat. She thought it possible that the bones of her face might melt. Inwardly she cursed her embarrassment and her inability to control it.

The mischievous spark returned to Madden's eyes. He asked her where she lived and she told him. "See you tonight, then," he said and then he stood and walked away, going toward the thick-set beckoning man, leaving Ellen somewhat astonished at herself, astounded both at the invitation she'd received and the fact that she'd so casually accepted it.

*   *   *

"I don't believe it," complained Bonnie. "My horoscope said it was *my* day. Not only did I probably not get the part but *you* end up with a date with a hunk of a man. What do you know about him?"

"Nothing. Except he's gorgeous. He's got the most wonderful blue eyes."

"Well, you know he's a liar," stated Bonnie. "Look there's an empty cab. Hail it over." Ellen waved the taxi to the curb and in a moment the two women were settled in the back seat giving instructions to the driver.

"What do you mean, he's a liar?" asked Ellen, her voice heavy with offense. "You don't even know him. How can you say such a nasty thing?"

"Easy," said Bonnie with a shrug. "All men are liars. That's what they do. Just like wearing pants."

"Oh don't talk like that. He seemed nice."

Bonnie laughed. "You sound like you really like him. Well, he's asked you to dinner but remember all he really wants to do is get your legs up in the air. Do you think you'll let him?"

Ellen raised a finger to her mouth. "Shhh." She wanted Bonnie to talk more softly as she was certain the cab driver could hear their conversation. She was simultaneously amused and appalled by Bonnie's words and her cheeks, (her terrible, undisciplined cheeks!) were red once more. "You're terrible, you know that?"

Bonnie grinned at her. "I'm only teasing. I hope, for your sake, he turns out to be the most wonderful man in the world, the best man ever."

And, with those words, Bonnie was giving voice to the very wish that was now residing in Ellen's heart, glowing like a newborn dream: *The best man, ever.*

Chapter Twenty-four

Ellen sat on the sofa, taking a strange immobilized nervous ride over a terrain of bumpy doubts. Her fingers patted the material of the brand-new silk dress on which she'd just spent too much money, a dress the color of Kelly green in which she looked beautiful. Was she wrong in accepting this invitation? *I don't know a thing about this man, John Madden. Except for his eyes, his kind, wonderful eyes. Will he come? Or will he stand me up? What if we have absolutely nothing in common? Maybe this whole night will be a total disaster? If he shows up at all.*

"Calm down, El," said Bonnie, sitting in a chair on the opposite side of the room. "I swear you look more nervous than a first-time actor on opening night. You're going to get the flop sweats."

Ellen smiled. "I'm not nervous," she lied. "Much."

"You look like one of those prisoners in a Western movie, looking out of a window with bars waiting for a gallows to be finished." She crossed her eyes and stared.

"I don't look *that* nervous, do I?" asked Ellen, concern appearing on her face.

"No, you look fine. Really good. Really."

The bell erupted, its buzz suddenly tremendous in the apartment. Ellen bounced in her chair, startled by the sound.

"There he is now, Miss Cool Calm and Collected," said Bonnie as she stood up. "I'll let him in."

Ellen felt a tremor, half-nervousness, half-exhilaration, shiver through her stomach and chided herself for it. *Stop acting like a silly schoolgirl,* she scolded herself as she pushed herself out of the chair and stood.

John Madden offered Bonnie a polite hello and introduction and came into the apartment. Seeing Ellen he smiled and greeted her with a nod of his head. She returned the smile, feeling gratitude for it.

He was wearing a suit very similar to the one he'd worn earlier that day, perhaps it was even the same suit, but tonight his shirt collar was opened, the formality of a tie abandoned in favor of relaxation. To Ellen's astonishment, in his hand he held one scarlet long-stemmed rose. At the sight of the flower, Ellen's uncertainty took to its heels. There was only John Madden, the rose he was extending toward her and the space in between them. For the instant, nothing else existed in the entire universe.

"You look absolutely beautiful," he told Ellen. To her surprise she found herself believing him.

Bonnie's face appeared behind John, looking at Ellen over Madden's shoulder. Bonnie rolled her eyes and offered a theatrical grin, putting her hands beside her face. "A rose. How sweet," she mouthed, moving her lips soundlessly. Ellen did her best to ignore her.

"Well," said John, "I've made reservations for seven-thirty and it's ten after now. We should be going. We can walk to the restaurant. It isn't far."

"Just let me get my coat," said Ellen. She turned to Bonnie and held the rose out toward her. "Could you put that in a vase for me, please?"

"Sure thing. I took a college class in NYU a year ago. How to put flowers in water. I actually failed, but I'll give it a shot . . . ."

Ellen disappeared, going into her bedroom for a minute before reemerging with her coat on. "Ready," she said.

"You really are beautiful," whispered John Madden and, with the repeat of the compliment, a miscreant blush began to heat Ellen's cheeks. A brief moment, then, to Ellen's relief, it was gone, scurrying from her cheeks and out of the room, leaving just steps in front of her and John's own departure.

*   *   *

The restaurant was perfect to Ellen's way of thinking, offering an ambiance of casual elegance romantically lit by soft overhead lights and the flickering glow from a working fireplace. They were seated near the hearth and its soft glow burnished their table, softly caressing their faces. It was clear, from the friendly greeting John Madden received from the headwaiter, that he'd dined here before, perhaps often. *How many other women has he taken here?* wondered Ellen.

"You've been here before?" she asserted, after they'd ordered their drinks.

"Once or twice," replied Madden. (*Or more*, thought Ellen.) "I like it here. The food is good." He fixed his striking blue eyes upon her, obviously admiring her features. His scrutiny once more made Ellen's cheeks glow pink. "Please don't do that," she asked him, looking at the tabletop.

"Do what?" He was surprised.

"Look at me like that."

"I'm sorry, I *was* staring." He smiled, a warm smile. "I can't help it. I find you to be very beautiful."

Ellen replied to the compliment with a smile of her own, certain that her face was glowing brighter than the flames in the nearby fireplace.

"I've embarrassed you," said John Madden. "You don't know how beautiful you are. You're not used to being told you're beautiful, are you?"

"No, no, not really," replied Ellen. "But it is nice to hear." She experienced a subtle tremor in her body. She wanted to know more about this man, this man named John Madden with the beautiful, magnetic blue eyes, and over dinner she made every effort to get him to talk about himself. But he had a disarming penchant for turning the conversation away from himself, which made it difficult to obtain anything but the most casual information. He glossed over the facts of his own past and turned the conversation to either Ellen's own life or to generalities.

The dinner was delicious and, by its completion, Ellen was completely charmed by Johnny, as she was now calling him. He was bright, witty, and complimentary. There was a vein of sincerity in his voice and within those eyes, which was appealing and which made Ellen believe every word he spoke. How could she doubt those eyes? *Like Da's eyes.*

She enjoyed being with him, being in his company, more than

she'd ever enjoyed being with anyone and now, over dinner, sitting and looking at him over the table in the soft illumination of the firelight, she found her thoughts wandering toward contemplations of what it would feel like to sleep beside him, to feel his skin against hers. The first time this salacious consideration came to her she was shocked by the audacity of her own mind, and blushed pink (again) over it, afraid that somehow he could see, or at least sense, what she was thinking. *I'm a blushing machine in front of him,* she thought to herself. *How do I stop it? Please God, help me stop it.*

An hour after midnight, he returned her to her home. "I had a wonderful time tonight, John," she told him, turning to face him and looking up into his face as they stood outside her apartment door. "Really I did. Thank you."

"Can I come in?" he asked. "I don't want the night to be over."

Her Catholic upbringing was shocked by the suggestion, but the woman in her was pleased. She thought of those nights when the headboard of Bonnie's bed was slapping against the wall and some part of her smiled at the thought of reversing roles. Still the words of her mum and the pressure of the years of the teachings and iron insistence of Catholic morality dominated her, this night at least. "No, I can't do that. Bonnie, my roommate is inside. She's very . . . . uh, uptight." *God,* she scolded herself, *I'm lying to him on the first date.*

"Really?" responded Madden, arching an eyebrow. "She didn't strike me that way. Well, then tell me at least that we can see each other again tomorrow night. We'll do this again."

"I'd love to. But I can't. I'm a working girl and I have to work. I'm going to be going to my job tomorrow with only five hours sleep. Two nights in a row and I'll be worthless."

His eyes fixed on hers. "I understand. It was thoughtless of me to keep you out this late on a weekday. If I promise to get you back earlier – no later than ten? What about it? You're quite a gal. I don't want to wait too long to see you again."

Ellen, staring into the keenness of his eyes, smiled and nodded her head.

"Good," he said simply. "Good." Placing a finger beneath her chin, he tilted her head back up to him. Ellen's lips parted slightly as he leaned down and placed his mouth upon hers, a long kiss that sent Ellen's heart rapping against her ribs. Then he turned and, with a final wave, descended the stairs. Ellen, watching him go, was already regretting saying no to his request to come inside.

Her mood as she went into her apartment was intensely buoyant, even ecstatic. She might have been a helium balloon, floating high above the floor. She was happy, more happy than she'd ever been, more happy than she'd previously thought it possible to be.

*   *   *

Incredibly, they were married just two months later, on a beautiful July day, the gleaming morning outdone only by the radiance of the young bride. Rose served as the Maid of Honor and Maggie, Teresa and Bonnie were there as bridesmaids. Jim, Rose's husband, walked her down the aisle, and, during the entire walk to the altar, Ellen could think of nothing but her father and her brother. Jimmy couldn't be with her, the cost of the double fare from Ireland and then back again simply too dear to allow him to travel to America for the wedding. It was an extravagance, one the family didn't have the money to pay for.

But once at the altar, Ellen felt like a princess. The pressure of preparation for the wedding, which had absorbed her for the last two weeks, and the soft sorrow of missing her da and Jimmy were left behind her as, standing beside John, she experienced nothing but pure bliss, a joy so abundant she thought she'd burst with the expansion of it.

All around her were the solemn warmth of the church, the smell of flowers on the altar, the embrace of a benevolent God, the man she loved. Her future held nothing less than the promise of a wonderful, happy life.

Ellen could not then perceive, in the midst of her newfound bliss, that the promise of happiness being held out before her was in fact a counterfeit jewel, a deception, as was the man she walked toward as she stepped slowly down the church aisle to the sound of the church organ playing *Here Comes the Bride*. The truth of her future was then hidden from her eyes as totally as was the genuineness of the true nature of the concealed and unknown man she'd chosen to marry.

Chapter Twenty-five

Ellen was, in her way, a coconspirator in the illusion that was John Madden. She *wanted* him to be what she imagined him to be, what her dreams wanted him to be, and so she dismissed any evidence of the contrary. How did he make a living? She'd asked him that before they were married and he'd told her in vague terms that he was an investor, a trader in the Stock Market, and was so successful at it that he had abandoned his former profession, that of carpentry. Did she doubt the truth of this? A little (Ellen never saw him check the prices on the Exchanges, nor did he ever show any interest in financial publications) but her own doubt stirred up something unpleasant inside of her and she wanted nothing to do with unpleasantness, not now. So she pushed all questions and doubts aside. He was charming and attentive and he loved her. What right did she have to betray his love with doubt?

They settled into an apartment on the Upper East Side. She remained awake half the night of the first day they moved in, staring at him as he slept in their bed (*our bed!*) after they'd made love for the second time, a long ebb and flow of slow and pleasing passion. The moonlight tinted the room a ghostly silver, the light falling pale upon his skin. She might have been sleeping with a wonderful phantom, or a glorified spirit, an angel's ghost, a gift from heaven.

A month into the marriage, she asked him if she should quit her job as his own success made her salary unnecessary. He told her to keep working for the time being. He was out of the house most of the day and she'd be bored sitting at home alone. It would be different when she became a mother.

He talked constantly about having children, beautiful children, beautiful just like their mother, and rhapsodized about how wonderful their children and their lives would be. Their future, the gospel according to John, would be bliss. "I promise, I'll never let anyone or anything hurt you," he told her. "Never. I never want my beautiful Ellen to be unhappy. Not for even one moment."

Just three months and one week after the day they were married, he came up missing. He kissed her goodbye in the morning, walked out the door and simply failed to return that night.

Ellen was frantic with worry, certain that something terrible had happened to him. In her mind, she saw visions of him beaten in an alley or crumpled in a heap by a curb having just been hit by a speeding car. *Oh please God, don't let him be hurt! Oh please God. Watch over him!*

Desperate for his safe return, she prayed, her heart hammering fear into her with greater intensity with each passing minute. Near eleven at night, she dialed the police and was mildly chastened for making the call. It was too soon according to their rules, a person could not be considered legally missing just for skipping dinner and staying out late one night. She returned to sit in her chair in tears, and continued to wait, confused and anxious, pressing the palms of her hands together as tears of fright ran down her cheeks, her heart a thick lump of aching ice in her chest.

She didn't sleep at all that night. *John is hurt. Dead? Is that possible?* No, that was a demon of a thought her mind could not, would not, accept as being conceivable. A thought similar to the image of one of the evil creatures in one of her father's stories, a frightening illusion in the telling of the tale but an impossibility in real life. John was hurt; that was as much pain as Ellen was willing to conceive of. Still, despite her denial of it, the demon refused to leave her entirely, its gleaming eyes blinking at her now and then in the dark of a back corner of her mind.

She went to the telephone in the morning and repeated her call to the police. This time a sympathetic police detective, hearing the frantic tone in her voice, "bent the rules" and took down the information of the missing husband. He then asked her to come down to the precinct to make a formal notification.

A search of her purse revealed she had only two dollars and some change. *I was supposed to go to the bank and take out some money,* she recalled. *I forgot to do it.* She would need money, for the cab ride to the police station and for getting to John once they locate him, wherever he was. The bank was just one block away. *I'll get some money and then grab a cab to the police station,* she told herself. *Please God, let Johnny be found by the time I talk to that detective again. Please God.*

*   *   *

Her prayer was, in a perverse way, answered by her trip to the bank. There, she learned that her bank account had been depleted, her hard-earned savings was gone, withdrawn by her husband the day before he'd disappeared. Only one dollar remained, and that so the account wouldn't be automatically closed. Upon learning this, a light exploded in Ellen's head, a painful Aurora Borealis composed of the reflected light coming off the shards of her broken illusions and shattered dreams. She stood, gaping at the bank teller, feeling as though she'd just been shot from a cannon straight into a stone wall. She had abruptly "found" Johnny, the true Johnny.

He left me! Just picked up and left me. Taking what money he could with him. I loved him . . . I loved him . . . .

It made Ellen sick. Looking into the eyes of the truth of what John Madden was. *Rose. Rose. Call my sister. Go to her. No. God, I'm so ashamed.* She felt suddenly dirty, filthy to the core of her soul, and, her eyes overrunning with tears, drawing the gazes of others she passed on the sidewalk on her way home, she rushed to her apartment, seeking the only shelter that remained to her, privacy behind a locked door.

Inside, she found that the newly born demon that was her sorrow refused to be left standing in the hall but rather insisted upon entering with her, not willing to relinquish its cruel opportunity to burrow itself deeper into the damage of her heart. She rushed to the bathroom, stripped off her clothes and jumped into the shower, remaining beneath the cleansing water a long time as electric palsies of pain throbbed inside her. There was little true respite offered by the water and the tears continued to run down her face as she stood in the shower. They continued to fall as she toweled herself off.

As painful as the initial shock of truth was, there was more pain coming. As she put her robe on, the hurt to her soul suddenly gained additional force inside her and abruptly hit her again with such renewed cruel intensity that her body convulsed with the overwhelming ache of it. She might have just touched an exposed live wire on which rode a powerful electric current. Her face twisted into a grotesque mask of distress and she doubled over as though kicked in the belly. Slowly, her eyes continuing to stream tears, she sank to the tiles of the floor.

She remained there, on the floor of the bathroom of the apartment she and John had rented just three months earlier, resting half on the bathroom mat and half on the tiles, curled up in a fetal position. She wept for almost an hour, until she found the power to stand and leave the bathroom, still weeping.

She climbed into bed. And stayed there the rest of the day. Evening came and the sun departed, its leaving offering Ellen the small sympathy of darkness while she continued sobbing the pain of her utterly broken and devastated heart.

*　　*　　*

Ellen called in sick to her job and cried and stumbled about her apartment for two days, ceasing her tears only now and then, and only to later find their force returning with renewed vigor. But then on the third day she discovered she was finally cried out, at least for the time being. That day she contacted Bonnie and, in a voice overflowing with urgency, asked her friend if she'd yet found a new roommate. When Bonnie replied with a "no" Ellen exhaled a great sigh of relief and told her to stop looking; she'd be moving back in with her.

"What's wrong?" inquired a concerned Bonnie, responding to the agitation in Ellen's voice as much as to the surprise of her words. This was the first time she'd been contacted by Ellen in the past month. She had no idea up to the moment of this call that Ellen's marriage was anything but heaven.

"Tonight," replied Ellen. "I'll move back in tonight. All right?"

Bonnie was about to insist that Ellen explain what was wrong but decided against it. Perhaps, hearing the trembling in Ellen's voice, she sensed that her friend was neither prepared nor equipped to talk about it, or perhaps she immediately concluded that it didn't matter what was wrong. Not at that moment anyway. *Something* was wrong, her friend was hurt, and that was enough knowledge for the present.

"Great," she told Ellen. "Great."

Chapter Twenty-six

Ellen awoke gasping, clutching at her bedsheet with both hands, and stared sharply, fearfully, about the room. The images of her dream, the nightmare that had shoved her roughly from her sleep, remained with her, clinging to her.

Two months and a week had passed since she'd returned to Bonnie's apartment, Christmas was only days away.

A frightening dream: A return to Ireland, walking the path that ran through the bog near the old farm. As a consequence of an absence of moon and stars overhead there was almost no light on the path and deep darkness flooded the bog like the incoming tide of a stormy ocean. She could barely see more than a couple of feet in front of her as she walked, lost and seeking to find her way home.

A light appeared. One glimmering dim light floating in the air a few feet before her, a shimmering will-o'-the-wisp. Come to lead her, or so she hoped, to her home. She followed it. The night air was like cold water to her face, the result of a wet soaking wind, so frigid she thought her face would freeze into a block of ice.

She followed the light but home was not where it led her. Instead she was brought to the stone of a great mountain, to the bottom of a craggy wall. An entrance to a cave, a jagged cut in the rock, was before her, and, without remembering actually stepping inside, she found herself standing on the other side of it, in a corridor with walls of stone. The will-o'-the-wisp light was gone, evaporated perhaps into the stone, and Ellen was left alone, wet, cold and shuddering in the cave of the mountain, her heart pounding with fright.

Though the light that brought her here had abandoned her, she could still see as a hint of illumination, a soft, pale glow that seemed to come from within the midst of the stone walls now surrounding her, offered her a dim, muted light. The entrance she'd walked through had dissolved with her passing through it and she was now enclosed within a cave with no exit, sealed inside the mountain as securely as a corpse within a nailed coffin. A new fear gripped her. *I'm trapped! How can I get out of here?!*

"God help me," murmured Ellen. She repeated the plea several times before letting her feet do the only thing possible to do, walk. To where, she of course had no clue. She only knew, with certainty, that she was scared half to death. As she walked she perceived to her horror that the very nature of the cave, the corridor that held her, was changing, and not for the better. The floor shifted from rock to slippery muddy ground and an odor of foul decay began to assail her. Her heart beat now with such fear that she was certain it would burst from behind her ribs. Ellen turned around, wanting now only to go back, deciding it would be safer to return than to continue on this way. But, turning, she was terrified to find that the corridor behind her had been closed off! To her shock, she was facing a wall of stone that stood only two feet from her eyes! *God! I'm being sealed in! Buried alive!* One thought hammered in her brain: *I've got to get out! I'll be all right if I can get out!*

The ceiling of rock above her began to press her down, coming lower with each shuffling step she took and she was forced first to bend and then at last to drop to her hands and knees. "I'm being buried alive!" she shouted. "Please God!" The darkness surrounding her ignored her pain and simply absorbed her cries . . .

. . . and she awoke from her dream, sitting straight up in her bed, her chest rising and falling in quick gasps. So real was the nightmare, so tenacious and persistent its terror, that it required a few ticks of the clock before she could believe she was truly still tucked in the safety of her own bed.

She tossed away the ashes of the dream with a shake of her head and climbed out of the bed. Pressing her feet into her slippers, she crossed the room to the window. The faintest glimmer of dawn was peeping through the glass. The hard edges of the city, at least for now, were softened into graceful curves. The dawn glistened everywhere, so faint it fabricated the illusion that the light it offered came from a source within the brick and mortar of the city rather than from the sky above it. Like the walls of the cave of her nightmare, the city glowed mysteriously, each brick a little chip of phosphorescence.

Ellen stood, gazing at the scene through her window, for almost a full minute, then unexpectedly she began to cry. *John, you hurt me so much!* A sudden anguished acid-burning thought. *So much. So much . . .*

A wave of nausea washed over her and abruptly she felt desperately sick. She rushed to the bathroom and, after a few moments, vomited into the sink. With that retching, the sense of nausea passed and, inhaling a few deep breaths, she began to feel better. Wiping the residue of vomit from her mouth and chin, she flushed the sink and returned to her bed.

Placing her hands on her belly she rubbed herself. She was going to have John's child. *At such a time a husband and wife should be together with their love. Shouldn't they? Why am I alone? Why God? Why?* With the back of her hands she wiped away, now with a measure of disgust, the incipient tears forming in the corners of her eyes. It seemed she was always crying, always wiping away tears.

Then, with an effort of will, she banished the sorrow from her. *No more feeling sorry for yourself, Ellen! No more!*

She'd demanded that from herself days ago and she demanded it again now. And she'd keep that mandate to herself as best she could. She'd damn well keep it. Her hands moved to her middle and she looked down at herself. Her lips, compressed at first into a thin tight line, relaxed and formed a soft smile. *A new life.* At first she'd thought of this life inside her, within her, as something alien to her but no longer. Now it was part of her, *her* baby. She was creating a new life out of herself. A miracle. A true and real miracle.

A baby. The future would be difficult, but Ellen knew she had to find the strength and courage to face up to that future. Whatever it brought her she had no choice but to live it, day by day, and she'd be damned if she'd do it mewling and whining, bathed in self-pity.

She still had her own two feet to stand on and she'd damn well do her best to keep standing on them. As tall and straight as she could.

As tall and straight as she could.

Chapter Twenty-seven

Ellen tossed her friend a look of disapproval as Bonnie poured herself one more full glass of wine. "Don't drink so much," she scolded her. "It's not good."

"Well, you *are* getting into the mother mode, aren't you?" replied Bonnie, smiling. Hell, a few glasses of wine never hurt anyone." She giggled, already lightheaded from the Merlot. There were two bottles near by, one already empty, the other filled but waiting to repeat the destiny of its deceased comrade, understanding its life span was very limited. If it could speak, it would have requested a blindfold.

They sat on a newly purchased orange and red hooked rug that covered a quarter of the living room floor, their legs crossed American-Indian-like. The wine, together with a couple of boxes of Ritz crackers, a large slab of cheese and a white plastic knife on a plate, rested between them. Following Ellen's reprimand, duly ignored, they sat silent for a few seconds (Bonnie topping off her glass of wine) until Bonnie spoke up, giving voice at last to a question that was on her mind ever since she'd first learned her friend was pregnant. The wine loosened her tongue and so granted her the freedom to at last speak her mind: "You'll keep it, then?" Bonnie's eyes remained fixed on the box of crackers as she made the query.

Ellen stared at her, confused. "What – ?"

"You know," came back Bonnie, at last lifting her eyes to Ellen. "*Keep* it. There's people I know who'll help you get rid of it. It'll be as if you were never pregnant."

Ellen was shocked. "Abortion . . . ?"

"Yes. Don't look at me like that. Laws against abortion are just society's way of keeping women down. Did you know it was made legal in Russia after the revolution? Lenin thought it was immoral to force a woman to have a baby against her will. That's the way it should be everywhere."

"No, it isn't," stated Ellen adamantly, anger raising her voice a notch. "I'm not a barbarian who kills children, am I? It's not my baby's fault my husband was a liar and a thief and I'm in the plight I'm in, is it? It's not my baby's fault that I was such a foolish hen that I fell for a *moddhereen* like John, is it?"

"Well, it *is* an option, isn't it?" responded Bonnie, surprised at Ellen's venom. "I mean otherwise you're going to be alone raising a baby. He did leave you. So it'll be his fault it has to be done, won't it?"

"No, it won't be," replied Ellen with as much force as previously. "It'd be *my* fault since I'm the one who did it. I don't want to talk about this anymore."

"Well, even if you have the baby you could still give it up later. For adoption, I mean."

"Oh, Bonnie, it's part of me. Isn't it? Could I give my hand away? Or one of my eyes? It's part of me." She placed her hand gently upon the small bulge of her waist and lowered her eyes to her midsection. "Part of me . . . ."

"It'll be hard," came back Bonnie. "Raising it. Looking after it and working too. And expensive too."

"Stop calling my baby 'it'," demanded Ellen, looking up again at her friend, a frown on her lips. "My baby is not an 'it'. Call my baby 'your baby'." Then, lowering her eyes again to her waist, "My father used to say everything costs something and the cost is not always measured in money. If I gave up my baby just to give me less work and more money I don't think I could live with myself. And what would I spend the money on? A few new dresses and some pairs of shoes? They'd last a few months and then be thrown away anyway. A diamond broach? What do I want with that? I want my baby. I want to hold him in my arms, nurse him, see him grow, watch as he takes his first steps. I want to see him become a person. I guess I'm just a mother at heart."

"You keep saying *him*. How do you know it's a boy?"

"I just think it's a boy, that's all," replied Ellen. "It's a feeling. I don't know for certain. If it's a girl, that's fine too."

"No, girls are better. My aunt used to say girls are sugar and spice and everything nice and boys are slugs and snails and little gray mice. In my experience she's right. And she said baby boys squirt up at you when you change them. Disgusting."

"Either way, boy or girl, it'll be fine. I just have a feeling it's a boy."

Bonnie shook her head. "You're amazing. You sound as though this is the most wonderful thing that could happen."

"It happened. I'll make the best of it. And who knows, maybe it is the most wonderful thing . . . ." Ellen was surprised to see tears welling up in Bonnie's eyes. "Bonnie. What's wrong?"

Bonnie squinted the tears out of her eyes. "N-Nothing," she replied, stretching an arm to the coffee table and tugging a tissue loose from a box of Kleenex.

"It's certainly nothing if its pity for me," declared Ellen, "I tell you I don't need it."

"N-No, I was just thinking . . . remembering . . . ." She stared at Ellen with wide eyes. "I never told you. I-I had a baby. When I was sixteen." She would have said more except a sob caught at her throat, followed by another, forcing her to silence.

*　　*　　*

The memory, stirred up by Ellen's pregnancy, had been pressing itself periodically over the past few weeks into Bonnie's consciousness. A painful memory, a white blur of ache in the dark recesses of her mind. Bonnie would have preferred for it to remain *away*, but it chose otherwise, an indistinct recollection except for the image of her father. His face, his enraged face, part of the overall remembrance, was acid-burned forever sharp into her brain.

She was sixteen, and scared half out of her wits at the sight of the alteration taking place before her eyes on her father's face. Anger, a frightful terrible anger, jumped onto his features immediately after she revealed her secret to him, and the sight shattered any small hope she had for gentleness from him. Alarm filled her heart as he screwed up his eyes and glared at her, as she watched the slow deliberate manner in which he rose out of his chair and, standing, approached her with what seemed to her to be nothing less than the threat of murder in his eyes. "Daddy – please – " she pleaded, backing away from him, her hands held out in front of her as though she was a traffic cop holding a truck convoy at an intersection. He ignored her and her upraised hands, grabbed her shoulders tightly and shook her hard, as if he wanted to shock the second life she now held right out of her. She thought her head would snap off her neck. "D-Daddy – p-please."

He stopped, but only to throw her away from him, his face now becoming a visage of absolute disgust, looking as though he no longer wanted to touch something dirty, flinging her away so hard that when she hit the wall behind her it knocked the wind out of her. "Is that what I raised," he growled. "A slut, a filthy little whore!" His hard callused hand whipped through the air and struck her hard on the cheek. A weak cry of pain escaped from her, the sound of a small mouse caught in the jaws of a tomcat.

He struck her again, harder, this time closing his hand into a fist, seeking heavier damage. The inside of her head exploded with the force of the punch and blood began to pour from her mouth over her chin. She was dazed for a half-minute, and then, her eyes able to focus once more, she saw that her father's expression had become one of shock, surprised as he was by the blood he'd drawn from his daughter. That shock was her savior, her rescuer from further harm, for it kept him from delivering another blow. Perhaps many more.

He turned, presenting his back to her. "A damned whore," he hissed, and then he stepped away, a final step away from her, for he never reversed it, he never came back.

Bonnie ran from the room, the walls of which were now wavy lines though the water of her tears, fleeing from the house in which she lived, the house in which she was born, the place suddenly remade into a place of fright and apprehension.

She returned much later, but only because she had to. There was, for the time, no other place she could go.

*　　*　　*

"Don't cry, Bonnie," murmured Ellen consolingly, wondering what in heaven's name was making her friend so sad. "What's wrong?"

Bonnie dabbed at her eyes with the tissue. "I'm just being stupid," she declared, her voice containing a layer of self-reproach. She sniffed twice and blew her nose, then, in the tone of one finalizing a decision, said, "I want to tell you about it." Her hand, trembling, pulled another tissue from the box. "Yes, I do." Then, lifting her head and turning her body so as to be facing Ellen, she began:

"I think I told you I'm from a place in North Dakota. No? I thought I did. Well I am. A place called Valley City. All my family's friends were prim and proper which doesn't mean they were proper at all. It just means they kept their dirty laundry out of sight. I was sixteen and thought I was in love. He was eighteen and seemed so grownup. God, how beautiful he was. Physically beautiful. Like Rock Hudson. We went out a lot, in his sedan mostly, and parked and made out. Well, he was getting frustrated and I was getting tired of always stopping him, you know. I wanted to do it as much as he wanted to. Does that sound horrible? Well, it's true. So one night we did. After that first time there was no stopping us. I mean we were like two rabbits in heat. He'd peel my clothes off me almost anywhere we could be alone. For three months," Bonnie tossed an impish grin to Ellen even as she continued to dab at her damp cheek with the tissue, "I have to say it was great.

"Then I got knocked up and everything changed. When I told him he just stood and looked at me. I could just about see the gears turning in his head like it was made of clear plastic. He was thinking: Uh oh, how can I get out of this? I suddenly felt like an idiot. I got angry and demanded he marry me."

"And he said no. How terrible for you," remarked Ellen.

"No, he said yes. But you're right, he meant no. He promised he'd marry me but he didn't mean it. Said it just to shut me up. Still I believed him. Maybe because I wanted to. Because I had no other choice. After that night, he avoided me like the plague. I swear – I thought he really loved me. Wasn't I a little moron?" A sad smile fluttered upon Bonnie's mouth and then was gone.

"A few days later, I called him to set a date for the wedding. That's when I learned he left home. Just packed up and was gone – poof. I tell you *that* hit me like a ton of bricks. He's gone and I'm pregnant, sixteen and still in school. I was scared, really scared. What was I going to do? I thought of giving myself an abortion, even had the hanger in my hand, but that was scary too. I thought I'd kill myself. Or it would hurt. I don't like to hurt. Not even a little bit. Finally I got up the nerve to tell my dad. My mother was dead then, died a couple of years before. When I told him, he – hit me – " Bonnie's lower lip quivered as these last words tumbled out of her mouth. "He hit me so very hard. And the way he looked at me. That hurt too. I remember feeling as though I . . . I was *disappearing*, right in front of his eyes, even though I was still standing there. He called me a filthy whore – and looked at me like I was . . . less than dirt."

"Oh, Bonnie," murmured Ellen. "I'm sorry." Ellen pushed herself along the rug, went to her friend and draped an arm around her.

"I ran out of the house," continued Bonnie, wiping some tears from her cheeks. "I had no place to go so I ended up at the park, sitting on a bench. I cried – cried a long time. Later of course I went home. He was in the kitchen, sitting at the table, having a drink. He looked at me but didn't say anything and neither did I. I went up to my bedroom and threw myself onto my bed. I cried all night, El, my pillow was soaked through with my tears that night.

"I wanted an abortion. I begged my dad to let me have one but he wouldn't hear of it. Eventually I went to my aunt's house, in Illinois, and had the baby. I-I gave it away. Let it be adopted." Bonnie stared thoughtfully at her feet for a few seconds. "I hated my father then," she said at last. "I loved him but hated him too. But I think he was right about me having the baby. *Now* I think that way. But he could have been – nicer – to me then, couldn't he Ellen? I mean he treated me afterwards like I was nothing to him. Like I was less than nothing."

Ellen thought of her own father and how much she loved him. *He* would have been kinder. "Yes, Bonnie, he could have been nicer to you. It must have hurt you very much – for him to treat you like that."

"Me and him . . . we don't talk anymore . . . ." There passed a few seconds of silence, then Bonnie, attempting to change emotional gears, dismissed the topic with an abrupt wave of her hands. "Well, I've turned this into a cheery little den, haven't I? I'm sorry, El." She took another swallow of wine from her glass.

"It must be terrible to have a child out in the world somewhere and not be able to see it," said Ellen.

Bonnie smiled after she wiped her mouth with the back of her hand. "Terrible? No. Sometimes I do get curious a little and – " she shrugged, " – and think about it, wonder what he looks like. It was a boy. If he looks like me. If he's happy. Things like that. But terrible. No. Not terrible. But enough talking about me. Let's talk about you. I want to tell you that I think you've been great through this thing. Your husband leaving and all. God, you're stronger than I was. I don't think I could go through what you're going through and not go all to pieces."

Ellen frowned at the compliment. *Strong? Me?* She didn't believe it, not totally. She knew only too well how much she'd been frightened at the beginning, how much weeping she'd done. *Not go to pieces? I cried my heart out on the bathroom floor for God's sake* "Don't be anointing me for sainthood. No Bonnie. You'd be as strong as me or more so. And I don't deserve praise. Not a bit of it. Not for being a little fool. Let's face it, I'm just an Irish hick who fell for a line of blarney from the first good-looking tinker who came along and paid her a little attention. Not much to praise in that. I'm in a bit of a fix, yes, but no worse than many others and still better off than many. And from here on I'll do the best I can with what happened. Which is what we all try to do anyway, isn't it? What else is there for us to do? No, I'm not brave. I'm not strong." She inhaled, a deep sigh, and, with a shrug of her shoulders, added, "No, I'm just getting on with it. With living, that is. Just getting on with the business of living."

Chapter Twenty-eight

Ellen rubbed her belly, now rounded and swollen as a balloon, and smiled. Beneath the skin upon which her hand rested was new life, life yet unborn, floating in time, but soon to emerge to be held, to grow and walk, to smile and frown, to live and breathe. She thought of her parents, of her mother and father. Would there be a resemblance to them? A kind of reappearance of their generous natures, their intelligence, their courage? Ellen hoped so.

"The doctor just today," spoke up Ellen suddenly, "decided I might be carrying twins. He believes he's hearing two heartbeats in me."

Teresa's mouth dropped open. "Twins? Dear God in – I don't know whether to laugh or cry. Well, it's possible of course. Mum was a twin and they say twins jump every generation. Goodness. What a burden."

They were in Rose's apartment, seated at the kitchen table. Their sister Teresa had come down from 78th Street to visit Rose this day and it so happened that Ellen was visiting too. Rose was standing, busy at the counter, preparing three cups of tea. She came up beside Ellen, leaned down and gave her sister a kiss on the temple. "Twins," she said in a voice so soft it was almost a whisper, looking down at Ellen with her gentle eyes, "how wonderful for you."

How powerful simple words can be at times! Rose's "how wonderful" filled Ellen with a complete and profound sense of happiness, so forceful it nearly brought tears to her eyes. She looked again at her swelling middle. *Yes,* she decided, agreeing with Rose's soft words. *How wonderful. How perfectly wonderful.*

*   *   *

It was near the end of the eighth month of her pregnancy that the lives within her were suddenly threatened, as was her own.

Late on a lazy Sunday afternoon, Ellen lounged alone on the couch, Bonnie being out at rehearsals for a new play, with the TV turned on for company and with a copy of the Daily News on her lap. She offered her attention to both television and paper, glancing away from the TV now and then to scan an article that caught her attention in the paper. Ellen's eyes had just been snared by a story about Richard Nixon's wife, Pat, when she was suddenly jerked violently forward by a slash of furious pain that cut across her abdomen, a sneak attack delivered by a berserk invisible knife wielder.

"Ahhhhh!" she screamed as the agony hit her. Her hands leaped instinctively to her middle, wanting to protect what was inside. The newspaper dropped from her lap to the floor with a flutter.

The pain, carrying no sympathy within it but rather a lunatic's joy for inflicting hurt, increased as she doubled over. She cried out again, her eyes squeezing themselves shut as though they believed the hurting could be stopped by denying themselves sight of the world. She inhaled deeply and held her breath as the torment tore at her, ripping at her from side to side. The world transformed to all searing pain for a few moments and then, blessedly, as abruptly as it came, the pain was gone, vanished, leaving Ellen gasping and stunned by its hit-and-run assault against her.

Oh God – Ellen's heart pounded in her chest with fright. *Something's wrong!* She stared at the floor in front of the talking television set without looking, her mind shuttering her eyes to her surroundings as she concentrated upon the meaning of her pain. *God! Please God. Is this normal? They say having children can be very painful. Maybe this is normal. But it hurt so much!* Her midsection felt like a sheet of paper torn first into two or three pieces and then hastily taped back together. Her mind was suddenly whirling, spinning like a confused weathervane, threatening to pull her consciousness away from her. Concerned now that she would pass out, she leaned forward and placed her forehead onto her knees. *Deep, slow breaths. In and out.* It helped, the reeling sensation drifted away and, feeling better, she straightened up. A layer of perspiration stood out on her forehead.

A few additional deep breaths eliminated the residue of the dizziness. *Maybe this pain is a signal the babies are getting ready to be born! But that couldn't be, could it? I still have a month to go. But maybe the doctors are wrong about the time. Could that be?*

Maybe I better haul myself to the hospital to let them have a look at me. With that decision instantly finalized, she stood and retrieved her purse. *Bonnie. Better tell her where I'm going.* She spent a few seconds searching for a pencil and then, after scribbling a hasty note, left the apartment. The idea of calling and asking one of her sisters to accompany her on the trip briefly entered her mind and was summarily dismissed, Ellen concluding it would just waste time to sit and wait for someone to come over. *Silly. By the time one of them gets here I could already be at the hospital. Best to just go. Get there quicker that way.* She tossed her purse over her right shoulder and left.

Ellen did not have a personal physician, the costs being too substantial. The hospital clinic was, in her opinion, just as good and cheaper to go to. Convenient too, as there was no need to make an appointment. You just went in, gave your name, sat down and waited to be called. And that was fine.

Her first experience with clinic service was in New York Hospital, located in the Upper East Side, on York Avenue. She'd gone there while living with her husband uptown and went to it twice more even after moving back downtown. It was there she learned of her pregnancy. For a time she'd thought of it as *her* hospital but its lack of convenience due to distance eroded that sense of ownership and so she became an explorer of new territory, going one day to Saint Vincent's Hospital located so much nearer on Fifteenth Street. The staff proved to be so nice, the place so efficient, that it was immediately adopted by her as her new hospital and it was now where she went when any need of something medical was required.

The day was warm, not unusual for the time of year, but a cooling breeze came from somewhere to caress Ellen's face. A hot day's kindness. Like having a pixie on the shoulder waving a fan, she thought. A group of young boys, Chinese and Italians, walked by her, all laughing about something one of them said. Ellen tensed as they passed by, fearful that one of them might accidentally push against her, and relaxed again only when they were some steps past.

She found herself walking as though threading water. *Oh, God, I feel strange, but thank God I'm not getting that dizzy feeling again.*

Her original intent was to walk the entire distance. She'd been a walker in Ireland and continued to be one in New York. But then, on the spur of the moment, unexpectedly feeling fatigued to the bone, she turned and headed toward the subway entrance a block away from where she now was. Going on foot all the way to Saint Vincent's suddenly seemed a monumental and daunting task and so she would ride the train. Hailing a taxi never occurred to her, riding in cabs being an indulgence and an extravagance. Money was too precious and, once the two babies were in the world, would be more precious still.

As Ellen approached the steps leading down from the sidewalk to the subway platform, she was suddenly aware of a chilling sensation, a physical sense of impending harm. An omen of sorts? Or an illusion? Perhaps nothing more than a bad feeling inspired by her leaving behind the sunlight and entering into the darkness of the subway?

In the next moment, the sensation passed and Ellen, assigning it to her imagination, gave it no further thought as she descended the steps. At the bottom, she went to the token booth, pushed her fifteen cents toward the attendant and purchased her token for the ride uptown.

The train roared into the station, its wheels offering a noisy irritation to the ears of those waiting on the platform for its arrival. A station announcement to passengers was made and transformed to total incomprehension by the less than adequate speaking system, which reduced the announcement to a blare of useless noise that rolled across the station like a kind of shouting surf. Ellen, frowning at the unwelcome incomprehensible clamor banging at her ears, stepped onto the train and sat down, glad to be leaving it behind.

As the train rumbled along, Ellen noticed she was suddenly hot and sweating, her stomach tumbling as though being plowed up and turned over, like the earth of the Rawdon farm at planting time. *Is it the close atmosphere of the train making me feel ill, or something else?* Her forehead was damp with perspiration again. *Almost there. One more stop.*

As the train entered the Union Square station and slowed, she stood to get near the doors to exit. Immediately upon standing, the world blurred before her eyes and her sense of balance threatened to abandon her, tugging itself away from her like a dog straining at its leash. "Oh, dear – " she peeped, surprised by the hazy gray mist suddenly surrounding her sight. Her hand shot out toward the nearby pole in an attempt to steady herself and keep from falling, and it is likely she would have succeeded had not the train at that moment begun to brake to an abrupt stop. The high pitch of screeching brakes filled the air, the keening sound causing some passengers to wince, and the cars of the train pushed with force into their couplings. Riders braced themselves against the sudden forward momentum but Ellen, her reaction slowed by the gray haze floating over her, had no chance to do the same. A yelp, a protest against falling, escaped her as she was spun off-balance and thrown roughly to the floor, hitting it with a jarring thump. A bolt of profound, searing pain ran up her spine and instantly an explosion detonated inside her skull, offering her a display of flashing electric lights. Stunned, she emitted a gasp of shock and, as though that small gasp escaping from her lips contained within it the last remaining shred of her consciousness, her eyes closed and she fell into a void of absolute darkness.

Some passengers shouted their concern as they watched the pregnant woman fall. A few kind souls rushed forward to kneel beside her, seeking to offer any assistance they could, wanting to be certain she was all right.

Ellen remained unconscious.

In less than a minute the train was moving forward again, crawling slowly once more into the station. Within the short time it had taken for the train to resume movement the concern of the passengers surrounding Ellen increased dramatically, transforming into fear and consternation for the very life of the young woman. One elderly man began to shout, pleading loudly for help, calling for a doctor to come forward if one was aboard.

"I'm going to get the conductor," mumbled a young man and immediately he went and pulled open the door leading out to the coupling and the adjoining car.

Blood could now be seen beginning to soak through the fabric of Ellen's dress.

Chapter Twenty-nine

Ellen's eyes fluttered open and she gazed wearily at a florescent light flickering in the midst of a ceiling coated with cracked and peeling paint. "Where – ?"

A disembodied female voice came from somewhere. "You're in Saint Vincent's Hospital, Sweetheart. We're going to take care of you. Do you understand?"

The hospital? I made it here, thought Ellen. *Funny, I don't remember getting off the train and walking.* "H-How . . . are my . . . babies," she asked, throwing the inquiry up to the florescent light overhead.

"You've hemorrhaged a bit. Lost some blood. But the babies are fine."

"They're – f-fine," Ellen replied weakly, a wan smile curling across her mouth and, with that sweet assurance offered her, she closed her eyes once more.

"Yes, everything's under control," came the soothing voice.

"Sweet Jesus, thank you," murmured Ellen and then, still smiling, she drifted back down into the heavy haze from which she'd just for the moment emerged. In seconds, she was once more asleep.

*   *   *

"Try and stay still. Rest. You've had a hard delivery. You've been through a lot." The voice came to Ellen from within the same haze through which she'd heard it earlier. But something was different now. Yes, the light above her was gone, and her mouth tasted odd. Her tongue had the consistency of a ball of dry cotton. A vague pain demanded her attention from below. *Am I all right?* she wondered.

Someone's in the room. Ellen was aware of movement around her. *The nurse didn't leave,* she concluded, and this time was capable of summoning the energy, the strength, to turn her head, wanting to put a face to the gentle, reassuring voice. There she was. A plump tired face, framed with glistening blue-black hair pulled straight back. The face returned her gaze and offered her a smile that was somehow tender and severe at the same time. "Hello there," the nurse said simply. "How're you feeling?"

"Uh, good, I guess," replied Ellen, not certain at all how she was feeling. "How are the babies?"

"They're fine. The little darlings. They're small. Just a little bit under four pounds each. That's what they get for being impatient. But they're healthy. That's what counts."

"M-My God. So tiny . . ." Then, with a smile, "But they're all right."

"Yes, and you need to sleep. So close your eyes."

"Can I see them?"

"They're premature and so we've got them in incubators for now. You rest and you'll see them soon enough."

Ellen's heart was as happy as a child entering its first ice cream parlor. *They're healthy! My babies are healthy!* The elation lasted only seconds, being no match for the weight of the powerful fatigue filling her. "Yes, I . . . am tired . . . really . . ." she murmured, turning her head away from the nurse. She ceased to resist the desire of her eyes to shut and let the weariness inside her have its way. By the next tick of the clock she'd drifted off to sleep again.

*   *   *

She slept only for an hour or so. When she woke again, the haze that surrounded her previously had all but dissipated. The world, as well as Ellen's own thoughts and emotions, formerly filtered by that haze, were in focus once again. She turned her head and saw a white curtain, pulled halfway down the bed, separating her from wall and window. On her right was another bed. Empty. *I'm in a hospital room,* determined

Ellen. *I hope I'm all right. I don't feel sick. Did something happen to me when I had my babies?*

My babies. With that thought a great spiral of emotion manifested itself within her and her eyes glowed with happiness, reflecting that inner emotion. *My babies! My babies!* The thought filled her with fire and excitement and, fueled by that excitement, she lifted her head from the pillow upon which it rested, pushed herself up and twisted herself around, climbing out of the bed. *My babies.*

I'm dressed in a hospital gown, she noticed. *What happened to my things? Where's my dress? My purse?* The questions came and were dismissed. It didn't matter right now. *My babies. I want to see my babies.*

Walking on bare feet and still unsteady legs, Ellen made her way out of the room and down the corridor, hoping to find the way to the hospital nursery or, failing that, to find a nurse to point out the way to her. The hall's black linoleum was cold to the soles of Ellen's bare feet. The walls were covered with cream-colored tiles halfway to the ceiling. Her nose inhaled the odor, the clean odor, of disinfectant. Overhead were a series of long fluorescent tube lights that lit the corridor too brightly. Ellen saw, on the wall, a sign bearing a small arrow pointing the direction to the nursery, to her children. *That way.*

There they are. Ellen's heart leaped and trembled inside her as her eyes first fell upon her babies, gazing through the large plate-glass window and over the rows of other new-borns in their cribs to the back of the nursery, to the incubators against the wall.

There they are. She could see their faces, their bodies, so tiny, so frail and helpless, each in a separate incubator. One was on his back, his arms at his side, the other curled up in a ball. Each asleep in their isolette. A rush of overwhelming love for both of them rose up inside her, flooding her, a geyser of love having its origins in her holy soul. She suddenly longed desperately to pick them up, to hold them, to caress them, understanding at the same time that, for now at least, she couldn't do those things. She had to content herself with staring at them through the glass. She couldn't hold them. Not yet, but soon.

"There you are, you bitch!"

Bonnie. Ellen turned to the voice with a smile on her face. "Hello to you too."

Bonnie came up to her. "You leave me a note telling me you went to the hospital. You scared me half to death," she complained. "I thought I'd find you half dead and here you are looking fine. The least you could be is on death's door so's I wouldn't feel stupid rushing up here." She frowned and then her face went through a sudden convolution of expression, shifting rapidly to concern. "You *are* OK, right?"

Ellen's smile widened as she nodded her head. Then she placed her hand on her stomach and rubbed it a bit, wanting to draw Bonnie's attention to it.

"Holy crap!" exclaimed Bonnie. "Your belly's gone!" With that she grabbed Ellen by the shoulders. "You had the babies! You had the babies!" She was bouncing up and down now as though the soles of her shoes had become springs. She pulled Ellen to her, gripped her in an emotional hug for a few seconds and then, releasing her, turned toward the glass window. "They're in there, aren't they? Which ones? Where are yours? Oh, that one can't be yours," she proclaimed, her eyes descending to a baby very near the window. "Look at the black mop of hair on its head. And that nose! A bugle. Oh Lordy."

"That's one of mine," said Ellen.

Bonnie's eyes widened as she turned to face Ellen. "Oh I'm so sorry, El. I-I didn't mean – It's beautiful. Really. It's – "

"I'm only fooling. Mine are in the back."

Bonnie slapped Ellen on the top of her arm. "You bitch. Playing with me. You've got a mean streak, you know that?" Then she turned back to look through the glass. "Oh, those two. How sweet. Look at them. So small. But they are beautiful. Look at their little faces. They're all right, aren't they?"

"They're too small, but fine otherwise." Ellen placed a hand on the glass. "Oh," she said, "I suddenly feel a little woozy."

"Of course you do," came back Bonnie, concern landing on her face once more. "You just had two babies. You're probably not even supposed to be out of bed. Is that so? Should you be walking around like this?"

"I don't know. I was told to rest – "

"So of course you're walking around. Come on, we'll go back to your room. Goodbye, little babies, we'll see you later."

Ellen bid goodbye to her babies with a smile and a loving glance that pressed against the window like a kiss, leaving them with a small ache in her heart as a large part of her wanted to keep her babies at least within her sight if not in her arms.

"Goodness," she piped up as she and Bonnie began to walk, "I haven't told my sisters yet. They don't even know I'm in the hospital. I'd better call them. Is there a pay phone here?"

"Look, you give me the numbers and I'll call. You get back to bed. Look at you. Your face is white as a sheet and you're walking like somebody's great grandmother." Bonnie shook her head. "People think *I'm* crazy. You come down here all by yourself, don't tell anyone except for leaving me a note, a note that scared the living heebie-jeebies out of me, and people think I'm crazy."

"I'm sorry," said Ellen. "But I've gone to the hospital by myself before. I didn't think this time was any different. I didn't want to bother everyone if I came up here and just went home again. I didn't know everything was going to happen so fast. I don't even know what happened to tell the truth. I-I can't remember most of it."

Ellen lay back in bed and placed her head on the pillow. "Only a couple of weeks and then I'm gone." she said.

"Gone? Why? What – ?"

"Gone from the apartment. What we talked about," replied Ellen. "Me, moving in with my sister, Rose."

"Oh, that. Yeah. I know." Her eyes started to tear up. "Why'd you bring that up now? God, I'm going to miss you."

"I'll miss you too, Bonnie, but as I said it's got to be, for the children's sake. Rose is home all day and she can just as easily watch her kids and my two as watch hers alone. Have you got any potential new roommates yet?"

"No, I haven't even asked anyone yet."

Ellen chuckled. "Bonnie, always the last minute. If you need help with the rent after I'm gone, I can help you out until you get a roommate."

"What? No way. No freaking way." She wiped a tear from her cheek. "Now you've got me all mushy. God, I'm going to miss you.

You're the best roommate I've ever had. The others were too much like me. I can't live with people like me. I don't know how you could do it."

"It's easy. You're a good person. Better than you give yourself credit for. Look, I won't exactly be leaving America. We can still get together, after I move, can't we? Now and then?"

"This is supposed to be a happy day. And now look, you're making me cry." She rummaged through her own purse and produced a small pen and a pad of paper. "Here, write your sisters' phone numbers down."

"Ellen took the pen and pad and did as requested while Bonnie stood wiping tears from her cheeks.

"All right," said Bonnie as she accepted the pad and pen back. "I'm going out to call your sisters – " She made a gesture toward the door leading out of the room and to the hall. " – I'll be back in a minute." Her hands continued to wipe tears from her eyes as she turned and walked out of the room.

She's a good friend, thought Ellen, as she watched Bonnie leave. It was then, with that thought, that she realized how altered her life would be. Friends, her family, even her own wants and dreams, were now relegated, through the birth of her twins, to a lesser level of importance in her life. Her babies came first. Now and always.

She turned onto her side and pressed her face into the pillow, like her dog Tinker used to do when pushing his nose into her stomach, seeking to be petted. *I should stay awake,* she told herself, *Bonnie'll be back, but I'm so tired . . . .*

Thank you God, she prayed. *For my children being healthy. Thank you.*

As she closed her eyes, she saw the first vision of an approaching dream: The hill in Ireland that was once her favorite spot, the trees and rocks coated on their edges with gold from a setting sun, yellow syrup highlighting the contours of the landscape and the sparkling water beyond, stretching out as far as the eye could see. *God was there. On that hill. And God is here as well.* They say God is everywhere, but Ellen knew that couldn't be true. God was where love existed, where need existed and where prayers were spoken to Him from the heart. That wasn't everywhere. Not at all.

But it was here, today, in this hospital room.

She closed her eyes and smiled as a vision of herself as a young girl filled her head, a young girl running once more to the top of her hill, laughing as she ran, filled with the joy and pleasure, the gift, of simply being alive.

Chapter Thirty

Ellen waited until Bonnie had finished kissing her boyfriend goodbye before coming out of the bedroom. During the night, she'd felt at times she should put ear plugs in the ears of her newborn twins, to keep them from hearing the sounds of physical pleasure that poured through the wall. *Funny,* she thought, *how our sense of morality becomes more important regarding our children.*

She was home, Bonnie's apartment still her home for now, but was increasingly anxious to leave. She'd be glad to finally move in with Rose. Part of that gladness was the sense of security living with her sister would grant her. Rose could help with the children much more than Bonnie was capable of doing. Also, Rose was family and was, like Ellen now, a mother of children. Ellen understood for the first time in her life what that word truly meant. Mother. She had created new life and so was no longer an individual, but rather a living extension of her own creation. She wanted so much to protect her new twins, to have them grow up fine, to have Life treat them well. Rose and she had more in common now then did she and Bonnie.

Ellen felt as though she'd crossed over an unseen threshold and entered into another world, a world entirely separate from the one in which Bonnie continued to exist, her friend remaining on the other side of the doorstep.

Only when she heard the front door of the apartment close, did Ellen step out of her bedroom. Bonnie turned to her with sparkling eyes, her complexion flushed, ecstatic. If her eyes had legs they'd have been kicking like Radio City Rocketts in their sockets. "Hello, El. Isn't he dreamy?"

"He seemed nice," replied Ellen, not stopping to talk but going straight to the kitchen to prepare a cup of morning coffee. "You didn't do much dreaming last night, did you?" There was an undercurrent of reprimand in Ellen's voice.

"Did you hear us?" asked Bonnie, the smile remaining on her face.

"Did I hear you? I think the whole building heard you. I looked out the window once last night and I swear I saw the moon put its fingers in its ears."

Bonnie laughed. "Oh, poop, I wasn't that bad." Her eyes fell onto the clock on the wall above the sink. "Oh no, look at the time. I've got to get to work." With that, Bonnie rushed back into her own room, reappearing minutes later just as Ellen was sitting at the table with her coffee.

"I'm off," she told Ellen. "Have a good one. I'll see you later. God, you're lucky, you get to stay home."

I'm lucky . . . . Ellen took a sip of her coffee as the front door opened and closed. Quiet reigned for a moment, but only for a moment, as almost immediately after Bonnie's departure the twins began to cry. First one, then the other, apparently in sympathy of the first. Their cries had the effect of a gravitational pull upon Ellen and she immediately abandoned her coffee to go straight to her wailing babies.

A new mother's dilemma: How to soothe and comfort *two* crying babies at the same time? A dilemma Ellen still hadn't resolved to her satisfaction. They shared the same crib and Ellen talked softly to both, leaning over one of the barred sides, not picking either baby up but gently stroking first one and then the other as they lay side by side bawling. Her desire was to gather both of them to her but how do you hold two babies at the same time? And she didn't want to choose one over the other. To hold one and leave the other in its crib seemed unfair. At least while they were crying.

Her soft voice worked magic and in just moments the twins' dual assault on her ears faded. They quieted down and stared up at her with their big and beautiful blue eyes. Wearing only their diapers, their bellies and chests bare, Ellen thought she could see their little hearts beating, barely perceptibly beneath the skin and small ribs. They were identical, each a mirror image of the other and Ellen, unable to distinguish between them, had resorted to painting red the toenail of the big toe of one with nail polish, the baby she'd named Thomas, so as to keep track of their identities.

The name Thomas was selected because she liked it. The other she christened Philip, after her father.

"Well, boys, now that you've calmed down, I'll tell you a story." The two round faces looked up at her as though understanding her words. "It's one my father told me a long time ago. Want to hear it? Very well, I'll tell it. It starts with a rhyme: There once were two cats in Kilkenny. Each thought there was one cat too many. So they fought and they hit. They scratched and they bit, 'til excepting their nails, and the tips of their tails, instead of two cats there weren't any.

"If you haven't guessed yet, it's about two cats living in Kilkenny – you too boys aren't going to fight like that, are you? Anyway, these cats lived way back when, in the days of Cromwell. Who's that, you ask? Well you go to school and study and you'll find out. Well, these two cats didn't like each other at all. Not at all – "

Ellen's narration was interrupted by the doorbell. "That's Mrs. McGuire, boys. She's going to the store for us again. Isn't that nice of her? I'll be right back. Don't start your crying again until I get back."

The McGuires were a family residing directly across the hall from Ellen and Bonnie, replacing Warren the transvestite who'd moved out weeks ago. Maureen McGuire was a stout, pleasant middle-aged woman who had three boys of her own, all teenagers now, a woman who understood the difficult demands placed upon new parents. Difficulties she rightfully concluded were multiplied by the fact that Ellen was alone and so didn't have the help of a husband. In calling upon Ellen to congratulate her for the birth of her babies, she'd volunteered to pick up whatever Ellen needed when she went to the stores. Ellen protested, not wanting to be an imposition, but the kind lady was as stubborn as she was and wouldn't hear of it. It wasn't any trouble, the sweet lady insisted, and, after Ellen heard for the third time "I will not take no for an answer" she put aside her Rawdon independence and agreed to let the woman help her.

"Shopping list, shopping list – where?" mumbled Ellen. "In the kitchen," she proclaimed, recalling where she'd left her list of needed things, and ran to retrieve it as the bell buzzed once more.

Mrs. McGuire's smile was dominated by her perfect and pristine white teeth. *Are they false?* wondered Ellen each time she spoke to her. "Morning, Maureen," she said, greeting her neighbor as she opened the door. "How're you today?"

"Just fine. Off to the market. Do you need anything?" In response to this expected query, Ellen extended to Maureen the written list of items. "Please and thank you," she said.

"Are you feeling all right?" inquired Maureen, scrutinizing Ellen's face as she accepted the list. With a frown, she lifted her purse, opened it and shoved the paper into the midst of the paraphernalia it held.

"Sure, fine." came back Ellen.

"You look feverish," stated Maureen, still frowning. "Are you sure?"

"No really, I'm fine," insisted Ellen. "I was just running to answer the door. Maybe I got a little red in the face."

"I'll pick you up a little flu medicine," declared Maureen. She was, as Ellen was quickly learning, a woman who, having determined that something was so, could not be easily veered from her point of view. Ellen smiled approvingly in response. Best at times to win by acceding. "Thank you. Actually now that you mention it, I do feel a little funny," she fibbed, offering a placating prevarication. "A bit of a temperature."

"Didn't I tell you?" said Maureen, beaming at her. "Mother knows best. With three children and a husband who never complains, God bless him, I have to notice these things. All right, dear, I'll be back shortly."

"Bye, and thanks again," said Ellen as she shut the door. *Now where was I? The story, that's right. The Kilkenny Cats.*

Her father had told her the tale more than once. But it wasn't until she was much older that he'd explained the facts behind the playful rhyme, telling her of the blood sport practiced by English soldiers stationed at Kilkenny. For sport, they'd bind two cats together by knotting a length of cord around their tails, then throw them over a clothesline or a tree branch so they'd be hanging next to each other by their tails, swinging on the rope. The cats, so suspended, would then fight and claw each other until one or both was killed. Brutality was the truth behind the rhyme. But the tale as told to her by her father had none of that, being just a pleasant story of two cats who didn't get along and so plotted pranks against each other. A humorous morality tale for a child. Of course her babies were too young to understand what she was saying to them now, but she enjoyed telling them stories anyway. It made her feel somehow closer to her father. She could almost hear his soft voice in her ear speaking the very words she was now repeating to her babies. There was a kind of connection of generations with her telling the twins her father's stories, as though he was himself speaking to them, with her being the link between Da and the twins.

Ellen returned to the bedroom and, finding that both babies were now sound asleep, immediately retreated on tiptoes, softly closing the bedroom door shut as she left.

The doorbell buzzed once again. *Mrs. McGuire again? I hope she doesn't make me see a doctor for the fever she thinks I have.* Ellen chuckled at her own silent comment as she stepped to the door.

The person Ellen saw when she opened the door was absolutely the last person on the entire planet she expected to see. There, standing before her thoroughly stunned and astounded eyes, was John Madden, clad in suit and tie and looking essentially the same as on the first day she'd ever set eyes upon him.

Here was the thief and liar she'd been foolish enough to marry almost a full year earlier, a man who remained, in the eyes of the law and of the Church if not in her heart, her husband. Her heart faltered and fell inside her at the sight of him, dropping like a heavy stone to the bottom of her stomach.

"Hello, El," he said, presenting her with the audacity of a sunny smile. "Good to see you again."

Chapter Thirty-one

John had emerged from sleep that morning to be greeted by the ghostly image of his own poverty as seen through the after-haze of the drunkenness he'd enjoyed the previous night. Through bleary eyes he gazed at the faded, grimy walls of the cheap hotel room in which he'd slept.

For three nights he boarded here and it irritated him that he could afford no better, for of course he deserved better. The best. He had the best coming to him. Nothing but. Life was unfair. To him.

Rising up, he shook his head in an attempt to dislodge the fuzziness clinging to his mind. It remained, sticking to his thoughts like lint to a shirt crackling with static electricity. Not until he dragged himself into the shower and felt the hot water sluicing over his body did he at last begin to leave behind the effects of the hangover.

He hated being down on his luck, being low on money, hated the desperation of it, feeling at such times like an army grunt on the front lines in the midst of battle, a grunt down to his last bullet and staring at a line of attacking enemy soldiers. All holding IOUs instead of rifles. It wasn't right! He deserved better. The best! He deserved the best. Nothing but. He grumbled another curse, angry at the bias of Life that caused him to suffer unfairly, to suffer through no fault of his own. *I deserve better.*

John Madden was a man with a closet for a soul, a closet containing an assortment of masks and costumes that he could, at any time, take off a hook, put on and wear. He could be what he had to be, whenever it pleased him or when advantageous to him. One of his costumes was the silk of love and charm and it was that costume he would clad himself in today, for it was necessary today. Love and charm, that would be the attire he'd have on when he approached Ellen once again.

She was, after all, his wife and she loved him. *I'm the father of her kids. That has to get me points!* And having the children would make her anxious, no, *desperate,* to have him back. *Yeah, she'll jump at the chance to have me back.* Of that he was convinced. In his mind he held an idea of exactly how the reunion would take place, of how she would look as she yielded herself into his arms, so very grateful for his return.

Regarding money, she was a good saver, was Ellen. John had learned that about her at least. And she'd time enough in a year to put aside some riches since he'd left her. He wouldn't get much from her, a few hundred dollars, maybe a thousand. But it would be quick money and it was better than the few nickels he now held in his hands.

He actually married her! He hadn't intended to. Not at first, but as the joke went on, it amused him to consider it. To walk Ellen down the aisle. To play a different kind of game.

Comical, actually, but as it turned out, it was also the best way to get the most money out of the woman.

For the last few days, he'd been watching the apartment building in which his wife lived, careful to avoid being seen in return, and, in so doing, gained a knowledge of her schedule. He knew when she was alone.

And there was no new man in her life. No doubt because she was still pining away for him.

*　　*　　*

"You!" blurted Ellen at the sight of him, not calling him by name. And how much significance was contained that instinctual "You" that burst from her, the word uttered as it was with such complete disdain. That single declaration spoke volumes about the visceral contempt Ellen now felt for the man.

John Madden's attempt at charming Ellen into a feigned reconciliation, of winning her back for the short period of time needed to enable him to steal from her once more, was doomed right from the moment of Ellen's pronouncement of that particular "You". But of course John Madden didn't understand that at the time, and wouldn't have accepted the truth of it even if he did.

He greeted her, his face wearing his best confident little-boy smile. A proven winner.

A cold spot of confusion sat at the base of Ellen's skull. *Why is he back?* She stared at him trying to understand his presence while he smiled engagingly at her, a hint of hesitant regret in his eyes. *Why is he back?*

John was now talking to her. *What is he saying? Something about being sorry. I'm sorry for hurting you.* Ellen could hardly make out his words, so loud was the roar of the surf pounding upon her heart and mind. It rushed at her like waves blown by a raging storm onto a beach.

A little bit awkward now, he continued to attempt to set the tone for their reunion, still affecting charm but faltering now beneath her silence, beneath the glare of her burning eyes. Her eyes bothered him, enough to make him stumble in his speech as he offered Ellen his practiced expressions of his pretend-sincere regrets for hurting her.

Then the storm inside her was gone, and she was standing straight and tall in its departing wake. She studied him, watching him attempting to win her over, her eyes turning cold as gravestones.

Talk. Empty words. Meaningless words.

What's he saying? What does it matter? She saw the intensity of his doubt increasing beneath the ice of her gaze. How dare he believe that he could be so nonchalant regarding his betrayal of her! *How dare he come back!*

"Please, El," he implored her, wanting to say something winning, striving to erase the hardness he saw now residing in her eyes. "Please, it wasn't easy for me to come here. Please, I was wrong. Horribly wrong. Please, I want us to start over. I thought I could leave you, but I can't live without you, El. You're different. I can't live without you. And there's the children, El. I know they'll need a father. I had to come back, El. For you – and for them. Please."

He was shameless.

Is it possible he really thinks it would be so easy? So easy for me to forget what he did to me, to trust him again?

"Please, El. Don't look at me like that. I love you, El. I want to come back to you. I want us to be a family again."

"Do you? Want to come back?" spoke up Ellen at last, the words hitting at the air between them like the swipe of the blade of a knife.

She seems so strong, thought John as he gazed at her. Where was the naive tenderhearted farm girl he'd married? "I want it to be the way it was between us, El. Remember how it was? I never really meant to hurt you."

His apologies, his pleas to her, were not having the effect he'd imagined. *What's wrong?* He had visualized her to be pining for him, wanting nothing more than his return, praying for him to reappear. It served as an illustration of how little he knew of Ellen's character that he could now be taken aback by the disdain so evident in her face, in her glaring eyes, in the stern cold way she spoke to him.

"You never meant to hurt me?" returned Ellen, raising her voice. "Nothing! Nothing can be the way it was! Nothing! Liar! Thief! You left me!" She was shouting at him now. "I was pregnant with your children and you left me! And robbed me as you were leaving! I had to go to the hospital – alone – " Tears gleamed on the rims of Ellen's eyes but she willed them back, banning them by the fiat issued by her pride and anger, not wanting to show weakness in front of him.

"I want to come back, Ellen," he insisted. *God, she's making me work for this.* "When I left I didn't know you were going to have my kids. That's why I'm back. I just learned about them. I can't abandon them. They'll need me. You'll need me. Please understand. For our children's sake." He reached out and gripped her by the wrist, attempting to pull her closer to him and she was forced to twist her arm free from him.

"Keep your hands off me!" she screamed, her face livid with rage. For a moment John froze, fearful that someone would hear, that someone would come and throw him out of the building.

"You left me!" yelled Ellen. "Now you come strolling back, spewing sweet words like you made some kind of noble decision to come back! I don't know which is the greater insult; your leaving or your believing you can just march back when you feel like it! As though nothing happened at all! Am I supposed to be grateful to you?!" She straightened her back, standing even taller. "Well, I don't want you back! You left once and you can turn right around and leave again! Go! Go away!"

John stared at her incredulously, looking for a moment like a baby being scolded but not quite comprehending why. Not for one moment, in deciding to come here, did he believe he'd be turned away. "You want me to go?" He continued to stare at her. "But El, I love you."

"Love me. You love yourself, you mean."

"I do love you El," he protested, running his fingers through his hair like a claw. "You're the most important thing in my life. You and my kids. I had to leave to find that out. No El, I love – "

"I'm sorry it took your leaving for you to realize how important I was to you because it also made it impossible for me to ever love you again. Besides, I don't believe you have the slightest idea of what love is. Now there's nothing left to say. I want you to go. If you don't I'll call the police."

"Ellen, I-I've never seen you like this." John was unsure how to proceed and gazed at her with that uncertainty evident in his eyes, still not fully accepting the fact that she really wanted him to leave. "Just go? Just get out? Is that it?" John's conciliatory tone now began to shift to disbelief and anger.

"That *is* it!" replied Ellen emphatically.

"I want to be with *my* children." He raised his own voice now.

"Your children! I was pregnant with *your* children when you walked out! I had to go to the hospital without their father being there when they were born!" Suddenly her voice cracked. "God, I wanted to die when you left. Do you know how much you hurt me? Do you have any idea?" Ellen's lips trembled with emotion. "I-I really wanted to die – "

Is this my chance? considered John. He reached out to her, thinking that perhaps it was, but was immediately pushed roughly away.

"Don't touch me!" shouted Ellen, her face twisting with bitter loathing over the contact his hands made with her. "It's the children and me now! You're not a part of us. Nor will you ever be! You're a miserable excuse of a human being! To do what you did to me! After you left, I cried. Well, I'm through crying over you. I don't want you back. I'm not that big a fool!"

"Damn *you* then," growled Madden, his eyes suddenly locking in combat with hers. "You bitch. I can see I made a mistake in thinking you had a heart."

"Oh why are you here?" cried Ellen in exasperation. "Why don't you go? Just go away. For God's sake, leave me alone!"

These last words, their heartfelt tone, struck John like a series of stones flung at his forehead. "You black-hearted bitch," he growled as he reached out and gripped her forearm tightly, hurting her, wanting to hurt her. Again she was able to pull away, although with much more effort this time, and this time grimacing with pain.

"Keep your hands off me!" Her freed hand came up as though with a will of its own and she slapped his face, hard, the sound cracking the air like the violent slamming of a door.

John's face turned red with rage. His eyes tightened with animosity as he scowled at her, the veins standing out on his neck. His hands balled up into fists so tightly it seemed he might splinter the bones of his hands. For a few seconds, they stood glaring at each other, their hostility crackling in the air between them.

Then, into the midst of their anger, came the sound of the twins bawling, the babies awakened and frightened by the commotion of the violence occurring in the next room. Ellen twisted her head toward the sound and then back to John. "Now my babies are crying. Oh, please go away. Just go!"

There was a dismissive tone in Ellen's voice that John found more infuriating than her anger in its perceived insult of him and it roused him to a new height of fury, to a ferociousness approaching irrationality. He suddenly was no longer thinking but simply desired, with all his heart, to do something to hurt Ellen, to hurt her in any way possible.

"*Your* babies?" he growled. "Your babies?!" Abruptly he rushed past her, running toward the room in which the babies were, following the sounds of their cries, pushing her so hard as he went by that she stumbled back and fell to the floor.

Suddenly a new fear pressed against Ellen's heart. "What're you doing?" she shouted to his back even as she lifted herself up from the floor and ran into the bedroom after him. When she entered, he already had possession of the twins and was holding them upside down, the ankle of a baby's leg gripped in each hand, looking like a man with two sacks of garbage searching for a trash can. The babies were bawling louder than ever, uncertain as to what was happening to them.

John lifted them high above his head as both infants, red-faced with the efforts of their cries, flailed their small arms and wailed their protest. "You think more of these two little shits than me!" he screamed, his eyes unnatural, opened wide and glittering with the momentary insanity of his rage. "These little shits mean more to you than me!"

"Put them down, John," pleaded Ellen, forcing her voice to be soft and coaxing, not wanting to antagonize him further. "Please. Put them down."

"Put them down?!" he shrieked. "Is that what you want?" A terrible grin appeared on his face and then just as quickly skittered away as a maniacal decision was made. He ran to the nearest window and, using the foot of one baby, the toenail-polished foot of Tommy, pushed it up and open, not caring that, in the act of opening the window, Tommy's head cracked hard against the glass. Luckily, the glass didn't break and there was no real harm done to the child. Not yet. Ellen stared at John, goggle-eyed, frightened to the core of her soul, fearful for the very lives of her children, for their continued existence. Seeing this madman in possession of her babies she experienced a deeper terror than she'd ever dreamed possible; every cell in her body felt as though it would explode with fright.

"Put them down?!" he screamed again, thrusting his arms and hands and the shrieking babies he held through the open window, dangling the flailing bodies of his own sons two stories above the pavement below. Bright sunlight flowed over the struggling infants. "Want me to put them down?! Is that what you want?! Is it?!"

Ellen's heart shuddered in her chest at the monstrous sight. "Sweet Jesus – " she murmured. Her knees went weak. For a moment she felt her head spin and thought she'd pass out.

Was it an effect of her briefly murmured prayer? John suddenly froze in mid-stance and his face slackened with the sudden release of his rage. Surprise flooded his features as though he was abruptly amazed to find himself where he was. In a flash he appreciated the horror of the act he was in the midst of committing and, comprehending it, slowly withdrew the children from the outside, pulling them back into the safety of the room. Silently he walked over and placed them again into their crib where, once again on their backs, they continued to bawl.

John then stumbled over to the nearest chair, walking like a drunken man, and sat down. "Look what you made me do – " he moaned, prepared to blame Ellen for his insane actions and already wallowing in self-pity. *Why won't she do what she should?* "Look what you made me do . . . ."

Ellen went directly to the twins, studying them to assure herself they were not injured. The wails of both filled the room but they were unhurt, and were safe again.

When Ellen at last released her gaze from her babies and turned to look once more at John, her eyes contained nothing but absolute naked loathing, a profound pedigreed hatred. If her eyes were lasers, John would have been reduced to ashes before he was able to draw his next breath. "Bastard!" she shrieked, and then she shot across the room, hurling herself at him, her fingers extended toward his face like the claws of a wild carnivore pouncing on prey, wanting to shred that prey to edible bits.

The nails of her fingers succeeded in raking one cheek, producing parallel lines of ragged bleeding scratches down the side of his face, before he could grab her wrists to stop the infliction of worse damage. Still she fought for the privilege, hating him now, deeply, purely, wanting only the satisfaction of tearing at his flesh, of ripping his face away down to the bone with her nails. John held her wrists tightly, holding those claws from his already damaged face, struggling to stand up and out of the chair as Ellen continued to shout a stream of curses down at him. Her raw fury stunned him.

"Stop it Ellen!" he screamed. "I'm warning you!"

But Ellen was relentless and her perfect loathing made her deaf to warnings. She continued to struggle against the grip he had on her wrists, kicking and spitting curses at him even while he held her. John, with a shouted obscenity of his own, released one wrist and swiftly struck Ellen hard with his own freed fist, striking her in the temple. She was stunned to immobility by the blow, by the sudden shock of pain filling her skull, and John took the opportunity to swing his fist once more, this time knocking her half-conscious to the floor.

She lay there at his feet, moaning her pain. The babies continued to bawl and she heard them vaguely now, as though they had been moved to another room.

He stood over her, dabbing at the torn flesh of his face tenderly with the fingertips of his hand, the same one he'd just struck Ellen with. When he pulled his fingers away, there was blood on them. *God, she really ripped me!*

"Goddamned stupid bitch." A thought came to Ellen then through her pain and shock: *He's going to kick me. He wants to kill me.*

To her blessed relief he did neither but simply repeated his name-calling. "Goddamned stupid bitch!" Having thrown this final insult down to her, he turned and walked out of the room. Ellen, still on the floor, heard the front door of the apartment slam shut.

He's gone.

Thank you Jesus. He's gone.

A minute had to go by before she could summon the power to stand and stagger to a chair, the same one John had just vacated. There she burst into tears, sobbing into the palms of her hands.

They were all crying now, mother and baby twins together, as though all were part of one large sorrow, which in fact they were.

*   *   *

John's "Goddamned stupid bitch" were the last words he ever said to her, his final farewell. After that terrible day, Ellen never laid eyes upon him again, nor did she ever hear another word spoken about him. She didn't want to see or hear of him, no longer caring if the man lived or died. Yet, in the future, almost paradoxically, she would see him many times, often observing him in those small moments when, gazing at her children, she would recognize bits of his image floating in their eyes or tucked in the corners of their mouths. In her children, there was John, a phantom in hiding, shifting like a reflection in a rippling brook, stirring beneath the surface of the faces of the two children he'd created through her.

The man had abandoned her, wounding her heart terribly, and she wanted nothing to do with him any longer, yet at the same time he'd given her everything that was now important to her, what was most important to her. John was gone, little more than a bad dream now, a despicable memory to be ignored, yet, while gone he also remained behind, residing within the bodies of her precious children. While gone, he would be with her as long as she was alive, as long as she still had eyes to see with and a heart with which to love.

Her babies, now her great joy, had come to her through a terrible sorrow. How could she not ultimately be grateful for it, that sorrow? Even while continuing to hold the man who'd broken her heart in utter contempt for what he was.

Chapter Thirty-two

Within two weeks of John's sudden reappearance, Ellen was back in Rose's apartment, her sister once again surrendering a bedroom for her benefit. She remained in Rose's apartment for the next few years, dutifully putting away what money she could for the boy's future needs, necessities that she knew would come as they grew. Money was also saved (once again) in anticipation of eventually finding a place of her own. The latter was years away. Probably, she thought, when the boys were old enough to go to school and so had less need of babysitting.

The next few years formed a landscape of relative peace, of tranquillity. Time became a topography of small hills and valleys composed of hard work and quiet love; love not from men but rather showered by Ellen onto her two little boys and offered back to her in turn by them. The twins were the focal point of her life now and she spent her days dedicated to the chore (and joy) of caring for them. With their blond hair, blue eyes and round Irish faces, she thought them to be the most beautiful creations alive on Earth.

She worked hard both at her job and then, after coming home, in spending as much time as she was able with her children, which more often than not depleted more of her energy than did work. At night, going to bed, she would sink blissfully into weary sleep in order to regain the energy necessary to wake and begin all over again tomorrow. It didn't trouble her, this almost constant sense of fatigue, indeed, a secret part of her accepted it as a friend, for, with fatigue, she became more insensate to the world existing beyond the boundaries of her work and her children. Fatigue was a protection of sorts, a shield that softened her life. Ellen's heart didn't hurt as much when she was worn out, her energy depleted. And she didn't want to hurt anymore. Being tired was better.

The final divorce decree came and she read it, neither understanding fully the words nor wanting to comprehend them, a mix of legal phrases and Latin. She threw the paper into the bottom drawer of her bureau, thankful it was delivered to her, and immediately put it out of her mind.

The boys offered her all she needed for now. She nearly jumped for joy when they, within minutes of each other, spoke their first words; she marveled at their efforts to stand and take their first steps, and was entertained by their sense of wonder at all they saw, at the impression of mystery and magic they seemed to sense existed behind the mechanisms of the world's machinery. Yes, John was there, in her babies, but she was there as well and she saw more of herself in her children each day. She often imagined that it was bits of herself, living pieces of her own heart and soul, miraculously running free of herself, living outside herself, existing in the forms of the bodies of her children.

Ellen was, in her own way, as dependent upon the twins as they were upon her, for their dependency gave her life purpose, and that purpose filled her with a courage she may otherwise have lacked. She subconsciously viewed her boys as a psychological solidity, an emotional rock in the ever-shifting sands of the world, the dishonest, hurting world. They were her true Forever Love.

As the twins got older, Ellen began sleeping on the sofa, giving the room over totally to the boys. She needed her own place, but how could she give up the help Rose offered her with the children? Who would stay with them if she moved to another place? A stranger?

Rose's own set of twins were now as close as brothers to Ellen's Tommy and Philip. The two sets of twins, one pair fraternal and one pair identical, were seen together often throughout the neighborhood, walking together on the sidewalks or climbing up fire escapes to explore the rooftops of buildings. Often, the four would appear at the firehouse across the street, Patrick's love of fire engines and firefighters showing no signs of waning as he grew older. It was he who insisted they go to the firehouse. They were welcome there by the easygoing firefighters and invited to come as often as they liked.

A few months back, after some pleading, Patrick was allowed up to the second story of the firehouse where the men slept and cooked while waiting for calls. Since that first time he'd been granted the freedom to go upstairs whenever he wanted. At times he'd run upstairs for no other reason than to slide down the fire pole, then storm up the stairs once more to do it again. He encouraged Philip and Tommy to follow him down the pole but they, being younger, thought the distance from the second floor to the first to be mountain-high. Both twins, only three years and some months old the first time the invitation was offered to them, simply stared down through the large hole in the floor and shook their heads. Got to be crazy to do that.

Some additional time was needed, a few more months, before Philip and Tommy were finally able to summon the vast courage required to jump the great chasm, the vast empty distance from floorboards to pole, and grab on tightly to the pole to slide down to the floor below. On that day, the bell of the fire engine was rung in their honor, clamoring the firefighters' pride in them.

When the twins turned five years old and started school, it was Rose who, each morning, took them to Kindergarten and who, at noon, walked back to the school to take them home again. All this while taking care of her own children as well. Ellen often, when saying her prayers at night, thanked the Lord for blessing her with Rose.

Approximately five and a half years after moving in (the second time) with Rose, a one-bedroom apartment in the same building became available for rent. It was just one floor below Rose's apartment and Ellen, hearing of its availability, rushed straight down to the superintendent to request it for herself. The super, knowing Ellen and Rose and Jimmy and liking them, put no impediment in the way of Ellen obtaining the vacant apartment, this despite the landlord specifically telling him not to rent to single women. A week later it became officially hers. A godsend and a blessing, for it offered her the perfect logistical situation. She was now able to offer Rose and Jimmy their privacy (and obtain her own) but still remain close enough so that her sister could continue to walk the twins to school and care for them while Ellen went to work.

Once burned by fire, one is more frightened by sparks. Ellen was now more cautious with men than ever before. Almost afraid of them, or, more precisely, fearful of granting them her trust. Over the years since her divorce, she went out with men only sporadically, rarely. Some of them shocked her with what they expected of her after buying her a dinner and a drink. One, learning she was the mother of two children by a previous marriage, simply got up, walked away and never called her again. All who attempted to bed her left disappointed.

Her children and her family were two of three primary pillars of support in her life. The third source of Ellen's strength was her religion, her belief in Jesus, in God. She believed with all her heart that God's compassionate love for her was real, a solid shining truth. This kind of deep belief in God is what impels humankind to be more than bones and flesh, to be more than simple chemical-based automatons as some scientists would have it; for it grants people souls with which to fill their bodies and so allows them the potential to be more than what Nature itself may offer them.

It also, at times, grants individuals more strength than they would otherwise be capable of. It did so for Ellen. She was convinced with all her heart that, with God, she would never truly be lost and alone. This profound belief was as real to her as were her cherished children, as real as the moon, the stars and the shining sun.

Chapter Thirty-three

The twins, having completed their year of kindergarten, were each thrilled to receive documentation of their achievement, a small facsimile of a diploma. They took it out, unrolled it, stared at it, put it away and then took it out again, all the way home, amazed and delighted at the sight of their names printed upon the thick paper.

How quickly they're growing up, thought Ellen. It seemed to her only yesterday that she'd ridden the subway with them still in her belly.

*　　*　　*

The summer sped by and autumn followed as quickly on its heels. The twins now entered into the First Grade at the public school to begin their true education. This was the first time the boys would be going to a full day of school (kindergarten being never more than a half-day) and Ellen, determined to be with them on their first morning, called her job to tell her boss she would be late as the sink faucet in her kitchen was broken, the sink overflowing and the apartment in danger of being flooded. She was waiting for the plumber. A lie, but to her the lesser of two crimes. The greater would be her failure to be with her boys on this momentous day.

So it was that Philip and Tommy toddled along to school accompanied by their mother, one twin on each side of her, each yellow-haired boy a mirror image of the other, both clinging onto the security of one of her hands with one chubby little fist while holding in their other hand a tin Roy Rogers lunchbox. They walked for two blocks when, turning a corner, the large school building, its windows covered with wire cages, came into view. The eyes of the twins frowned slightly at the stern sight of it, both boys becoming somewhat apprehensive at the rather severe appearance of the building in which they were to spend the largest portion of many of their future days. Staying at home instead was suddenly a more attractive alternative but neither boy gave voice to this thought as they walked with their mother toward the school.

Inside the entrance they knew their mother would leave them and they stood by a bit nervous and frightened as she spoke some words to a studious-faced, pleasant, matronly woman with gray hair. They stared about them, taking the place in. There were so many others, grown-ups and children, all of various colors, sizes and ages. One child, a third-grader two years older than the twins, seeing the two boys, stuck his tongue out at them, and then roared with laughter as though it was the funniest thing he could imagine. He continued laughing as he walked away down the hall.

Then came the inevitable. Ellen knelt down on one knee and offered to both Philip and Tommy a few words of encouragement, punctuated by a hug and a kiss. Then she stood to leave. "Be good, boys," she told them and then, tousling the blond hair of each boy and offering them both a final smile of departure, she turned and walked away, tossing them a last wave when she was a few feet distance from them. The twins returned the wave unenthusiastically, gazing at her with very doubtful eyes.

They were taken to a small pack of children their own age, and then walked with the pack to their classroom by a different matronly woman with dyed black hair. There they were assigned desks at which they sat and listened to the teacher standing and talking in front of a large blackboard soiled with smears of wiped-away chalk. At first they were attentive but then, as their uneasiness dissipated and they grew bored, they began to wiggle in their seats. The benches were of hard wood, an illogical choice by a school system seeking to keep children's attention. Bored, their rear ends tired of the wood, their minds seeking entertainment, they began to make faces at each other across the row of other children that separated them, and began giggling at their efforts.

"There'll be none of that!" came the sharp voice of the teacher, snapping like the crack of a whip in the air midway between them. Their eyes shot to the front of the room where the teacher stood. "Sit, fold your hands in front of you, and look front!"

The two boys straightened their backs and did exactly as told.

During recess they were released into the schoolyard and there were allowed to mingle with other children their own age. Being identical, they were unusual enough to be objects of curiosity. One boy and a girl even came over to investigate the oddity and the two stood silently, staring at the twins like a pair of geologists viewing an unusual rock formation.

Tommy spoke first. "Hi," he greeted them and the little boy and girl immediately returned the greeting and stepped closer. Soon the initial curiosity passed and the four were playing and laughing with each other with the simple acceptance that most children offer each other. They stayed together until recess was over and all the children were summoned back into the authoritarian atmosphere of the classroom.

Within three weeks the boys declared to their mother that they "liked very much going to school" and that their teacher, Mrs. Campfield, was not the "mean lady" they'd first determined her to be. In fact, she was "kinda nice".

As the twins had got older, Ellen tried more than once to relate to them a few of the tales her father had offered her as a child, the Irish tales and legends she loved as a child, but she soon discovered, to her own disappointment, that she had little real talent for storytelling. The words of the tales came out of her mouth like lifeless marionettes with slackened strings, strings she was incapable of pulling and tugging in just the right manner to give the puppets life. Whatever skill her father had as a storyteller, and it was more than grand, was not passed along to her, or, if granted to her initially, had since been lost. Philip and Tommy sat politely in front of her, listening to her as best they could, but were so obviously quickly bored by her attempts that she felt nothing but sympathy for them in her continuing to keep them there. Knowing they preferred the television, Ellen very soon abandoned further efforts to make them suffer. Accepting the truth that her Irish tales were so poorly told as to be sleep inducing to both listener and narrator, she released them from any obligation to listen. She didn't have the gift, it was that simple, and the Blarney castle was too far away from her now to try to improve her storytelling with a kiss to the stone.

As the twins were identical to most who saw them (Ellen could now easily tell them apart) there was confusion among the friends they'd made in school as to who was whom at any given time. As a consequence, the boys developed the habit of responding to both names, either his own or his brother's, for each boy could never be certain, when they heard the other's name, that it wasn't him who was being called. This habit only served to confuse their friends (and their teachers) even further. It was as if each boy was, in a small way, also the other.

*　　*　　*

In little more than a blink of an eye, or so it seemed to Ellen, the twins were entering into the Second Grade at school, and were now becoming more like independent little men than babies. Seven years old now, they were transforming before her eyes, growing like mung-bean sprouts planted beneath a southern sun, their eyes already up past her elbows. Their hair remained blond, beginning to turn an even brighter gold as they spent more time playing in the sun.

In the Second Grade, for the first time in their young lives, the twins were forced to fight, to defend themselves, when another boy, a classmate, bullied them to the point where a battle for honor was necessary and unavoidable.

He was a stout boy named Peter McNally, bull-necked at the age of seven. Bigger and wider than his classmates he experimented with the potential rewards of being the Second Grade Schoolyard Bully, doing so for no other reason than he was able and, by gosh, it was fun. Being the infantile tough guy was not a bad thing. Bullying others was good. What a fine thing to have others be scared of you. Better to be the lion than the lamb. Peter discovered what tyrants and oppressors have always discovered, that the fear you inspire in others could grant you an equal amount of self-gratification and sense of self-importance. Every action has an equal but opposite reaction. And that was good. Especially when the reaction was respect (out of fear) for you. Good because it made Peter feel special. He reveled in the fact that most of the other children his own age were easily intimidated by his growls and angry looks.

He was, through his bullying, transformed into a seven-year-old Napoleon, daily scanning the schoolyard as though its fences held the plains of Europe. The schoolyard was a great land to be conquered, and its varied peoples waited to be subjected to his whims.

Peter was a conqueror with, as yet, no knowledge of defeat. But his Waterloo was on the horizon, appearing to him in the form of two young boys, each fully equipped with an Irish temper and the strong backbone not to be cowed by him.

As with nations so with children, Peter always began his attack with words, and this time was no different. On a fine sunny day, in the schoolyard at recess time, he approached his newly determined enemy, walking up to them with the arrogance of the leader of the Vandals approaching the gates of a weary Rome.

"You two look like a coupl'a freaks. Lookin' alike and all. Are you freaks? You reek, freaks." A chuckle escaped him, evidence of his pride in his own wit and poetic way with words.

To his surprise, one of the boys answered him back. "And you're a big tub of lard," snapped Tommy.

"A big *stupid* tub of lard," added Philip a moment later. Neither remark was the most witty of retorts but both were sufficient on the moment to make their point. Not only did the boys answer the seven-year-old-tough back, but – insult to injury – they had the audacity to grow angry with him, both their identical faces screwing up sternly and glaring at him with a look of reprimand, a look that reminded Peter of the way his own father's face scrunched up when scolding him for misbehaving at home. This reaction was, for this budding dictator of the world, intolerable, but what to do? How best to respond?

Immediately he decided that some rougher treatment was necessary to put the two insolent upstarts in their proper places. He'd have to teach the twins a proper lesson. With that thought prodding him, he marched up to the boys and challenged them to a fight then and there, a challenge delivered with the contemptuous audacity that a fox might toss to the populace of a chicken coop (a fox that had yet to learn of the existence of farmers with shotguns).

Here was a challenge spoken with the certainty that neither of the twins would muster the courage to answer it. He was, after all, Peter the Invincible, Peter the Mighty, Peter the Ruler of the Schoolyard. All must kneel before Emperor Peter.

At first his assessment proved correct, or more correctly, circumstance offered him the *appearance* of it being correct. Both boys, never challenged to a fight before, simply stared at him, not certain at all what to do. The young Napoleon, mistaking confusion for fright, decided to push further. He went to Philip, stuck his face close to his and gave him a sudden shove so that Philip lost his balance, toppled and fell backwards, bumping his head hard on the ground. Thump! The bully pointed and laughed, enjoying the sight of the fallen boy, relishing his schoolyard victory.

But he was thinking victory before he had actually achieved it. It came as a complete and profound shock to him when, in the midst of his celebratory braying, Tommy took a step forward and, swinging as hard a punch as any seven-year-old is capable of, cracked his brother's attacker square on the nose with his fist. *Bang!* The little Napoleon's laughter ceased on the moment of the mashing of his nostrils and Peter went two, three and then four stumbling steps back, stunned, before half-falling and half-sitting on his rump. His hand leaped up to his wounded face and, taking the hand away again, his gaping eyes saw his own blood smeared red on the palm. A like smear ran across his upper lip.

"You hit me?" he hollered to Tommy in a voice that indicated plainly this was a brand new experience for him. "You hit me!"

Tommy looked at his rolled-up fist. He did hit him, didn't he? He was almost as surprised as was Peter. Perhaps his fist had done the thinking for him, the tail wagging the dog, and he was little more than a spectator to the nose-whapping punch. Immediately he was proud of what his fist had done.

Some bullies are secret crybabies and some are not. To his credit, Peter, subjected now to the same test of courage he offered the twins, proved to be the latter. In a moment he was back up on his feet and charging at Tommy like an angry goat. The top of his head rammed into the standing twin's stomach, pushing Tommy back, and then Peter wrapped his arms around Tommy's waist in the seven-year-old equivalent of a bear hug. Together the boys went tumbling to the ground and there they fought and scuffled for a minute or two before at last being separated by an irate and very upset Mrs. Campfield. She scolded them, checked all three for injury and, finding to her relief that none of the children were seriously hurt, informed them that they would all be sent directly to the principal's office and, worse punishment still, their parents would be told of their misconduct.

It was quickly determined that Peter had instigated the fight (the bully having no shortage of other students ready and willing to tattle on him) and his swift punishment followed, coming to the boy from two directions. First, from the school in the form of detention and extra homework and, second, from his father in the form of a spanking that must have had his rear-end dreaming of detaching itself from the rest of him and running away to the inner recesses of the Appalachian Mountains, there to hide in a cave so as to shield itself from any future discipline.

The double punishment quickly cured little Peter of his desire to conquer the world through intimidation. Bullying had been fun at first but now he'd learned that aggression held its dangers too. Pushing and hitting people was fine, fun even, until and unless people started pushing and hitting back. Best to live and let live. A lesson for the ages.

As occurs now and then between fierce opponents, the twins and a reformed Peter McNally thereafter became staunch and loyal friends, mutual esteem arriving even before the small injuries incurred on both sides had fully healed.

Chapter Thirty-four

The tragic day began innocently enough, just two days after the twins' eighth birthday.

The boys played in the morning, ate lunch and, at one o'clock, were laying on the rug in the living room watching one of their favorite television shows, "The Lone Ranger" with Clayton Moore, while their mother and Bonnie sat a few feet away in the kitchen, the two women chatting over cups of coffee and a plate of sugar-dusted donuts. Ellen's apartment was small, and, as the twins were growing bigger and bigger, she had to consider the need (and the cost) of obtaining a larger one. It would have to be in the same building or very nearby of course and, given that necessity, it might be years before a two bedroom became available. "By that time," opined Ellen to her friend, as Bonnie grabbed up another donut, her third, "the boys might very well be married and have children of their own."

"Why don't you go away for a few days?" suggested Bonnie, switching topics to the two free weeks that Ellen would shortly have. "You've got vacation time but you're not going anywhere. You should go away. The last few vacations all you did was hang around your apartment here."

"It's relaxing. Staying home. Vacations can be work," said Ellen. "Sometimes you come back more tired than when you went."

"Just take a couple of days. You know where you could go? Up to Newport, in Rhode Island. Just to get out of the city heat. I went there last year with a boyfriend. The beaches are nice and you should see the mansions up there. They were the summerhouses of the hoity-toity years back. Summerhouses! They're great mansions! You wouldn't believe some of these homes! Ceilings as high as the sky, and some painted like that famous chapel, what's its name. Rooms of carved wood and marble, beds as big as your whole apartment. That's living."

"I suppose . . ." responded Ellen unenthusiastically. She turned her head toward the living room when she heard the buzz of the bell of her apartment. In moments Tommy appeared in the kitchen. "Mommy, it's Pete. Can we go out and play?"

"Sure," said Ellen. "But stay close to home, and play nice. I don't want to hear of any shenanigans from either of you."

"Thanks, Mom," said Tommy, already turning to run out of the kitchen. Ellen listened as the twins, together with their friend, left the apartment, laughing as they went out the door.

"I remember," continued Bonnie, "we were with a group of tourists in this great dining room. The table was at least eighty feet long and there were chairs with backs on them taller than me. The guide tells everybody that these chairs are made of solid brass and each weighs about a hundred and fifty pounds. The guy who owned the house had to have servants standing by just to move these chairs so people could sit down at the table to eat and get up to pee. Anyway, there was this black couple in the crowd and all of a sudden the black man speaks up, loud enough for us all to hear: 'Yeah and you know the color of the men who had to move the chairs.' We all laughed."

Ellen smiled. "They could have been Irish. The ones moving the chairs. We have a history of being servants. And of being put down, mistreated. Treated like slaves – and worse. Worse because no one cared if we lived or died. I suppose at different times a lot of people have been taken advantage of. I know the Irish had it bad. Some still do, at least in Northern Ireland, the Catholics there are still treated like second class, although they're not as bad off as all of Ireland was when it was ruled by the English. Then, throughout Ireland, we were all treated like used tin cans. Use it until it's empty and then throw it away."

"Really? I didn't know that," said Bonnie.

"Sure, there was a time, and not that long ago, when the Irish couldn't own property in their own country. There was a law passed in

1801 called "The Act of Union" that transferred political power from Ireland to London. I remember that from my school lessons but I'd know it anyway, from my father's telling me of it. Irish weren't even allowed to pray in their own churches. They had to sneak off to pray in caves. And the priests had to say their prayers with a mask over their faces so no parishioner could turn him in if captured and tortured to give a name. Worse, the people were allowed to starve, children too. Left to die like unwanted dogs. Ever hear of the Irish *An Gorta Mor*, the Great Hunger?"

Bonnie shook her head. "No, not really."

"They call it the "Great Potato Famine" here. The potato was a primary crop in Ireland at the time, like rice in China. One time in the 1800's, 1845 through about 1850, something happened, a blight hit and ruined half the crop. Blights happened before and after but never as bad as then. That was bad enough but here's the real terrible part, the landlords who now controlled the property took much of the other half of the crop, the part that wasn't ruined, and shipped it out of the country, exported it, so as to keep making their money on the land. Most of the landowners were in London and they just wanted their profits from the farms. They literally took the food out of the starving mouths of the Irish people, leaving them with the choice of either eating the stones of their houses or starving to death. Many did starve. Whole families, whole towns."

"Damn – for real – ?"

"Absolutely for real," replied Ellen. "So many people died there weren't enough coffins to bury them. People made reusable coffins, boxes with a false bottom in them. The body of the latest dead person was carried to the churchyard and then dropped through the bottom of the coffin into the grave. The coffin then taken back to be used again. Some people, so terribly hungry, resorted to trying to eat the bad crop, the blighted crop, and as a result ended up with cholera or typhoid. It was like the European plague, only in one place. Some of the hungry resorted to "bleeding". Know what that is?"

"No," said Bonnie.

"Those that had livestock, cows, took to draining some of the animals' blood and mixing it with the rotten potatoes to make a soup of sorts. The only meal they could get and, terrible as it was, they were glad to get it. Others, those that could, fled the country. They sailed in what is now known, in Ireland anyway, as "coffin ships", trying to get to America. These ships were overcrowded and filled with disease. It's said that sharks followed these ships waiting for the bodies to be tossed over. Those that made it here were the lucky ones. Many a poor Irishman and lady just fed the sharks on the trip over."

"God, that's horrible." Bonnie shook her head. "I suppose as long as two people are alive, there'll be somebody fighting over something . . . ."

"I suppose it's so. Maybe that's the whole point of the Cain and Abel story in the bible."

A few seconds ticked by and Bonnie picked up another donut. "So you're not going on a vacation?" she asked, eager to change the subject back to what it was.

"Likely not," returned Ellen. "It's just too much money. Even going away just a couple of days is too dear. I need my money for other things besides vacations. For my two boys. They come first."

*   *   *

"Here, you can see it through the window," said Peter, speaking around a mouth filled with a large bite of the peanut butter and jelly sandwich that he held in his hand. Another sandwich sat on a plate in front of him, both prepared by his mother. The twins, when offered a like sandwich, had declined with a polite and simultaneous "No, thank you, Mrs. McNally". They weren't big eaters and were increasingly amazed at their friend's seemingly prodigious capacity to consume food.

Peter lifted the flower-print curtain covering the window, revealing to the twins' eyes the sight of the decaying, vacant brick building directly behind the apartment house in which he lived. The vacant building's abandonment lent it an air of mystery that intrigued the twins immediately.

"Does a ghost really live there?" asked Philip.

Peter nodded his head as he shoved the last portion of sandwich number one into his mouth and reached for number two on his plate. "Huh-huh, it does," he replied after swallowing. "My brother told me so." His eyes widened, following the lead of the twins, whose eyes had grown as big as goose eggs. "From my brother's room he can see it at night. He's told me it's all white and glowy with red eyes and long teeth. Oh, there's a ghost there all right." He snapped his teeth with certainty into his sandwich.

The apartment in which the McNally family lived sat on the third floor of a weary six-story tenement walk-up, situated above a small Italian barber shop with a large candy cane red and white striped pole in front of it. Minutes earlier, on their way into the building, they'd passed the barbershop and saw the gray-haired barber, Mr. Calducci, clad in a white jacket and sitting in his own barber's chair waiting for customers. Hearing the boys going by, he glanced up to look out the window and Peter, who had his own hair cut by the man, waved to him. "Hello, Mr. Calducci," he shouted. The old man waved back, nodding a smile. Peter then led the twins through the narrow door immediately adjacent to the shop and, one behind the other, the boys clambered up the dimly lit narrow stairs leading to the apartments above.

"There's no such thing as ghosts," ventured Tommy, not certain if there was such a thing or not.

"If my brother says there's a ghost then it's so," declared Peter adamantly. "Yep, you can bet on it. Says it scared the pants off him."

The twins looked again out the window, glanced down at the unkempt chaos of the neglected yard, a rectangle of cracked and broken concrete bordered by a tangle of untrimmed hedges, weeds and a cyclone fence, and then up again at the scarred brick wall and boarded windows of the abandoned building. In the act of their looking the old building became transformed, becoming suddenly a mysterious unworldly place, a supernatural place, and both boys were transfixed as they imagined vaguely the shape and movement of the alien creature moving about deep within its ruined walls. Yes, if ghosts did exist then one would certainly be living in a building like that.

"Let's go see," whispered Philip excitedly. "C'mon."

Peter was so taken aback by the suggestion that, for a moment, he forgot to chew his sandwich. "What? No way," he declared at last. "I'm not allowed over there. No way."

"C'mon," insisted Tommy.

"You scared?" challenged Philip.

Peter thought it over and concluded that yes, he was scared, but he wasn't going to admit it. "All right, we'll go," he conceded. "But when we find that ghost, you both better get out of my way 'cause I'll be moving. That blur you see going by will be me. We can go out my brother's room window. That's where the fire escape is. Then go down to the yard. I do it all the time. It's easy. The only hard part is you gotta drop from the ladder. I'll show you. But be quiet so my mom doesn't hear."

With Peter leading the way, the boys went into Pete's brother's bedroom, opened the window and climbed out onto the fire escape in the back of the building. Each boy had to suspend himself by his arms from the ladder's last rung, stretching to his fullest length, before dropping from the fire escape ladder onto the ground below. Here was a feat that required a certain amount of courage and daring on the part of each of the twins. Peter was used to it, but the twins were not, and the distance from their eyes to the ground below appeared substantial to the point of danger. But after watching their friend drop down safely, and after daring him to go in the first place, they felt they had little choice but to muster their courage and go ahead and do it. Both boys were very pleased with themselves after landing safely on the ground.

The trio made their way over the wire link fence separating the yard of the apartment building from that of the abandoned structure and then fought their way through the tangle of hedge that lined the fence on the other side. Each felt a slight bit of exhilaration, mingled with a thrill of trepidation, as they approached the rear entrance of the now *looming* brick structure. As they came slowly closer to it, it seemed to be forming a *personality*, an intelligence of sorts that was now looking back at the small boys, staring down at them with contempt for their audacity in daring to approach it.

There were three old concrete steps leading up to a weathered door. Weeds, some quite tall, grew wildly between the cracks of the steps. The door's black paint was peeling off leaving jagged scars of exposed wood. As a consequence, the wood, in parts, was deteriorating, rotting with decay. Two boards were stretched across the door, nailed to the frame with nails orange with rust. Washed reddish-brown lines ran down the boards from the exposed nail-heads.

Peter turned to the twins. "Do ghosts come out in the daytime?" he asked, his eyes brimming with fearful doubt.

"I-I don't know," murmured Philip, his own courage faltering. "Maybe we should go back."

"C'mon, let's go in," chimed in Tommy. "We can open that door, can't we? I think we can."

"Y-Yeah . . . I suppose . . . ." It was clear from Peter's tone that he hoped he was more wrong than right.

The boards came away easily, the rusted nails gasping their last and breaking almost at the first touch the boys pressed upon the wood. They had to jump back quickly to avoid having their shins and feet hit by the falling boards.

Peter reached out his hand toward the doorknob, fearfully, as though afraid it might burst into flame at the touch of a fingertip. The door offered a little resistance but no more and soon relented to the boy's pushing, swinging open on creaking hinges.

The trio of explorers stared inside, eyes wide, looking into the musty dark shadows of the interior of the building, trying to make sense of the vague shapes they saw. Some slight illumination squeezed into the building through the boarded and grime-coated windows.

Peter cleared his throat. "It's dark," he whispered, stating the obvious.

"Sure is," replied the twins simultaneously.

The courageous trio stepped over the threshold and stood there, not immediately willing to abandon the safety of the door and the quick exit it provided them should they need it. Their wide staring eyes gazed into the gloom, observing in the dim light the accumulation of years of dust, dirt and decay. Soft billows of cobwebs laced the ceiling and the walls in many places. The boy's noses quivered at the dank odor of rot and degeneration that floated everywhere.

What's that?! They drew up sharply in fright when they heard a low, rustling sound somewhere in the shadowy murk before them. Each boy held his breath, listening intently, trying to determine exactly what could have made the sound, waiting for a repeat of the noise, or the appearance of the demon behind it. Both encore of sound and demon failed to materialize, the maker of the noise remaining hidden behind the curtain of darkness. Listening, the boys heard only absolute silence.

"Was that – a mouse?" whispered Peter. "It must have been, right?" Frozen in place for a few ticks, they at last began to relax, deciding that, whatever the cause of the noise, since it hadn't come leaping out of the shadows snarling at them, it was most likely nothing they had to fear.

"Sure, that's what it was," decided Philip. "A mouse."

Tommy and Peter nodded their heads in agreement, hoping it was so.

"It's sure spooky in here," commented Tommy as the three boys continued forward into the house, walking from the light of the doorway slowly into the murk. They moved much like three ancient exploring ships at sea sailing into a fog bank that obliterated sight, the fog hovering over that part of the hissing ocean labeled on the captains' charts as: *Parts Unknown. Monsters Exist Here.*

"Where does the ghost stay?" murmured Philip, the question was meant for Peter, the expert on phantoms within the group.

"My brother says he's seen it in different places, walking all over the house. So it could be anywhere here, I guess."

"Oohh, maaan," complained Philip, evidently not thrilled by the thought of a ghost that could be *anywhere*, even nearby. He was no longer completely certain he wanted to hunt around in the dark to find it.

They passed through the first room into a short, narrow corridor holding a flight of stairs that twisted up to the next floor. There was evidently an uncovered window up there as hazy sunlight, originating from some unknown point, could be seen straining to push against the shadows coating the stairs. It succeeded in dispelling some of the murk and that small success was sufficient enough for Philip. "Let's go up there," he suggested, for no other reason than he wanted to go toward a place where it was less dark. He didn't like the dark one bit. No telling when something with sharp teeth would come bounding out of shadows at him.

"No, wait, there's a room right here," said Tommy. "Let's see what's in there first." Without waiting for agreement, he went right in. The others followed, the three marching to a spooky tune offered by the old, rotting floorboards groaning now beneath their hesitant footsteps. *Creak, creeaak.* This room, filled with dirt and decay as were the others, was also streaked with charred wood and plaster, evidence of a fire in the room at sometime in the past. Here were bare walls and a floor devoid of furniture and decoration, and the boys quickly decided that nothing of interest would be found inside.

"Nothing here," concluded Peter and the twins nodded their agreement of the now plain to see.

They went out and back to the stairs, which they ascended, going up slowly, one delicate step at a time, feeling the old wood give way under their feet as they walked up, first to the small landing where the stairs turned at a sharp angle and then to the second floor of the house.

At the top of the stairs was a small grime-covered window, the source of the little light they had, a pale suggestion of sunshine managing to creep in past the heavy buildup of dirt on the glass.

Before them, against a wall a short distance away they could discern in the murk the rounded silhouette of a dark heap of rags resting on the floor. Or were the rags covering something underneath? Was something hiding there?

"What's that?" whispered Peter, fright in his voice, pointing to the rounded heap. "What's that?"

"Don't know . . ." whispered Philip back.

Movement! Their hearts immediately leaped into their throats as suddenly the inert bundle rolled over and came to terrifying life, groaning and rising up in front of them like a sea monster proving its questioned existence by lifting its great head and neck out of the waters of the ocean! A dark shadowy form rising up taller and taller.

"Monster!! Ghost!!" came the cries of the boys. To the three friends this shifting, growing silhouette was nothing less than a manifestation of their worst fears, the grisly materialization of the ghost they'd been seeking.

A monster to the boys, a tramp in life; the form rising up before the trio's amazed and terror filled eyes was that of a derelict who spent the night curled up and sleeping on the floor beneath a great mound of old rags serving as his bed blankets. The tramp, stirred to wakefulness by the sounds of the boys, now pushed himself up off the floor, shedding blankets like a sea serpent tossing off large scales as he stood. It looked like pieces of himself coming away from him. His unshaven, gaunt and grimy face, a face containing features without any real congruity in the shadows, wobbled at the boys like a snake's head prepared to strike.

The boys, screaming, were rooted to the spots on which they stood with terror. Then the tramp stepped forward and a sliver of sunlight fell upon his features, displaying a face ugly to the point of deformity. Dirt-rimmed orbs stared bleary-eyed and fearful at the children. The face was such that it could have served as an artist's rendering designed to do nothing but strike horror into the heart of the beholder and it succeeded in doing exactly that to the young boys gaping at it now.

Their eyes sighting the apparition, they realized immediately they wanted absolutely no part of it. Still emitting screams of terror, they backed away, seeking safety beyond the creature's reach. A blare of sound, a cry not unlike the howl of a wounded beast, was added to their own screams as the derelict, himself frightened by the appearance and shouts of these strangers, began to yell and bellow his own terror in return.

Had the boys simply been able to run away as they wanted, to escape back down the stairs, the occasion would have ended with them fleeing the building and, once safely outside, would have no doubt concluded with them laughing and giggling over how scared they'd been. But fate today wanted no part of a happy conclusion, opting instead for misfortune and cruel tragedy. As the boys backed away in fear of the apparition rising before them, they, all three, pressed their bodies against the aged banister behind them. The dry, rotten wood squealed at the sudden stress and then splintered and gave way, coming apart with cracking explosive sounds of destruction. Peter, Tommy and Philip toppled over as one and fell to the bottom of the stairs, their descent accompanied by pieces of railing and broken wood, all landing hard on the floor below.

The tramp stepped over to the destroyed banister and peered down into the darkness. He couldn't see the children in the lake of shadow below but heard them well enough as, rising through the dust-filled obscurity, there came from below the moans and sobbings of pain and injury. "They're just kids," he mumbled and then he shuffled down the steps to reach them.

Downstairs, there was barely light enough to see through the gloom, the air now thickened with dust. Peter was crying and groaning as was Philip who'd landed beside him. Both were too dazed to move except to weakly wave an arm or bend a leg. But it was Tommy who appeared the most grievously injured. He lay unconscious, his little body twisted terribly amidst the debris and wood. Blood matted his blond hair and covered half his face.

"I-I'll get help for youse boys," muttered the tramp after gazing at them for a few seconds. He then turned and walked away, reiterating his purpose as he went, as though fearful he might forget it as soon as the boys were out of sight: "Yes, I will. Get help. Get help, Get help . . ."

*   *   *

The words of the patrolman coming through the telephone were like a boxer's pounding blows to Ellen's head; her heart constricted with fear and her knuckles turned white with the tightening of her grip on the receiver she held to her ear. "My boys – hurt? But how? It's not serious, is it?"

In reply she was given only the broadest sketch of the accident and the name of Saint Vincent's Hospital, the hospital to which the boys were taken by ambulance. Anything else, she was told, she would have to learn from the doctors caring for the children.

It was there, at the hospital, she was told her Tommy was gone.

Chapter Thirty-five

It was her son, her baby, in the closed white casket in the aisle before the church altar. *My baby! My . . . little Tommy . . . .*

The interior of the church grew hazy. The voice of the priest on the altar, delivering Tommy's eulogy, faded as though controlled by a volume dial being turned down by an unseen hand. Ellen's head ached as dots of light danced before her eyes. The altar swayed and wavered and she mumbled something, indistinct even to her. In the pew to Ellen's right sat little Philip, then Rose followed by her husband Jim. Maggie and Teresa, together with Philip and Patrick, Rose's sons, sat in the pew behind them. Each head turned with concern toward Ellen upon hearing her voice.

"Are you all right?" asked Rose, leaning into Ellen and whispering the inquiry into her ear.

It was a moment before Ellen could reply, before the sensation of dizziness passed. She nodded. "I-I think so . . . ."

Rose picked up the palm of Ellen's hand and cupped it gently within her own two hands, holding it as though she'd picked up a fallen sparrow with a broken wing. *I'm here*, implied that gesture. *I will help you anyway I can.*

The casket was closed now for the funeral mass taking place, but Ellen's mind was back in the funeral parlor, at the wake of the night before. She saw her Tommy resting inside the casket, encased in satin, his chubby hands folded across his small chest and holding a small brass crucifix, the few freckles dotting his cheeks amplified by the pale color of the surrounding skin. He looked like he was casually asleep, napping just like he used to do on the couch – in front of the still-turned-on television. A sob escaped Ellen as this image of her lost child floated before her, little Tommy in his casket, the last memory she'd ever have of him. She pulled her hand from Rose to press her fingers hard against her mouth, as though wanting to keep her grief contained and preserved within her, to retain the last emotion she would experience for her little boy before he was placed into the ground, even though that emotion was nothing less than the pain of a shattered heart.

Bonnie, sitting two pews behind Ellen, emitted a choking sob of her own. That sob proved to be a catalyst for others and soon many of the almost fifty people attending the mass, men and women alike, were wiping tears away from their cheeks and eyes. Ellen continued to struggle not to burst completely into tears. Her efforts were successful until the moment the mass ended and the small coffin was being wheeled back up the aisle to be placed in the waiting hearse. The reality of the finality of Tommy's death came crashing down upon her heart then, the full terrible sense of the finality of death somehow made more stark and real now that Mass was over and her lost son was going to the graveyard. Ellen wept without restraint as she followed behind her forever lost baby, her little son truly and unretrievably gone from her.

A few pedestrians outside stopped and watched as the casket was lifted and pushed into the back of the hearse, the funeral an occurrence of momentary interest to them. Ellen, Rose and her husband Jim, and little Philip, sat together in the back seat of the limousine that would follow the hearse to Calvary Cemetery. All others would follow the limousine in other cars.

*   *   *

Two days prior to Tommy's funeral Ellen had gone to the hospital room in which Philip was recovering from his own slight injuries, and, for the first time, told the boy of the death of his brother. A hard thing for Ellen to do. The two boys looked so much alike; mirror images of each other; Ellen felt as though she was talking to Tommy's ghost rather than to his brother, trying to explain the mystery of his own death to him.

Tommy's death was difficult for Philip to comprehend, to accept. Tears rolled down the poor boy's face as, sitting up in his hospital bed, she told him that his brother would not be coming home again, that he'd gone to live with God.

"But we want him home," complained Philip, his tears swiftly renewing themselves as fast as he wiped them away. "He'll miss us being there in heaven, won't he? He wants to be here with us, doesn't he?"

Ellen leaned over the bed and kissed him. "Honey, in heaven he'll never be sad. He'll always . . . always be happy there. In two days you'll come to church with me, and together we'll say goodbye . . ." She tried to say more but found she couldn't, not another syllable, her heart suddenly all pain again, her voice nothing more than ashes and dust incapable of forming words.

*   *   *

A lattice of steel and elevated highway, a roadway that curved past the perimeter of the graveyard, cut a gash across the bottom of the gloomy, tattered sky. A fragile white mist crawled amidst the tombstones, imparting to the graveyard an eerie, ethereal sense of true eternity. The tombstones seemed to be authentic markers indicating a precise point of transition from this world to the next. Mid-morning on a damp and dreary day. In an hour or so the mist would dissipate, fade and be gone.

The mourners had to wait, and most did so by remaining seated in their cars, while the casket was removed from the hearse and placed near the cavity dug in the earth waiting to accept it. When that was done, all climbed out (excepting the limousine driver) and walked toward the casket and the priest now making his appearance beside it.

A few workmen, the gravediggers, were a respectful distance away, down the road a few yards, standing beside an old and battered truck that resembled, to Ellen's mind, the one Jimmy used to work on back on the old farm. Years ago. *Thank God he was finally able to get a newer one a couple of years ago.*

As the priest spoke, Ellen saw a bird flutter up from the ground; her eyes followed it as it lifted itself and flew away, forming a graceful arc against the steel-gray sky. *How free it seems,* she thought. *How nice to have that freedom. Is my Tommy's soul like that? Free and flying up to heaven? Happy?* Then she lowered her gaze back to the small white coffin and, in staring at it once again, felt the full weight of her sorrow once more, pressing down so hard she thought she might be pushed down and absorbed into the very dirt on which she stood, buried here with her lost child.

My Tommy. Gone from me. Gone . . . .

Chapter Thirty-six

For a long time following Tommy's death, Ellen's heart remained all desolation and sorrow. Dazed with the loss, angry with fate and even with God, her soul was harsh with it. Her mind focused on Tommy constantly as though through the act of thinking of him, of remembering him completely, she could bring him back to have him standing to be hugged in front of her once more. She longed to hold him again, one more time, to tickle him in play, to hear his laugh.

That Philip had survived offered her little solace at first. How could she look at the living twin without feeling the pain of the loss of the other?

*   *   *

One night, two weeks afterward, she was pulled from her sleep by the sound of her son calling to her: "Mommy! Mommy!"

Sitting up, she imagined for an instant, an instant in which her heart leaped with happiness inside her, that it was her Tommy calling out of the dark for her. *Tommy's alive!* The whole nightmare of his injury, the hospital, his death and funeral, was just that, a nightmare, a terrible dream that would now fade away. But the next moment of being awake shattered the brief illusion. No, it was Philip calling to her. Tommy was still beneath the earth, unable to call her, still forever in his coffin with only the sound of the wind passing over his grave to soothe him. Still alone, with her no longer able to offer a mother's love to comfort him.

She lay back on her pillow and closed her eyes, waiting for Philip to stop calling her, not able to summon the energy to go to the surviving boy.

At last Philip stopped calling out to her, and, perhaps, drifted back to sleep.

* * *

Coexistent with her painful grief was Ellen's stunned disbelief. She'd always believed in a benevolent God, the Christian God of love and compassion. Why did such a God let this happen? Why allow her beautiful boy to be born, just to grant him a few short years? Letting him be killed before he could even start to truly live his life? *What kind of God did that?*

What kind of God did that?

There was no danger that Ellen would, in her grief, cease to believe in God. No, her belief went too deep for that. The real hazard was that she'd alter her concept of *what God was.* That she'd come to think of Christ as a God of sadistic cruelty. For Him to allow her son to die, to permit her mother's love to be transformed to nothing but profound pain and suffering, seemed to be a cruelty of the worst sort. An act of evil, or so she thought.

An unseen force was deep within Ellen, and that spiral of pain turned and twisted again and again, tearing at her. How often can the same wound be ripped and reopened? Yet it occurred within Ellen again and again, bringing unbidden tears again and again – and again.

* * *

Little Philip slept alone in his room. The small bed beside his own now empty in the dark. He wasn't used to that, to being alone. To not hearing the sound of his brother's breathing in the night as Tommy slept; to no longer having a brother to play with or to joke with as a prelude to sleep; to no longer being able to simply talk over the day's adventures. All of his life he'd had a brother near him. It was lonely without him.

Philip was afraid too. Vaguely the little boy felt as though something threatening had replaced Tommy, something indistinct yet something to be feared, like that monster in the vacant house that had taken Tommy's life. Sometimes at night, Philip was certain the terrible entity was sitting somewhere within the gray gauze of the shadows of his room at night, looking at him, looking – and waiting.

*   *   *

Every cliché is an ancient truth, otherwise it would not exist as a cliché. *Time heals all wounds* it's said and time, as it passed by, did indeed heal Ellen's torn heart as well. A healing that took place almost without her awareness of it, almost against her will.

Healing of the soul is nearly always indicated by small events.

Weeks after Tommy's funeral, Philip was alone on the living room floor amusing himself by playing. He'd taken the cushions off the sofa and chairs and arranged them so as to create a small tunnel into which he could crawl. A great adventure was taking place here on the apartment floor. Within that cave of cushions existed a powerful but evil magician who'd just transformed himself into a great dragon (resembling to a great degree the plastic toy dragon Philip had placed in the cave of cushions). An immense fire-breather of a dragon, an evil creature that could only be conquered by great daring and courage. *A bomb wouldn't hurt either,* decided Philip, and he reached for a small figurine sitting on the end table by the couch. A bomb if he'd ever seen one. He needed it for the dragon had moved, trying to attack him while he was unaware, and was now lurking somewhere behind the sofa. He, the newly appointed Protector of the World, appointed by The Mighty King of the Universe himself, now had the awesome task and duty to stop the thing from walking its path of destruction, to save all the poor and helpless people that would be harmed by the dragon's rampage. He would do his best to succeed.

Ellen came into the room and, seeing her son playing, was suddenly driven on a happy impulse to join him. She got down on all fours beside him on the floor and there, together, truly together for the first time since Tommy's death, the two played, crawling on the floor, fighting the evil magician/dragon roaming and hiding amidst the furniture of the room. With his mother's help, Philip defeated the evil dragon at last and, victory acknowledged and praised, Ellen offered to take the White Knight out for a walk and a treat of ice cream to celebrate the triumph.

Now early evening, the sun, a ball of glowing pink-orange, was moving behind the buildings, sending streaks of pink and gold across the white bellies of the small tufts of cloud floating in the blue sky. That beauty pleased Ellen today, but more pleasing was the *feel* of her son's happiness in being with his mother now, in their simply being able to walk beside each other, unaccompanied by the presence of sorrow and gloom. Ellen felt a sense of happiness, of true happiness, so long absent that it seemed to her now to be almost a strange experience.

Was her being happy a betrayal to her lost son? No, she no longer thought that. Tommy was with God, and so he was happy. She believed that with all her heart. And she was alive and holding the hand of her own little Philip who loved her and whom she loved in return. And that was a blessing. A warm and wonderful blessing. A small shining gem resting in the mud of her sorrow.

Chapter Thirty-seven

A betrayal of sorts . . .

That was the sense of guilt thumping at Ellen's heart as she packed away her little Tommy's things; his clothes, a few comic books; some baseball cards and other little treasures. Like putting the boy himself away, tucking him into the back of a dark drawer, there to rest forgotten. Like burying him a second time.

She'd told Philip to take and keep whatever he wanted of Tommy's, but she didn't think he'd taken anything. Everything seemed the same to her. Maybe Philip felt it to be as much a kind of violation as she did.

Is it wrong? Wrong to put his things out of sight? Wrong to feel any happiness, ever again . . . ? Does it mean I didn't love him enough . . . ?

As Ellen took the cardboard box that held Tommy's things, the things that had remained untouched in the twins' bedroom since his death, she found herself shedding fresh tears over his loss. She held the box in front of her and walked behind it toward the hall closet, there to place it upon a shelf inside, feeling all the time as though she was once again walking down the aisle of her church behind his small coffin.

A second burial. A kind of betrayal . . . .

*   *   *

The following Saturday, with the help of a partially hung-over Bonnie, Ellen took the sheets and pillow cases off the bed that was Tommy's and placed them in the hamper to be washed. She returned to the twins' room to remove the mattress, disassemble the bed frame and to move the separated pieces, mattress, frame and headboard, outside for discard. Her heart was pounding in her chest all the time, not from her exertions, the bed was small and each piece, once separated, was well within her and Bonnie's physical capabilities to lift and move, but rather from that same sense of guilt she'd felt days earlier when packing the remnants of Tommy's short existence into a cardboard box.

Bonnie, more for show than anything else, attempting to lighten the mood by playing the clown, huffed and puffed as they moved the mattress and pieces of bed about. She might have been practicing for an audition to play the role of a female Samson struggling to bring down the temple. But, in truth, even the headboard, the largest piece of the deconstructed bed, offered little challenge to their combined strength.

"Why don't you sell this bed?" asked Bonnie. "It's worth something. Why throw it away?"

"I-I couldn't," replied Ellen. "It's actually easier just to put it out. If someone wants it they can just take it, and be welcome to it."

During the whole time Ellen was working to remove the bed there was the conflict occurring once more within her, returning now to pound against her heart like an aggrieved surf on a rocky shore, a secret dissension caused by the lingering sense that this, this removal of what was Tommy's, was somehow *wrong*. That it constituted a kind of treachery against her lost son, an abandonment of sorts. *Does it mean I didn't love him enough . . . ?*

Her mind offered her Reason, telling her it wasn't so, but Reason was a weak foe against the power of what her heart was feeling. *Sorry, Tommy . . . .*

Once again her faith in God was her blessing. Ellen believed deeply that her Tommy was now with the Almighty, together with the souls of her parents, Tommy's grandparents. Her little boy, although separated from her, was now happy in God, happy with God.

Only those left behind suffered.

Belief in the soul renders the material less necessary. Ellen understood that retaining the physical reminders of her son's existence was not as important as her heart declared it was, but still her heart ached with the pain of removing the things that were once the proud possessions of her deceased son. The image of Tommy resting in his coffin, the last sight of him she possessed, an image that for now dominated all previous memories of him, kept appearing and vanishing in her mind as she worked, as though someone or something was flipping a projector's switch on and off inside her skull.

She would always ache for her missing son, and always a part of her would grieve for his absence from her, but it would be a different softer grief than the terrible pain of the past few bitter weeks.

A *softer* pain . . . . Was that too a betrayal . . . ?

On the twins' bureau she discovered a small crayon drawing of a smiling face atop a red triangle of a dress. A small drawing Tommy had made years earlier in Kindergarten and which had once hung in a place of honor on the refrigerator door. *Tommy,* it was signed in big block letters that were less than straight, his portrait of her.

Another small scrap remaining of a small scrap of a little life. This one she would not discard or lock away. Ellen took the drawing to her room and placed it on her bureau. Soon she'd buy a frame and hang it on a wall. There to rest beside the crucifix Tommy had held in his lifeless hands, the funeral parlor offering the cross to her before closing the coffin.

It wasn't until later, after Bonnie had left and Philip was in bed, that she picked up the drawing again and wept copiously over it, looking down at the rough lines of crayon on the cream-colored paper, sitting alone on her bed, wiping her tears from her face like a child, cloistered by solitude and sorrow.

Later, going to sleep in her bed, she whispered a prayer into the dark shadows of her room, and, as part of that prayer, greeted Tommy once again with a whispered "Hello. I hope you're happy, Tommy." A soft wish that, smoke-like, dissipated and was absorbed into the undisturbed darkness surrounding her. A wish that, Ellen believed, would be accepted by the Timeless Existence that stood unseen beyond the limits of human sight and, in that acceptance, then be passed along to be whispered in her baby's ear.

This kind of belief is thought to be an absurd notion by some but is as real as the ground underfoot to many others. It is a belief that can only exist in the human heart and cannot be viewed by curious scientific eyes. A sense of God's true love cannot be felt anywhere except within the faculty of faith that resides within the depths of the human soul.

A belief beyond understanding.

Tommy was now in the midst of God's pure love, and there he would wait patiently until it was time for her to see and hug him once again. "I love you, Tommy." Another whisper into the dark, and then, this declaration of love being her "good night" to her lost son, Ellen closed her weary red-rimmed eyes to the night.

And still the last thought that came to her mind as she drifted off to sleep was the same one that had haunted her for days now:

Maybe I don't love him enough . . . .

Chapter Thirty-eight

Following Tommy's death, Ellen lived her life half detached from what was going on around her. As though a part of her, a true living part of her, had severed itself and ran away, leaving only a partial Ellen behind. It's true she felt happiness again, now and then, but it always came to her in a watered-down version of what joy should be, a happiness that came to her feebly, bedraggled, as through it came traveling on foot and had walked too many miles in the gray of a drizzling rain.

Five months after Tommy's funeral, she and Philip rode the subway to Queens, to Calvary Cemetery, to the ground that now held her son's coffin. She'd gone there previously following the funeral but never before with Philip, believing it would be best for the boy not to go. This time Philip insisted that he accompany her and so together they went, mother and surviving twin.

They stood together, holding hands, looking at the stone that now held her Tommy's name and the dates of his birth and death, dates so very close together, a mere blink of a blink of time.

So young, he'd already shown signs of intelligence, of being strong-willed, of being courageous and of being kind. Wouldn't he have been a good person once he was grown?

Why God . . . Why take such a good little boy, so soon? Before he had a chance to grow up? Wouldn't he have done good things?

Together, she and Philip said an "Our Father" and a "Hail Mary" over the grave, and then, still holding hands, they walked away. Ellen, absorbed in her own sorrow, didn't notice the tears that Philip was wiping away from his eyes with his free hand as they both stepped away from the grave.

She didn't return to the grave again after that visit until the day of the first anniversary of Tommy's death. This time she went alone, leaving Philip with his Aunt Rose. Hard to believe, a full year had passed since her son's fatal accident.

A full year . . .

And the question, as she stood on the ground that now held her baby's bones, was still the same:

Why God? Why take such a good little boy, so soon? Before he even had a chance to grow up? Why God, Why?

*   *   *

Bonnie looked up from the open, untidy and over-packed suitcase and glanced at the clock: 11:30.

"Oh God, El, I've got to hurry. My plane leaves in less than an hour."

Ellen, sitting on the bed very near the suitcase, nodded her head. "I've been telling you to hurry for an hour now, haven't I?" she said, a tone of reprimand in her voice.

"Yes, you have," replied Bonnie, sticking her tongue out at Ellen. "Oh, thanks for coming over. I wanted to say goodbye to you in person. And you're good luck. For me. Isn't it nuts? Life, I mean," she added excitedly. "Oh, what else can I take?" She gazed at the litter of clothes strewn helter-skelter over the bed and the furniture. "I've got to hurry."

"You can't fit anything else in there," declared Ellen. "And if you waste more time, you'll miss your flight."

"You're right, you're right. When you're right, you're right. And you're right. Where's my elephant hair bracelet? That's good luck. I've got to wear that." Her head began to whirl like the beacon of a confused lighthouse on a stormy night.

"It's right here," Ellen told her, pointing a finger to it. It lay on the bureau in the midst of a heap of papers, jewelry, perfume bottles and underwear. Bonnie grabbed it up and slipped it over her hand onto her wrist.

"I'm going to miss you, Bonnie. I'm happy for you and I wish you nothing but luck, but I'm going to miss you."

Bonnie halted in her movement and smiled. "Oh, El, I'll miss you too," she responded, her voice rising as her eyes turned sad. Then, with a shrug of her shoulders, "But I probably won't be gone long enough for you to miss me too much. The odds are this part I got in this movie will lead nowhere, to Nowhere's-Ville and I'll be back here before you know I'm gone. With my luck, the movie'll be a bow-wow dog."

"No, don't say that. I hope this leads to a lot of success for you. You've worked hard enough for a long time. You deserve a break."

"Yeah, I do, but that doesn't mean I'll get it. But thanks El." Bonnie smiled with appreciation and fondness at Ellen. "You're a true good friend. Oh God, I'm so excited about this! Who'd have thought a bit part in a second-rate off-Broadway play would've led to a part in a movie! God, I hope it's the best movie ever made in Hollywood!"

"Your plane?"

"I'm ready, I'm ready." Bonnie grew serious again. "I was starting to think about giving up acting. I thought I'd never get a break. It can hurt, El, to dream of something and never get it. There comes a point when dreams start to weigh you down, you know what I mean? They weigh you down rather than pick you up. And then from out of the blue my agent calls me to audition for this part. And I get it! Oh God El, I'm so happy."

"I'm happy too. Shouldn't we call for a cab to come?"

"Call a cab? On the phone? This is New York. There's more cabs on the streets than beers in one of your Irish pubs. I'll grab one outside at the corner. Come on El, park your big fat fanny on top of this suitcase so I can close it."

Bonnie pulled the suitcase to the corner of the bed and Ellen, as requested, sat on it while Bonnie grunted it shut and snapped the catches together. "Thanks El, I'm glad you're still eating those marshmallow vanilla wafer things. That suitcase called for a plump derriere."

"Thanks. You're sweet. That's what I like about you," responded Ellen, chuckling at the friendly (and false) jibe. "Always a kind word."

"Only kidding," came back Bonnie. "Kinda anyway," she added as she pushed her arm through the sleeve of her jacket. She went to the bed and picked up her crammed suitcase. "Well, off I go. Walk me to the curb?"

"Of course."

In the hall they stood outside the apartment as Bonnie rummaged through her purse, searching for her keys to lock up. "Keys . . . keys . . . keys . . . ." Ellen rolled her eyes.

"Found them," declared Bonnie and she held them up, displaying them to Ellen as though she was a magician who'd just pulled a twitching rabbit from a high hat and wanted applause for a trick well done.

"So lock the door and let's go."

"I'm going to continue to pay the rent here," said Bonnie as she twisted a key in the lock and the dead bolt clicked into place. "I'll need a place to come back to if things don't work out. Which is probably what'll happen. If I don't pay the rent I'd have to come and live with you again then. Wouldn't that be something? Geez, don't make such a face. It wouldn't be that bad. Well, then again maybe it would . . . ."

To the accompaniment of Bonnie's chattering, the two descended the stairs and exited the building. Outside, they walked to the corner of the street and there, within just two minutes, Bonnie hailed a taxi to the curb. She opened the door and shoved her suitcase inside, placing it onto the floor of the back of the cab.

Tears now glittering in her eyes, she turned to Ellen to offer her a final goodbye. The two friends embraced for a moment, separated and Bonnie climbed onto the back seat, her legs straddling her suitcase. "Idlewild Airport," she told the driver as she pulled the door shut.

As the taxi pulled away, Bonnie turned in her seat to wave a last farewell through the glass of the rear window and Ellen returned the wave, lifting her hand and waggling her fingers.

Will I see her again? Ever? wondered Ellen. It was possible she wouldn't. She stood and gazed at Bonnie as the yellow cab pulled away, keeping her eyes upon her until the taxi was absorbed into the city traffic and was gone from sight.

"Ellen, Ellen Rawdon? Is that you?"

Ellen, surprised to hear her name, turned toward the voice and gazed up into the face of a rather handsome, smiling man whom, at first, she didn't think she knew.

Who is this? A stranger somehow in possession of her name? Then, in the next instant, recognition came to her and she realized she did know the man after all, older now but much the same as he once was. "Sean? Sean O'Reilly? Is it you?"

The man nodded his head and at last Ellen returned the wonderful smile.

Chapter Thirty-nine

The same sun that had failed to penetrate the layer of gray clouds covering the sky above Calvary Cemetery more than a year ago on the day of little Tommy's funeral, shone bright and warm against the skin of Sean O'Reilly's face as he stood leaning against the aged railing of a ship at sea. Aboard a freighter bound for Brazil, Sean enjoyed the feel of the sun's warmth and the touch of the salty breeze against his face as he gazed out at the gray-blue ocean extending out to the horizon, where the blue sky pressed down upon the water. White foam curled against the bow as the nose of the ship cut its way through the next resisting swell of ocean; then the foam disappeared, only to be replaced in the next few seconds by another splash of wave. To Sean, the sound of the ocean lapping against the bow of the ship sounded like the Earth breathing.

An old ship, it moved through the sea with a sense of weary fatigue. Throughout its elderly body, except for its engine room, which was fairly well cared for, it exhibited telltale signs of its age and casual maintenance. Here and there, like liver spots on an octogenarian, sat orange stains of rust. The old hull was layered with barnacles, no one, not even the owner, willing to invest the time and money it would take to remove them.

The crew was a composite of nationalities, many Germans and Scandinavians, a few Poles, some Moroccans, two Americans and one Irishman. Most were not here by choice but rather pushed to the task by their poor education and economic need. Sean, having signed on simply for the adventure of it, was, in that sense at least, unique among the crewmen.

As he leaned against the rail, a man came up beside him and Sean turned his head at the approach, forsaking sight of the sea to see whom it was. Abraham Tait, one of two Yanks on board. *Tait with the untidy face,* thought Sean to himself. He, Tait, was a rough looking man with a countenance marred by bad proportions, the pieces put together not quite right. Whether that was a result of past confrontations or an accident of birth, Sean couldn't venture a guess.

Tait was not friendly with many on board, was even openly contemptuous of some, but was friendly enough with Sean. "We're moving into good weather," he said, his greeting to Sean as he took up a place beside him on the railing. "It'll stay all sunshine tomorrow."

Sean nodded. The bow of the ship plunged slightly as the swells increased. Droplets of spray came up over the rail.

"We'll be nearing land as well then," continued Tait. "Tomorrow, 'bout noon we'll see the coast." With this pronouncement he turned from the sea and placed a scrutinizing eye on Sean. "With your permission," he said, "I'm going to ask you a question. I'm acquainted with you three weeks now and I've been wondering most of that time why a young educated gentleman like yourself would want to be here. I can't figure why a young, smart, educated lad would come to work on a tub like this. Most of us are here because we can't be anywhere else. This is a crew of losers and misfits, some villains and thieves. You're out of place – unless you're on the lam from the law."

Sean smiled. "Which are you? Villain or thief? Loser or misfit?"

Tait snorted a laugh. "Part loser, I suppose. Part villain too if truth be told. Reformed of course. Mostly." A chain hanging loosely around Tait's neck caught a ray of sunlight and glinted gold into Sean's eyes.

Sean liked the answer. He also believed it to be true, at least the villain part of it. Tait was an imposing man who carried an antagonistic aura about him. His sense of humor was harsh. Sean noticed for the first time the small dot of gold in Tait's earlobe as it too flashed in the sun, imitating the necklace. "You're wearing an earring," he said, an inquiry as much as a statement.

"Yea, worn it for years. They say it improves the eyes. That's why pirates wore them. Used to think it was an old wives' tale myself, then I read somewhere that the acupuncture point for the eyes is in the earlobe. So who's to say, maybe there's truth in it? Me? I wear it 'cause I like it. I've got my twenty-twenty. Both here – " Tait pointed a finger to his eyes, "– and here as well." He tapped the finger on his temple.

Sean asked him what he meant by the finger on the temple.

"Why, it does no good to see with your eyes and not understand what you see, does it? That's what I mean. That's another kind of being blind." Tait narrowed his eyes slightly against the wind and mist coming over the rail and dug a hand into a pocket of his pea jacket. In a moment, he produced a package of small, thin, black cigars. After two attempts to light one up, the wind fighting against him and extinguishing the first of his matches, he released a puff of smoke into the breeze.

"I look at you, I see someone out of place," he said, returning to his original conversation. "Like seeing a racehorse pulling a farm plow. And I have to wonder why such a capable and educated young man chooses to be on a floating tin can like this."

"No mystery. I decided to do some traveling and this is a way of doing it – and earning a little money at the same time. Worked for a few years after college, in a bank, sent money home and all that, but then both my parents passed on. Suddenly there was little reason to keep working. I was working primarily for them, I realized. Always felt out of place doing it. At least in the bank. Not quite ready to stay in one place, I guess."

Tait grunted. "Infected with a bit o' the wanderlust. Me too, when I was younger." He rolled his hand closed and expelled a rough cough into it. "Too much smoking. I've switched from cigarettes to cigars because of this cough. Don't inhale the cigars." His hand came up again to catch another cough.

"Me?" he continued, speaking as though responding to a question, "I've always liked to travel. Always liked the sea. Though now, after all these years, I can't say there's much point to it. Excepting it beats staying still by a long shot. And I've gathered a lot of stories over the years." He grinned and pointed to a white sliver of a jagged scar that ran along the bottom of his jaw and up toward the corner of his mouth. "Next time we talk remind me to tell you about the sonofabitch Scotsman who gave me this, and the woman with the long, red hair who was worth the cut. See you later, boy." With that, he turned and walked away, trailing a white cloud of cigar smoke that billowed out from his head, was grabbed by the wind and blown off the deck. Sean watched the man's back for a moment before turning his attention back to the sea.

*   *   *

Tait was right, the weather the next day was sunny. As it neared noon, Sean returned to the railing to gaze out toward the smoky horizon now coming nearer, slowly and steadily. First it was all white haze, holding within it the merest suggestion of land, then the city rolled forward to present itself more clearly and Sean could make out its rooftops, the outline of an infrastructure. Finally, as the ship continued forward, the smaller details of the various elements of the city came into view.

The ship glided into port, moving to take its place by a Russian freighter, and Sean watched as pieces of the city slid by. Houses and buildings, closely compacted near the shore, some brightly colored, others drab and gray, were near enough now for him to be able to look in the windows. Fishing boats bobbed in the water, reminding him of the port in Donegal. Looking up into the hills behind the houses, he saw peasant women walking a trail, carrying bundles, no doubt wares to either sell or barter in the city below. Off in the far distance, bordering the edge of the water, he saw a long ribbon of yellow, a sandy beach, touched now with shadows of blue and purple. The scene was a painting, needing only an artist's talent to transpose to canvas.

That evening after supper, except for a skeleton crew forced to remain on board, the men were given permission to disembark. A couple of separate groups set off to sniff out that part of the city that held the bars and houses of prostitution. Tait was not among them. "I've given up the pleasure mongers," he told the men when they asked him to join them. "There's only so much pleasure an old body can take." Tait looked to be near sixty years of age although no one knew exactly how old he was.

Sean declined to go with the men as well and later left the ship alone with the intention of enjoying a solitary walk through the city streets, taking it in, being content to be a visitor exploring new surroundings. The setting sun offered him a soft light to show him the way. He walked a primary avenue, what looked to be one of the main streets of the city, continuing on until curiosity turned him down an intersection. Here the streets squeezed narrow. The closeness of the houses on either side kept what little sunlight the day still offered away and the corresponding shadows made the air chillier. He passed some fine adobe homes topped with orange slated roofs, kept aloof from the street by black wrought iron fences. Then, continuing on, he stepped through a slow transition to a neighborhood of poverty. He walked one street odd in its contrast. Worn, tired, frame houses stood between new and expensive appearing stores with plate glass windows. Poverty standing cheek to cheek with wealth. The landlord and the hobo side by side and holding hands. Another short distance and all suggestions of wealth were left behind, Sean walking now in an area of dilapidated homes, grimy with neglect and cracked with lack of care.

He passed a group of ill-dressed little children, the oldest perhaps six years old, playing without supervision in the streets, running like excited puppies beside chickens and small livestock. A little boy, no more than four years of age, scabby kneed, with skin the color of mocha, stared at him with dark shining eyes. Sean smiled and offered the child a "hello". In response, the boy turned and ran from him, disappearing into a cluttered and littered alley. Sean was surprised; having anticipated that the boy would approach him for money, his hand was already in his pocket feeling for change and he removed it now, spreading his fingers in a "too bad" gesture.

He walked for almost an hour, and then, with night having chased away all but the slightest remnants of daylight, began circling his way back toward the water where his ship was docked.

A stone steeple peered up at the sky from behind a series of rooftops and, at the sight of it, he was reminded of how long it'd been since he'd last visited a church. Spurred by a sudden impulse he turned at the corner of the street and walked in the direction of the steeple.

Some street entertainers were performing in front of the church, a group of woolly-haired mulatto urchins hoping to glean a little money from pedestrians and tourists, poorly dressed and dancing to the rhythm of a drum. Sean had heard the drum-pounding well before he saw the entertainers and wondered about the purpose of the noise. Now he knew. He watched the drummer for a minute. Little skill there. Simply a young man pounding a large drum with the palms of his hand with all his energy, looking more like a wild-eyed child throwing a tantrum than a trained musician. Still, he threw some change into the hat resting on the sidewalk, a petitioner for money.

Sean went up the aged stone steps, pulled the church door open and entered inside. The vestibule was dark, cool and somehow immediately comforting. Walking down the center aisle, he went toward a wonderfully carved wooden crucifix, down to the front of the nave, and there settled into the first pew, nearest the altar.

"Long time," he murmured to the figure on the cross as he tapped his forehead to begin the sign of the cross. "Long time."

His eyes wandered over the frosted white windows, dull now but windows that no doubt gleamed bright in sunlight, then his gaze lowered to pass over the few statues and representations of the Stations of the Cross that sat at intervals on the walls. A statue of the Virgin, carved out of ebony wood, was snuggled within a nook to the left of the altar, standing almost shyly behind two rows of candles. A few of the candles were burning.

There was someone there in the shadows, kneeling in front of the candles and praying fervently to the statue. A foreigner. Sean's gaze stuck itself to the worshiper but it required a few seconds of looking before he realized, with no small surprise, that the kneeling man was none other than his shipmate, Tait. Tait with the untidy face.

*   *   *

"Yea, found religion a while back. In that very church we was in. Thanks to that wood Madonna. Want to hear 'bout it?"

Sean and Tait were seated at a table in a small out-of-the-way bar on a back street familiar to the older man. A cheap and dingy place, dark, with bare, blackened wood floors and walls wearing little decoration. Except for the shock of the bright blue and yellow feathers of a macaw seated on a perch by the bar, the place was colorless. The heavy, blackened wood and sparse atmosphere created a medieval sense in the room, Sean feeling as though he'd gone back a few centuries in time when he and Tait first entered the place. Tait had selected the table they now sat at.

"Sure, why not?" replied Sean to Tait's question as he picked up the bottle of beer he'd carried from the bar, put it to his mouth and took a swallow. Tait imitated him with his own bottle, also taking a swig of beer.

"You know, you remind me of me. When I was younger I was a lot like you. Not quite as tall but a lot like you. You look like a fighter. Built like one, I mean. I was one once. A career fighter, a pugilist." Tait said the word with an affected high-class accent. "Had a nice career going for a time, a middleweight with a shot. But – " Tait shrugged, " – it all fell apart. I was tough as nails. That's how it is at your age. You feel immortal, as though nothing can touch you. You feel like you'll live forever." He chuckled and took another swallow of beer. "But when you reach my age you start thinking that Old Man Death is waiting for you round every corner, and he's not inviting you to the pub for a drink, but holding a blade in each hand to stick between your ribs. Yeah, it's all dreams and wishes when you're young. But, unless you're lucky boy, it all changes. Dreams break and you're left with nothing but an old body, a sense that time is running out and there's nothing you can do to stop it. Life's like a wild animal, boy. When you're young you can grab it by the tail and make it behave but when you get older and start to lose your strength, it turns on you. Bares its claws. Then you know it's just a matter of time before the beast tears you up. But you're young and I might as well be talking a foreign language to you. Right, boy? Do you have a woman at home?"

Sean smiled at the suddenness of the question, tacked on as it was to the tail end of Tait's soliloquy. "No. No one special."

"Good. Keep it that way. Ain't a woman in the world worth a damn." He lifted the bottle of beer and drained its contents without putting it down. Then he waited until he caught the bartender's eye and waved for another. "Again for you, Sean?" he asked at the last second. Sean shook his head and pointed a finger to Tait's scar. "What about the woman with the red hair?" he asked.

Tait's lips curled up in a smile. "Got me there, boy. Yeah, that was one woman worth more than a damn."

Tait, waiting for his beer, pulled out one of his black cigars and lit it up. Drawing deeply, he released a cloud of smoke into the air. Sean expected him to tell him the history of the scar and the one woman "worth more than a damn" but instead Tait spoke of the church they'd just left. "You remember that statue of Mary I was praying in front of?" he asked.

"Sure."

"But you don't know the story surrounding it. Someone told me that church is over three hundred years old. I have no reason to doubt it. I don't know how old the statue is. About thirty or so years back that statue created a ruckus in this city, in the whole country in fact, and beyond too. It was reported that the wooden Madonna, that same carving of Mary, was actually shedding tears. Crying. As though it was alive."

"Really?" responded Sean, his eyes widening with interest.

"The story goes that a priest was in the church one morning, on the altar, maybe preparing for the next sermon. It doesn't matter. An old woman was praying in front of the statue of Mary when suddenly she starts shouting, screaming hysterical-like, like someone set her panties on fire. Naturally the priest comes running over to see what's wrong. She points to the weeping Madonna and when he sees the tears rolling down the wood cheeks of the statue he nearly falls on the seat of his pants. He scans the ceiling to check for leaks but there aren't any. He steps past the candles and pats the cloth covering the stand on which the statue sits. It's soaking wet. The few other people in the church are drawn to the commotion and, when they see and hear what's happening, they drop to their knees and pray, convinced they're witnessing a miraculous sign from God. The priest runs to tell his superior what's happened and soon a big piece of the world is involved.

"Word of the miracle spreads quickly. First in the city and then through the country and then finally to the outside world. In the following weeks thousands of people make the journey, a pilgrimage, to come here."

"To this bar?" broke in Sean, smiling.

"What? No, wiseass." Tait was chuckling, he wasn't angry. "To the church. To view the weeping Mary. Many come to witness the miracle for themselves as the Madonna continues, now and then, to shed her tears."

"That's quite a story," commented Sean as Tait halted in his narrative to drink from another freshly arrived bottle of beer. "I've heard of other stories like it. Statues and icons, even paintings, that cry. Do you believe it?"

Tait ignored the question. "It created such a reaction in the city that it couldn't be ignored by the Church. A high official came from Rome to investigate the truth of it. Scientists came too, to ferret out the real reason for what they knew couldn't be true. They failed. Even while these scientists were there, the moisture formed again and tears dropped from the Madonna's wooden eyes. They never could explain it. I heard the story years later. Years after the first teardrops fell. They stopped as suddenly as they started. Every time I come here I go to that church and ask the statue to weep for me. It never does."

"So you won't believe it until you see it for yourself?" asked Sean.

Tait stared at him. "You misunderstand me," he said. "I believe it. I believe it all just as it was reported. I believe it one hundred percent."

*   *   *

After Tait and Sean split up, with Tait returning to the ship and Sean deciding to remain on shore, Sean strolled back to the church in which he'd met Tait earlier. Tait's history of the Madonna had prodded his interest enough to make him want to view the carving one more time. He'd barely glanced at it previously.

The church interior greeted him with its solemn hush. At this hour the place was almost entirely empty with just two worshipers inside, each alone, sitting near opposite walls. Sean went directly to the front and stood before the once renowned statue. A beautiful carving, cut from the wood with care and love. The sculptor clearly was talented, and probably a true believer besides. The statue's pose however was standard. The Madonna stood with her head slightly bowed and with her hands open, the palms up. The beauty was in the details, in the folds of the cloth and the features of the face. Certainly in the eyes, which seemed almost alive with love. The carving alone, the work itself, was a small miracle. A miracle of the human spirit's ability to transform a common piece of wood into Art.

He kneeled before it, as he'd seen Tait do, and prayed a demand, the same demand Tait had told him he'd made to it: *Cry for me. Cry for me.*

Of course nothing occurred. And, after granting the statue a couple of minutes to make the decision to perform for him, Sean stood up and went out of the church, concluding that the wooden Madonna, like Sean himself, did not respond well to unreasonable demands. He knew that, in making such kinds of "prayers" one was treating God and saints as though they were part of some kind of vending machine. *Drop the coin of a prayer into a slot and watch them perform for you. Dance for me. Doesn't work that way, does it?* Still, it was worth a try.

He walked away from the church with the intention of returning to the ship, but then, seeing a tight path that seemed to lead up a hill, and once again yielding to impulse, he changed his mind and walked the path, a narrow, meandering trail that led up through trees toward higher ground. It almost immediately grew steep enough to make it a task to walk upon it. He followed the trail to its end and found himself, after a quarter-hour of walking uphill, standing on a hilltop.

From this vantage point he was able to look down over the harbor, now crowded with masts and smokestacks. Lights gleamed in the night, striving to out-sparkle the stars overhead and failing to do it, for the sky above was ablaze with many stars. A shoreline in the distant black night wore a curving necklace of lights, lights gleaming from the homes and shops standing on the city's main street so very near the water. Closer to him, a freighter was getting up a good head of steam, preparing to depart. Sean saw, to his left, his own anchored ship. It would be leaving in the morning. Around him, in the trees, he heard the sounds of birds, loud, as if complaining, disturbed by his presence here.

And perhaps, in that moment, as Sean stared out at the sea, the miracle he'd demanded half-seriously earlier in church occurred, taking shape not in the blatancy of tears falling from a shrine's wooden eyes but rather in the form of an internal shifting of *purpose* within Sean himself. *The United States*, he thought as he stared out toward the dark horizon. *I've never been there. I'd like to go.*

Fate? Perhaps if one had supernatural ears, one would have heard at that moment the sound of a metaphysical gearbox turning and grinding into action. Perhaps, at this moment, the Power represented by the church Sean had prayed in suddenly chose to intervene in the random rumblings of the world He created, and intervened to push the thought, the desire to go to the United States, into Sean's head. The Almighty pays attention to so-called great events and to individual private affairs equally it is said, offering love to all, the great and the small, and, if that is so, it may also be true that He is continually offering the world little miracles too subtle for sight and appreciation.

Standing on the Brazilian hilltop, staring into the dark starlit night shrouding the harbor, Sean suddenly made the up-to-then never contemplated choice to travel to New York City in the United States. Was this decision on his part a small miracle, unseen and unnoticed as such? A miracle of wooden eyes without the tears? For a miracle of sorts is what it was. Here was a decision that would ultimately change his life, and Ellen's as well

For the decision made on that hilltop ultimately put him upon a course that would, in little more than a year's time, place him on the corner of Christopher and Bleeker streets in the Greenwich Village section of New York City. Walking there, he chanced to glance to his right and, in that moment, thought he saw someone he once knew.

Ellen? Is that Ellen Rawdon?

Yes, he was certain of it. It was Ellen Rawdon, his old boyhood friend's little sister.

Jimmy's little sister, Ellen.

Chapter Forty

The Ellen that Sean was looking at was little no longer. For a moment he was motionless, startled at the maturity and beauty of the woman before him, comparing the living person to the image of the little girl he still held in his memory. Momentarily, the Ellen in front of him and the image of the little girl of the past sat juxtaposed side-by-side in his mind and he was astounded at the difference between the two.

"You're staring," said Ellen with a smile, her cheeks flushing pink.

"Am I? Yes, I'm sorry," apologized Sean. "I'm just – amazed. You're all grown up. Hey, can I invite you for a bite to eat? Tea or coffee? Let me treat you to a lunch. We can talk about the Old Sod and catch up. Look, there's a place right across the street. We can go right there."

"Sure," responded Ellen, without hesitation. "Let's go."

"That's what I like about this city," commented Sean as he started across the street with Ellen beside him. "Everything is always just across the street." They squeezed between two parked cars and crossed over to the little restaurant Sean had pointed to. Inside, they settled in at a small table.

A waitress appeared, brusquely handed them Saturday brunch menus and asked if they wanted anything to drink. Ellen indicated she wanted tea and Sean, who wanted a beer, went along. "Two teas," he told the waitress who then, with a grunt, departed. The only other customers in the place were two gray-haired men sitting and staring with stern expressions at a backgammon game. Mugs of steaming coffee sat near the fingertips of each man. A wonderful smell of fresh baked goods floated in the air, and it made Ellen think of her home in Ireland.

A large, brightly polished brass Expresso machine sat behind a counter at the rear of the room.

"So tell me 'bout yourself, Ellen Rawdon," invited Sean. "And Jim. Tell me 'bout old Jim. How is he?"

"Jimmy's fine. He's stayed on the farm all these years. At first I know he hated it, staying there, but now he wouldn't dream of leaving. There were some lean years at first, but now he's doing better. And he's married – "

"Jim? Married?" Sean stared at Ellen as though she'd told him her brother had grown wings and was planning a flight to the highest hilltop in Donegal.

Ellen nodded. "In fact he sent me some pictures." She pulled her pocketbook up to the table and rummaged through it, finally producing a small packet of photos that she handed to Sean.

A smile appeared on Sean's face as he gazed at the images. There was his boyhood friend, much the same, older of course and a bit heavier about the middle, but much the same, standing in front of the Rawdon home. And there, beside him, also smiling for the camera, was a plump, brown-haired woman with soft eyes and a pretty, round Irish face.

As Sean studied the photos, Ellen scrutinized him, assimilating him. He was as handsome as ever and there was a gentleness about him that she found appealing. A relaxed, casual figure now in his tan corduroy jacket and open white shirt. Ellen recalled how her sisters idolized him years ago. They'd wanted to make him a god once.

"So Jim's been taken prisoner and brought before the firing squad," said Sean as he handed the photos back to Ellen. "She's pretty. And Jim looks as healthy as a horse. They both look happy."

"Yes. I'm happy for him. With everyone gone, he'd be alone on the farm. I'm glad he found someone."

The waitress returned with their teas. Apparently, in her short time away, she'd also discovered the secret spot in which she'd hidden her good humor for this time she smiled at them. "Ready to order? Or do you need more time?"

"Just give us a couple of minutes, thanks," replied Sean. The woman nodded and walked away.

"And you, Ellen," said Sean, pointing a finger to the wedding band on her finger. "I see you've found someone too."

Ellen dropped her eyes to her hand. "Oh, that. Yes – but – " (*Should I tell him?*) "It didn't work out. I'm divorced actually. I wear the ring though. I learned it helps – helps keep the undesirables away."

"Divorced? I'm sorry."

Ellen waved the words away. "No, it's all right. It was a while ago."

"The ring doesn't always work," commented Sean, smiling now. "Does it?"

"What – ?" Ellen didn't understand.

"You said it's to keep the undesirables away. Yet here I am."

Ellen laughed. "Well, if the ring doesn't work, I still have my blackthorn stick to beat you with. I just have to ask you to wait while I go back to my apartment and get it. Enough about me. Let's talk about you. What have you been doing all these years? What brings you to New York?"

"I don't know. It seemed like the place to come to. Now it's work keeping me here, I suppose. I was lucky. I'm now working for a television news station of all things. I sort of stumbled into it. After school I went straight to work in the Bank of Ireland, stayed there for a few years, making money to send home to the farm. Thought I had to do that so I did it. Then my parents passed on – "

Ellen gasped. "Oh, Sean, I'm sorry," she told him. "I liked them so much. What happened?"

"Da went with a sudden heart attack," replied Sean. "And his passing really took a toll on my mother I guess. She followed him a few months after. Broken heart I think. Can you imagine loving someone that much?"

Ellen didn't answer and Sean went on. "After my mother passed, I traveled a couple of years. Wanted to see a bit of the world. Worked aboard old freighters and went where they took me. Up to last year. After that time I guess I had enough. Maybe it was something a shipmate said to me. He'd been on ships for almost his whole life and, after all that time, he told me he couldn't see much point in doing it. Years of traveling he meant. Years of just looking at things. Being outside and looking in. I thought about that and decided I wanted my life to have some point to it. No matter how insignificant. I suppose I decided New

York was a good place to start. I made my way here and got lucky right away. Landed a job with the television news. ABC. I write the words to tell the stories. Pays more money than I ever thought I'd be making. Pretty lucky, actually. The way it all turned out."

The waitress returned and they gave her their order. Ellen, over the food that very quickly arrived, spoke a little of her own history, hesitantly, which was natural enough as she hadn't seen Sean in so many years. She relaxed more when the conversation turned away from her and focused instead on the general past. They spoke of common memories and events in Moville, of their homes and mutual friends, of times that seemed now to have existed so long ago. Ellen felt it was a pleasure to have Sean to talk about old times to, to have him sitting across a table from her.

They talked on for more than two hours. It might have been much less than that, or so it seemed to Ellen. Glancing at her wristwatch, she was surprised by how much time had passed and announced she had to leave. Unspoken was the reason, that she had to get home to her son. She hadn't spoken to Sean at all about her children, about the death of one, about the survival of the other, keeping that part of her past private, at least for now.

As they parted, Sean asked to see her again, inviting her to the theater and dinner. Ellen happily accepted, without a moment's hesitation. Unusual for her. Especially now.

For his part, Sean had no real desire to see a Broadway play or eat in a fancy restaurant, what he did want was the pleasure of looking once again into Ellen's eyes, of hearing her voice speaking to him once more. He wanted her company again. As soon as possible he wanted that. Suddenly, mysteriously, it was one of the most important things in his life.

They parted, each offering the other a wave and smile as they walked in opposite directions, and Ellen found her mind crammed with nothing but thoughts of Sean as she returned to her home, walking uptown, seeing little of the streets through which she passed.

Chapter Forty-one

The following Saturday night, Ellen and Sean went to the theater and enjoyed a presentation of the popular drama, "Cat on a Tin Roof". Afterwards, over dinner, Ellen said she felt sorry for the old man who complained about mendacity. She sympathized with him. "It was an interesting play."

"Depressing though. I actually thought I was buying tickets to a musical. Let's eat."

They chatted only a little bit about the play they'd just seen, neither one really that interested in Tennessee Williams' philosophy of life. Both events, the play and dinner, were made extraordinary primarily because they, Ellen and Sean, were together. Nothing really mattered to Ellen other than the fact that she was with Sean and he was with her. Sean, for his part, felt exactly the same way. He could have spent the evening sitting on a park bench being entertained by sleeping pigeons and it would have been all the same to him, as long as it was Ellen sitting on the bench beside him.

*   *   *

At that time in her life, Ellen's heart was a place broken into sections, a garden in which a not insignificant portion was effectively shrouded in thick shadow, a result of the profound hurts she had endured over the past few years. Those sorrows had not simply come and gone but had thrown off seeds of wary fear that rooted themselves in the most private place of her soul. There, unbidden, the seeds had grown into weeds thick and dense enough to forbid the entry of sunlight beyond the tangled wall of their own existence. In that special and secret section of the heart, that recess that is the sole place in which the rich and multiple colors of passionate love can truly bloom, there was in Ellen only deep darkness, a heavy obscurity that seemed increasingly to be absolute, more immutable than stone.

Until she met Sean. Then, in a series of amazing moments, first occurring as she sat in that small eatery on Bleeker Street and then again on the Saturday she went to the theater, she felt her heart begin to alter itself, to begin to accept a new brightness. Somehow, sunlight was creeping past the shadows.

Later, sitting home alone, with Philip long ago tucked away in his bed, Ellen found herself incapable of doing anything except sitting and thinking of Sean and, in thinking of him, she was suddenly acutely aware of how long it had been since she had made love to a man. Thinking of him, she found herself contemplating what it would be like to be held by him, to recline beside him and hold him tightly in return. That speculation sent a sense of excitement through her, an excitement that sat warm and smiling on the cheeks of her face.

With the same elusive mystery and magic with which Life transforms inanimate matter into living, sentient creatures, so Love, true Love, can infuse and transform Life into something more than what it otherwise is. Sitting on the sofa, in one amazing instant, Ellen felt her heart fill with an incandescent and gleaming brilliance, as though the sun in one final tremendous effort had at last burst through the twisted growth of past tragedy to obliterate all remaining shadow existing there. Suddenly, miraculously, her heart was bursting with colors and springtime again. Ellen felt alive, fully alive, once more.

She'd put Sean off that Saturday night, that first time, but she knew afterwards, sitting alone on her couch, her mind filled with thoughts of him and her heart suddenly filled with love and desire for him, that she'd never deny him again.

And she didn't. Only the very next night, she didn't.

*   *   *

They saw each other almost constantly over the next few months and Ellen's heart during that time was more enthusiastically happy than it had been in many years, but human beings do not exist by their hearts alone, they have minds and souls as well. As happy as Ellen was, it was happiness still tainted, for at its edges, outside the walls of her heart, there remained the remnants of the sorrows she'd suffered in the past. There remained too the sense of morality she'd been taught as a child. Caution and Morality were outcasts for now but they still lurked at the borders of her thoughts, staring at her, always vaguely threatening to invade.

Years ago, when she was a small girl in Ireland, how safe everything appeared to be then. How *solid* was the world around her. There was a time when her home, her parents, her existence, seemed as permanent as the hills of Donegal, but she'd learned since what an illusion the idea of permanence was. All things, Love, the people she cared for, the world about her, now lacked the solidity they formally held for that little girl in Donegal. The world was now a volatile place, a place of never-ending change and alteration. A place of harsh wind and shifting shadow that not only gave but also took away, doing so at times with cruelty. She'd once dreamed that some things were forever, that she'd meet a Forever Love. That was an illusion too, wasn't it? Of course. Forever doesn't exist.

All things disappear; either instantly, snatched out of existence like a buzzing fly grabbed up by the tongue of a hungry toad, or more slowly, over time, taken to oblivion almost gently, fading lazily like a morning mist destroyed by the sun, or melting away like a sugar cube in warm water. Many things vanished with their own loss almost unseen in the vanishing.

All things come into existence to be taken away. All things exist to be taken away, here one moment and then, with either a scream of pain or within a cushion of silence and without a murmur of protest, they are gone to nothing.

But her love for Sean was real now. As was his for her. For today. Who could say how long it would last? Best to enjoy the sun while it's shining and not worry about the threat of rain or the night drawing near. *Forget about Forever and enjoy what you can when you can.*

Ellen, older and wiser these days, felt she understood that truth now.

Over the next few months she was happier than she'd been in years, feeling like a teenager, a young girl in love again for the first time. She'd do her best to be grateful for Sean's love, for as long as it lasted.

Then, when it was gone, she would try not to regret that she accepted it. Instead, she would suffer through the price of its loss, and endure the falling of her tears and the ripping of her heart.

The day would surely come when Sean would at last walk away from her with no intention of returning, when he would walk away from her for the last time, when he would be gone and she would not see sight of him again. For wasn't every joy always a prelude to fresh sorrows? Wasn't that another truth she had been forced to learn over the years?

Chapter Forty-two

The flowers were divided into small multi-colored bunches, the stems wrapped in rubber bands and then rolled in green tissue paper. The colorful bunches stood in their green tissue skirts in a few large containers outside the vegetable store next to crates of peas, potatoes, apples, pumpkins and assorted other vegetables that were there. Ellen, heading home, nearly rushed by them as she normally did, but this time, a few steps past, she turned around, went back and selected a couple of bunches of yellow daffodils to bring home with her. A rare thing, this purchase, for it was Ellen's opinion that flowers were an extravagance, a waste of hard-earned money, but the day was gray and damp, a Saturday filled with drizzle and dim light, and she wanted to bring some color into her apartment, so today, for once, she would surrender to extravagance.

An Asian man with gold-framed spectacles took her money, smiled and nodded. "See you," he said, offering her the slightest suggestion of a bow with a nod of his head and shoulders. Ellen wondered if he'd meant "Thank you" as she returned his smile and turned to leave.

A gust of chilly October air rustled the thin paper protecting her purchase and then swirled against her legs as she walked away. It caught the edge of the cloth of her skirt and lifted it up, the breeze suddenly deciding to act like a playful schoolboy teasing a girl student. A young man, catching a glimpse of exposed thigh, winked his approval as he walked by in the opposite direction.

As Ellen reached the entrance to her building, a break in the clouds appeared, granting momentary permission for the sun to peek through, albeit without enthusiasm, looking down at the Earth with a weak and watery gaze, that of an old man longing to close his tired eyes and return to rest.

Inside the apartment her son was seated by the window, craning his neck to see into the street below, waiting in anticipatory excitement of Sean's arrival, his eyes anxiously searching for the appearance of the man. Philip and Sean had, over the past few months, become the best of friends. Philip idolized him.

"Mom's home," called out Ellen. The boy offered her a perfunctory "Hi Mom," and returned his eyes to the window. *You're not Sean*, the boy's actions said. Ellen smiled, accepting that fact that her son had a case of hero worship and that she was now second on his list of "wanna-see" people. The radiator by the window began once again to hiss heat into the room.

Ellen unwrapped the daffodils and placed them in a glass vase that she then put on the coffee table. Their presence did indeed make the room brighter as she hoped, and somehow that splash of yellow made her feel better. The sacrifice of the daffodils had not been in vain.

The sun disappeared again, too weary to battle with the clouds, and the interior of the apartment became darker than was normal at this time of day. Ellen switched on a lamp to bring light into the room

It's chilly, she decided and went into the kitchen to make a pot of tea as Philip moved away from the window, driven away both by his own impatience and by the increasing heat of the radiator. He turned on the TV and plopped himself down on the floor in front of it.

Five minutes later when the bell rang he emitted a gleeful yelp. "It's Sean!" he shouted, leaping up and running to the door. If the coffee table had been in his way he'd have jumped over it like a steeplechase horse driving for the finish line. He greeted Sean with a face that was all grin and enthusiasm and stood by possessively as Sean and Ellen embraced. "C'mon Sean, let's go out. C'mon."

Sean looked down at the tugging "C'mons" that were yanking at him for attention. "Do you see the coat I'm wearing, Phil?" he asked.

"Sure."

"And what do you see on the coat?"

Philip's mouth dropped open. "Rain," he groaned, his voice suddenly heavy with disappointment. Evidencing an inherent scientific instinct for verification, he ran to the window and stared outside. It was teeming.

He turned and looked at Sean. "But we can go out anyway, can't we?"

"Only if we turn into ducks," replied Sean, taking his coat off and handing it to Ellen. "No, I'm afraid the elements are against us today, boyo. It started pouring just as I got here. And it doesn't look ready to stop any time soon, does it?"

Philip ran to the window again. The rain continued to fall in torrents. "Rats!" he muttered. He returned to Sean wearing a dark, angry frown of disappointment.

"Well, look at that dreary face," commented Sean. "It makes the day outside seem absolutely sunny." He turned to Ellen. "We might have a cloudburst in here too with that thundercloud about. Look, it's too wet to go to the park as we wanted but maybe the boy's right and we can still go out. How 'bout we take him to the Metropolitan Museum instead? He could use a little culture."

"Oh, so my boy needs culture, is it? I'm raising a little ignorant heathen, is that it? Well, you're right, Sean, he *is* a little heathen. Aren't you, Philip?" The boy nodded his head enthusiastically. "What's a heathen?" he asked.

"So we'd better get some culture into him," continued Ellen. "The sooner the better." She handed Sean's coat back to him.

"Good," responded Sean. "We can grab a taxi and shoot over there. How's that sound, Philip?"

Philip held his doubts and his expression evidenced it, but he nodded his head. Apparently it was the museum or nothing. "Great," he told Sean. The word half lie and half compromise.

"I'll have to put pants on," said Ellen. "And boots too."

"Hey, what's a heathen?" asked Philip once again.

*　　*　　*

The three of them couldn't fit beneath one umbrella so Sean walked alone under his own while Ellen and Philip shared another. As dreary as the weather was, it held some appeal too. Maybe it's in the Irish genes to consider shades of gray delightful in the same way Mediterranean cultures worship the sun. Ellen found herself enjoying the sound of the rain pelting the cloth of the umbrella overhead and relishing the sense of shelter the cloth offered her in its protection from the downpour.

Luck could still shine on them even if the sun would not. Empty taxis are less abundant in New York during a rainstorm, but after just a couple of minutes' wait, they were fortunate enough to see a vacant one coming along. Sean hailed it over and the three climbed quickly inside. In the seconds it took them to close their umbrellas and enter the cab, they got rained upon, becoming wet enough to complain about it.

"Some day, folks," commented the driver. "Where to?"

In twenty minutes they were running up the great slabs of steps in front of the Metropolitan Museum. The sidewalk, which in better weather would be filled with street entertainers, vendors and clusters of pedestrians and onlookers, was today almost deserted.

But inside, the museum was surprisingly crowded. "See these people, Phil?" whispered Sean to Philip. "Some of them actually sleep here. Inside the paintings." The boy stared at the crowds and considered the truth of the knowledge Sean had just imparted to him. Sean was always making up tales.

"That can't be . . . ." responded Philip at last. "Can it?"

"Yep. Some of them anyway. They're part of a magical race of people. They can go into the paintings as easily as you and I walk through a door."

Philip, not really believing Sean, but still considering the possibility, stared about him, trying to determine who the "magic" ones were as Sean paid the entrance fee. "Be good," he instructed Philip solemnly. "Or I won't be responsible for the terrible consequences. The guards here are armed with pistols. One or two carry hand grenades."

They walked up the great wide stairs that, Sean knew, would bring them up to the rooms holding the Impressionists works he admired. "Do you know what I like about this place, Philip?" he asked. The boy, drawn by the question away from his contemplation of the immensity of the stairs he was ascending, shook his head.

"Nope."

"It's like a time machine. You feel like you're walking through the centuries instead of just rooms. It makes us a little like time travelers." Philip's eyes took a moment to absorb the concept and then, appreciating it, he smiled up at Sean.

"Golly, Sean, Mom! Look at that!" They'd just reached the top of the stairs and Philip was pointing a finger toward a large statue that greeted them there. Ellen nearly covered her eyes. "Dear God – " she murmured. Philip put his hand over his mouth and giggled. "Didn't men wear pants back in time before?" he asked Sean.

"I suppose the museum people just forgot to put his BVD's on him this morning." He smiled at Ellen. "Dear God – " she repeated, her face blushing pink at the sight of the marble nakedness of the male statue.

"Come on Philip," directed Sean. "It's not polite to stare. "We'll go on in here."

They passed through a series of exhibition rooms. On the walls were displayed many works of Monet, Van Gogh, Degas and others. Each work, even the least of them, constituted a blend of talent, effort and determination on the part of the artist who created it. In some cases, even sacrifice went into the effort. Sean understood that any work of art, whether musical, written or pictorial, was in a sense the residue of a struggle, the victory prize of a battle fought and won. Philip of course couldn't yet see these works as great efforts of will and dedication. He was still too young. They were simply "pretty" or "nice" and if they failed this simple criterion, "crummy". He was indifferent to many.

Before leaving, they stopped in the museum shop where Philip found himself picking up a large book that contained photos of paintings and sculptures of horses. On the cover was Franz Marc's "Blue Horse". Flipping a few pages he gazed at Degas' racetrack pastels and was looking at Delacroix's "Arab Horses Fighting in a Stable" when Sean came up beside him. "You like horses, Philip?" he asked.

"I guess." He closed the book and displayed the cover to Sean. "Can horses be blue?" he asked.

"Well, maybe, but I have to say I've never seen a horse that color. But then who knows for sure? That's a big horse, looks like. If it was meaner looking it might be a pooka. Maybe that's what it is. Pookas could be any color, I think."

Philip didn't know the word. "Pookas? What's that?"

Sean feigned amazement. "Now, don't tell me your mother never told you of the pooka, the great demon horse that is all phantom shadow some of the time but can become substance, can materialize, when it wants to. They're devils, Philip. Devils to be feared. Demon horses black as midnight, when they're not blue as the sky, with great red eyes that glow like burning hot coals and with teeth like saber points."

Philip's face looked like he'd just been seized from behind. He gazed down at the book in his hand suddenly considering the possibility that the blue horse might be capable of peeling itself from the cover and transforming itself into a creature of weight and substance right before his eyes, coming to life so as to stampede him to death beneath its hooves right then and there. Didn't Sean say some of the people here were magic, and living inside the paintings? Could that be true of horses too?

"Don't be telling the boy any of those tales," broke in Ellen. "Look at him, you'll be scaring him so he won't sleep."

"Aw, El, it was your own father told me the pooka's tale. And I was no older than Philip."

"I know. I know too I had nightmares from half my father's stories. I still have nightmares."

"Come to think of it, so did I. I was scared to walk alone at night for a long while. Maybe that's the point in telling it."

"Please, Sean, tell me the story," pleaded Philip. "Please." Sean shot a glance to Ellen who shrugged her defeat.

"Well, tonight then, Phil," responded Sean to the boy. "But only if you're as good as you can be. Then I'll tell you."

"Aw, tell me now," protested Philip. "Please."

"No, Ellen's father, your grandfather, warned me that the story can't be told in large places like this. Nor in the presence of too many people. It must be told in private, and then in low voices and whispers so that nothing can be overheard. Otherwise word might get back to the pooka that it's being talked about and almost nothing gets a pooka as mad as being talked about. From this point on, Philip, we've got to be cautious. Very cautious indeed. Understand?"

Philip's face was dubious, not certain if Sean was pulling his leg or was actually as serious as he pretended to be. But, despite his doubts, he nodded his head, indicating that he did understand. If Sean said so, then this could very well be very serious stuff indeed.

Unless it was just another one of Sean's pretend-stories.

Chapter Forty-three

The elements that had conspired to very nearly ruin the day for Sean, Ellen and Philip now became a willing participant, a stage director, in creating the appropriate atmosphere for the telling of Sean's version of the Irish legend of the terrible pooka, the demon steed. Thunder periodically growled and rumbled like the passing of a thousand train wheels bearing massive weight, rattling the windows and vibrating the walls of Ellen's apartment. The rain, which continued to fall heavily, hissed against the windows as though the very faces and snarling mouths of angry demons were pressing against the panes, seeking entry into the apartment, frustrated at their failure to find a way inside.

Ellen accepted Sean's compliment on the dinner she'd prepared and turned down his offer to help with the dishes, pushing Sean away from the sink. "I'll clean and make tea. You have a promise to keep, remember?"

"Promise?"

"You're going to tell Philip the story of the pooka." Philip, nearby, nodded his head vigorously. "You said you would, Sean," he pleaded.

"So I did and so I shall. C'mon, we'll go inside and get comfortable."

"Remember," called out Ellen to Sean's back as he and Philip left the room, "when the boy's awake with bad dreams in the middle of the night, it's your fault."

"I'll take the blame," responded Sean with a laugh. "What's life without a few bad dreams anyway, right, Phil?"

"Absolutely," agreed the boy, grinning up at Sean. The thought of his questioning the notion that bad dreams might be good for you only briefly occurred to the boy. He decided that if Sean said it was good to have bad dreams now and then, then it most definitely must be so.

*   *   *

Sean, appreciating the atmosphere created by the storm, became an assistant stage director to it. In the living room he put the lamp on low to keep the room in shadows. He made a grand show of peering about the room cautiously while Philip watched him. "Sit, Phil, while I make sure it's safe," he whispered, speaking like a convict planning a jailbreak within five feet of the prison warden's office. "The storm is raging – and nasty, but is it *just* a storm? Or something else?" He let the question hang in the air a moment. "There's always danger when you talk of the pooka, Philip. One must be careful. Although you can never, never, be one hundred percent safe. There's those who would have you think the pooka is just a story, a made-up thing, but I know better. It's real, and it's dangerous, as dangerous as anything can be."

Philip, increasingly wondering if he really wanted to hear about the demon, sat quietly on the sofa, his eyes expanding wider and wider as he gazed at Sean and absorbed each word of caution. "M-Maybe, maybe then we shouldn't talk about it," he suggested in a low voice.

"Maybe. No, I think it's safe enough here," replied Sean as he came over and joined the boy on the sofa. "Although, as I say, you can never be absolutely certain about these things. Well now, at a great risk to my personal safety, let me tell you about the pooka." Seeing Philip's frown tighten and finally realizing his playacting was really beginning to frighten the boy to the point where Philip might be close to wetting the couch, he quickly added: "See, *I* have to be careful. But right now I'm the only one in danger. The pooka is forbidden to hurt little children. Those who are twelve years old or less. How old are you, Philip?"

"Ten!" declared the boy, loud enough for any demon in the local vicinity to hear him, unless the demon had his fingers in his ears. Philip immediately exhaled a sigh of relief but then, in the very next moment, was frowning again. "But I don't want *you* to get hurt," he proclaimed with real concern as he comprehended the fact that, while the pooka-rules protected him, they still left Sean vulnerable. Sean could still be in danger from the demon.

"Thank you for that, Phil," responded Sean. "But I really think we're as safe as we could be." His words were belied by the expression he struck. He looked at Philip with a conspirator's eyes, a conspirator fearing that his life was in fact in mortal danger. "I *think* so, anyway," he added. "All right. Here goes:

"Long ago, so long ago that it was before even time existed, and well before men and women were on the Earth, the world was filled with strange, unusual creatures. It was a hard time, Philip, filled with war, fighting. A time of constant threats and battles between evil demons and good creatures. Between devils and good angels too. The world then was in chaos, in danger of being ruined altogether with all the battling that was going on and God, looking down from Heaven, wasn't happy with it, not a bit. Warring factions irritate God, Philip. Very much – "

"Factions?" broke in Philip. "What's that?"

"A group. A gang. Some did bad, and God, well, He created all his creatures to do good, not bad, so He was angry that some had turned bad in spite of what He wanted. But He'd given them free will, which is the ability to choose their own way, and some, much to God's disappointment, chose to do bad. This both saddened God and made Him angry as well. But despite His displeasure with these evil creatures He was hesitant to destroy them for God doesn't like to destroy anything.

"And God also wanted the Earth now to be the home for his newest creation, human beings, men and women. Could humans survive in the world as it was? God knew that they couldn't, Philip. Not in such a world, a world in which so many mighty creatures and demons (they weren't called demons until after they became evil) existed. So what could He do? He didn't want to destroy these demons and yet He didn't want them destroying people. What could He do?"

Philip stared up at him and frowned his ignorance. "Don't know – "

"God divided the world into dimensions, Philip. These were unseen walls, invisible, composed of space and time, walls that allowed men and demons to both share the world and yet remain separate from each other. These invisible walls were meant to keep people and demons forever apart. The angels God took up into Heaven where they are now. Some of the good creatures, a very few, He let stay here."

Philip nodded his head indicating his enthusiasm for God's good judgment.

"But while these unseen walls were being formed, some of the demons decided they preferred to remain on this side of the wall. They wanted to stay here for no other reason than they were being forced to live on the other side. And so they hid. They hid themselves wherever they could. Don't forget that many had great and magic powers. One hid inside a moonbeam, having changed his shape and form to resemble moonlight. One turned green and slimy and hid in a mossy, slithery swamp. They were evil but they were also smart. Demons can be cunning, Philip, and they can be very tricky."

"Didn't God see them hiding? God sees everything, doesn't He?"

"Of course," replied Sean. "Nothing can hide from God. But remember, some of the good creatures, good witches, fairies and elves, and others as well were allowed to stay here and so God decided to let some of the evil ones remain behind as well, to balance everything out. You see, Philip, God knew that a major part of being good is fighting evil. And that people would never really be as good as they could be unless there was some evil in the world for them to resist. So He let a few of these demons remain hidden.

"But God also realized that these demons were much too powerful to be allowed to remain on Earth exactly as they were. Left alone, they would continue to roam and destroy. It was too dangerous for people. So God did something else. He protected the world by limiting the powers of the spirits and demons in various ways. Some could only use their power at night. Some were forbidden to first approach people but could use their evil powers only when people invited them to use them or threatened them in some way. Others are limited to living in only one place, such as a deep cave, and are forever forbidden to leave under penalty of death. Others can interact with people only under certain very specific circumstances. The *banshee* is an example of that kind of spirit. Do you know what a *banshee* is?"

Philip shook his head.

"It's a spirit that's allowed to appear to people only when the death of a loved one is near. Then all they're permitted to do is wail and howl, which is enough, for the howls are such they generally scare the bejabbers out of anyone who hears them screaming. These kinds of limitations are common to all spirits, and they apply to the pooka as well. The pooka is only permitted to take the shape of a horse. Well, sometimes another animal or two, a goat now and then, but usually it's a horse. But it's never a common horse. No, it's a creature greater in size than an ordinary horse, and it's usually as black as a moonless midnight so it's hard to see in the night, you see. But I suppose if it came out in the daytime it might be blue like in that book. Blue like the sky so that when it flew overhead no one would see it. Dangerous creatures, the pookas. Their heads resemble the head of any horse in shape except for the eyes and the teeth. The eyes glow like red coals smoldering in a hearth and their teeth, Philip, their teeth are rat-like, small and needle-sharp. Oh, Phil, it's a sight to make your eyes run screaming away from your head. The pooka's face can strike terror into a brave man's heart and freeze it solid with icy fear. It's said there's nothing more frightening than staring into a pooka's glowing red eyes and watching the mouth, with its rat teeth, curl into an evil grin, a grin of happiness, for when it grins it knows it's got you. The grin, Philip. That's when you know you're in the pooka's power. And then it's too late . . . much too late."

"G-Golly – " stammered Philip, who, to Sean's satisfaction, was now all eyes and open mouth. Somewhere in the child's imagination, he was standing in a vague darkness and gazing into the evil face and gleaming red eyes of the pooka at that very moment. The demon horse might have come up from under the couch to stand in front of him, grinning its rat-like grin at him.

"The pooka," continued Sean, "is very clever in its evil way, and has the power to dispel itself, to kind of evaporate itself until it almost disappears, becoming little more than a vague misty dark shadow. In this way it hides so that people can't see it, until it wants you to see it. In this way it can trap people into coming to it, for you see, the pooka is forbidden to approach people. People must go to it, except when people talk about it, that is. Then it's allowed to come after you.

"Another power it has is its magical ability to hold you on its back so that once you're riding it, you can't get off. No matter how much you try, no matter how much you squirm or kick or scream, you stay on the creature's back as though your hind end is sweating glue. You stay on until the pooka releases you or until you're dead, Philip. Whichever comes first."

"Can the pooka make you ride it?" asked Philip, his eyes opening a little bit wider.

"Ah, good question. No, the pooka cannot do that, force you on its back. A man must climb on of his own free will. But remember Philip, the pooka is very clever, and once you have a pooka after you, it wants nothing more than to get you. It will try to trick you onto its back. And it will keep trying until it has you."

Ellen came in carrying a cup of tea in each hand. "I heard you in the kitchen. You spin quite a tale," she said as she placed one cup on the coffee table in front of Sean. "Put something under that," she ordered and Sean obediently grabbed a magazine and placed it under the teacup. Ellen held onto the second cup as she went to a chair. "I swear it's like hearing Da again."

Sean smiled at her, accepting her words as a great compliment, and then turned back to Philip: "Your mother has doubts about the pooka being real. That's why she called it a tale. But I'm telling you, Philip, it's real. As real as that rain outside. And now that you know what a pooka is, I can tell you of poor Tom Donovan who lived in Greencastle very near the town of Moville where your mother and I grew up. Tom's story was told to me by your own grandpa.

"One fine morning Tom woke early from a sound sleep. Putting on his pants and shoes he left the bedroom and his sleeping wife and went off into the kitchen. There he started to boil water for some tea. As the sun wasn't up yet, it was very chilly and he wanted to put a little warmth into his belly.

"While he's waiting for the water to boil he goes to the window and inhales a deep breath of good clear Donegal air. Then he lets his eyes wander over his land. He was a man very proud of his farm. But, while proud of it, he wasn't entirely happy with it, for he wanted more profits out of it. He wanted more money, Philip. Now it happened that a large portion of his land was covered by a large and foul-smelling bog and this bog irritated Donovan no end. He wanted nothing more than to have it drained and the land made suitable for farming. So's he could make more money.

"And little by little he was doing it. Over the past couple of years Donovan had succeeded in draining large pieces of the bog, shrinking its size in direct proportion to how much draining he did. And he was happily increasing his profits, with more land being available for plowing. But what old Tom didn't know was that the bog was the home of a particularly nasty pooka and this particularly nasty pooka was not at all pleased with the shrinking of its home. It'd lived in that bog for centuries and liked living there. Oh, the demon was angry, Philip, so angry that its great tail was always twitching like that of an irritated cat and its red eyes glowed twice as red as normal, looking like they had pupils of red flame. It vowed to get Tom Donovan.

"Another harvest came and went and all the time, unknown to Tom, the pooka was waiting for its chance to get him. And one moonlit night, as Donovan drove home from the cobbles of the streets of Greencastle, as he passed over the countryside in his brand new car, the pooka got its chance. And the demon made the best of it.

"As he did every year, Donovan had spent a few hours in the pub. He was in high spirits, celebrating the success of the year's harvest and all the money he'd made and he was still feeling happy as he was driving home. He was a temperate man, was Donovan, not a heavy drinker at all, and so he'd only two or three pints of ale. It's not good to drink too much, Philip, it makes you stupid and careless. You don't want to have whisky-brains in your head."

Philip nodded his head, taking in the lesson.

"And Donovan, while stupid sometimes about certain things, was very rarely careless. He never went into the bog for example, for he knew bogs were dangerous even without pookas in them. And he certainly never went into the bog at night. In fact he seldom stayed out at all after sunset. That's why the pooka had to make a plan, a plan that'd succeed somehow in getting Tom into the bog – after dark.

"The pooka had realized over the years that every year Donovan went into town to celebrate the harvest and every year he came back late, although not quite at night. And with that knowledge the pooka saw its opportunity to get Tom Donovan. This particular year the demon was ready.

"This year, as Tom drove home and reached the old covered bridge spanning the stream that irrigated his land, he saw to his surprise in the evening twilight and the pale beams of the car's headlights, the destruction of that bridge. It was literally torn apart, shattered to bits as though it'd been the site of a sledge hammer contest. Planks and pieces of beams lay scattered along the road and by the banks of the stream. The bridge was totally destroyed."

"The pooka did it!" piped up Philip.

"Right on the money, Phil. It was indeed the pooka's work. But Donovan didn't know that. Now who could have done such a terrible thing to that fine old bridge? he wondered as he stared at the remains. Why would anyone want to do such a senseless thing? See, it was senseless to Donovan because he couldn't see the *plan* behind it. He clucked his tongue and then turned his thoughts to another problem. With the bridge gone, how was he to get to his home?

"The most direct route to Donovan's home (as the pooka knew) was a narrow, rutted path that led through a corner of what remained of the bog and, as Tom Donovan was a direct man, he decided that this path would be the way for him to go. With this decision, he was doing exactly what the pooka wanted, exactly what it had thought Tom would do.

"It was a narrow road but was still wide enough for his auto so Tom climbed back into the car and started off, believing he'd be home and tucked in bed in just a few more minutes. His car was rocking and bouncing as it rolled on the uneven path. It grew dark. The bulrushes and the branches were brushing up against the car, making hissing, scraping sounds, much like the rain and wind outside that window right now." Sean pointed to the window and, as if on command, a rumble of thunder vibrated in the distance, causing the window to shiver.

"Once Donovan entered the bog, unusual happenings occurred. Clouds of mist suddenly rose up on all sides, obscuring the road in front of him. A black cloud crawled like a great spider across the moon, making the night black as pitch. Another pooka trick. If not for the headlights of the car, Tom wouldn't have been able to see a thing. And then his car stopped moving entirely, Philip, its wheels spinning in the muck and mud of the bog. Donovan was forced to abandon his car and start walking."

"Uh-oh," whispered Philip. "That's bad."

"Very bad," confirmed Sean with a solemn nod. "Very bad. The mud was put there by the demon, which'd made certain to pour great quantities of water over the dirt. Donovan was now walking in the bog, walking in darkness so black he'd be unable to see his shoes if he took a moment to look down at his own feet. So he's walking, muttering to himself over his misfortune. The bog is damp and the night is cold and the chill is beginning to penetrate his coat and pants. He wants nothing more now than to get home and have a warm cup of tea. He's thinking about that cup of warm tea as the dark cloud that's covering the moon moves off, permitting again the moon's silvery glow to shimmer through the mist of the bog. That's good, thinks Tom, for now at least he can see again where he's going and he's glad for that. He doesn't know that his being able to see is also part of the pooka's plan.

"So he continued on his way, still muttering to himself, and went a distance more when he spied a black ridge in the path in front of him. It looks to him as though something, something indistinguishable in the darkness, is resting across the path. "What is that?" he asks himself, suddenly afraid. But neither the night air nor the darkness answers him.

"Moving closer, for he has to get past the thing to get home, he sees by the moonlight that it *seems to be* nothing more than a great lump of blackened rock. A large boulder protruding up on the path and nothing more. He chuckles now at his own fear. 'Afraid of the shadows now, Thomas,' he scolds himself.

The bog came up to the edge of the road at that point and so Donovan had no choice but to step onto the rock in order to continue. And the moment he steps on the rock, he really is in trouble.

For, as he steps onto the black rock, suddenly the ground shakes and trembles beneath his feet. "Lord Almighty!" he shouts in fright. A transformation of the most terrifying kind takes place then. What had looked to be just rock now becomes a living thing. In a furious, churning spasm of earth and wind, the pooka coalesces, comes together, and rises up beneath Donovan's feet, picking him up onto its back so quickly it makes the man gasp. Donovan, in one swift terrifying instant, finds himself seated upon the broad back of the terrible pooka!

"It's immense, the demon is, at least forty hands high, with a gleaming black hide as shiny and hard as black onyx. Great blasts of air are snorting from its flaring nostrils and its massive chest is heaving with power and evil glee. With Donovan on its back, the man is in its power. It has him!

"The pooka stomps its hooves as though dancing and issues a shrill triumphant peal of *banshee*-like laughter that makes Donovan's ears curl in fear. Then the demon-beast twists its great head around so its glowing red eyes gaze straight into Tom's face and its lips peel back into that hideous pooka grin, revealing its needle-sharp teeth. It hisses and flicks a snake-like tongue at him. Poor Donovan, seeing the pooka's face, its red eyes and sharp teeth just inches from his own face, screams like a little baby separated from its mommy. He screams with terror, and, even while he's screaming, the pooka leans back on its hindquarters and springs suddenly up into the air, moving with such power and speed that the wind is suddenly whistling past Donovan's ears. They, demon and man, are moving so fast that even Donovan's own terrified screams are left behind and, as far as he can tell, he's screaming in silence.

"They rise up, and up, high into the night sky. The bog is suddenly far below, looking no bigger now than a spread-out copy of an old black ink blot on a piece of gray paper. Tom sees for a moment his home, the pinpoints of light from its windows, and then he's carried even higher, right through the clouds, and he can see nothing. Nothing but the fog of the clouds surrounding him and the pooka upon which he rides. The pooka continues to move so fast that poor Donovan still can't hear his own screams of terror, for he's screaming still, Philip. Screaming his head off. He's so scared that, despite the height and knowing it would mean his certain death, he decides to jump off the pooka's back. But he finds he can't budge. He's held on as securely as if his buttocks have been nailed on."

Philip giggled at the word, buttocks, and Ellen, seeing him giggle, suddenly recalled her own giggle, many years back, sitting at the breakfast table when her father had said the words "Tinker's anus", so many years ago.

"They descend, Philip," continued Sean. "The pooka drops back to earth even faster than it's risen. Then it runs along the ground, as swift as sound, running over the worst of terrain and through the thickest of forests. The branches of trees tear across Donovan's face, ripping his clothes and skin. Pieces of rock gouge his legs, cutting him, and all the time, while Donovan is screaming, the pooka is hissing its evil laughter.

"For hours the pooka runs that way, until poor Tom's clothes and skin are cut to ribbons and then, just before the sun was to rise, the pooka returns the man to the doorstep of his home, still alive but barely so. The demon releases Tom from its back, letting the man fall to the ground and, with another high-pitched squeal of delight, turns away and gallops off.

"Donovan's wife, hearing the pooka's laugh, comes running outside and shrieks at the horrible sight of her poor bloodied husband laying on the ground. 'What's that?' In the distance, she hears the sound of the pooka's hooves fading into the moonlit silence, moving back toward the shadows of the bog, and she hears too the demon's words of warning. 'I'll do the same to anyone else who drains the bog.' This warning is followed by its hissing laughter that hangs in the air for a time and then fades away as the demon continues to run off.

"Donovan lived after that. He survived his ride on the pooka's back, but he was a broken man afterwards. He was never the same."

"Goodness," exclaimed Ellen. "You *do* tell a tale. Philip, you look like you want to press yourself beneath the cushion. Remember, it's just a tall tale. There's no such thing as pookas. Now thank Sean for telling you the story."

"The story's not over yet," said Sean.

"It's not?" responded Ellen.

"No, more facts have come to light since your father told it to us." Sean turned to Philip. "Now it turns out that Tom Donovan had a son," he said. "A boy just about your age. Maybe even *exactly* your age, and when Donovan's son learned what'd been done to his father by the pooka, he vowed to get even. He swore he'd have his revenge on the pooka living in the bog. Coincidentally, the boy's name was Philip, the same as your name.

"But how was Philip to get even? He'd no idea of how to even meet a pooka. You can't just go up and shake hands, can you? And, even if he did know how to meet a pooka he had no idea of how to win in a fight against it. So he thinks long and hard on this and finally he decides to go to the home of an old woman who lives in a cave atop one of the rocky hills of Donegal. For you see, it's known about the county that the woman is a witch. A witch who, so it was said, is at least two hundred and fifty years old and who is very knowledgeable in many things.

"By inquiring about town, Philip gains a general idea of where this witch lives and one afternoon he leaves the farm and starts off in the direction that he believes will take him to the correct hill holding the cave that is the old woman's home.

"And he finds it. Hours later. A cave with parts of its entrance coated with patches of strange mossy growth that give the rock a tinge of silver-green color. It looks like a giant's large snotty nostril. The sun is just setting behind a hilltop and owls are hooting and animal noises are growling nearby in the surrounding woods. There's something imposing, very scary, about this particular cave. Something that makes the boy think twice about going near it. Even the twisted old trees outside seem to lean *away* from the cave as though, if they could, they'd exchange their roots for feet and boots so as to be able to run down the hill.

"But Philip is a very brave boy and has no intention of running away. He gathers up his courage and steps slowly into the cave. It's terribly dark inside and he walks for a while without being able to see even his hand in front of his face, but then at last he sees, up ahead, a light, a fire burning beneath a caldron. The old witch is home.

"A voice like screaming gravel suddenly comes out of the dark from somewhere. 'Go away!' The sound makes Philip's heart jump inside him. 'Go away!' the voice shouts again and Philip replies that he can't go away. That he's come a long way and wants to know the secret of besting the demon pooka. He hears a soft rustling sound and a quiet cackling laughter. 'Come ahead then!' shouts the voice and Philip, his heart beating like a drum, goes forward to meet the witch. He steps forward into more light, but a place still very dark.

"The air here is thick and pungent. It smells like a kitchen in which a stew of bad cabbage and old snails has been overcooked, and it's all Philip can do to keep from wrinkling his nose up at the stink of it. And when he sees the witch, who then steps out into the light, it's all he can do to keep from turning around and running away from the sight of her. She's ugly as warts with warts. Her face is all gnarled bumps and crevices. A face that might be made out of the same stone as the slimy rocks of the cave in which she lives. Her teeth are brown and black and her wild gray hair flares out from her head in all directions, as though each hair in her own head is straining to escape from her, just like the trees outside the cave seem to want to run away. Her hands and neck are thick with wrinkles and veins. When she lifts her hand and points at Philip, it's with one lone bony finger that terminates in a yellow nail so long it curls back at the end so that its pointing at her while her finger is pointing at Philip. All of the nails on her hands are the same."

"Sounds like old Mrs. Dunphy," broke in Ellen. "She used to live over a pub in Moville and was ugly and nasty as sin. She was a hundred if she was a day."

"Hush" came back Sean. Then, returning to his tale: "The old hag points her finger at Philip and then, with a sweep of her arm, invites him into her living quarters. 'So you want to fight the pooka, boy?'

"Philip nods his head at the witch" – As Sean said this, Ellen's Philip too nodded his head, his eyes fixed on Sean – "Now, unknown to Philip is the fact that the old woman holds no love for the pooka either. She'd once been a victim of its foul temper and she too wants nothing more than to have revenge against it. She looks at Philip with fire in her eyes, studying him. 'You're a fool, boy,' she says at last. 'You're too small, too little, to fight the pooka. Go away!'

"A flame of indignation comes into Philip's eyes. 'I'm not afraid!' he declares loudly. 'I can beat it if you show me how!'

"The woman's expression changes, shifting to a kind of qualified approval, like your teacher's face when you give a right answer, Philip. 'All right, boy,' she says. 'You'll get your chance. Wait here.' She hobbles out of the room and, in a few moments, hobbles back, returning with a long, thick, black stick.

"'It's magic, boy,' she says, handing the stick to Philip. 'And very powerful. It'll enable you to best the pooka. But here's the hard part, in order for it to work, you must be on the back of the pooka itself. Do you have that kind of courage, boy? *Are you brave enough to climb up on the pooka's back?*

"Philip turned the stick over in his hands. It looked very ordinary. 'But I thought for a pooka to be able to hurt you, you *had* to be on its back?' he asks. The hag snorts, making a sound much like a pig blowing bubbles in the mud. 'The pooka can kill you in many ways. It can trample you if it chooses, for example. Or set traps for you. It saves its back for those it particularly wants to have suffer. For those it wants to give one of its rides to. A painful deadly ride, it is. It must have hated your father very much.'

"'How do you know about my father?' asked Philip.

"'I know many things,' replied the hag. 'Now listen, the pooka is vulnerable only when it materializes, when it becomes solid, and the only time it becomes solid is when it wants to attack something it hates. So, how will you get on its back, boy, to use the stick!? How!?'

"Philip considered the puzzle for a moment. 'Why, I suppose I must make the demon hate me. Only then will it show itself to me and trick me onto its back.'

"'The witch cackled with glee. 'Hee, hee, hee, a clever boy. But how, boy?'

"'Why, I'll do like my father done and continue to have the bog drained – "

"'Not necessary!' interrupted the woman. 'It's easier if you insult the pooka. Insult it without mercy. Ridicule the demon in public and in private. The pooka is vain. It cannot stand being insulted. And it nearly always finds out when it's being talked about in public.'

"'Can it hear us now?'

"The hag cackled another laugh. 'Such a clever boy. No, I have magic to keep the pooka's ears away. Now go! Avenge your father!' With a stomp of her foot on the floor of the cave and a swing of her arm, she waved Philip out of the cave. 'Go, boy! Before I grow tired of you and turn you into a pig's tail!'

"Philip left the cave pleased with himself, feeling he now had the means by which he could beat the pooka. But as he descended the hill another thought came to him. *Will the stick really work?* If no one has ever been of the back of a pooka to test it, how could anyone be sure? The question makes him nervous.

"He does as the witch advised and begins insulting the pooka everywhere he goes. Even when he's alone at home. The demon is, as the hag said, very vain, and its ears begin to grow hot with the insults it hears. Philip continues to speak insults and soon the pooka's ears begin to smoke with the heat, ready to burst into flames. The insults so enrage the pooka that it vows to get even with the boy who is speaking against it, just as Philip intended.

"So it comes to pass that one night, as Philip is strolling the bog at night (as he's been doing every night since his visit to the witch) he hears a voice in the darkness. It's a dark night with only a hole in the sky where the moon is supposed to be and Philip can barely see. The voice is shouting a call for help. It sounds like that of a young girl. 'Please help! Oh, please help, someone! I'm caught! Can anyone hear me? Please.'

"It's a pitiful cry and Philip's first thought was to help, for he was by nature a good and kind boy, but a second thought comes to him as well. The pooka can be cunning. *Could this be the pooka drawing me into a trap?* The voice calls out again and Philip runs to it anyway. Real trouble or the demon's trap? Either way, he had to go.

"He tightens his grip on the magic stick, which he carries everywhere now, and steps off the path, entering the gray mist of the bog. 'Where are you?' he calls out.

"Another plea for help, almost weeping, draws him into a labyrinth of narrow, rocky paths that eventually terminate in a large, open area. In the center he sees, by the light of the few stars shining in the sky, a swirling pond of murky water, dark as ink. A whirlpool. In the midst of this swift swirl of water he sees a small, terrified young girl being spun about as though caught in the wind of a small cyclone.

"She is about his age and with light blonde hair and she has good reason to be frightened. She's in grave danger of drowning. The outer edges of the whirlpool are already above her shoulders and she will be very soon pulled down. How can there be a whirlpool in a bog? wonders

Philip as he goes straight away to save her. He knows he has to act quickly or it'll be too late. Going to the water's edge, he extends the magic stick out over the swirling water as far as he can, stretching it out toward the girl. 'Grab it,' he screams to her, shouting above the sound of the rushing water, which is now a great roar like the wind of a hurricane. 'Grab it and I'll pull you to shore!'

"The small girl can only reach for the stick in those brief moments when she is closest to Philip, for she's being spun around in the midst of the whirlpool and goes pass him time after time like a horse on a carousel that is turning too fast. She tries once, goes by, then she tries again, stretching up, her little face grimacing with her effort to grab onto the stick, but each time she misses it. Philip, to his dismay, realizes that his arm is just a few inches too short to get the stick close enough to the girl to allow her to grab it. He stretches himself out even further. Just a bit more, he's thinking, and I'll save her. But, in doing so, he loses his balance and himself tumbles into the twisting, rushing water. Immediately he's swept away by the force of the raging whirlpool. In moments, he finds himself in the current next to the terrified girl he'd tried to save. Now it seems he'll suffer the same fate and drown in the pool.

"But the little girl doesn't remain a little girl for long. As Philip stares at her, her angelic little face begins to change, melting away and twisting itself into a grotesque shape, shedding its pink skin.

"Suddenly Philip found himself looking straight into the glowing red eyes of the demon pooka! From behind the rat-lips of its grinning mouth there came a laugh of glee, a hyena-like laugh that filled the air, louder than even the sound of the rushing water. It nearly stopped Philip's heart. He recalled then what the old hag of a witch had told him: 'The pooka can kill in many ways.' Philip understood then that he'd fallen into a trap of the pooka's and that he'd failed to avenge his father. He realized then that the pooka had won."

Sean leaned back on the sofa as though having completed the tale and then made a forlorn motion as if to say it's sad that all stories can't have happy endings. Philip, and even Ellen, protested mightily, insisting he continue.

"That can't be the end!" declared Ellen. She'd never heard this particular pooka story before and knew that Sean had either come upon a new version of the legend or embellished the tale with elements created out of his own imagination. "It'd better not be the end anyway!"

"That's not the end," piped up Philip, looking at Sean with pleading eyes. "Is it, Sean?"

"Well, it very well might have been," replied Sean, leaning forward again, "except for the courage of our little Philip Donovan. Even as the swirl of the whirlpool was whipping him about, even as the glowing red eyes of the pooka were staring dead at him and even with the chilling heart-stopping laugh of the pooka filling his ears, Philip had enough fortitude, and enough good old Irish temper, to get fighting mad. He also had enough presence of mind to remember that the witch had told him that he had to be on the pooka's back for the magic stick to work. So he does then what the pooka *least expects him to do.* He quickly reaches out his free hand, the one not holding the stick, grabs hold of a hunk of the pooka's mane and pulls himself up onto the back of the pooka! For a moment the pooka thinks the boy is crazy! It twists its head around, still grinning, and looks at Philip. Then its grin widens, becoming a grin meant to mock Philip for being stupid. 'So you want a ride, boy,' it hisses at him. At the same time Philip raises the magic stick high above his head and, swinging as hard as he possibly could, whams it! Pow! right down into the pooka's laughing face, hitting the demon right flush between its gleaming red eyes!

"With that blow, the pooka's eyes crossed and it howled in pain, howling so loud that people for miles around the bog began to climb out of their beds to throw their shoes and pots at the cats outside their windows. And, at the same time as the howl of the pooka splits the air, the force of the whirlpool begins to lessen. Whack! Another hit with the stick and the whirl of the water slows even more now until it's little more than a placid pond, and then even that water begins to disappear. For you see, Philip, it was the evil magic of the pooka that had created the whirlpool in the first place and the pooka had to remember to concentrate his power on the water to keep it spinning. But now, since Philip was hitting it with the powerful magic stick, the pooka could think of nothing but its pain, and so the evil magic went right out of the water.

"Philip raises the stick again and, once more, with all the strength he could gather, brings it down on the pooka's neck. The pooka howls so loud this time that many of the citizens of Donegal thought the same cats they'd just thrown their shoes at were now rising up in revolt against them. Some citizens even went to hide beneath their beds and wait for the end of the world, grabbing up their rosary beads to pray for the redemption of their souls.

"The pooka reared up, wanting now only to throw the boy off its back, but Philip's fist still clenched tightly a large lock of the pooka's mane and he wasn't about to let it go. He swung the stick again, and then once more. First on the neck and then on the pooka's hindquarters. And then again, on the head between the ears. The pain the pooka feels is terrible and, for the first time in its existence, the demon begins to plead for mercy. 'Please boy – stop – the pain – '

"'Did you listen to my father's cries!' shouts Philip. 'Or the cries of the many others you hurt or killed!' He lifts the magic stick again and again, raining blows on the pooka until the demon's forelegs crumple beneath it and it's kneeling on the ground, looking for a moment like a show horse in a circus taking a bow. Then its hind legs collapse as well and it falls heavily onto the ground. There it rests, broken beyond repair. 'You've destroyed me, boy,' it moans. 'You've destroyed me.' With those words the pooka exhaled its last breath, white mist on the night air, and was gone.

"'As you destroyed others,' murmured Philip. He pulled out a pocketknife from his pants pocket and cut off the long black tail of the pooka. This he brought back as proof that he'd killed the demon of the bog. As proof that even the most powerful of evildoers must eventually pay for the evil they do to others. I'm told," added Sean, "that the tail of the pooka hangs on a wall of the Donovan house to this very day – to the wonderment of all who gaze upon it."

"Yaayyy," cheered Philip. "That was a great story, Sean. Really good."

"Yes, merciful heavens, it *was* a story," said Ellen. "It took my breath away in parts."

"Tell another," pleaded Philip. "Please Sean, tell another."

"Hush, Philip," scolded Ellen. "It's not polite to insist on more.

Besides you have your homework. Say thank you to Sean and go off and get your schoolwork finished."

"There's nothing more important than learning, Philip," stated Sean, speaking to the frown on the boy's face. "Go on now, and next time I'll tell you of the terrible *Garrett Og* who long ago practiced the art of black magic. He was able to change himself into various shapes, into birds and animals."

"Promise, Sean?"

"Sure, but only if you do a really good job on your homework. Deal?"

"Deal," responded Philip and, wearing the smile of a stock trader who'd just bested the Dow, he snapped himself up off the couch and ran to his bedroom to tackle his schoolwork, carrying with him the wonderful sense of being an intrepid boy searching in shadowy bogs for demons to conquer.

Ellen came over to Sean, sat and leaned her body against his. "He thinks the world of you, you know that?" Sean draped an arm over her shoulders.

"He's a great kid," he replied. "Sometimes I wonder how he got to be such a good kid, considering the nasty mother he's saddled with." Ellen arched an eyebrow at him and he offered her a gentle kiss on her forehead to erase the feigned indignation over the pretended insult.

"I never heard that last part of the story before," said Ellen. The part about the boy hunting down the pooka and killing it."

"I invented that part. Never liked the original ending. Too depressing."

"You're good at telling tales. I swear you're as good as my father even."

"That *is* a compliment. He could really tell them. I like the old stories. That time I told you about, when I was at sea, one of the books I brought along was of the old Irish legends. I found myself reading it more than once. Now that I think of it, I guess one of the reasons I read it was that it reminded me of home. Of your father's stories. Home, it's always with us, isn't it? One way or another we always carry it with us, no matter where or how far we go."

*　　*　　*

Sean stood up and stepped to the closet to retrieve his coat. "Getting late, El. Time for me to get going." It was past eleven and Philip had long ago been tucked away with his dreams.

"I hate it when you go," said Ellen with a sad sigh. "I like having you around." It was true, she always felt a little colder and more alone when he left her. She stepped up to him and kissed him, a kiss meant to be a goodnight kiss but, like a spark falling accidentally onto a bed of crackling straw, it had greater consequences than it was meant to. In moments she and Sean were embracing each other with passion. It was Sean who, half against his will, put a halt to it. "Now, El," he told her. "You have a rule about doing anything with the boy near."

But the rules tonight were straw also. And Ellen let them burn. Sean saw the nervous flutter of her hand as, half in the delirium of passion, she raised it to touch his cheek. Inhaling deeply with her decision, she wet her lips with her tongue. "Come with me," she whispered and, taking his hand into hers, tugged him forward, leading him down the hall to her bedroom, signaling him to be quiet as they stepped by the closed door of the bedroom of her sleeping son.

Chapter Forty-four

Ellen awoke early the following morning in complete darkness after a night of contented sleep, and, for an instant, was surprised to feel the presence of Sean beside her in the bed. Her mind struggled with the fact that she wasn't alone for the most fleeting of moments and then she urgently shook Sean awake.

"Please," she whispered, "you've got to go outside, onto the couch. Pretend you slept there. I don't want Philip to know. Please, Sean."

Sean dressed quickly and, with the stealth of a thief, carrying over one arm a blanket that Ellen hastily pulled from a closet and handed him, he moved softly past the sleeping boy's room and down the hall into the living room. Laying down on the couch, he haphazardly covered himself with the blanket and, in moments, was asleep again. Ellen remained awake until the alarm clock's buzz drove her from her bed.

*　　*　　*

For days afterward, Ellen experienced a sense of shame over that night with Sean. She'd slept with him before of course, but never while her son was close by. Never had she made love with only a thin wall separating her sin from her boy. And sin is what she considered it. Her religious beliefs, her strict moral upbringing, could lead her to no other conclusion. Sin, pure and simple. And now a sin compounded by a worse one, for now she'd brought that sin close to her Philip, where it could perhaps touch and contaminate him.

Isn't that what sin and sinners do, contaminate others?

She'd lived with Bonnie and had often heard her through the walls. Now she was Bonnie and her son was the potential listener on the other side of the plaster. Did her son hear anything?

Not with the boy nearby. It was a firm rule, a rule meant to protect her son. And in one flash of passion she'd brushed the rule away. A traitorous moment, a moment in which she'd abandoned what was good and right for her child for the sake of the gratifying pleasure of the night. She had chosen her own pleasure over the good of her baby. It was a scalding truth.

So far she'd been able to live with her doubts over the rightfulness of her affair. She'd lived with it even while her mind fretted and paced, ill at ease over the stamp of wickedness her morality placed upon it. But now, with the events of this one night, she felt the frail equanimity she'd been able to sustain begin to weaken and start to crumble, a sand castle with the sea water that pasted it together evaporating into the heat of the sun, the sand now being blown away by ever increasing gusts of wind. Her happiness was, more and more, being overwhelmed by her expanding sense of shame.

And shame frightened her as well, for she loved Sean and wanted to keep him. Loneliness frightened her too. No, she didn't want to lose Sean's love.

Her trips to her church increased in frequency. She urgently prayed, petitioning God for an answer, knowing that what she was asking God for was a rationale that would excuse her sin. She was pleading for a justification she and God could live with, a way out of her moral dilemma. She wanted the sin taken away, but without losing Sean, the very cause of her sinning. And she understood that, in her wanting this, she was committing the offensive act of simply leaning one additional offense against the first. At times, when praying in church, she wondered why the statues of saints around her didn't angrily come to life, grip her by the shoulders and push her down right through the marble floor of the nave, condemning her to the place where immoral people belonged.

She began to vaguely suggest marriage, dropping her hints almost invisibly, and then grew frustrated that Sean, not seeing those transparent hints, ignored them. Her campaign of veiled suggestions, now a failure, was soon discarded and replaced with one of simple directness. She began to openly talk to Sean of marriage.

To her dismay, he dismissed the talk with bad jokes, laughing her suggestions away, telling her there was no *need* of marriage. All was fine and all would continue to be fine if all things remained the way they were. The thought of marrying, it was clear, did not appeal to him, or perhaps, and this thought held a temperature of less than zero as it passed through her, perhaps it was the thought of marrying *her* that held no appeal for him.

Outwardly she reacted in a nonchalant manner when he voiced his quick dismissal of the sacrament of marriage, but inwardly his words hit her like an elbow across the bridge of the nose. Ellen began to consider the possibility that perhaps Sean O'Reilly didn't love her as much as she believed he did, as much as she loved him.

*　　*　　*

Another few weeks passed by and Ellen increasingly felt as though she was walking through a world erected upon a lake of thinning ice, the sounds of the dark waters below her feet in her ears, the waters threatening to break through. Why couldn't she be happy with the way things were? Why not just leave things alone? She wanted to talk to a priest but her shame kept her away. Easier to talk to statues than a living priest. After all, she was still seeing Sean, still offering herself to him in bed, and had no intention of doing otherwise. Not yet. The fear of losing him still remained greater than her increasing shame.

But her heart was sore in her chest almost all the time now, and the condemnation of the saints was growing ever more strident in her ears each time she visited her church. Sean wanted things to remain as they were, but for Ellen that was increasingly becoming an impossibility. There were forces within her that were now growing greater and stronger than even her love and they intended to have their way, no matter what it took.

Chapter Forty-five

What it took was time. Ellen's heart was now as much an open wound as a place that held her love. Increasingly, over the passing weeks and months, she and Sean debated her growing desire, her expanding *need*, to legitimize their relationship before her Church and her God. Debate then slowly transformed to argument. She couldn't understand Sean's continuing adamant refusal to recognize and honor her need to marry. Nor could she endure the scrutiny of God's condemning gaze upon her.

Why not? she wondered. *Why not marry?* There was nothing extreme or unnatural in doing this. Wasn't it the expected progression of love? Ellen believed it was and was increasingly dismayed that Sean remained so immutable regarding her pleas. She offered him love and he was now returning that love with what she saw as rejection, a rejection increasingly incomprehensible to her. *Surely if he loved me, as he says he does, he would want this as much as I do!*

If he loved me! If.

If.

It was that increasing doubt of Sean's feelings for her, that ever expanding distrust of the depth of his love, that gave additional power to the hurt inside. Her soul was now each day bruised by it and she was each day more silently humiliated by it.

At last, after a buildup of weeks of tension, inevitably, the break came, in a final, bitter argument between the two.

*   *   *

It was afternoon. They were alone in Ellen's apartment, Philip being treated that day to a trip to the movies by his Aunt Rose, the main event a Disney film. Rose had invited Philip to join her own children and he happily went along.

Ellen, alone with Sean and dismissing the advice of her better judgment (being aware that Sean was not in the best of moods) once again broached the subject of their getting married.

"Please Ellen," he came back to her, exasperated. "Enough with that talk. Please. Let it be."

"I'm sorry if it *annoys* you," she told him, her anger beginning to flare, "but if you love me, why can't we marry?"

"There's no reason," he said, his voice rising, trying to keep his own temper down. "No reason not to do it, and equally no reason *to* do it. Things are fine the way they are."

"No reason to do it – ?" Ellen's face turned so deeply red that the heat radiating from it might have bent the air around her. Her throat tightened with anger. "No reason. No. Reason."

Sean stared at her, Ellen now sitting straight in her chair, her eyes turning angry. He was weary of explaining himself to her, of defending himself, of being made to feel like a villain. "That's what I said," he snapped back. "No reason."

The words had been said before, more than once, but this time Sean's manner and tone were different. This time the words were harder, more cruel, and this time Ellen was in no mood to hear them, feeling she'd endured listening to them for too long. Standing, she stepped toward him, close enough so that he had to look up at her.

"Things are not fine!" she shouted down at him. "I don't want to go on like this anymore! Not anymore. What am I to you?! Nothing but your mistress! Your whore!" She turned away and retreated to her chair, her legs trembling. Suddenly she was crying. "Your whore – " she hissed through her sobs. "That's all – "

Sean studied her, scrutinizing her. The ticks of the small clock on the wall and Ellen's rough sobs the only sounds in the room. *What's this?* he asked himself, *a feminine attempt to win an argument, to get her way?* "Perhaps if you feel that strongly about it, El, we should break this up."

The words were like a hard slap across her cheek, a slash of a knife blade across the surface of her heart. She actually flinched at them. Her blood was throbbing in her head, almost blinding her sight. Then she found herself speaking: "Maybe, maybe . . . we should . . . ." Her eyes stared at him, suddenly two wet wounds in her aching face. Somewhere inside, her heart was shrieking. She continued to sob, her breathing actually becoming painful for her.

Sean studied her with the cold eye of a soldier gazing down the sights of a rifle at the object of his bullets. "Your crying won't win it for you," he muttered after a long silence. "Is that it then? We're over?"

Ellen, looking at him, nodded her head, her whole upper body rocking with the motion.

Sean, angered now by what he interpreted as Ellen's rejection of him, stared at her for a long desperate moment, then he stood and, retrieving his coat, turned and strode out the door without another word. Ellen gasped piteously at the hollow sound of the door slamming shut, a sound akin to a trial defendant listening to a judge's gavel coming down to pound the announcing of a death sentence.

She remained in her chair, her heart crushed, her face white as chalk, tears streaming from her eyes, staring at the hole in the air where Sean was standing moments ago, the place where he should have been standing now.

*   *   *

Sean's feet slammed upon the steps as he descended the stairs and left the apartment house. His intent was to walk entirely away, but once outside on the sidewalk he halted and waited, standing in front of the building, somewhat bewildered, even stunned, by Ellen's dismissal of him. Shaking his head from side to side like an old man with palsy, he muttered curses to himself. An elderly woman, carrying a load of groceries in two shopping bags, one in each hand, scurried away from him, fearful he was indeed the lunatic he appeared to be, capable of God only knows what.

He stood, staring at the building's entrance, his mind in turmoil, harassed by conflicting emotions, his pride insulted by Ellen's ability to summarily dismiss him. She talked of love, but *she* ended their affair. How limited than was her love for him? If she loved him, then why couldn't she accept him on his terms? That was no different than her expecting him to accept her on the conditions she was throwing at him. Wasn't it so?

A damp drizzle was falling and the air was raw and cold, the weather offering him no balm. He started forward, as if to go back inside the building, but instantly, and with a mumbled curse, checked himself and instead turned and walked away. *The hell with it*, he decided. *Maybe it's better this way.*

Somewhere a small group of loving angels might have groaned, their sense of disappointment sounding very much like rumbling, distant thunder.

Chapter Forty-six

Love conquers all. It is a romantic's sentiment, a poet's dream. *Omnia vincit amor.* A better, truer statement would be: Love conquers all *except when it doesn't conquer at all.* Under the harsh realities of daily life, Love is often pushed into dark shadows, or thrown down the stairs and dragged outdoors to be abandoned to the whims of cold temperatures and hard winds, left to weep in an alley or by the curb. How often is Love mistreated before the allure of riches? Or ignored by the haughty disdain of pride? Or forsaken due to social demands and pressures? How often is Love left shuddering and teary-eyed because of its abandonment before the realities of Need and Necessity or before a greater sense of Sin and Shame?

Love conquers all, too often nothing but a poet's dream.

After leaving Ellen, Sean's emotions were in turmoil. Almost immediately he regretted what had occurred between them, but that regret was shoved aside by his anger and resentment. Ellen's intent was to manipulate him, to push him into making a commitment he wasn't ready to make, and, with the unbending instinct for resistance inherent in a disgruntled mule, Sean disliked being manipulated. He always did.

He went straight home wearing a scowl that caused the meek and mild to place extra distance between him and them. Once inside his apartment he turned on the radio, poured himself a healthy drink and placed himself into his favorite chair. The classical music helped, as did the Irish whisky. What did he want out of Life? *Why can't I marry Ellen? There's love there, isn't there? Real love. On both sides. Why not marry?* He questioned his own aversion to the idea. Why not? Perhaps because marriage seemed to him to exist in extreme opposition to his love of adventure and sense of freedom. Yes, that was part of it, perhaps it was all of it. Marriage had its stringent parameters that, if one married seriously, (and Sean was the type who could marry no other way) eliminated many other possibilities, many other choices. It made Life too *narrow*. It represented, for Sean, a voluntary taxi ride to a place of confinement, to a prison with barred windows and locked doors. A soft prison maybe, if you were lucky, but a prison nonetheless.

Who needs it?

*   *   *

Days passed by. Days that weighed Sean down with ambivalence, contradictions and uncertainty. At first, he wondered if there was a chance that Ellen would give in and call him. Time passed, and he began to understand there was a greater probability that she would not. And, even while his heart reproached her for it, he understood too that he couldn't condemn her for it. He loved Ellen not just for the charms of her body, but for her sense of honor, her courage, and her strength of will. As more time passed by, he ceased any and all speculation that there would soon be coming a call from an apologetic Ellen.

He experienced moments in which he realized he hadn't considered Ellen's feelings during their time together. A stab of anguish went through him at such times but then, in the next moment, in startling angry contradiction to his own regret, he'd be locked in a fit of anger in which he blamed Ellen (and only Ellen!) for what happened. It was her fault they were apart! No one else's. And, in his vanity, he would mutter words against her that he knew weren't true.

He was not immune to the torments of his own memories. So many intimate moments with Ellen, him holding her in his arms, her face smiling up at him, loving her, the feel of her soft skin. Gone.

Despite this roiling emotional turmoil within him the potentiality that Sean would ultimately give in to it and contact Ellen didn't exist. No, he would not one day appear before her with a bouquet of flowers in his hand and an apology in his mouth. It simply wasn't in his nature. Once, as a young boy, he'd gotten into a schoolyard fight with another boy who, being older and bigger, soon had Sean's face down in the dirt. The hulk, squatting on Sean's back, pushing Sean's face into the ground, demanded that he speak words of surrender. Despite the pain, Sean refused to speak the words, knowing that, despite the other bigger boy being on his back, he wasn't truly beaten until and unless he did.

He felt now very much the same sense of battle. His intellect and his pride were being pressed to the ground by his own heart, and he resented the power his own heart wanted to wield over him. He was determined not to let his heart wave its flag of victory over the prone body of his own beaten pride.

Love conquers all. Sometimes a truth. Sometimes nothing more than a frail sentiment, a poet's dream.

And the idea of a Forever Love just a young girl's silliness, an absurdity in a cold world.

Chapter Forty-seven

No one else was home when Philip broke his leprechaun bank and picked out the change and dollar bills from amidst the rubble of broken ceramic. He stuffed the money into a pocket of his denim jacket and then, with the sorrowful expression of one who no longer cares what happens to him, went out the door. There was no one to hear him, but he carefully closed the door silently anyway.

Leaving the apartment building he entered into the maze formed by the thousands of city sidewalks and streets, the tributaries of Manhattan. He walked a long time, passing first the familiar coffee houses, stores and restaurants of his neighborhood and then, further from his home, going by the bleak facades of places of manufacturing and past seedy apartment buildings and grime-stained bars advertising less than wholesome entertainment.

The entrance to one bar was open, music was playing and, out of curiosity, Philip stopped to look inside. Standing atop the long bar he saw a scantily clad woman slowly moving beneath a pale spotlight. He stayed and watched, waiting for something else to happen, but when after a time nothing else occurred, he grew bored and continued on. Just in time too, for a man with a strange bent face, baleful eyes and broad chin appeared in the open door and Philip was certain he would have been shooed away by the behemoth if he'd not already turned to leave.

Soon the bars and bleakness were left behind. He wandered now past stores and homes with high stoops. His stomach began to grumble over his neglect of it and he decided to bend to his belly's demand.

Entering into a small deli, he purchased a bottle of Coke and a two-pack of cupcakes, the kind he liked, with the white squiggle running through the middle of the chocolate icing. The soda and cupcakes were placed into a small brown paper bag and, back outside, Philip carried this with him, looking now for a place where he could sit and eat, walking as though he was a factory worker heading out for a day of labor, and brown-bagging his lunch to work.

He found his place to eat in the form of a small children's park shaped in a triangle on the corner of a city block. It held a row of four swings, a small monkey bars and five benches, all of which were empty. Philip went to one, sat and opened his paper bag. Nearby a mother was pushing a smiling baby on one of the swings, the only other people in the park. The monkey bars were as deserted as the benches.

It was only when he held the small bottle of Coke in his hand that he remembered he needed a bottle opener to get it open, the age of twist-off bottlecaps being still years away. The bottlecap with its crimped edges stared at him with the same baleful gaze that the behemoth had carried when he blocked the door to the wiggling lady he'd seen just an hour earlier. A problem. But maybe a problem with a solution. It took Philip only a moment to remember that Sean, a couple of weeks back, had solved the very same enigma by placing the edge of the bottlecap on a hard surface and, bringing his open hand down like a hammer onto the cap, popped the cap off. After considering the memory for a few seconds, Philip concluded that he too could pop the cap off just as Sean had done.

He went to the side of the bench and, placing the bottle against one of the thick pieces of wood forming the seat of the bench, caught the rim of the bottlecap on its edge. He then raised his hand high overhead and, frowning seriously with narrowed eyes at the bottlecap, brought the palm of his hand down on the top of the bottle with a determination that would have made a blacksmith from a former century turn from the heat of his furnace and bellows to offer him a smile of appreciation. Wham!

Failure. The bottlecap with its pleated skirt remained resolutely fixed on the bottle. The only reward Philip received for his effort was the feel of a sharp, stinging pain running through his hand and up his arm. He felt like a carpenter who'd just hit his thumb with a hammer. "Owwwwww," he murmured (instead of yelling), waving his hand like a seal's flipper. "That really hurt."

His complaint was directed to the obstinate bottlecap, which he glared at as though expecting it to grow lips and offer him an apology. It didn't and, as the pain in his hand faded, he found the problem remained. He still had his closed bottle of soda with the stubborn bottlecap sealing it shut, and still had the problem of separating one from the other.

A few moments of additional thought, and then he pulled his right hand up into the sleeve of his jacket, covering all but the fingertips with the denim, seeking some protection for his hand with the heavy cloth. And he'd learned from his first attempt that, if he was going to hit the top of the bottle again, and he was, it might be best to do it with the heel of his hand rather than the palm. Things hurt less when you hit them that way. He raised his hand again, looking like Captain Hook gesticulating without the hook and, holding his breath, started to bring his hand down – and stopped, exhaling mightily. *Gosh, would this hurt again? It sure hurt the first time.* A frown and then he regrouped his courage. If it hurt, then it hurt. The alternative was to let the bottlecap have its victory and for him to go thirsty.

He swung his hand, and this time was rewarded with partial success. The bottlecap, although still clinging to the bottle, was clearly bent up on one side. And hitting it this time, with the heel of his hand and his hand covered with denim, caused barely any pain at all. Philip knew that victory was now clearly within his reach and he repeated the process, once and then again until at last he received the satisfaction of having the cap fly off and hearing the sound of it hitting and bouncing on the ground. The sound of victory! His success was deemed fully complete when he sat down and raised the bottle to his lips, enjoying the spoils of battle.

After finishing the eating of his cupcakes and drinking half the bottle of Coke, he felt better. He continued to sit on the bench, entertaining himself by puffing air in and out of his cheeks, swinging his legs and looking over at the mother pushing her smiling baby on the swing. Having run away and now having eaten lunch, he wasn't certain at all what he should do next.

Perhaps it was the warmth of the sun shining on him, or the contentment he'd gained from eating, or maybe he was simply weary from his walking, but he found himself suddenly juggling sleepiness and the desire to remain awake inside him. He put the bottle of Coke down beside him and, after a few minutes, the juggled ball that was "stay awake" dropped to the floor and he let his eyelids slowly slide shut.

*   *   *

"Philip, come help me with the groceries," called out Ellen as she entered her apartment. When her son didn't appear, she concluded he'd gone out to be with a friend. "Probably at Peter's," she decided, and went straight into the kitchen to empty the groceries from the two large bags she'd brought home. It wasn't until she went into Philip's room and saw the broken remains of his bank that she began to give more thought to the absence of her son. *Why would he break open his bank?* she wondered. He loved that bank and liked the process of squirreling away his nickels and dimes. *A born penny-pincher. Why break it open now?*

*   *   *

Philip woke hours later, his face chilled, his nose cold. The sunshine that had been beaming warmth upon him when he'd fallen asleep had since moved away to be replaced with the shadow of the six-story building forming one boundary wall of the small playground. Philip woke shivering inside his jacket. The mother pushing her baby was gone but the playground wasn't empty. There were a few children now on the monkey bars and two on the swings. All were smaller and younger than Philip and were with either their mothers or baby-sitters. It was the laughter and soft hollers of the children on the monkey bars that had awakened Philip.

When in doubt, puff up your cheeks and huff. Philip was now reexamining his decision to run away. He'd given no consideration at all to the question of where he should run *to*, but only to running *away*.

He'd vaguely assumed that, once away, a destination would readily present itself to him. Now he was becoming a bit disconcerted that it had not. So he sat and puffed his cheeks and let the air out with a pop of his lips while he thought about what to do now.

"Hey, kid," a voice said. Philip turned his head and found himself perilously close to a scruffy looking man with an unshaved greasy face and eyes like two rusty razor blades. His old, long coat needed a bath. "Ya got money, kid? Huh, ya got money?" Philip was immediately afraid of the man but, inherently honest, nodded his head. Yes, he had money.

The man, who was standing, grinned and placed himself on the bench beside Philip, the miserable suddenly looking at the boy as if they'd been friends for life. He talked quickly, slurring his words, and Philip's mouth hung open as he struggled to understand what the man was saying to him.

*   *   *

"Oh, God, Rose, where would he go!" moaned Ellen. "It's not like him to do something like this. What got into him?"

"Don't start imagining the worst," came back Rose, trying to soothe Ellen's worries. "He's probably out buying something. Or he went to a movie, maybe. Did you call all his friends?" The two sisters sat on the couch in Ellen's apartment, the same couch Sean had at times slept upon.

"Yes, of course," said Ellen. "I called all of them. Sean too. No one's seen him. No one." Anxiety seemed to stream from every pore on Ellen's body. Her face was an etched panorama of concern. "Oh God, Rose, what if something's happened – ?"

Rose told Ellen to relax, not to worry, knowing it was an impossible request, one that Rose herself found it impossible to comply with even as she asked Ellen to strive for it. It *was* so out of character for the boy to disappear like this. And what would compel him to break his bank and take his money with him? Rose used to joke about the way Philip saved, calling him "the little banker".

"I called the police," she told Ellen. "They said to wait, that he'll probably come home soon. And they're right, he will. He'll turn up any time now. If he doesn't come back by tonight, they said to call them again. But you watch, El, he'll turn up any time now."

Tears welled up in Ellen's eyes. She barely heard her sister's words, staring in front of her in a trance of apprehension. She'd lost faith long ago in happy endings. She'd lost too many people who were dear to her, her father and mother, her husband whom she loved so much when she first married, Sean too, and, most heart-breaking of all, her son Tommy. No, happy endings were for dreamers and school children. Ellen's personal history was now like a great magnifying glass intensifying the light of her worry into a burning beam of profound fright. She'd lost *everything* except her son Philip, hadn't she? *Am I going to lose him too?*

Ellen's years of living had taught her that Life was a cold, uncaring thief, taking what it wanted, when it wanted. Sometimes grabbing with cruelty, in as vicious a manner as was possible, enjoying the suffering and pain it inflicted upon its victims. Life could be a grinning destroyer who threw acid in your face for the sheer joy of it. No, Ellen couldn't blithely believe in happy endings, not any more. Unless God helped. Ellen prayed silently, *Please God, you've already got one of my babies. Please leave me the other. Please keep my Philip safe. Oh please God –*

A sound at the door, and both women turned toward the noise with expectation flooding their faces, only to be disappointed when their anxious eyes fell upon the sight of Jim, Rose's husband. He appeared in the doorway, entering alone. They were further disappointed by the shake of Jim's head and the beaten expression on his face. "I looked everywhere I could think of," he told them. "The candy stores, the movie theater. Went over to the schoolyard. Thought maybe he was playing over there. Some of the kids climb the locked fence to play there on Saturdays. Nothing – "

Ellen had stopped listening, not caring to learn where Philip *wasn't*. She withdrew once again into her cocoon of worry and prayer. *Please God, not my Philip too. Please God, not him too . . . .*

* * *

"Hey, kid, ya say ya money, how 'bout ya le' me see, uh, kid? Le' ol' Henry see ya money."

Philip's instinct for Proper Banking Procedures took command of him at that moment, for he doubted it would be wise to let Ol' Henry see the money he had in his pocket, reasoning, with the acuity of a budding J. P. Morgan, that if the man saw the money he would "borrow" it, leaving Philip holding an IOU against an uncollateralized loan. But Philip was frightened of the man, and so was hesitant of simply saying no to Ol' Henry. This might possibly anger him, so instead Philip picked up the half-empty bottle of Coke beside him and extended it toward the slovenly man, thinking that maybe the man would leave him alone if he, Philip, gave him his soda as a gesture of good will.

The gesture succeeded but for a different reason. Ol' Henry immediately concluded that the boy, in declaring he had money, had meant only the two pennies he could get for the return of the Coke bottle. "Whasis? A sodabot'l? Dat wha ya call money, kid? Two stinkin' cents?" Henry's unshaven face clenched in a tight expression of disappointment. Even so, he still took the bottle from Philip. Then he closed one eye and studied it with the other, like an archeologist examining a fragment of bone just pulled from the ground.

At that moment a voice came between Philip and Ol' Henry. "What's going on? Sonny, is this old bag of dirt bothering you?" The voice held both strength and authority and when Philip turned toward it he was pleased to see it belonged to the largest police officer he'd ever seen. Before he could speak however, Henry was talking. "No, now no bothering," he replied as though the question had been directed at him. "We ja pals, ain't so, kid?" He grinned hideously up at the cop, who remained somehow undazzled by the derelict's charms.

"Shut up," commanded the cop, pointing his nightstick at the derelict and Henry did exactly that, his mouth snapping closed instantly.

The patrolman lowered his nightstick. "I told you not to come into the playground, didn't I? Well, didn't I?"

Henry stared sheepishly at his scarred shoes and nodded his head.

"Go on with you," ordered the patrolman. "And don't come in here again." Henry, still holding the bottle of Coke that Philip had given him, rose to his feet and, without another word, shuffled away from the bench and out through the gates of the playground.

The cop watched the old man leave, before offering Philip a smile and walking away, following the same path out of the playground that Henry had taken.

An elderly woman, holding the hand of a young golden-curled girl who looked to be five or six years of age came over to Philip. "Are you all right?" she inquired with real concern. "That dirty man comes in here every now and then. We've asked the police to get rid of him but they say all they can do is chase him away. It's disgraceful."

Philip nodded his head, supposing that, if she said so, it must be disgraceful. "I'm fine, thank you, ma'am."

"Well, aren't you the little gentleman," responded the woman, beaming sunshine down at him. "See, Claudine, that's the way you should behave. With politeness. C'mon, Grandma is going to take you to the ice cream parlor now. Bye, bye, little boy."

Claudine, still holding the hand of her grandmother, scowled and stuck out her tongue at Philip as the old woman turned to walk away. Philip was taken aback by the action and, watching the backs of the woman and child as they walked away, wondered what he'd done to get the girl mad at him. "I wanna big vanilla sundae," Philip heard the girl demanding as she and the old woman went toward the playground gates. "Un'erstand, Gran'ma?"

Philip began again to reconsider his decision to run away from home, examining it now with the perplexed analytic thoroughness of a mathematician considering the possibility that a beloved theorem might be false. *This running away isn't easy,* he decided. And it was with that new illumination prodding him, that he made his way to his next decision. He'd been told by his mother that he couldn't go *there*, but she hadn't bothered to answer his question: "Why not?" And so, with one final ballooning of his cheeks and with one last puff of air exploding from his lips, Philip got off the bench and left the playground, granting himself permission to do what his mother had expressly told him was forbidden. He would go to Sean's place.

Chapter Forty-eight

It started drizzling when Philip was only part of the way to Sean's building so that by the time he actually arrived his hair was damp with wet. An absence of assurance shone in his eyes as he went up the steps to the entrance as he was not certain at all if he was doing the right thing by disobeying his mother to come here. He was also fearful that Sean, apparently no longer wanting to be his friend, would only yell at him and chase him away.

The building was an old one, five stories high, with an ornate lintel over the entrance that held, in its center, the face of a staring gargoyle. Philip liked the face. It reminded him somehow of Sean's Irish tales and it seemed fitting somehow that it should be in the front of the building where Sean lived. The image gazed down at Philip as he went up the steps. Behind the gargoyle, a few pigeons pressed themselves against the brick of the building, seeking to avoid the wet of the weather.

He entered into the foyer, which contained the mailboxes and doorbells but was stopped from going further, from entering the interior of the building, by a second door that was securely locked. He thought of ringing Sean's bell but decided against it, for no other reason than he was afraid Sean would simply tell him through the intercom to go away. So he waited a few minutes until a tenant, leaving the building, opened the door and went past him. Then he walked though the open door.

*   *   *

Sean at last responded to the insistence of the doorbell, not the entrance bell but the one at his own apartment door. Someone was in the hall outside. *The super, maybe.* He was surprised, happily, when, opening the door, he saw Philip instead of the Russian who cared for the building. Philip's hands were jammed into the pockets of his denim jacket and he looked up at him with faltering resolution in his eyes, wondering if he'd be welcome, fearful he'd be shooed away. Then, to his great joy and relief, he discovered that Sean was glad to see him.

"Phil!" exclaimed Sean. "Hey, it's good to see you! Come on inside. Hey, your mother's worried about you. She called to tell me you were missing. Where've you been?"

Philip face lit up as he responded to the warmth of Sean's greeting, but to Sean's question he replied with only a shrug and a word. "Around," he said.

"Ah, around," responded Sean, grinning as he twisted the door lock shut. "And a more enlightening answer couldn't be given. Take your jacket off, it's wet. Your head's wet too, isn't it? But you can leave that on. Let me get you a towel" Sean disappeared into the kitchenette and came back seconds later with a dishtowel. "Here Philip, rub your head with that. You don't want to catch cold. Are you hungry? I just got some good roast beef and potato salad from the deli. Want some?"

Philip, rubbing his head with the towel, said that he would, thank you.

"Good, I'll make you a sandwich. First though, I've got to call your mum and let her know you're safe. She's worried sick about you, you know. You shouldn't go out all day and not let people know where you are." It was as close to a scolding as Philip would hear from Sean and the boy's eyes turned sad in response to the words. Not knowing what else to do or say he simply mumbled: "I'm sorry." Uncertainty leaped again for a moment onto his face. *Is Sean mad at me?* Then the flash of consternation was extinguished as Sean offered him a smile and ruffled his now dry hair. "Go," said Sean as he took the towel from Philip. "Sit at the table and I'll make you your sandwich, right after I call your mother."

Philip sat at the table and gazed at the accumulation of clutter that covered most of it. There was no place for him to even put his elbows down. He had to push some of the clutter aside.

"Get yourself some minerals from the fridge, if you want," called out Sean from the other room.

Philip went and poured himself some soda. When Sean returned, Philip was again seated at the table, this time with a large tumbler of Nedick's orange soda sitting in front of him.

"Your mum's really glad to hear you're all right," announced Sean when he returned. "I offered to take you home, but she wants to pick you up. She'll be over in a few minutes."

"This place is really messy," stated Philip, with the truthful candor often tolerable only in children.

Sean laughed, "Hey, don't you know you never tell a hog its pigpen is dirty? That's an old Irish saying I just made up. At least I think I made it up. Who knows? Someone probably said something just like it before. Besides, it's cluttered, not dirty. Let me make you that sandwich I promised. I'll have one too I think."

Sean and Philip were silent while Sean prepared the sandwiches, Philip sipping occasionally at his glass of soda. There were tears rimming his eyes. He had the imploring gaze of someone contemplating a sorrowful thought and getting up the courage to give voice to it.

"Hey, what's wrong, champ?" questioned Sean as he placed two plates on the table, each holding a sandwich, a mound of potato salad and a fork. "You look like you're bothered by something."

Philip's feet, which didn't reach the floor, began to swing. They were crossed at the ankles. Rather than talk, he reached for his glass and took another sip of soda. His big eyes gazed up at Sean.

"Come on," coaxed Sean in a soft voice, as he sat down. "Spit it out. What's on your mind?"

"Mom misses you," declared Philip, as two large tears fell from the corners of both eyes. "I can't go home."

"What? I don't understand. Why can't you go home?"

The boy's face twisted up and his vision blurred as tears began to run in earnest. "You – you left her 'cause of *me*," he blurted out, the words broken by sobs, at last releasing in speech the pent-up thought that had harried him for days now. "If I'm not there y-you'd come back to her. Then – then she'll be happy again – " A small hand came up to wipe away the tears running down his cheek.

Sean's heart ached in sympathy for Philip's sorrow and he sat on his haunches directly in front of the sitting boy, placing his eyes on the same level as the child. "Philip, I didn't leave your mother because of you. That was between your mum and me. What would make you think that?"

"M-My dad – he left." He took a deep breath and exhaled. "'Cause of me and Tommy. And – and you left too. 'Cause of me."

"Aw, Philip," whispered Sean as he stood up and gathered the head and chest of the crying sitting boy into his arms. "Don't cry, Philip. It's not true. Not true at all. You're a fine boy. The best. Your dad didn't leave because of you and your brother. How'd you come up with such a thought?" He held Philip for a few seconds and then separated, going to the kitchen counter to grab a Kleenex tissue from a box. "Here, Phil, wipe your face and blow your nose."

Philip did as requested.

"Why then Sean? Why did my dad go away then?"

"What does your mother say?"

"Mom – she doesn't say anything. Only – only that – that he had to go. But not why."

Sean sat in the chair beside Philip. "Why?" he replied with a shrug. "Sometimes *why* is a big word. The biggest word of all sometimes. Sometimes people themselves don't even know why they do things. I can't say why. I can only guess. Maybe he was a man who wasn't ready to have a family. Sometimes people find that kind of responsibility too heavy. Like a big black stone on their shoulders. Or sometimes, people leave each other because they stop being able to get along with each other. I don't know exactly why your dad left, Philip, but I do know, absolutely, that he didn't go because of you. Or because of your brother. I know because of the type of boy you are. You're a fine boy. The best I know. And I sure didn't leave your mum because of you. Or because of anything you did. Not at all. Don't ever think that."

The words worked magic. Relief began to flood into Philip like the clear water of a stream released from an earthen dam flowing over parched land. With Sean's declaration, the weight of guilt and self-doubt Philip had borne for so long was lifted and washed away. Philip, without another word, got up from his chair and stepped over to Sean to place his arms around the man's neck, to lean his head against Sean's chest.

And Philip's own action worked its own amazing magic, he and Sean suddenly trading little miracles, for, in that moment, with Philip's head pressed against Sean's chest, *something* was altered within Sean. All his own doubts ran away from him, fleeing like phantoms that can only live in the dark and running from the sunshine of Philip's hug. Sean understood on the moment that he and Ellen were *meant* to marry. Nothing else mattered. His own doubts were nothing more than mere foolishness. This transformation came to him with a rapidity that was startling, almost overwhelming. *I'm in love with Ellen. I'm absolutely and totally in love. In LOVE with capital letters. Nothing else matters. Nothing else.*

Ellen arrived ten minutes later, her heart applauding the sight of her son. Gleefully, going down on one knee, she pulled Philip close to her, first hugging him tightly, then holding him at arms' length, her eyes running over him, tears of joy on her cheeks, examining him in order to assure herself after so many hours of the worst apprehension that a mother can endure that he was indeed as unharmed as he seemed. Immediately, having made the determination that her son was fine, she scolded him for making her worry. "Don't ever do this again, young man! Do you know how worried I was?! Do you know – " Her joyful heart interrupted her in the midst of her reprimand and she pulled Philip to her once again to hug him again, briefly, until she once more pushed him away to scold him again, waggling her finger in front of his astounded face, all the while as tears of relief and happiness ran down her cheeks. Her son was all right. This time, her son was coming home safe and sound.

Philip stood as if mesmerized by the flood of confusing emotions streaming from his mother. Ellen, lost in the complete joy of holding her little boy momentarily forgot where she was. When her senses returned to the point she was able to comprehend the world once more, she glanced up to look at Sean, and, in the act of seeing him, experienced a twist of sharp pain behind her ribs. Suddenly her heart was pounding inside her and her knees were trembling. Behind her eyes, tears of sorrow were racing to compete with those shed for the joy she felt over the safe return of her son. She wanted then to leave, as quickly as possible. "Get your jacket, Philip," she told her son, standing up. "We'll go now. Thank you, Sean. For c-calling – thank you – " she murmured, her back to Sean, not daring to look at him again, fearful her heart would break anew at the sight. Her throat was suddenly constricted, forbidding her the ability to talk further. Grabbing Philip's hand, she started to leave.

Sean reached out and placed his fingertips gently on the arm of her coat. "El, don't go," he said softly. His words stopped her in her tracks and she turned to face him.

"El, I've been a fool. I want to get married. If you'll still have me, that is. Will you, El? Marry me?"

Ellen's mouth dropped open and for a moment it was as if everything in her body stopped, her ability to breathe halting, her heart forgetting to beat. Her wet eyes stared at him, stupefied. Was she hearing correctly? "W-What?" she gasped finally.

"Let's get married, El," repeated Sean, slipping his arms around her. "I love you. More than anything."

A third miracle, three in short order. Ellen's soul ignited and she uttered a small peep of joy as she went up on her toes, immediately seeking Sean's lips. Together they met in a kiss of tender love. Tears once more sprang from her eyes, tears of joy this time, as she smothered Sean with kisses and uttered words of love to him. Little Philip, standing beside them, grinned up at them.

Somewhere deep inside her, Ellen was a child again, running up the hill of her youth, racing toward the clouds, and, in the weightless acceleration of happiness, flying up into the clear ether of the blue sky, running into the midst of the sunshine overhead.

*   *   *

Joy and Love, so fleeting at times, comes to us wearing costumes, masquerading as objects of timelessness, offering us the possibility they will endure. That endurance is an illusion, say some. All things pass away. Love is no different.

If that is so, then the profound love of Sean and Ellen would no doubt eventually pass into oblivion, just as all things pass away.

Perhaps.

Or perhaps it is Love alone that, when true and absolute, holds the ability to avoid the destruction that otherwise comes to all things. Perhaps it is Love that is held in special regard by the Creator and so it is Love that is granted the special power to survive, to make the transit from this world to the next. Perhaps the love of Ellen and Sean would triumphantly endure forever.

Perhaps there is such a thing as a Forever Love.

A poet's dream? A foolish thought?

Or not?

Author's Note

This book is essentially a love letter to the past and so, like all love letters, it is as much romantic fancy as truth.

Moville is a true town in Ireland, but residents there will note that the Moville described in this novel bears only a cursory resemblance to the reality of their town. A few true facts of the existing Moville have been incorporated into this book but much of the description here is not fact at all. That is certainly true of the "church within a church" that I placed within Moville.

The tale of Tom Donavan and the pooka is an old Irish tale. I've embellished it here a bit, giving the demon "rat-like teeth" and red eyes, for example, and have added the story of Tom's son seeking revenge for what was done to his father.

Ellen's life is also much fiction mixed with some fact. Some of the major events that occur to Ellen parallel those that occurred to my own mother, Ellen Carraher, nee Rawdon, but, at the same time, much is drawn out of imagination and is not fact.

Lest I be accused of melodrama however, let me hastily add that the scene in which Ellen's two newborn twins are dangled out the window by their irate father is one based upon a true event. I was one of those twins. Tommy was the other.

There is one major difference that will be noticed by all who knew Ellen. That is, in this small novel, I gave my mother's life the happiness of finding a new love after she was deserted by her husband. Life itself was not as kind to her. There was no happy ending for Ellen.

But I couldn't write this book any other way.

I believe in the Sun . . .

       When it is not shining.

I believe in Love . . .

       Even when I feel it not.

I believe in God . . .

       Even when He is silent.

           – An Irish Adage

Printed in the United States
24223LVS00001B/67-78